참전 16개국 전적지 답사기

The exploratory records to honor the favor in the War

신인범

6 · 25 한국전쟁 UN 16국 보은 답사기

The exploratory records to honor the favor of
UN 16 nations during the 6.25 Korean War

도서
출판 **가온미디어**

역사를 잊고사는 민족은 미래가 없다

독일의 철학자 헤겔은 역사를 잊고 사는 민족은 미래가 없다고 하였다. 특히 전쟁의 아픈 역사적 상처를 가슴에 묻고 살아가는 민족은 평화를 위해 평시에도 항상 국력배양에 전력투구해야 할 것으로 생각한다. 그 이유는 너무나 자명하다. 현대 전쟁은 총력전 양상이기 때문이다.

우리는 1950년 6월 25일 새벽, 북한의 불법적이고 기습적인 남침으로 3년여 동안 전쟁의 뼈아픈 상처와 흔적을 갖고 있다.

특히 6.25 한국전쟁은 우리들 만의 비극과 희생이 아닌 가슴 아픈 역사적 사실이다. 전쟁기간 동안 UN 연합국 중 22개 나라에서 572만여명이 전투에 참전하였고, 당시 불법적으로 개입한 중공군이 약675만 여명에 달하였는데 그중 약 42만명과 UN군 15만명이 목숨을 잃은 유일무이한 큰 상흔을 남긴 전쟁 이었다.

한국전쟁 당시 모택동의 아들도 참전하여 사망하였고 미국대통령 아이젠하워, 워커장군, 밴플리트장군 그리고 해군 항공단장인 헤리스 장

군 아들 역시 참전하여 산화하였다는 사실을 전사의 기록을 통해 확인할
수 있었다.

  따라서 필자는 한국전쟁 당시 이름 모를 산하를 헤메다 산화한 UN군
선배 전우와 자랑스런 그들의 유가족분들에게 조금이라도 보답 드리고
싶은 순수한 열정으로 그들이 목숨 걸고 혈투를 벌였던 격전지를 찾아
전장의 생생한 기록을 남겨두고자 기획하였다.

  아울러 자라나는 후세들에게도 전쟁의 역사적 교훈이 되기를 소망하여
본다.

  이 책이 완성되기까지 시공간적으로 제약적인 요소가 많았지만 물심
양면으로 함께해 주신 모든 분과 한국전쟁 당시 피와 땀을 아낌없이 바
치신 모든 분들에게 보은의 뜻을 담아 이 책을 바치고자 한다.

2024년 6월 엮은이 신 인 범

German philosopher Hegel said that a nation that forgets its history has no future.

In particular, people who live with the painful historical wounds of war buried in their hearts strive for peace.

I believe that even in peacetime, we must always put all our effort into cultivating national power. the reason is you

Everything is self-evident. This is because modern war is a total war.

We suffered for over three years due to North Korea's illegal and surprise invasion of the South in the early morning of June 25, 1950.

It has painful scars and traces of the war.

In particular, the heartbreaking history that the Korean War of 6.25 was not just our own tragedy and sacrifice.

It's true. During the war, approximately 5.72 million people from 22 UN allied countries fought.

participated in the war, and the number of Chinese soldiers who illegally intervened at the time amounted to approximately 6.75 million.

Of these, approximately 420,000 people and 150,000 UN soldiers lost their lives, a war that left a unique legacy of mourning.

It was this.

During the Korean War, Mao Zedong's son also participated and died, as did US President Eisenhower.

General Walker, General Van Fleet, and the son of General Harris, head of the Naval Air Corps, also participated in the war.

The fact that it was oxidized could be confirmed through company-wide records.

Therefore, the author is a senior member of the UN Forces who lost his name after wandering around an unknown branch during the Korean War.

Wow, I just want to give some repayment to their proud bereaved families.

A vivid record of the battlefield by visiting the fierce battlefield where they fought for their lives and blood with passion.

It was planned to leave behind the historical lessons of war for future generations.

I hope this happens.

Although there were many constraints in terms of time and space before this book was completed,

Everyone who was with us and everyone who generously gave their blood and sweat during the Korean War.

I would like to dedicate this book to you as a thank you.

Edited by June, 2024

6·25전쟁의 비극을
체득하는 계기

우리나라는 미, 일, 중, 러 4강의 국익에 민감한 지정학적 요충지로서 한반도는 유일하게 남, 북 분단국가로 자리하고 있으며 한국전쟁의 포성이 멈춘지 70년 지난 오늘날까지 준전시 휴전 상태로 존재한다는 것이 참으로 안타까운 사실이 아닐 수 없다.

6.25 한국전쟁 당시 UN군 자격으로 군수물자 및 의료지원을 포함해 22개 국가에서 수백만 명의 참전하여 아까운 목숨을 앗아간 사실을 한국 전쟁사를 통해 인지하고 있지만 마땅히 일목요연하게 정리된 자료가 없었고 다른 한편으로는 이국땅 이역만리에서 희생한 전사자와 유가족분들에게 조금이라도 위로를 드리고 순수한 보은의 열정으로 격전지와 전적비를 직접 답사하여 한국어와 영어와 일부 해당 국가어로 번역하여 기록한 점도 매우 눈에 띄게 특이하다.

자유와 평화를 지키겠다는 신념 하나로 생면부지의 타국 전장에서 목숨을 걸고 싸우다가 희생된 그분들의 넋을 기리고 아울러 오직 구국 일념으로 조국을 지키겠다는 마음 하나로 전장에 참여하여 산화한 선배 호국영령과 유가족 여러분들에게 이 책을 통해 조금이라도 위로가 되기를 진심으로 기원해 본다.

아울러 자라나는 후세들에게도 이 땅에 다시는 전쟁이라는 동족상잔의 비극과 아픈 상처를 이 책을 통해 직, 간접적으로 체득하는 계기가 되기를 바라는 마음이다.

이 책은 전국 각지 산재해 있는 UN군 전적비 위치와 주소가 일목요연하게 기록되어있어 안보 현장 답사시 참고하기에도 유용할 것으로 생각한다.

이 책은 보은의 열정으로 격전지와 UN군 전적비 등을 답사하여 엮은 생생한 전장 기록서 이기도 하다.

엮은이는 현재 인천시 계양구 상이군경회 회원으로 투철한 국가 안보관을 견지한 모범적인 회원이기에 그 열정과 노고를 치하하면서 많은 분들이 이 책과 함께 해주실 것으로 바라면서 미력하나마 감히 추천의 글을 바칩니다.

대한민국 상이군경회 인천시 계양구
지회장 안 성 윤
전상군경 4급

7

Our country is a geopolitical strategic point sensitive to the national interests of the four major powers: the United States, Japan, China, and Russia. It is the only divided country between South and North Korea, and the gunfire of the Korean War has stopped. It is truly unfortunate that 70 years later, we still exist in a state of quasi-war truce. It can't be true.

During the 6.25 Korean War, as a UN force, it provided military supplies and medical support to 22 countries. Through the history of the Korean War, we can see that millions of people lost their precious lives in the war. Although we are aware of this, there was no data clearly organized, and on the other hand, We wish to offer some consolation to the fallen soldiers and their bereaved families who sacrificed their lives in this foreign land, 10,000 miles away.

With a passion of pure gratitude, I personally visited the battle sites and monuments during this period. It is said that the charter of the Korean War was recorded vividly in Korean, English, and some national languages.

Risking your life on the battlefield of a foreign country, unfamiliar to you, with the belief that you will protect freedom and peace.

We honor the souls of those who sacrificed their lives while fighting, and we protect our country with the sole intention of saving our country. The senior patriotic spirit and bereaved family members who participated in the battlefield with the sole intention of protecting their country and died. I sincerely hope that this book will provide some comfort to you.

In addition, the growing generations will never again experience the tragedy of fratricidal war and war.

I hope that this book will be an opportunity to experience painful wounds directly or indirectly. It's um.

This book provides a clear overview of the locations and addresses of UN military monuments scattered throughout the country.

Since it is recorded, I think it will be useful for reference when visiting security sites. This book is a vivid account of the battlefield compiled from five years of field trips to battlefields and UN military monuments. It is also a rock book. The editor is currently a member of the Disabled Persons Association in Gyeyang-gu, Incheon.

As he is an exemplary member who adheres to the national security view, we praise his passion and hard work and give him many blessings. I dare to write a recommendation, even if only in a small way, in the hope that others will enjoy this book. I dedicate it.

Gyeyang-gu,Incheon, Republic of Korea Disabled Veterans Association
Planning Manager Ahn Seong-yoon

16개 한국전쟁 참전국에
보은하는 마음으로

군 생활 20여 년을 마치고 예편, 사회생활도 거의 끝난 후에 이 땅에 태어났으니 나를 키워준 고마운 한국 땅을 여행하고 싶었다. 그래서 전국을 10바퀴 외곽을 돌았다. 11바퀴 돌 때 파주지역 감악산 지역 설마리에 도착했다.

영국군 부대의 격전지, 전적지를 돌아보고 큰 감동을 받고 맘이 결심했다. 전국에 흩어져 있는 한국전쟁 참전국 16개국의 격전지와 전적지를 답사해 보고 싶었다.

부족한 필력과 제한된 자료를 들고 무지하면서 용감하게 6.25 한국전쟁 전투병력을 지원한 16개국 격전지와 의료지원국 6개국을 답사했다. 참전 순서대로 1. 미국, 2. 영국, 3. 네덜란드, 4. 캐나다, 5. 프랑스, 6. 필리핀, 7. 호주, 8. 튀르키예, 9. 태국, 10. 남아공, 11. 그리스, 12. 뉴질랜드, 13. 벨기에, 14. 룩셈부르크, 15. 에티오피아, 16. 콜롬비아 순으로 기록했다. 한국군의 주요 격전지도 답사했다.

나는 가장 가까운 지역의 전적지 인천부터 인제, 원통, 양구 민통선, 부산, 경남지역과 낙동강지역을 답사하고 중요지역은 하룻밤을 자면서 그날을 상상해 보기도 했다. UN군 연천지역 화장장이 있는 곳에서는 나도 모르게 눈물이 흘렀고, 왜관 작오산 북괴군에 의한 미군학살 현장에서는 새벽부터 현장에서 통곡을 했다. 나도 몰래 태국군 전적비 답사시에는 까닭모를 흐느낌이 와서 내가 왜 이런지도 몰랐다. 아마 전생이 있었다면 나는 태국인이었나 보다 라고 생각되었다. 때로는 가슴이 떨리고 눈물이 앞을 가려 참전비를 쳐다 볼 수 없었다.

한국전쟁 때 UN군이 도와주지 않았다면 우리는 노예가 되었다. 지구상에 존재하지도 않았다. 미군과 UN군이 없었다면 적화통일이 되었을 것이다. 지금 우리가 누리고 있는 자유에 대하여 조금이라도 생각해 보았다면 종북 주사파는 없을 것이다.

한국전쟁은 미국에서 잊혀진 전쟁이라고 한다. 역사를 잊으면 역사는 반복한다. 원주지역에서 부상 당한 윌리엄 Bill Weber 중위는 한국인이 자유를 얻었으니 의무가 생긴 거란다. 북쪽에 있는 동포에게 자유를 전달하는 것, 그 의무를 다했으면 한다.

우리는 미국과 유엔과 22개국에 아주 큰 빚을 지고 살아가고 있음을 알아야 한다. 다시는 이 땅에서 전쟁이 일어나지 않기를 기원하며 미국과 UN군의 숭고한 희생에 감사를 드립니다.

2024년 6월 신인범 (육군항공 대위 예편)

After had retired 20 years of military service, at the end of the civilian life, I wanted to travel to thankful ROK which I was born and raised. So I had traveled 10 times outside of whole nation. During the 11 times travel, I arrived at Seolmari of Gamak Mountain in Paju area.

After looking around the fierce and former battlefields of the British Army, I was deeply moved and made up my mind. I wanted to visit the nationwide fierce and former battlefields of 16 nations that participated in the Korean War.

Despite my ignorance, I visit bravely 16 nations providing military support and 6 nations providing medical support with poor writing skills and limited data. I have written in order of participation in the Korean War: 1. United States, 2, U.K., 3. Netherlands, 4. Canada, 5. France, 6. Philippines, 7. Australia, 8. Tьrkiye, 9. Thailand, 10. South Africa, 11. Greece, 12. New Zealand, 13. Belgium, 14. Luxembourg, 15. Ethiopia, and 16 Colombia. I also visited the major battlefields of the ROK military.

I visited starting with Incheon which is the nearest battlefields, Inje, Wontong, Yanggu Civilian Control Line, Busan, Gyeongnam. I explored the Nakdong River area 7 times and stayed overnight in critical areas to reflect on the day. At the UN military crematorium in Yeoncheon, I wept tears without realizing. At the site of the massacre of U.S. soldiers by nK puppet Army on Mt. Jako, Waegwan, I wept bitterly at dawn. Without even knowing, I started sobbing for no reason when I visited the monument Thai military. Might if I had a past life, I would have been Thai. Sometimes my heart trembled and tears blocked my vision so I couldn't look at the war memorials.

If the UN forces had not helped us during the Korean War, we would have become slaves. Even we are not on earth. Without the US and UN forces, unification would have occurred under communism. If we have ever thought about the freedom we are enjoying, there would be no pro-nK, Juche ideology(Kim Il-Sungism) following group. The Korean War is said to be the forgotten war in U.S.. If you forget history, it will be repeated. Former Lieutenant William Bill Weber, wounded in the Wonju area, said that the ROK people have a duty due to winning freedom. We have to fulfill the duty to deliver to our compatriots in nK.(Photographer; Rami Hyeon)

We must realize that we live with big debts on the United States, the United Nations, and 22 nations. While I hope that wars will never break out in my country again, I appreciate noble sacrifice of U.S. and UN forces.

June 2024, Shin In-Beom (Reserved Captain of Army Aviation)

차례

1부 : 한국전쟁 배경
Background of the Korean War

2부 : UN군 국가별 전투참전 기념비 답사
Exploring Forces Warfare Memorials by Country

미국(United States of America)

1부

한국전쟁 배경
Background of the Korean War

PART 01

6·25 한국전쟁

1950년 6월 25일 새벽 4시, 북한 김일성은 소련 스탈린의 군사장비*를 지원받고, 중공의 마오쩌둥의 승인 및 지원을 받아 38도선을 넘어 대한민국을 공산화할 목적으로 침략전쟁을 감행했다. 이러한 내용들은 구소련의 외교 문서의 공개로 백일하에 드러났다.

*군사장비: T-34전차 242대, 야포 565문, 대전차포 552문, 고사포 72문, 박격포 875문, 자주포 186문, 장갑차 59대, 모터싸이클 500대, 함정 115척, 전투기 전폭기 226대.

- 북한병력 188,297명. 중공군 380,000명 지원.

6·25 한국전쟁 때 대한민국을 도우려고 파병한 16개국과, 의료지원 6개국 등 총 22개국이 우리들의 아버지와 함께 목숨을 바쳐 대한민국을 지켜주었다. 모든 참전용사 분들과 유공자 가족, 그리고 파병국의 모든 국민분들께 고맙고 감사함을 드린다.

파병 16개국 - 미국, 프랑스, 영국, 네덜란드, 벨기에, 룩셈부르크, 캐나다, 필리핀, 태국, 뉴질랜드, 호주, 콜롬비아, 남아프리카공화국, 에디오피아, 터키, 그리스.

의료지원 6개국 - 스웨덴, 덴마크, 노르웨이, 이탈리아, 인도, 독일.

6. 25 Korean War

At 0400(I) 25th June 1950, Kim Il-sung from nK(north Korea) who was supported by Stalin's military equipments and got an approval & supports from Mao Zedong conducted illegal invasion war to communize Republic of Korea(ROK). These had come to light with the disclosure of diplomatic documents from the former Soviet Union.

*Military equipments: 242×T-34 tanks, 565×field guns, 552×anti-tank guns, 72×anti-aircraft guns, 875×mortars, 186×self-propelled guns, 59×armored vehicles, 500×motor cycles, 115×battle ships, 226×fighter&bombers.

- 188,297 North Korean Soldiers. 380,000 soldiers supported from Communist Chinese Army.

Those 22 nations including 16 nations which dispatched troops and 6 nations which supported medical assistance and our father protected ROK with their lives together. I am really grateful for all the Korean War veterans, their family and all the people of those 22 nations.

16 nations which dispatched armed forces
United States, France, United Kingdom, Netherlands, Belgium, Luxembourg, Canada, Philippines, Thailand, New Zealand, Australia, Colombia, South Africa, Ethiopia, Türkiye and Greece.

6 nations which supported medical supports
Sweden, Denmark, Norway, Italy, India and Germany.

PART 02

결초보은의 뜻과 나의 마음

* 결초보은(結草報恩) ; 죽어 혼령이 되어도 은혜를 잊지 않고 갚는 것. 남의 은혜에 깊이 감사할 때 하는 말.

결초보은의 유래

춘추시대 (BC770-BC403) 진(晉)나라에 젊고 예쁜 첩을 둔 위무자(魏武子)라는 사람이 있었다.

그가 늙어 병이 들자 본처의 아들인 과(顆)를 불러서 유언을 했다. "내가 죽거든 네 서모를 다른 데로 시집보내도록 하여라!" 후에 병세가 악화되어 곧 죽을 지경에 이르자 다시 아들을 불러 당부하였다. "내가 죽거든 네 서모를 내 무덤에 함께 묻거라!" 순장(殉葬)하라고 했다.

아버지가 죽자 아들은 두 가지 유언 가운데 어떤 것을 따라야 좋을지 골똘히 생각한 끝에, '사람이 위독하면 정신이 혼란해지기 마련이니, 정신이 조금이라도 맑았을 때 하신 말씀을 따르는 것이 좋겠다.' 라고 마음을 정하고는 아버지의 처음 유언에 따라 서모를 살려 주어 다른 데로 시집(結婚)가게 하였다.

몇 년 뒤 이웃 나라가 쳐들어와 전쟁이 일어나자 아들 위과(魏顆)는 진나라 장수로 임명되어 싸움터에 나갔다.

적국에는 힘이 세기로 이름난 두회(杜回)라는 장수가 있었다.

위과는 두회와 결전을 벌이게 되었는데, 싸움은 위과에게 불리하게 진행되었다. 그러던 중에 적의 장수 두회가 탄 말(馬)이 어떤 무덤에 엮어져 있는 풀에 발이 걸려 넘어졌다. 그 순간 위과는 두회를 덮쳐 사로잡아, 큰 공을 세우게 되었다.

그날 밤 위과의 꿈에 무덤의 혼령이 나타나 이렇게 말했다. "나는 당신이 살려 준 서모의 아비 되는 사람이오. 그대가 아버지의 두 유언 가운데 옳은 것을 따랐기 때문에 내 딸이 목숨을 유지할 수 있었고, 지금은 새 남편을 만나 잘 살고 있다오.

나는 당신의 그 고마운 은혜(恩)에 보답(報) 하고자 내 무덤에 풀(草)을 엮어(結) 놓았던 것이오" 그때 이후로 나는 그대에게 보답할 길을 찾았는데 이제야 그 은혜를 갚는 것이라고 했다.

-출처: 춘추좌씨전

The meannig of "Returning the favor by weaving grass" and my mind

* "Returning the favor by weaving grass": To return one's favor even when someone died and became a soul.

An expression that when someone feels grateful deeply for the others' favor.

The origin of "Returning the favor by weaving grass"

In the Qin Dynasty during the Spring and Autumn Period, there was a man called Wimuja who had a young and pretty concubine. When Wimuja became old and sick, he called in Wigua, the son of his first wife, and made a will. "When I die, merry your second mother to another." When time had passed, Wimuja's condition had deteriorated and he was about to die, he called in his son again and made another will. "When I die, bury your second mother in my grave together."

After the father had died, the son had thought deeply about which of the two wills to follow and made up his mind. 'when a man is critically ill, one's mind is bound to be confused. It's better to follow what he said when his mind is more clear.' So according to his father's first will, he saved his second mother and married other person. A few years later, when a neighbor country invaded and a war broke out, the son Wigua was appointed as a general of the Qin Dynasty and went to the battlefield. In the enemy country, there was a general Duhoe who was famous for his strength. Wigua had a decisive battle with Duhoe, but the fight went against Wigua. In the meantime, the horse ridden by the enemy general Duhoe tripped on the woven grass of grave and fell over. At that moment, Wigua attacked Duhoe and captured him, so Wigua contributed to a great victory. That night, in Wigua's dream, the spirit of the tomb appeared and said, "I am the father of your second mother, whom you saved. Because you followed the right one of your father's two wills, my daughter's life was saved, and now she is happy with her new husband. I tied grass knot on my grave to return your big favor. I have been trying to found a way to repay you since my daughter was saved. Finally I have returned the favor."

- source: A commentary "Spring and Autumn" written by Gongja

6·25 한국전쟁 때 풍전등화에 처한 긴박한 시기에 죽을 수밖에 없는 한국을 살려서 재가하게 되었고, 아들 위과는 UN 지원군이 되었고, 순장되어 죽을 수밖에 없는 처지의 딸을 살려서 시집까지 보냈으니 친정아버지가 된 한국은 전쟁을 지원한 UN 16국 나라의 은혜를 어찌 잊으랴? 죽어서도 은혜를 갚아야 한다.

United Nations(UN) forces saved ROK which was forced to die in a tense period like a lantern in front of wind during the Korean War and married a second time. If the son, Wigua were UN forces and ROK were Wigua's second mother who was forced to die, how could ROK forget the favor of the 16 UN nations that supported the war? We must return the favor even if we die.

PART 03

6·25 한국 전쟁의 발발 원인

70년 전(2020년 기준) 1950년 6월 25일 북의 남침 "남한 곧 적화될 것"을 주장한 김일성은 스탈린·마오쩌둥의 지원을 약속받았다.

전쟁이 계속되고, 스탈린이 죽고 나서야 휴전할 때 북침설과 남침 유도설이 나왔지만 북의 남침설에 근거하는 정보들이 쏟아져 나왔다.

1990년대 중반 이후 러시아와 공산권 국가들의 기밀자료가 공개되었다.

북한 김일성이 소련의 지원 약속을 받아낸 뒤 일으킨 전쟁이라는 사실이 명확해졌다. 구 소련 기밀문서가 해제되면서 김일성이 구 소련을 설득해 지원받아 일으킨 철저하게 계획된 남침임이 밝혀졌다.

스탈린은 심지어 수백 명의 한국계 소련인을 중앙아시아에서 차출해 북한 편에서 싸우도록 했다. 13년 전 스탈린의 명령으로 강제 이주되었던 그 조선인들이다.

김일성이 마오쩌둥의 군사지원을 약속받고 6·25가 발발했다. 전쟁 직전 중국이 북에 넘긴 조선인 사단 2개는 남침의 주력부대였다.

김일성은 18만 명의 병력과 T-34 전차 242대, 자주포 142문, 100대의 전투기와 폭격기를 앞세워 남침했다.

6·25 전쟁은 500만 명의 인명피해를 야기시켰다. 남침 때 최일선에서 인민군을 이끌었던 장교의 80%와 18만명 인민군 중 6만여 명이 모택동의 중국 공산당이 북한에 보낸 조선족 병력이었다.

한국전쟁은 명백하게 김일성·모택동 합작의 남침 전쟁이다.

The causes of the Korean War

70 years ago(as of 2020), on 25th June, Kim Il-sung who claimed that "ROK would be communized soon" by nK's Invasion which was promised aids from Stalin and Mao Zedong.

The war had continued, when armistice was signed after Stalin died. There were rumors who was subject of invasion causing the war, nK or ROK. But informations based on invasion from nK poured out.

Confidential documents from Russia and communist countries had been released since the mid-1990s. It became clear that the Korean War was caused by Kim Il-sung who had gotten the promise of aids from former Soviet Union.

With the release of confidential documents from former Soviet Union , It was revealed that Kim Il-sung thoroughly planned to invade to ROK by persuading former Soviet Union and being assisted by former Soviet Union.

Stalin even transferred hundreds of Korean-Soviet people from Central Asia to fight on the nK side.
They were Koreans who were forcibly relocated by Stalin's order 13 years ago(as of that time).

Kim Il-sung launched the Korean War after receiving Mao Zedong's promise of military support.

The two divisions consisted of Koreans which China handed over to nK just prior to the war were the main forces for invasion to ROK.

Kim Il-sung invaded ROK with 180,000 soldiers, 242×T-34 tanks, 142×self-propelled guns, and 100×fighters and bombers.

The Korean War caused 5 million casualties.

When nK Invaded to ROK, 80% of the officers who led the Korean People's Army(KPA) at the forefront of the war and 60,000 of the 180,000 KPA who were dispatched from the Chinese Communist Party that is led by Mao Zedong were Korean-Chinese soldiers. Korean War was clearly caused by illegal invasion from nK to ROK which had been planned Kim Il-sung and Mao Zedong together.

전쟁 시작

한국전쟁은 1950년 6월 25일 새벽 4시, 한반도를 가로지르는 38도 선상의 전 전선에서 선전포고 없이 북한의 남침으로부터 시작되었다.

그로부터 2일 후인 6월 27일, UN 창립 후 최초로 침략당한 대한민국을 돕기 위한 UN 안전보장이사회의 결의로 UN군이 한국전쟁에 참전하게 되었다.

UN군의 일원으로 참가한 국가는 전투병력 지원 16개국, 의료지원 6개국, 물자지원국 63개국이었다.

전쟁 중 200만 명의 민간인이 희생되었다. 그분들의 고귀한 생명의 댓가로 오늘의 대한민국은 세계 10위권 내의 경제 대국을 이룩하였다.

2020년 6월 25일, 한국전쟁 70주년을 맞이했다.

한국전쟁은 잊혀져가는 세계 전쟁으로 그 과정들을 요약한다.

6·25 전쟁의 결초보은 같은 고마움을 잊어가는 대한민국 국민들에게 그 고마웠던 혼을 깨우고 싶다. 특히 한국전쟁 때 병력을 지원한 16개국에 대한 고마움을 글로 써서 그들의 나라에 잊혀져가는 자국민들에게 고마움을 전하기 위하여 이 책을 펴낸다.

Start of war

The Korean War began at 0400(I) on 25th June, 1950, when nK invaded ROK without declaring war on the 38th parallel which across the Korean Peninsula.

Two days later, on 27th June , the UN forces participated in Korean War in accordance with the UN Security Council's resolution to help the invaded ROK for the first time since the UN establishment.

16 countries supported combat forces, 6 countries provided medical support, and 63 countries supported materials as members of the UN forces.

Two million civilians were sacrificed during the war. In return for their noble lives, today's ROK has become to have the world's top 10 economic power.

25th June, 2020 marked the 70th anniversary of the Korean War. The Korean War summarizes its processes as a being forgotten world war. I want to awaken the grateful soul of "retuning the favor by waving the grass" to ROK people.

In particular, the reason why I publish this book to express my gratitude to the people of the 16 countries who supported their troops during the Korean War.

UN군의 국가별 참전시기

1950년

6월 27일 : 미 해 · 공군 참전

6월 28일 : 영국 해군 참전

7월 1일 : 미 지상군 스미스부대 참전, 호주 해 · 공군 참전

7월 13일 : 미 제8군사령부 대구지휘소 개소

7월 16일 : 네덜란드 해군 참전

7월 26일 : 캐나다 공군 참전

7월 29일 : 프랑스 해군 참전

7월 30일 : 캐나다, 뉴질랜드 해군 참전

8월 28일 : 영국 지상군 참전

9월 20일 : 필리핀 지상군 참전

9월 27일 : 호주 지상군 참전

9월 28일 : 스웨덴 적십자병원 파견

10월 17일 : 터키 지상군 참전

11월 7일 : 태국 지상군 참전

11월 16일 : 남아공 공군 참전

11월 20일 : 인도 야전병원 파견

11월 29일 : 프랑스 지상군 참전

12월 1일 : 그리스 공군 참전

12월 9일 : 그리스 지상군 참전

12월 18일 : 캐나다 지상군 참전

12월 31일 : 뉴질랜드 지상군 참전

1951년

　1월 31일 : 벨기에, 룩셈부르크 지상군 참전

　3월 7일 : 덴마크 적십자 병원선 파견

　5월 6일 : 에티오피아 지상군 참전

　5월 8일 : 콜롬비아 해군 참전

　6월 15일 : 콜롬비아 지상군 참전

　6월 22일 : 노르웨이 이동외과병원 파견

11월 16일 : 이탈리아 제68 적십자병원 파견

Timeline of UN forces' participation

1950

1. 27th June: United States of America Navy and Air Force participated

2. 28th June: British Navy participated

3. 1st July: Task force Smith of United States Ground forces, the Australian Navy and Air Force participated

4. 13th July: Daegu command post of U.S. 8th army established

5. 16th July: Dutch Navy Participated

6. 26th July: Canadian Air Force Participated

7. 29th July: French Navy Participated

8. 30th July: Canadian, New Zealand Navy Participation

9. 28th August: British Ground forces participated

10. 20th September: Philippine Ground forces participated

11. 27th September: Australian Ground forces participated

12. 28th September: Swedish Red Cross Hospital was dispatched

13. 17th October: Türkiye Ground forces participated

14. 7th November: Thai Ground forces participated
15. 16th November: South African Air Force participated
16. 20th November: Indian Field Hospital was dispatched
17. 29th November: French Ground forces participated
18. 1st December: Greek Air Force Participated
19. 9th December: Greek Ground forces participated
20. 18th December: Canadian Ground forces Participated
21. 31st December: New Zealand Ground forces participated

1951
1. 31st January: Belgian and Luxembourg Ground forces participated
2. 7th March: Danish Red Cross Hospital Ship was dispatched
3. 6th May: Ethiopian Ground forces participated
4. 8th May: Columbian Navy participated
5. 15th June: Colombian Ground forces participated
6. 22nd June: Norwegian Mobile Surgery Hospital was Dispatched
7. 16th November: Italian 68th Red Cross Hospital dispatched

PART 06

물자 원조 국가

1816년부터 1965년까지 150년간 동맹을 맺었던 나라는 177개이었다. 이들 중에 전쟁 시 동맹의 의무를 이행한 나라는 48개국이다. 채 30%가 안 된다. 108국은 중립을 택했다. 심지어 21개국은 동맹을 배반했다. 동맹관리의 중요성이 여기서 필요하다.

6·25 한국전쟁 당시 지상군을 파견한 16개국과 의료지원 6개국 외에도 수많은 나라에서 물자를 보내 주었다. 그때 우방국에서 한국을 지원해 주지 않았다면 아마 지금과 같은 경제성장은 물론이거니와 국가의 존립 문제가 어떻게 되었을지 아찔하다.

한국전쟁 때 물자를 보내준 국가는 다음과 같다. (27개국)

레바논: 5만 달러

우루과이: 20만 달러, 모포 7,000매

호주: 의료품

이스라엘: 의료품

파라과이: 의료품

프랑스: 의료품

영국: 의료품 60만톤, 소금

베네수엘라: 10만 달러 상당의 의료품

인도: 야전구호대, 압박붕대 40만개, 의료품

에콰도르: 의료품, 쌀 1만톤

튀르키예: 혈청

필리핀: 혈청 500점, 쌀 1,000톤 , 비누 5,000개

쿠바: 혈청, 사탕 2,000톤, 알코올 1만 갤런

파키스탄: 소맥 5,000톤

태국: 백미 4,000톤, 수송선 2척

대만: 백미 1,000톤, 석탄 1만 톤, 소금 3,000톤, DDT 20톤

아이슬란드: 간유 125톤

칠레: 동, 소금

멕시코: 콩(두류)

네덜란드: 두류

아르헨티나: 소고기 통조림

코스타리카: 해군 및 공군기지 지원병 수제 보유

리비아: 천연고무

노르웨이: 상선

엘살바도르: 경제원조

콜롬비아: 경제적 일반원조

아이티: 2,000달러.

* 참고자료 : 6·25 사변사 / 육군본부 발행. (49개국 지원함)

Countries which aided Materials

From 1816 to 1965, there were 177 countries that had been allied for 150 years. Among them, 48 countries fulfilled their alliance obligations during the Korean war. It was less than 30 percent. The 108 countries chose neutrality. Even 21 countries betrayed the alliance. We can find out the importance of alliance management here.

There were 16 countries that sent ground forces, 6 countries that sent medical support during the Korean War, and numerous countries sent supplies. If the allies did not support ROK at that time, it is dizzying to see what would have happened to existence of ROK as well as economic growth as it is now.

The following countries sent supplies during the Korean War. (27 countries)

1. Lebanon: $50,000
2. Uruguay: $200,000, 7,000 blankets
3. Australia: Medical supplies
4. Israel: Medical supplies
5. Paraguay: Medical supplies
6. France: Medical supplies
7. UK: 600,000 tons of medical supplies, salt
8. Venezuela: $100,000 worth of medical supplies
9. India: Field relief, 400,000 compression bands, medical supplies
10. Ecuador: Medical supplies, 10,000 tons of rice
11. Türkiye: Serum
12. Philippines: 500 pieces of serum, 1,000 tons of rice, 5,000 soap
13. Cuba: Serum, 2,000 tons of candy, 10,000 gallons of alcohol
14. Pakistan: 5,000 tons of wheat
15. Thailand: 4,000 tons of white rice, two transport ships
16. Taiwan: 1,000 tons of white rice, 10,000 tons of coal, 3,000 tons of salt, and 20 tons of DDT

17. Iceland: 125 tons of liver oil

18. Chile: Copper and salt

19. Mexico: Soybeans (Kinds of beans)

20. Netherlands: Kinds of beans

21. Argentina: Canned beef

22. Costa Rica: materials for Navy and Air Force Base Volunteers

23. Libya: Natural rubber

24. Norway: Merchant ships

25. El Salvador: Economic aids

26. Colombia: Economic general Aids

27. Haiti: $2,000.

* Reference: History of 6·25 Korean War / Army Headquarters
  Published. (49 countries supported)

PART 07

유엔

6 · 25 한국전쟁이 발발하자 유엔은 안전보장이사회를 소집하고, 북한군의 침략중지 및 격퇴를 위하여 결의안을 승인하였다.

이 결의안에 따라 유엔 회원국은 육 · 해 · 공군을 참선시킴으로써 본격적으로 전쟁에 참가할 수 있게 되었다.

16개국이 전투부대를 파병하고, 6개국이 의료 또는 시설을 지원하기 위해 참전하였다. 이외에도 40여개의 나라들이 대한민국을 위해 물자를 지원하였다.

United Nations

When the Korea War broke out, UN had convened the Security Council and approved the resolution to stop and defeat nK's aggression. As the resolution, UN members enabled to participate the war by dispatching their Army, Navy, and Air Force. 16 nations dispatched combat troops and 6 nations sent units to aid the facility and medical. In addition, about 40 nations provided the supplies for ROK.

2부

유엔군 국가별
전투참전 기념비 답사

Exploring U.N. Forces Warfare Memorials by Country

미국은 유엔 참전국 중에서 제일 먼저 그리고 가장 많이 한국에 전투부대를 파병하였으며, 유엔군 사령부를 지도하며 한국에 파병된 유엔 참전국 부대를 통합 지휘 하였다.

전쟁 동안 수행한 주요 전투는 오산(죽미령) 전투, 대전 전투, 낙동강 방어작전, 인천상륙작전, 평양탈환작전, 장진호 전투, 지평리 전투이다.

United States of America(U.S.) was not only the first nation to send troops but also the nation which dispatched the largest number of combat troops to ROK among the United Nations member nations during the Korea War. U.S. led United Nations Command(UNC) and fulfilled combined command and control of the UN forces which were dispatched to ROK. Its major battles include the battle of Osan (Jukmiryeong(hill of Jukmi)), battle of Daejeon, defensive operation of the Nakdong River, Incheon landing Operation, Pyeonyang secure operation, battle of Jangjin Lake, and battle of Jipyeong-ri.

- 참전기간 (Date of Participation) : 1950. 6. 27 – 1955. 3
- 참전규모 (Troops Provided) : 8군 (8th army), 극동해군(Far East Naval Forces), 극동공군(Far East Air Forces)
- 참전연인원 (Total Participants) : 1,789,000
- 부상자 (Wounded in Action) : 92,134
- 전사자 (Killed in Action) : 36,595

미국

한국군 지원부대 (카투사) 전사자: 7,174명 / 합: 43,769 명.
Killed in Action of Korean Augmentation to the United States Army
(KATUSA) : 7,174 / total: 43,769

미국: 보병 7개 사단, 해병 1개 사단, 극동함대 261척, 극동공군 66개 대대.
U.S.: 7×Infantry Divisions, 1×Marine Division, 261×Far East Naval ships,
      66×Far East Air Force Squadron.

01

미국군 참전기념비

위치: 경기도 파주시 문산읍 사목리 490-1(임진각 공원 내)

1950년 6월 25일, 공산 괴뢰집단이 불법 남침하니 미국군은 UN의 한국전 참전을 결정하고 7월 5일에 최초 참전했다. 16개국 파병 국가 중에 가장 많은 병력인 572,000명이 참전하고, 한국전쟁에서 표현할 수 없는 많은 희생을 했다.

1953년 7월 27일에 휴전할 때까지 한국전에 참전하여 북한 공산괴 뢰집단과 중공군을 격퇴시켜 승리를 이끌었다.

어찌 잊으랴! 이름도 모르고 가보지도 못한 미지의 땅 한국을 향한 미국의 귀한 아들, 딸들의 고귀한 생명들, 참전용사의 그 고마운 은공 을 어찌 보답하랴!

아직도 이름 모를 산골짝에서 부모의 품으로 돌아가지 못하고 싸늘 한 시신 무명용사의 희생을 어찌 잊으랴?

2020년 9월 26일(토), 임진각에 위치한 '미국군 참전기념비'를 답 사하고 참배했다. 사상자 142,108명, 그중에 전사 36,595명, 부상자 103,284명, 실종 5,178명이다.

대한민국은 미국에게 갚을 수 없는 은혜의 빚을 아주 많이 졌다.

특히 미국 트루먼 대통령은 한국인에게는 구세주다. 그의 결심이 없 었다면 한국의 자유 민주주의는 없었다. 그의 단호한 결기로 한국 남 자는 공산당의 노예에서 벗어났고, 아녀자들은 기쁨조(공산당의 노리 개 역할)에서 벗어났다.

한국은 자유민주주의 국가가 되었다. 머리 숙여 깊은 감사를 하는 신삿갓입니다.

The Monument to U.S. participation in Korean War

Location: 490-1, Samok-ri, Munsan-eup, Paju-si, Gyeonggi-do(in Imjingak Park)

On 25th June, 1950, as the communist puppet nK invaded ROK, UN made a decision to participate in war and the UN forces participated in Korean War on 5th July for the first time.

U.S. dispatched 572,000 soldiers, the largest number of troops among the 16 nations, and sacrificed numerous soldiers during the Korean War.

Until the armistice agreement was made on 27th July, 1953, the U.S. led the war by defeating and repelling both nK Communist puppet Army and Communist Chinese Army.

We cannot forget their sacrifice! How can we return precious U.S. sons and daughters' lives and veteran's favor whom had never known ROK.

How can we forget the sacrifice of soldiers who became unknown cold bodies and cannot return to their parents from unknown mountain valley.

On Sat, 20th September, 2020, I explored and worshiped to the monument to U.S. participation in Korean War which is located at Imjingak.

Total of Causalities: 142,108, among them Killed in Action(KIA)：36,595, Wounded in Action(WIA): 103,284, Missing in Action(MIA): 5,278

ROK owes indelible debts of favor to U.S..

In particular, U.S. president, Harry Truman was a savior for ROK people. If he didn't made a decision, there would be no liberal democracy for ROK.

With his firm resolution freed ROK men from the possibility of slavery byway of the communists, and women from becoming the Gifuemjo(sex slaves for the Communist Party).

I, gleeman Shin, expresses deep gratitude for the sacrifice of U.S..

北韓傀儡　不法南侵
美軍參戰　最初作戰
支援國中　最大兵力
韓國戰爭　多死犧牲
休戰協定　參戰至續
退共産軍　勝利牽引
戰亂忘焉　不知名也

未去觀韓　高貴生命
參戰勇士　恩供答焉
無名戰士　未知山谷
回而母胸　屍身魂靈
犧牲將兵　千秋忘焉

02 유엔군 초전 전적비; 1950년 7월 5일 (오산 竹美嶺 전투)

위치: 경기 오산시 외삼미동 600-1번지

1. 북괴군 이리떼가 38선을 넘은지 10여일 후에 미군 스미스 특수임무 부대가 이곳에 전개되고

2. 오산 죽미령에 진지를 구축하고 유엔군 첫 전투의 서막이 열렸다.

3. 새벽 3시 죽미령은 비가 내리는데, 좌측 능선에 B중대 우측 능선에 C중대, 후방에 포대를 배치 완료했다.

4. 오전 10시 긴 행렬의 북한군 트럭 보병 출현, 북한군 향해 스미스 부대는 박격포와 기관총을 쏘아댔고 피아 가릴 것 없이 수많은 병사 쓰러졌다.

5. 이 전투에서 특수임무부대는 540명 중 보병 150명, 포병 31명이 전사하고, 북괴군 역시 5천명 중 150명이 전사했고, 전차 4대가 파괴되었다.

6. 6시간 15분 동안 죽미령 전선은 피바다 되었다.

7. 이 전투선이 낙동강으로 이어지고, 한 품은 외로운 고혼은 이곳에 잠이 드니 혈맹의 우리가 어찌 잊으랴!

8. 이곳 미군의 젊은이들이 희생한 숭고한 전투지역에서 한국의 자유와 평화를 위해 희생한 스미스 특수임무 부대원에게 눈물 젖은 머리를 숙인다.

20년 8월 12일 UN 초전 기념비와 기념관을 답사하며 1950년 7월 5일 미 24사단 21연대 1대대 대대장 스미스 중령은 그 이후 준장으로 진급했고 1967년 예편, 1975년 7월 한국을 방문하여 박정희 대통령으

로부터 태극무공훈장을 받았다.

The Monument to UN forces' first battle: On 5th July 1950 (Jukmiryeong in Osan battle)

Location: 600-1, Oesammi-dong, Osan-si, Gyeonggi-do

1. About 10 days after the nK puppet Army which like a pack of wolves crossed the 38th parallel, Task force Smith of U.S. Army deployed here.

2. And they established positions at Jukmiryeong in Osan, and there was prelude the first battle of the UN forces.

3. At 0300(I), when it rained at Jukmiryeong, Company B on the left ridge, Company C on the right ridge and battery C on the rear had been deployed.

오산 죽미령 사진 A photo of Jukmiryeong in Osan

4. nK vehicle infantries appeared in a long procession at 1000(I). Task Force Smith fired mortars and machine guns at the nK Army and a lot of soldiers were dead, regardless of enemies or friendly forces.

5. In this battle, the Task Force Smith lost 150 infantry guys and 31 artillerymen out of 540 soldiers, nK Army also lost 150 soldiers out of 5,000, and four tanks.

6. For 6 hours and 15 minutes, the Jukmiryeong front line was flooded with blood.

7. This front line have been leading to the Nakdong River, and the lonely souls fell asleep here, so how can we forget about our blood alliance!

8. In the noble battle area where young American soldiers sacrificed, I bow down with tear to show my thanks to members of Task Force Smith who sacrificed for freedom and peace of ROK.

On 12th August, 2020, I visited the monument to UN forces' first battle and Memorial Hall.

On 5th July, 1950, Smith, U.S. 1st Battalion commander of 21st Regiment of 24th Division, had been promoted to brigadier general and retired in 1967.

He visited Korea and received the Taegeuk Order of Military Merit from President Park Chung-hee in July 1975.

北傀越線　十日後也
美特殊隊　戰鬪展開
烏山戰鬪　陳地具築
特殊部隊　戰鬪準備
三更雨中　左右中隊
配置完了　砲隊後方
北傀出現　砲擊開時
無次彼我　兵士戰死
戰線血海　戰連洛東
孤魂寢亂　血盟不忘
靑年美軍　崇高犧牲
韓國自由　爲平忘焉

03

천안지구 미군 추모비(마틴공원)

위치: 충남 천안시 동남구 삼룡동 401

한국전쟁에서 두 번째로 전투한 천안전투다.

1950년 7월 8일 미 24사단 제34연대가 북괴군 4사단, 6사단, 105기 갑사단과 접전한 장소다.

파죽지세로 밀고 들어오는 북한군 전차는 천안읍내 시가전으로 혼전 상황인데 로버트 마틴(Robert R. Martin) 연대장까지 소총수처럼 무기를 들고 싸워야 하는 긴박한 처지였다.

적 전차 파괴 목적으로 2.36인치 바주카포를 들고 제리 크리스틴스(Jerry C. Christenson)상사가 탄약수 역할을 했다.

마틴 대령 전차를 조준, 피아간 거의 동시에 포탄 발사했다. 불행하게도 85mm 전차 포탄이 대령을 덮치고 말았다.

이 전투에서 전사자는 연대장을 포함해서 129명이다. 한국 자유, 평화위해 헌신한 전몰장병의 은혜를 잊을 수 없다.

2020년 11월 7일 천안시 천안삼거리 주변 구성동에 있는 "마틴거리"와 마틴공원을 답사했다.

마틴 대령 전사 후 한 달 뒤인 8월, 마틴 부인은 딸 제인(Jane Martin) 출산한다. 1999년 제인은 아버지가 전사한 한국을 방문했다. 구성동에서 한 줌 흙만 가지고 돌아갔다.

현재 미국에는 20여명의 마틴 후손들이 살고 있다. 한국에 할아버지 이름의 도로와 공원이 있다는 사실에 너무나 감격한단다.

손자 마틴은 "또다시 한국에 위기가 생기면 기꺼이 할아버지처럼 한국을 돕기 위해 달려가겠다." 라고 한다.

미군 129명 전원이 마틴 대령이 된 공원 기념탑에서 참배하고 추모하는 신삿갓 입니다.

The Memorial Monument to the U.S. Army in Cheonan District(Martin Park)

Location: 401, Samryong-dong, Dongnam-gu, Cheonan-si, Chungcheongnam-do

Cheonan battle was the second battle in the Korean War.

Cheonan was the engagement place where the 34th Regiment of U.S. 24th Infantry Division fought against nK puppet 4th, 6th, and 105th Armored Divisions.

While Cheonan-eup was very confused due to street battle, nK Army tanks were advancing south fiercely.

It was an urgent situation that even Robert R. Martin, the regiment commander had to fight like a rifleman.

With a 2.36-inch bazooka to destroy enemy tanks, master sergeant Jerry C. Christenson took the role of ammunition bearer.

The tank which Colonel Martin boarded and enemy's tank aimed and fired each other almost simultaneously.

Unfortunately, an 85mm tank ammunition hit the tank which

Colonel Martin boarded.

KIA were 129 in this battle, including the regiment commander.

I can forget the favor of the fallen heros who devoted themselves to freedom and peace of ROK.

On 7th November, 2020, I explored "Martin Street" and Martin Park in Guseong-dong around Cheonan junction of three roads in Cheonan-si. After a month later Colonel Martin died, Mrs. Martin gave birth to her daughter, Jane Martin in August.

In 1999, Jane visited Korea where her father had died. She went back U.S. with only a handful of soil from Guseong-dong.

Currently about 20 Martin's descendants are living in the United States. They are thrilled because of the fact that there's a road and a park named after their grandfather in Korea. Colonel Martin's grandson said, "If there were another crisis in Korea,

"I would gladly run to help ROK like my grandfather."

I, gleeman Shin, worshiped and cherished at memorial tower in the park which all 129 U.S. soldiers became Colonel Martin.

美軍二次　天安戰鬪
北機甲師　美市街戰
破竹之勢　北傀戰車
彼我熾烈　邑內混戰
同時發射　命中戰車
赤彈發射　戰死聯長
韓國平和　爲國獻身
戰歿將兵　恩惠不忘

04

개미고개 전투 전적비(조치원)

위치: 세종시 전동면 운주산로 836번지 일대.

1950년 7월 10일 조치원 북쪽 고마고개(높다는 뜻)에서 북괴군 3사단과 미 21연대가 접전했다.

북괴군 2천 명이 개미떼처럼 기어올라왔다고 하여 개미고개라 불렸다.

적 전차 38대 격파, 반궤도 차량 7대, 트럭 117대를 격파해 최대 전과를 올렸다. 반면 대대장 칼C. 젠슨 중령과 인사, 정보, 작전장교, L중대장 등 195명이 전사했다. 이날 A중대는 181명 중 27명이 전사하고 30명이 실종되었다.

치열했던 6·25 격전지 연기군, 개미허리같이 잘록한 개미고개 격전지의 현실은 전설이 되었다.

미국 청년의 피를 뿌린 자유, 평화의 빛이 전투 전적비 기념탑 뒤 벽면에 빛나는 이름으로 새겨져 있다. 대한민국은 이 은혜의 피 값을 잊지 않고 갚아야 한다.

20년 11월 7일 경부선 철로와 1번 국도가 협소한 지역을 통과하는 6·25 격전지 개미고개 격전지를 청토마와 답사했다.

61년이 흐른 후 2011년 6월 전쟁 유해 발굴작업 중에 U.S. 마크 찍힌 수통이 나오고, 군화 크기 290mm의 유해 1구와 방망이 수류탄과 뒤엉켜 있는 9구의 유골을 발굴했다.

추정컨대 미군과 북한군 간 백병전 같았다. 훗날 판명 감식에 그들은 미군과 북한군으로 밝혀졌다.

현재 고지 정상에서 매년 7월 10일 개미고개전투 기념행사가 열린다.

미국 청년이 이름도 모르는 곳에 자유를 위해, 이역만리를 달려와 평화를 위해 생명을 버린 곳. 자유는 거저 얻어지는 것이 아니었다.

The Monument to Gaemi(Ants) pass Battle (Chochiwon)

Location: Region of 836 Unjusan-ro, JeonDong-myeon, Sejong-si.

On July 10, 1950, at Goma Pass (meaning high) in the north of Jochiwon.

The nK 3rd Division and the U.S. 21st Regiment had engagement.

Goma pass was called as ants pass because 2,000 soldiers of nK puppet climbed up it like ants.

U.S. 21st Regiment made the most results during the Korean War as destroyed enermy's 38×tanks, 7×semi-orbital vehicles, and 117×trucks. On the other hand, 195 friendly soldiers were killed in action, including battalion commander, Lieutenant Colonel Carl C. Jensen, personnel, intelligence, operations officer, and L company commander.

On this day, 30 soldiers were killed in action and 30 soldiers were missing in action of 181 soldiers from Company A.

The fierce battlefield with a narrow pass like an ant's waist of Korean War which took place in Yeongi-gun has become a legend.

Freedom, light of peace through blood of U.S. youth were engraved on the wall behind memorial tower as the honored names. ROK must not forget the favor of U.S soldiers' blood and pay it back.

On 7th November, I visit Gaemi(Ants) pass, a hard-fought field of Korean War, which Gyeongbu railroad and national route 1 passes through the narrow area with my Cheongtoma(my truck's nickname).

61 years later, while carrying out war remains excavation in June 2011, a U.S.-marked water bottle was found and a 290mm foot size body, mixed nine other bodies with bat-shaped grenade were excavated.

It seemed like that there was hand to hand fight between U.S. soldiers and nK soldiers. Later, the results of inspection revealed that they were U.S. soldiers and nK soldiers.

Today, the Gaemi(Ants) pass battle memorial is held every 10th July at the top of the pass.
This is the place where U.S. youth had run to protect freedom and peace of unknown far nation.
Freedom was not free.

北鳥致院　高魔地形
北傀三師　對美聯隊
蟻群集團　蟻嶺峽路
二日血戰　擊戰地域
最大戰果　最大避害
熾熱擊戰　自由平和

05

대전지구 전적비

위치 : 대전 중구 대사동 산3-71 (보문산 공원 내)

1950년 7월 5일, 최초 오산 전투 이후 경부축선을 따라서 지연전을 전개했다. 미 24사단은 대전에서 북괴군의 중과부적으로 많은 적을 대적하지 못했다.

방어전을 전개하면서 시가전을 치렀다.

포위공격을 당했다. 악전고투했다.

3.5인치 로켓포를 최초 사용하여 북괴군 전차를 파괴하는 성과를 올렸다. 진두지휘하던 윌리엄 에프 딘(William F. Dean) 사단장이 실종되는 비운을 겪었다. 이 전투가 낙동강 최후방어 준비시간을 벌어 주었다.

대전에서 용감히 싸운 영웅을 잊어서는 안 된다. 혈맹의 우의를 길이길이 전해야 한다.

약 2개월 후 9월 17일 미 24사단은 낙동강지역 창녕에서 사단을 재정비했다. 인천상륙작전 성공으로 한 많은 대전지역을 북괴군에 설욕을 갚고 탈환했다.

2021월 5월 3월 대전 중구 대사동 산 3번지 보문산 공원에 있는 대전지구 전적비를 답사하고 참배했다.

The Monument to Daejeon district battle

Location: San 3-71 in Daesa-dong, Jung-gu, Daejeon (in Bomunsan Park)

On 5th July, 1950, after the first Battle of Osan, U.S. 24th Infantry Division engaged delaying actions along the Gyeongbu Axis. The U.S 24th Division failed to stand against lots of enemies in Daejeon because of numerical inferiority.

While conducting defensive operation, U.S. 24th Division engaged street battle. It was enveloped and had a hard time to fight.

The first use of a 3.5-inch rocket launcher resulted in the destruction of nK puppet tanks. But U.S. 24th Division suffered the misfortune that William F. Dean, commander of division was missing.

This battle earned time to prepare for the final defense line along the Nakdong River. Don't forget the heroes who fought bravely in Daejeon. The friendship of blood alliance must be conveyed forever.

About two months later, on 17th September, the U.S. 24th Division reorganized itself in Changnyeong, in Nakdong River region. With the success of Incheon landing operation, U.S. 24th Division revenged on nK puppet Army and recaptured a lot of Daejeon areas which have many stories.

On 3rd May, 2021, I explored and paid tribute to the monument to the Daejeon district in Bomunsan Park, San 3, Daesa-dong, Jung-gu, Daejeon.

初戰以後　遲延展開
大田地域　衆寡不敵
包圍攻擊　苦戰惡鬪
展開攻防　爲市街戰
北傀戰車　破壞成果
師團將焉　失終悲劇
最後防禦　洛東防備
師再整備　大田奪還

06

대전지구 승전비

위치: 대전 중구 보문산공원로 426-83 (대사동)

　1950년 6월 25일 북괴군의 불법 남침으로 미 24사단 스미스 특수부대는 오산에서 첫 전투를 했다. 첫 전투는 중과부적으로 지연전을 전개했다.

　천안전투는 시가전으로 지연작전을 수행했다. 개미고개 전투에서 많은 전과를 내고, 큰 피해도 있었다.

　방어전에 실패하여 대전지역이 포위당했다.

　미 8군 사령관인 워커장군의 명령으로 7월 20일까지 사수를 했다. 20사단은 대전에서 결사 방어전을 수행했다. 시내는 피아혼전이다. 시내를 적의 T-34 전차가 휩쓸고 다녔다.

　사단장인 딘 소장이 직접 지시, 3.5인치 바주카포로 대항, 북괴군의 전차를 파괴했다.

　미군 20사단은 대전지구 전투에서 3,933명이 참전했다.

　그중에 전사 48명, 부상 228명, 실종 874명의 피해를 보았다.

　3.5인치 바주카포로 전차 8대를 격파하고. 포격으로 2대, 항공기로 5대 총 전차 15대를 파괴했다.

　미 24사단은 7월 5일부터 21일까지 17일간의 전투를 치루고 제1해병사단에 인계했다.

　대전전투로 낙동강 방어 준비에 황금 같은 시간을 획득했다.

　사단 병력 7,305명이 희생되고 장비 60%를 잃고, 사단장이 실종되었다.

24사단은 낙동강 지역인 창녕과 남지에서 재편성에 들어갔다.

2020년 11월 7일 대전 보문산 공원에 있는 유엔군 대전지구 전승비와 전투 전적비를 참배했다. 인류의 신성한 이상의 자유와 평화는 거저 얻어지는 것이 아님을 알았다.

사단장은 전북 진안 상천면에서 부역자의 신고로 포로가 되었다. 그후 딘 소장은 1953년 9월 4일 포로교환 때 귀환했다.

우리는 이러한 6·25 전사를 알아야 된다는 신삿갓이다.

The Monument to victory of Daejeon district

Location: 426-83, Bomunsan Park-ro, Jung-gu, Daejeon (Daesa-dong)

On 25th June, 1950, Task Force Smith of U.S. 24th Division conducted their first battle in Osan after the illegal Invasion from nK puppet. Task Force Smith conducted delaying action because of numerical inferiority.

The Battle of Cheonan was carried out by delayed operations with a street battle. There were many military achievements but severe damages as well in Gaemi(Ants) pass battle.

The Daejeon area was enveloped by nK Army due to failure of defense. As General Walker's order, commander of U.S. 8th army, 24th Division depend positions to the last until 20th July.

The division fought desperately in Daejeon. Downtown was confused with engagement between friendly forces and enemies. Enemy's T-34 tanks kept sweeping through the city.

Major General Dean, the division commander, destroyed the anti 3.5-inch Bazuka tank by direct command.

3,933 soldiers of U.S. 24th Division participated in the Battle of Daejeon District.

Among them, 48 were killed, 228 were wounded in action, and 874 were missing.

U.S. 24th Division destroyed eight tanks with a 3-5-inch bazooka. It also destroyed two tanks with artillery shelling and five tanks aircraft attack. U.S. 24th Division destroyed a total of 15 tanks.

U.S. 24th division had fought for 17 days from 5th to 21st July and then handed over their operation area to U.S. 1st Marine division.

Thanks to the Battle of Daejeon, friendly forces earned a golden time to prepare for the defense of the Nakdong River.

7,305 soldiers were sacrificed, 60% of equipments were lost, and the division commander was missing. The division began to reorganize in Changnyeong and Namji, region of Nakdong River.

On 7th November, 2020, I paid tribute to monument to victory and memorial monument of UN forces at Bomun mountain Park in Daejeon. I found out that freedom and peace which sacred and ideal of mankind were not gained for free. The division commander was taken prisoner at the report of a servant in Sangcheon-myeon, Jinan, Jeollabuk-do. After that major general Dean returned when the prisoner exchange was held on 4th September, 1953. I am gleeman

Shin who appeals to ROK people to learn history of Korean War.

北傀南侵　美軍先逢
烏山戰鬪　衆寡不敵
天安戰鬪　爲遲延戰
蟻腰嶺戰　二次遲延
大田戰鬪　結死抗戰
大田包圍　市街混戰
大田市內　對戰車戰
上部命令　死守遲延
遲延作戰　最後防禦
洛東防備　金科獲時

07

창녕지구 UN군 승전비

위치: 경남 창녕군 창녕읍 교상리 28-1 (만옥정 공원 내)

6·25 한국전쟁은 불법 남침으로 동족을 죽이는 비극, 괴뢰군 적 4사단은 서부 경남 함양과 거창을 점령하고 낙동강 도강해서 현풍과 창녕지역 공격했다.

대구를 포위 공격할 계획으로 낙동강 돌출부 남지읍 박진나루와 오향나루 건너 부곡방향으로 공격했다.

재편성 완료한 미 제24사단과 미 제2사단의 치열한 역습으로 북괴군 9사단, 10사단을 저지했다.

8월 13일은 6회에 걸친 발악적인 공격을 저지했다. 미 8군 사령관 워커 중장은 미 5해병연대를 투입했다. 9월 15일까지 1달여 간 일진일퇴의 혈투가 지속되고 육박전까지 벌어졌다. 보급지원이 끊어진 북괴 3개 사단은 지리멸렬되니 대전시 지연작전에 큰 피해 본 미 24사단은 이로써 설욕을 하게 되었고 창녕읍에 UN군 승전비가 세워졌다.

이 불후의 낙동강 전투 공훈을 길이 빛나며, 참전한 미국 젊은 청년들을 깊이 위로한다.

2020년 12월 23일 창녕읍에 있는 창녕지구 UN군 승전비를 답사하고 참배했다.

전쟁사를 알수록 한국의 자유와 평화를 지키기 위해 이역만리 달려온 미국 청년들의 살신성인 정신을 우리 젊은 청년도 알고 살아가기를 소망하는 신삿갓 입니다.

The Monument to UN forces' victory in Changnyeong District

Location: 28-1, Gyosang-ri, Changnyeong-eup, Changnyeong-gun, Gyeongsangnam-do (in Manokjeong Park)

The Korean War is a tragedy of killing relatives with illegal invasion from nK puppet. 4th division of puppet nK Army secured western of Hamyang and Geochang in Gyeongsangnam-do and attacked Hyeonpung and Changnyeong areas after crossing Nakdong River.

As nK 4th division's plans of Daegu envelopment, It had crossed Bakjin ferry and Ohyang ferry in Namji-eup, the protrusion of the Nakdong River and advanced toward Bugok.

U.S. 24th Division which completed the reorganization and 2nd Division blocked nK puppet 9th and 10th divisions with fierce counterattacks.

On 13th August, U.S. forces blocked six vicious attacks.
Lt. Gen. Walker, commander of U.S. 8th army, deployed U.S. 5th Marine Regiment.

A month-long bloody battle continued Until 15th September. Even there were hand to hand fights.

The three nK divisions which had been cut off sustainment were dissolved.

U.S. 24th division which suffered heavy damages from delay operation in Daejeon could vindicate. And then the monument to victory of UN forces was elected in Changnyeong-eup.

I honor that immortal merits of Nakdong River battle and deeply comfort U.S. youth who participated in Korean War.

On 23rd December, 2020, I visited and paid tribute to monument to victory of UN forces in Changnyeong district. As I know more about the history of Korean War, I, gleeman Shin, hope that our young people will know the spirit of sacrifice of U.S. youth who had run to far ROK and fought to protect freedom and peace of ROK.

韓國戰爭　同族相殘
居昌占領　洛東渡江
爲包大邱　攻擊計劃
渡江進擊　釜谷向攻
美軍逆襲　企圖座切
一進一退　攻擊沮止
一月攻防　肉薄戰鬪
赤軍滅切　美軍勝利

창녕지구 승전비
A photo of the monument to
victory in Changnyeong district.jpg

08

박진지구 전적비(박진전쟁 기념관)

위치: 경남 창녕군 남지읍 월하리 산 180 (박진전쟁기념관 언덕 위)

북한군은 전차를 앞세우고 기습 남침했다.

공산군은 일거에 38선을 돌파하고 3일 만에 수도 서울을 섬령했다. 한강을 건너서 남쪽으로 공격했다.

우리는 약한 군사력으로 UN군과 힘을 모아 혈전을 계속했다. 지연전으로 40여일 후 8월 초에 낙동강을 끼고 최후 방어선을 구축했다. 북괴군은 대구와 부산을 점령하기 위해 박진지역으로 도하했다.

박진지역은 북한군 제4사단, 제2사단, 제9사단, 제10사단의 4개 사단과 미 제24사단, 제2사단, 제5해병연대가 일진일퇴를 거듭한 격전지다.

당시 북한의 최정예부대 제4사단은 이목나루로 은밀히 기습침투를 했다. 강변을 방어하고 있던 미군과 치열한 전투를 했다. UN군은 대구와 마산지역의 예비 병력을 박진지구에 집중했다. 8월 19일에 적에게 치명적인 타격을 입히고 적을 강 건너편으로 격퇴시켰다.

이 전투에서의 승리로 전세가 역전되었다.

UN군은 이곳 박진지구에서 자유를 위해 산화한 UN군의 수많은 젊은 영령들에게 나는 충심으로 명복을 빈다.

자유는 그냥 얻어지는 것이 아니다.

2020년 12월 23일 남지읍 박진지구 전적비를 답사했다.

조용했던 낙동강변 월하리 마을에는 전쟁기념관과 격전지 능선에는 전적비가 피에 젖은 땅 위에 세워 있었다.

The Monument to battle of Park Jin District(BaKJin War Memorial Hall)

Location: 180 Wolha-ri, Namji-eup, Changnyeong-gun, Gyeongsangnam-do (on the hill of the BakJin War Memorial Hall)

The nK Army invaded the ROK with tanks at the forefront.

The Communist Army penetrated the 38th parallel at once, and three days later, it secured the capital of Seoul. They crossed the Han River and attacked south.

ROK Army with weak military power and UN forces fought fiercly against nK Army. About 40 days later, in early August, the last line of defense along the Nakdong River was established.

nK puppet Army crossed river to Bakjin district to occupy Daegu and Busan. Bakjin district was a series of fierce battle place between nK 4th, 2nd, 9th, 10th divisions and U.S. 24th, 2nd Divisions, 5th Marine Regiment.

박진지역 전적비
A photo of the monument to bakjin district

At that time nK elite unit, 4th Division conducted surprising infiltration secretly to Imok ferry. and then it fought fiercly against the U.S. forces defending the riverside. UN forces concentrated reserved forces of Daegu and Masan to Bakjin district.

On 19th August, the enemies were dealt a fatal blow and defeated across the river. The momentum of Korean War reversed in this battle.

I pray with all my heart to the young spirits that died in glorious in bakjin district. Freedom is not free.

On 23rd December, 2020, I explored the monument to Bakjin district in Namji-eup. In the quiet village of Wolha-ri along the Nakdong River, a monument was erected on blood-soaked land on the ridge of the war memorial and battlefield.

奇襲南侵　北韓傀儡
破三八線　首都占領
弱軍士力　血戰返復
四十餘後　防禦構築
爲釜山占　渡河洛東
最後發惡　美軍擊戰
奇襲侵鬪　防禦熾熱
預備兵力　集中防禦
赤致命打　江越擊退
全勢易戰　祈冥福也

박진전투기념비

왜관 작오산 미군학살 추모비

위치: 경북 칠곡군 왜관읍 아곡리 431번지 (안질마을)

1950년 8월 15일, 미 1기갑사단 제5연대 H중대 박격포 소대원 45명은 북한군을 증원하러 오는 북한군을 국군으로 오인하는 바람에 저항 없이 포로가 되었다.

포로로 잡힌 미군 소대원들은 신발과 옷까지 모두 발가벗겨졌다. 군화 끈으로 두 손을 뒤로 묶인 채 2일간 작오산 303고지 일대를 끌려 다녔다. 비인간적 대우를 하면서 말이다. 그리고 17일 왜관 작오산 자락에서 처참하게 학살당했다.

북괴군은 확인 사살까지 했다. 그러나 동료의 시체 더미에 깔려있던 '프레드릭 라이언' 이병을 포함한 5명이 극적으로 목숨을 건졌다. 그때 입은 총상으로 고통에 시달리고 있다.

그들은 한국의 자유와 평화를 위해 싸웠다.

미국 젊은이들은 한국이 어딘지도 몰랐다. 그럼에도 다른 나라의 자유를 위해 자신의 목숨을 내놓고 싸우고 희생했다.

이처럼 대한민국의 평화와 자유를 수호하기 위해 수만리에서 온 미군용사의 넋을 나는 위로했다.

추모비가 있는 포로학살 현장인 안질마을 답사하고 추모하면서 명복을 빌었다. 식전 아침부터 눈물바람이 불었다.

2021년 5월 1일 왜관읍 아곡리 431번지에 있는 작오산 자락 안질마을에 갔다. 미군 학살 추모비가 잘 정비 되어 있다.

Memorial Monument to the massacre of U.S. soldiers in Jakosan Mountain, Waegwan

Location: 431 Agok-ri, Waegwan-eup, Chilgok-gun, Gyeongsangbuk-do (Anjil Village)

On 15th August, 1950, 45 platoon members of H Company mortar of 5th Regiment of U.S. 1st Armored Division were taken prisoner without resistance because they mistook nK Army as ROK augmented forces. Captured U.S. platoon members were forced to take off all their shoes and clothes. nK Army dragged captured U.S. platoon members with their hands tied behind back with strings of military boots around the 303 highland area of Jako Mountain for two days. nK Army treated them inhuman.

On 17th August, nK Army was brutally massacred at the lower edges of Jako Mountain in Waegwan. nK Army even shoot to confirm U.S. soldiers' death. But there were five dramatic survivors who had been buried in a pile of his colleagues' bodies, including Private Frederick Ryan. They have been suffering from a gunshot wound. They fought for freedom and peace in ROK. Young Americans didn't even know where ROK was. Nevertheless they fought and sacrificed their lives for the freedom of another country.

In order to protect the peace and freedom of ROK, I consoled for the spirits of U.S. soldiers from far away. I visited Anjil Village, the site of the prisoner's massacre where the memorial monument is located. I prayed for the repose of their souls in memory. I had tears in my eyes early in the morning before the breakfast.

1st May, 2021, I went to Anjil Village where the lower edges of Jako Mountain at 431 Agok-ri, Waegwan-eup. The memorial to the massacre of U.S. soldiers was well maintained.

國軍誤認　無抗獲捕
捕虜裸體　束手非人
悽慘虐殺　確因死殺
同僚屍下　劇的五活
生存五命　銃傷苦痛
自由守護　美軍靑年
平和韓國　爲美犧牲
現場踏査　朝淚冥福

10

왜관지구 전적비(칠곡 낙동강 전투)

위치: 경북 칠곡군 석적읍 226 (중지리)

　1950년 8월 1일~9월 24일, 55일간의 낙동강 방어 전투는 칠곡 왜관이 최대의 격전지다.

　미 제1기병사단 장병은 바람앞에 등불같은 대한민국을 위기에서 구하는 큰 공을 세웠다. 낙동강 방어선 240km에서 가장 중요한 전력적 요충지로서 전국토의 10%만 남은 상황이다.

　미 제1기병 사단장(Hobert Raymond Gay)은 삶과 죽음의 경계선에서 8월 3일 20시 30분 적 전차 도하 저지를 위해 왜관 철교를 폭파했다.

　8월 16일 11시 58분부터 12시 24분까지 26분간 B-29 폭격기가 960톤의 폭탄을 낙동강 서쪽 대안과 약목지역 일대를 폭격하여 적 4만명과 지원물자를 융단 폭격했다. 포로와 귀순자의 증언에 의하면 이로써 북한군은 전쟁 승리의 확신 의지를 상실했단다.

　다윗과 골리앗의 싸움으로 328고지는 주인이 15번 바뀌었다.

　양보할 수 없는 핵심 거점지역이다. 가장 치열한 고지전이다. 적 3사단과 105기갑사단 6천명과 맞딱드렸다.

　혈전과 혈전으로 시체가 산이 되고 피가 하천이 되는 '시산혈하' 지역이다. 백병전과 야간 기습공격의 심한 고통으로 울부짖는 아비규환의 참상이다. 결국 8월 23일 국군 1사단 15연대가 최종 탈환했다.

　역사를 기억하지 못하는 자는 다시 그 역사를 반복할 것이다.(Those who Forget History are Doomed to Repeat It.)

한국은 미국에 갚지 못할 큰 빚을 지고 살고 있다. 한국이 어딘지도 모르고 평화와 자유를 지키기 위해 왔다. 이들의 용기와 희생이 우리 후손에게 대대손손 기억되어야 한다.

2021월 5월 1일, 칠곡군 왜관 작오산 아래 칠곡 호국평화기념관 지역을 답사했다. 이곳은 '호국의 성지'로 군인과 공무원, 교사가 한 번씩 답사해야 한다. 애국자는 답사 필수 코스다.

워커 사령관의 (Stand or Die) 죽음을 각오하고 전선을 사수하라는 명령이 지금도 유효하다. 우리는 전쟁하다 잠시 쉬는 휴전 중이니까.

왜관지구 전적비를 참배했다.

*제안합니다. 대한민국의 모든 공직자들은 임용 시 첫 부임지를 가기 전에 꼭 1회 이상 답사하기 바랍니다. 나라사랑으로 애국심을 고취하기 위해서 입니다.

The Monument to Waegwan district Battle(Chilgok Nakdong river battle)

Location: 226 Seokjeok-eup, Chilgok-gun, Gyeongsangbuk-do (Jungji-ri)

Chilgok of Waegwan was the largest battleground in the Nakdong River defense battle. The battle continued for 55 days from 1st August to 24th September, 1950. The soldiers of the U.S. 1st cavalry division made a great contribution to ROK in crisis, which was like a lantern in front of the wind. Waegwan district was the most critical strategic point on the 240km defense line along the Nakdong River, when only 10% of the country territory remained.

At 2030(I) on 3rd August, U.S. 1st cavalry division commander Hobert Raymond Gay blew up the Waegwan Railway(br) to block crossing enemy tanks on the border between life and death.

For 26 minutes from 1158(I) to 1224(I) on 16th August, B-29 bombers bombed the area of opposite bank and Yakmok, west of the Nakdong River, carpet bombing 40,000 enemies and support materials. As a result the nK Army lost its will to fight, according to the testimony of the captives and defectors.

As the battle between David and Goliath, the owner of the

328 highland 15 times. It was a key lodgment area that cannot be compromised. It was the fiercest highland battle. Friendly forces met 6,000 enemies of 3rd division and 105th armored division.

It was a area where the bodies became a mountain and blood became a river due to bloody battles in a row. It was a devastation of chaos, severe pain due to hand to hand fight and night surprise attacks. On 23th August, the 15th Regiment of the ROK 1st Division secured 328 highland eventually.

Those who forget history are doomed to repeat it. ROK owes big debt that can't repay. Young Americans came here to protect peace and freedom without knowing where ROK was. Their courage and sacrifice should be remembered by our descendants from generation to generation.

On 1st May, 2021, I toured the Chilgok National Peace Memorial Hall area under Jako Mountain, Waegwan, Chilgok-gun. This place is a 'holy place of defense' so soldiers, government officials, and teachers should explore this place at least once. This place is a must-see course for patriots. General Walker said "Stand or Die", stood by the front line. The order is still in effect. Because we're in the armistice. I paid tribute to the monument in Waegwan district.

*I suggest that all public officials in Korea should visit at least once before going to their first position after appointment. The purpose is to promote their patriotism with love for the country.

洛東防禦　最激戰地
風前燈火　大韓民國
絶體絶命　戰車渡河
倭館鐵橋　爆破決行
絨緞爆擊　若木一垈
戰爭勝利　意志傷失
高地爭奪　屍山血河
夜間奇襲　阿鼻叫喚
歷史忘失　再返復也
美國大債　代孫記憶

11

최초의 전차전 볼링엘리전투(多富戰勝碑)

위치: 경북 칠곡군 가산면 금화리 125

1950년 8월 21일~23일 다부동 천평계곡 진목정에서 한국전쟁 중에 최초의 전차전이 벌어졌다.

북괴군은 전차와 자주포, 차량을 앞세우고 왔다. 중공은 보전포 공격으로 국군 1사단 11연대 앞으로 공격했다. 중공은 미 제27연대 정면으로 야간공격 감행했다.

미 27연대는 가용포를 집중했다. M26 전차 8대와 자주포 3문을 소이리 협곡에 배치했다. 전차와 보병은 분리했다. 아군 전차를 추진해서 적에 대응을 사격했다.

미 장병은 협곡주변 산에 배치했다.

천평계곡은 피아전차에서 발사되는 철갑탄이 5시간 동안 교차하면서 불꽃이 튀었다. 미 27연대 장병은 철갑탄이 어둠을 뚫고 좁은 계곡에 적 전차를 향해 날아가는 광경을 보았다. 마치 볼링공이 핀을 향해서 재빠르게 미끄러져 가는 모습과 같았단다. 그래서 볼링 엘리(Bowling Alley) 전투라 했다.

날이 밝자 적 전차 9대, 자주포 4문, 수 대의 불탄 트럭과 1,300여구의 사체가 확인되었다. 더구나 다음날인 22일에 적 13사단 포병연대장 정봉욱 중좌가 작전지도를 가지고 병사와 귀순을 했다. 23일 밤 12연대는 밤에 야간 기습으로 유학산을 탈환했다. 이로써 국군 1사단(백선엽 사단장)과 미 제27연대장 존. H. 마이켈리스 대령은 최초 연합작전으로 찬란한 무훈을 남기고 다부동에 승전비가 세워졌다.

2021월 5월 1일 경북 칠곡군 가산면 금화리 125번지에 있는 다부동 전승비를 답사하고 참배했다.

당시 이날 밤 적 13사단의 공격을 막지 못했다면 대구는 함락되었을 것이다. 아찔한 생각이 들었다. 혼자 만세를 불렀다.

The Battle of Bowling Alley, the First tanks battle

Location: 125, Geumhwa-ri, Gasan-myeon, Chilgok-gun, Gyeongbuk

On 21st~23rd August, 1950, There was the first tanks battle took pin Jinmokjeong, Cheonpyeong Valley, Dabu-dong during the Korean War. nK puppet Army came with tanks, self-propelled guns, and vehicles. The supporting attack troops attacked ROK on front of 11st Regiment of 1st Division by infantries and tanks. The main attack troops conducted night attack on front of U.S. 27th Regiment.

The 27th U.S. Regiment concentrated its artillery fires. Eight M26 tanks and three self-propelled guns were deployed in the Soiri gorge. They separated the infantries and tanks. They had propelled their tanks and fired back at the enemies. U.S. soldiers were placed in the mountain around the canyon.

The Cheonpyeong Valley sparkled as ironclad ammunitions fired from friendly tanks and enemies for five hours. Soldiers from the 27th U.S. Regiment saw an ironclad ammunitions flying through the darkness toward enemy's tanks in a narrow valley. It was like that a bowling ball slided quickly toward bowling pins. So the battle is called Bowling Alley battle.

Next morning, 9 enemy tanks, 4 self-propelled artillery, several burned trucks and more than 1,300 enemy's bodies were found. Moreover next day(22nd) Jeong Bong-wook, commander of the nK 13th Infantry Division's artillery regiment and a soldier submitted to ROK with an operation map. On 23th night, the 12th regiment took back youhak mountain by night surprise.

As a result, Colonel John H. Michaelis, commander of the U.S. 27th Regiment and ROK 1st infantry division (Commander Baek Seon-yeop) erected the monument to victory through first combined operation with amazing military merits in Tabu-dong.

I visited the monument in Dabu-dong at 125 Geumhwa-ri, Gasan-myeon, Chilgok-gun, North Gyeongsang Province on 1st May, 2021. Daegu would have been destroyed if we couldn't defeat the enemies, attack from nK 13th division on that night. I had a dizzying thought. I called out "Hurrah" by myself.

韓國戰爭　初戰車戰
北傀步戰　夜間攻敢
韓美聯合　可用集中
步戰分離　狹谷配置
泉坪繼谷　彼我戰車
發射鐵甲　適破戰車
將兵視覺　飛彈鐵砲
似而飛球　如而株破
明朝確認　戰果擴大
夜間奇襲　奪還遊鶴

12

다부동 전적비(유학산 전투)

위치: 경북 칠곡군 가산면 호국로 1486 (가산면 다부리)

1950년 8월 13일~23일 낙동강 방어선은 왜관을 기준으로 동북 측은 국군이 맡았다. 북괴군은 전선의 약한 고리인 국군 지역을 집중 공격했다. 그래서 가장 치열한 곳이 대구 가는 길목 다부동 유학산 진출이다.

치열한 고지 쟁탈전이다. 아군이 2,300여 명 전사했다. 적군을 5,690여 명 사살했다. 대구까지 불과 20km, 대한민국의 운명이 달려 있던 생명선이다.

경찰이 대구 사수를 위해 1만 5천 명을 투입했다. 1,100명이 전사했다. 수많은 학도병이 이름도 군번도 없이 쓰러져갔다. 노무부대인 지게부대(A-Frame Army) 1개 대대에 60여 명, 황금 덩어리 같은 주먹밥, 탄약, 부상자 후송을 맡았다.

매일 700여 명이 죽어 나갔다.

9월 6일 국군 8사단이 방어하던 영천이 점령당했다. 국군이 동서로 분할 약화 되었다. 미군이 전면 철수를 고려했다. 이때 국군 1사단장(백선엽 장군) "내가 물러서면 나를 쏴라" 반격했다. 10일 영천에서 북한군을 격퇴하니 방어선이 안정되고 전면 철수는 없던 일로 하게 되었다. 14일까지 전선이 교착상태로 있었다.

9월 15일 인천상륙작전이 성공했다. 16일 오전 9시 한미 연합군이 총반격했다. 모든 방어선에서 공격으로 전환했다.

2021년 5월 1일, 다부동 전적기념관을 3번째 답사했다. 구국 용사 충혼비, 구국 경찰 충혼비에 참배했다. 반가운 것은 7년간 조종했던 UH-1H 헬기가 나와 같이 퇴역해 전시되어 있었다. 특히 마지막 조종사가 내가 가르친 기장 김00 준위였고 그의 이름이 있었다.

군가; 전우여 잘 자라
전우의 시체를 넘고 넘어 앞으로 앞으로..
낙동강아 잘 있거라 우리는 전진한다..
원한이야 피에 맺힌 적군을 무찌르고서
꽃잎처럼 떨어져 간 전우여 잘 자라.
-가수 현인; 당시 북진하는 상황의 군가.

The Dabu−dong Battle Monument (Battle of Yuhak Mountain)

Location: 1486 Hoguk-ro, Gasan-myeon, Chilgok-gun, Gyeongsangbuk-do (Daburi, Gasan-myeon)

From 13th to 23rd August, 1950, the Nakdong River defense line was handled by the ROK Army on the northeast side based on Waegwan. nK puppet Army attacked weak links of Nakdong River defense line which was covered by ROK Army. So youhak mountain in dabu-dong was the fierce battle place on the way to Daegu.

It was a fierce battle to secure the heights. More than 2,300 soldiers were killed in action. More than 5,690 enemy soldiers

were killed. It was only 20Km away from Daegu which was a lifeline that could affect the fate of ROK.

15,000 polices were deployed to defend Daegu. 1,100 polices were killed in action. Numerous student soldiers had passed away without names and service numbers. A-Frame battalion, a labor unit, consisted of 60 soldiers were in charge of transporting rice balls like gold, ammunitions, and evacuation of the injured. More than 700 people died every day.

On 6th September, Yeongcheon, which was defended by ROK 8th Division, was occupied by nK puppet Army. ROK Army was

divided from east to west and weakened. U.S. military considered a full withdrawal. At that time, General Baek Sun-yeop, the commander of ROK 1st Division, fought back, saying, "If I stepped back, shoot me." When nK puppet Army was defeated in Yeongcheon on 10th, the defense line was stabilized and there was no full withdrawal.

The frontline was deadlocked until 14th. The Incheon Landing Operation was successful on 15th September. At 0900(I) on 16th, ROK-U.S. combined forces launched a total counterattack. ROK-U.S. transitioned its operation to attack on every line of defense.

On 1st May, 2021, I visited the Dabu-dong Memorial Hall for the third time. I paid tribute to monument, soldiers, police officers who saved our country. The good thing is that a UH-1H helicopter, which I had piloted for seven years, was retired like me and being displayed. In particular, the last captain was warrant officer Kim who I taught pilot skill. His name was there.

A military song; good night, comrades

Go over the bodies of comrades, go forward, go forward/
Goodbye, Nakdong River. We are moving forward/
It's a grudge against bloody enemies/
Good night, comrades who fell like a flower petal.

-Singer Hun-In; a military song in the situation of advancing
north at the time.

高地爭奪　守生命線
救國警察　祐學徒兵
勞務部隊　彈藥補給
移動物資　移負傷者
傀儡占領　永川地域
東西分割　兩分弱化
全面撤收　美軍考慮
永川擊退　反擊機會
上陸成功　反擊命令
屍山血河　赤退滅裂

13 영산지구 전적비(낙동강 방어전투)

위치 : 경남 창녕군 영산면 동리 산 4번지 (호국공원 내)

1950년 8월 6일~9월 6일, 김일성이 가장 신뢰하는 최정예부대 4사단이 함양과 거창을 경유해 창녕에 왔다. 밀양을 탈취하고 부산을 점령하기 위함이다. 이를 미군의 결사 방어로 저지시킨 곳이 영산격전지다.

북괴 4사단은 낙동강 도강, 남지일대와 창녕 인근을 압박했다. 북괴 9사단은 주력 4사단을 따랐다. 미 24사단과 미 제5해병연대가 퇴각했다. 24사단과 교대한 미 2사단이 북괴군을 격퇴했다. 미 72 전차대대는 영산을 방어했다.

8월 11일 낙동강 돌출부 박천 월하리로 기습 도하했다. 사단은 공방전이 계속 되었다. 미 27연대가 남지에서 영산 쪽으로 적 후방을 역공격했다. 적에게 타격을 입히고 12정의 기관총과 대전차포를 노획했다.

9월 1일 북괴군 9사단이 박진나루를 건너왔다.

적 전차 43대가 지원해 영산이 점령되었다. 2일 미 9연대가 미 공군 전폭기 200여 대를 지원 및 폭격했다. 북괴군을 낙동강 서쪽으로 밀어냈다. 영산을 탈환했다.

9월 5일, 3일 동안 미군의 반격으로 큰 피해입은 북괴군 4사단, 9사단이 점차 공격 의지 잃고 와해되었다. 해병 5연대는 9연대에 작전지역을 인계하고 인천상륙작전을 위해서 부산으로 떠났다. 북한군 공격이 사라졌다.

2021년 5월 2일 경남 창녕군 영산면 동리 산 4번지, 호국공원을 답사하고 참배했다.

미 24사단, 2사단, 해병 5연대 백전불굴의 투혼을 발휘했다.

한국의 자유, 민주, 평화를 위한 거룩한 영혼에 한국인은 많은 빚을 지고 살고 있다. 점차 잊고 사는 듯해서 꼭 교육이 필요하다는 신삿갓이다.

The Monument to Yeongsan District Battle(Nakdong River Defense Battle)

Location: San 4, Dongri, Yeongsan-myeon, Changnyeong-gun, Gyeongsangnam-do (in Hoguk Park)

From 6th August to 6th September, 1950, Kim Il-sung's most trusted nK puppet 4th Infantry Division came to Changnyeong via Hamyang and Geochang. That's why to seize Miryang and occupy Busan. As a result, Yeongsan Battlefield was blocked by U.S. Army desperate defense.

The nK puppet 4th Division pressured the southern part of the Nakdong River and in vicinity of Changnyeong. nK puppet 9th Division followed 4th Division which was main force of nK Army. U.S. 24th Division and the 5th Marine Regiment withdrew. U.S. 2nd infantry division, which replaced 24th Division, defeated nK puppet Army. U.S. 72nd tank battalion defended Yeongsan.

On 11th August, nK Army surprisingly crossed into Wolha-ri, Bakcheon, at the protrusion of the Nakdong River. The Division continued its battle. U.S. 27th Regiment attacked the enemy's rear from Namji toward Yeongsan. The enemies were defeated and friendly forces captured 12 machine guns and anti-tank guns.

On 1st September, nK puppet 9th Division crossed Bakjin ferry. And the division occupied Yeongsan by supporting 43 enemy tanks. On 2nd September, U.S. 9th Regiment bombed with more than 200 U.S. Air Force bombers. So friendly forces could push nK puppet Army west of the Nakdong river. Friendly forces recaptured Yeongsan.

On 5th September, nK 4th and 9th Divisions, which were severely damaged by U.S. counterattacks for 3 days, gradually lost their will to attack and collapsed. U.S. 5th Marine Regiment had handed over its operation area to U.S. 9th regiment and left for Busan to prepare Incheon Landing Operation. nK attack disappeared.

On 2nd May, 2021, I visited Hoguk Park at San 4, Dongri, Yeongsan-myeon, Changnyeong-gun, Gyeongsangnam-do. U.S. 24th Division, 2nd Division, and 5th Marine Regiment fought with a heart of 'never surrender'. ROK people owe a lot to holy souls for ROK's freedom, democracy, and peace. I, gleeman Shin, insist needs of education for U.S. soldiers sacrifice because it seems to be being forgotten gradually form our memories.

最强北軍　精銳四師
咸居經由　攻擊靈山
渡江洛東　壓迫昌寧
美軍退脚　交代擊戰
北傀奇襲　攻擊靈山
美軍易攻　背後攻擊
北傀再攻　突出月下
空軍戰爆　靈山奪還
九師反擊　打擊北傀
北軍瓦解　美軍勝利

6 · 25 격전 함안 민안비 (艅航山, 갓뎀산 전투)

위치: 경남 함안군 여항면 주동리 483번지

1950년 8월 1일~ 9월 15일까지 45일간 전투했다. 적은 진주를 거쳐 왔다. 북괴군 최정예부대 6사단 2만명이다. 마산을 탈취하기 위해 함안 여항산 770m, 서북산 738m로 몰려왔다.

미군 제25사단은 낙동강이 최후 방어선이다. 민기식 혼성부대, 전투 경찰대, 학도병도 배속되었다. 너무나 위급상황, 정식 편성이 안 된 임시 부대들이 적과 맞섰다.

여항산은 야간에는 북한군 점령했다. 낮에는 미군이 점령했다. 이 고지들은 주인이 19번 바뀌었다. 미군은 울분을 나타내는 갓뎀 goddam* 이라했다.

지금도 민간에는 갓데미 산이라 부

른다.

1달 반 동안 처절한 전투는 계속되었다. 시체가 산을 이루고, 땅이 피로 물들었다. 산과 들판과 마을 주변에는 북한군 시체가 즐비했다. 적 6사단은 와해되었다. 최후는 미군의 승리로 끝났다.

*goddam 뜻: 망할, 빌어먹을, 지랄 맞다, 제기랄.

2021년 6월 12일(토), 함안 여항면 주동리 483번지를 답사하고 참배했다.

민기식 씨가 이끄는 부대는 여자도 참전한 것이 특별했다.

미 25사단의 아름다운 청년들이, 한국의 자유를 위한 수많은 미군의 숭고한 정신이 이렇게 아름다운 산에 있다. 처절한 전투지에 전승비가 없다.

우리 보훈처와 미 25사단이 협력해 전승비 설립을 건의하고 싶다.

The Monument to Peace of people in Haman where a Fierce battle occurred(Battle of Goddam mountain)

Location: 483 Judeong-ri, Yeohang-myeon, Haman-gun, Gyeongsangnam-do

The battle lasted for 45 days from 1st August to 15th September, 1950. The enemies came from Jinju. There were 20,000 soldiers of nK 6th Division, elite unit of nK puppet Army. In order to seize Masan, they flocked to 770m of Yeohang mountain and 738m of Seobuk mountain in Haman-gun.

The U.S. 25th Division's last line of defense was Nakdong river. Min Gi-sik mixed unit, combat police force, and student soldiers were also assigned. In too emergency situation, the temporary units which were not organized fought against enemies.

Mt. Yeohang was occupied by nK at night. During the day, U.S. forces occupied it. These highlands' owner had changed 19 times. U.S. Army said it was Goddam*, a expression of resentment. Even now, it is called Mt. God Demi among civilians.

For a month and a half, the bitter battle continued. The bodies formed a mountain, and the ground was stained with blood. nK soldier's bodies stood closely together at the mountain, fields, and villages. nK 6th Division was disrupted. U.S. Army ended in victory.

*goddam means: damn it.

On Saturday, 12th June, 2021, I explored 483 Judong-ri, Yeohang-myeon, Haman and worshiped.

The unit led by Min Gi-sik

was special because it had women who participated in the war.

The beautiful young men of U.S 25th Infantry Division which sacrificed for freedom of ROK are on this beautiful mountain. There is no victory in a desperate battlefield. I would like to ask the establishment a monument through cooperation between ROK Ministry of Patriots and Veterans Affairs.

最精銳隊　北傀六師
晋州經由　馬山奪取
最後防禦　美二五師
危急狀況　對適任隊
夜間占領　北韓軍也
晝間我領　我軍美軍
高地主人　拾九變主
血戰屍山　血濕山河
山野周邊　傀儡屍舒
激戰最後　美軍勝利

함안민안비

위치: 경남 창원시 마산합포구 진전면 평암리 산1-1 (서북산 정상)

1950년 8월 1일~9월 15일까지 45일간 전투했다.

북괴군 최정예부대 6사단과 서북산과 진동 일대에 미 25사단 5연대와 연대에 배속된 김성은 부대가 배치되어 있었다.

8월 6일 적 중화기에 의해 마산과 진동리 보급로가 차단되었다.

서북산 738m 일대로 적이 아귀처럼 달려들던 북괴군에 맞섰다. 이곳에서 5연대 중대장 티몬스 Timmons 대위와 중대원 100여 명이 부하들과 함께 장렬히 전사했다.

8월 7일 사단은 킨 Kean 특수부대 및 미 제1해병여단과 북한군 6사단 제 83모터싸이클 부대를 격파하고 진동지역을 탈환했다.

8월 17일 한국 해병대 최초의 상륙작전인 통영 상륙작전을 감행하고 성공했다. 해병대가 "귀신 잡는 해병대"* 신화를 창조했다.

한국의 자유와 평화를 수호하고자 장렬히 산화한 미군 장병과 국군의 숭고한 정신을 잊어서는 안 된다.

*귀신 잡는 해병대 : 마가렛 히킨스 미 종군기자가 전 세계에 상륙 성공 소식을 타전했다. 이 보도를 계기로 한국 해병대의 별칭으로 불렸다.

2021년 6월 12일(토), 마산 진동, 통영, 서북산 지역을 답사하고 참배했다. 특히 1995년 11월 미 8 군사령관 리챠드 티몬스(Richard Timmons) 중장은 함안 서북산 정상에 섰다. 한국전쟁 때 미 25사단 제5연대 중대장이었던 자신의 아버지 티몬스 대위의 전사 현장이다.
대한민국은 결초보은의 은혜를 갚아야 한다.

The Monument to Battles of Seobuk Mountain, Jindong, Tongyeong (Nakdong River Defense Battle)

Location: Mountain 1-1 Pyeongam-ri, Jinjin-myeon, Masanhappo-gu, Changwon-si, Gyeongsangnam-do (top of Seobuk Mountain)

The battle lasted 45 days from 1st August, 1950, to 15th September 1950. nK 6th Division, the elite unit of nK puppet Army deployed Seobuk mountain. U.S. 5th Regiment of 25th Infantry Division and Kim sung en unit which was assigned to the U.S. 5th Regiment deployed region of Jindong.

On 6th August, the supply routes of Masan and Jindong-ri were blocked by the enemy's heavy weapons. Friendly forces faced nK puppet Army, which rushed like a monkfish to the 738m area of Seobuk Mountain. At this place, Captain Timmons, a company commander of U.S. 5th Regiment, and about 100 members of the company died in honor.

On 7th August, the Kean Task Force and the U.S. 1st Marine Brigade defeated the 83rd Motor Cycle Unit of nK 6th Division and recaptured region of Jindong.

서북산 전적비

On 17th August, the Tongyeong Landing Operation, the first landing operation of ROK Marine Corps, was carried out and succeeded. The Marines created the myth of "Ghost-catching Marines."*

We must not forget the noble spirits of U.S. and ROK soldiers who died a glorious death to protect ROK's freedom and peace.

* Ghost−catching Marines: Margaret Higgins, a U.S. military reporter, reported the successful landing operation to the world. The report nicknamed the ROK Marine Corps.

On 12th June, 2021, I visited and paid tribute to the areas of Jindong, Masan, Tongyeong, and Seobuk mountain. In particular, in November 1995, Lieutenant General Richard Timmons, commander of U.S. 8th Army, stood at the top of Seobuk mountain in Haman. The place where his father, Captain Timmons, who died as a company commander of 5th Regiment of U.S. 25th Infantry Division in the Korean War. The Republic of Korea should repay the favor with "carrying our gratitude beyond the grave".

適精銳軍　對美五聯
晉州經由　馬山奪取
馬山鎭東　報給遮斷
赤西北山　功擊盡力
最後防禦　西北山頂
美軍死傷　一百戰死
特殊任務　鎭東奪還
海兵最初　上陸作戰

마산진동지구 전투 전적비
A photo of the monument to battle of Jindong distirct in Masan

위치 : 경남 창원시 마산합포구 진북면 지산리 314-3 (진동리지구 전적비)
Location: 314-3 Jisan-ri, Jinbuk-myeon, Masanhappo-gu, Changwon-si,
Gyeongsangnam-do (the monument to battle of Jindong-ri distirct

16

인천상륙작전 전초기지 영흥도

위치 : 인천 영흥도 십리포 해수욕장 해변.

맥아더 사령부는 특수침투요원을 구성하여 1950년 8월에 미군 클라크 대위와 한국해군 함명수 소령등 22명 첩보요원 편성했다.

8월 18일 새벽 1시 부산항을 출발 6일째 24일 인천 서해 영흥도에 도착했다. 특수첩보대는 3개조로 편성, 인천, 서울, 수원에 첩보 활동을 펼쳤다. 상륙 하루전 영흥도 거점을 철수했는데 해군첩보대 8명, 영흥도 청년방위대 6명 남아 있었다.

첩보활동을 감지한 북한군 1개 대대가 영흥도를 기습했다. 전투 중 14명이 전사하고 아군에게 협력한 동네 주민 50여명은 참살당했다.

상륙작전 성공확률 5,000분의 1, 공산전체주의를 물리치고 자유주의가 승리한 자랑스러운 역사다. 상륙작전에서 적의 수류탄을 몸으로 막으며 장렬히 산화한 ' 발로메로 로페스 ' 미 해병대 중위, '절대 후퇴하지 않겠다' 며 맥아더 장군을 감동하게 했던 백골부대 '신동수 일등병' 이런 결연한 용기와 희생이 승리의 원동력이다.

영흥도 십리포 해수욕장 해변에 그날의 역사현장을 비석으로 기념해 놓았다. 주변에는 해군참전비도 있다.

2023. 9. 16. 토, 인천상륙작전 시작점인 전초기지를 답사하면서 남쪽해변에는 해군 참전기념비를 답사했다.

★ 해군 영흥도 전적비, 섬 남쪽에 있다.

Incheon Landing Operation Outpost Yeongheungdo

Location: Shipnipo Beach, Yeongheungdo, Incheon.

MacArthur's headquarters formed a special infiltration unit, and in August 1950, it organized 22 intelligence agents, including Captain Clark of the US Army and Major Ham Myeong-su of the Korean Navy.

It departed Busan Port at 1 a.m. on August 18 and arrived at Yeongheung Island in the West Sea of Incheon on the 24th, the 6th day. The special intelligence unit was organized into three groups and carried out intelligence activities in Incheon, Seoul, and Suwon.

The Yeongheung Island base was evacuated the day before the landing, but 8 members of the Naval Intelligence Corps and 6 members of the Yeongheung Island Youth Defense Force remained.

A North Korean battalion, detecting espionage activities, raided Yeongheung Island. During the battle, 14 people were killed and about 50 local residents who cooperated with our troops were massacred.

The success rate of the landing operation was 1 in 5,000, and it is a proud history of liberalism defeating communist totalitarianism.

U.S. Marine Corps Lieutenant Balomero López, who died heroically by blocking an enemy grenade with his body during an amphibious landing operation.

Private First Class Shin Dong-soo, a member of the white-bone unit who impressed General MacArthur by saying, 'I will never retreat,' said that such resolute courage and sacrifice are the driving force behind victory.

The historical site of that day is commemorated with a monument on the beach of Simnipo Beach in Yeongheung Island. There is also a naval war memorial nearby.

On Saturday, September 16, 2023, while touring the outpost that was the starting point of the Incheon landing operation, we toured the Navy War Memorial on the southern beach.

★ Navy Yeongheungdo Battle Monument, located in the south of the island.

17

인천상륙 자유 수호탑

위치: 인천시 연수구 청량로 138 (옥련동)

6·25 한국전쟁 83일 차, 1950년 9월 15일, 전세를 일거에 뒤바꾼 작전이다.

인천항 앞 팔미도 등대 불을 15일 0시에 캘로부대* 6명이 침투 점령하여 등대 불을 밝히니 등대 불 따라 261척의 함선이 접근해, 함포사격이 시작되니 녹색 해안 월미도, 적색 해안 만석동, 청색 해안 용현동 3곳으로 75,000명이 상륙했다.

4일 만에 인천을 확보하고, 수도 서울 중앙청에 태극기를 게양하고, 낙동강 방어선 장병과 상륙군이 연결되니 전쟁 시작 91일차, 상륙 8일 만에 인민군에게 괴수 김일성의 총 후퇴 명령이 내려졌다. (9월 23일)

상륙작전 승리에 개가를 올려 자유를 찾은 옛 싸움터에서 산화한 미 해병 1사단 장병의 혼령을 만났다.

대한민국 자유민의 밑거름이 된 현장, 자유수호탑에서 머리 숙여 깊은 감사를 올립니다.

* 캘로부대 : KLO, Korea Liaison Office 약자, 주한연락처 특수전 부
　　　　　 대 ― 그 후 공수부대의 전신됨.

♥ 당시 미군3명, 국군 3명이 1조가 되었다.

20년 9월 28일(월), 인천 구송도, 당시 청색 해안에 있는 인천상륙작전 자유 수호탑을 답사하고 은혜에 감사를 올린 신삿갓,

주변 O-1 정찰기 보니 더 반갑다. 육군 항공 조종사 출신인 필자는

강원도 대성산, 적근산 백암산 북방 정찰기 비행시간 700시간 을 보유하고 있다.

★ 월미도 작전에서 북괴군 108명을 사살하고, 136명을 생포 했다.
상륙 피해는 한미 해병 21명 전 사, 부상 174명이다.

The Incheon Landing Freedom Guardian Tower

Location: 138, Cheongnyang-ro, Yeonsu-gu, Incheon (Okryeon-dong)

On the 83rd day of the Korean War, on 15th September, 1950, there was an operation that changed the war situation at once.

At midnight on 15th, 6 soldiers of KLO Unit* infiltrated & secured and lightened the Palmido Lighthouse in front of Incheon Port.

261 ships approached the lighthouse light, and as the gunfires began 75,000 soldiers landed in three places: Wolmido Island on the green coast, Manseok-dong on the red coast, and Yonghyeon-dong on the blue coast.

They had secured Incheon in four days, and the national flag was raised in the capital Seoul Central Office. As the landing forces and soldiers who were Nakdong river defense line are connected,

On eight days of landing operation, the 91st day of Korean War, the monster Kim Il-sung ordered general withdrawal to KPA.(23th September)

At the old battlefield where we found freedom by raising a shout of triumph in the landing operation,
I met the soldier's spirits of 1st Marine Corps that died in honor.
At the Freedom Guardian Tower, the foundation of ROK's freedom,
I bow my head and recalled their favor.

* KLO unit: KLO, an abbreviation for Korea Liaison Office, special warfare of USFK contact department – then transferred to airborne unit.

♥ At that time, each team consisted of three U.S. soldiers and three ROK soldiers.

On 28th September, I visit the Freedom Guardian Tower of Incheon Landing Operation at Incheon Gusong Island, on the blue coast and appreciated U.S. soldiers' favor.

I was even more glad to see the O-1 reconnaissance plane near that place.

I, a former Army aviation pilot, have 700 hours of flight time for northern reconnaissance in Daeseong mountain, Jeokgeun mountain, and Backam mountain in Gangwon-do.

★ 108 nK soldiers were killed and 136 were captured in Wolmido operation.

21 ROK and U.S. marines were killed and 174 wounded. The end.

韓國戰爭　戰勢急轉
仁川上陸　美軍作戰
美特殊戰　侵八尾島
燈臺占領　登火照明
艦船接近　艦砲射擊
上陸成功　韓美海兵
仁川擴保　首都中央
揭太極旗　連結作戰
傀首命令　退却傀儡
韓自由民　恩供感謝

18 인천지구 전적비

위치 : 인천 미추홀구 용현동 61-93 (인천수봉공원 정상)

기습남침을 자행한 북괴군은 승승장구로 낙동강 저지선 돌파를 서둘렀다.

UN군 사령관 맥아더 원수의 작전지휘로 미 10군단이 인천상륙작전을 1950년 9월 15일에 감행했다.

인천 앞바다 간만차 극심한 이곳에 미 해병 1사단과 국군 해병 1연대, 미 보병 제7사단, 국군보병 제17연대가 16일 인천시가를 탈환했다. 이로써 UN군과 국군이 38선을 넘어 북진의 결정적 계기를 마련했다.

이 언덕 수봉공원에서 그날의 인천 앞바다에 가득했던 전함들의 승리의 고동소리가 들린다.

낙동강 방어선에서 치열한 공방전의 전세를 일시에 역전시켜 북진의 발판을 마련한 곳이다. 민족의 사활을 가른 한국전쟁 결전의 옛터, 역사의 현장에서 이 땅에 정의와 자유를 지킨 용사들에게 하늘의 광명이 비치고 있었다.

2021년 1월 11일(월), 인천 수봉공원에 있는 인천지구 6·25 전적비를 참배했다.

그날의 영광의 하늘빛이 찬란히 빛나고 있다.

한국 자유와 평화를 사수한 자유수호역군 대 선배님들에게 감사를 올리는 신삿갓이다.

♥ 상륙작전 함선 : 261척 / 75,000명이 상륙했다.

★ 인천상륙작전을 계기로 괴수 김일성은 남침 91일차에
   총 북한군 전체 퇴각 명령을 9월 23일에 내렸다.

The Monument to battle of Incheon district

Location: 61-93 Yonghyeon-dong, Michuhol-gu, Incheon (top of Incheon Subong Park)

nK puppet Army which carried out a surprise invasion to the South, rushed to break through the Nakdong River blocking line with making a long drive taking advantage of victory. U.S. 10th corps carried out the Incheon Landing Operation on

15th September, 1950, under the operational command of UN commander Marshal MacArthur.

U.S. 1st Marine Division, ROK 1st Regiment of Marine Corps, U.S. 7th Division, and ROK 17th Regiment recaptured Incheon downtown on 16th where the in front of Incheon waters which has severe tide.

This provided a decisive opportunity for the UN and ROK forces to cross the 38th parallel. At this hill, Subong Park, I can hear the beating of the victory of battleships that filled the waters in front of Incheon that day.

It was the place where friendly forces reversed the Korean War situation for northern debouchment at once by the fierce battle on the Nakdong River defense line.

The ancient site of the decisive battle of the Korean War, which divided the lives and lives of the people, The light for soldiers who protected justice and freedom of ROK was shining.

On Monday, 11th January, 2021, I paid tribute to the monument to battle of Incheon district in Subong Park, Incheon. The glory of that day was shining brightly. ROK's Freedom and Peace Guard. I, gleeman shin, thank our seniors, guardians of freedom, who protected freedom and peace of ROK.

♥ Battle ships for Landing Operation：261 ships / 75,000 soldiers landed.

★ On the 91st day of the Korean War, Kim Il-sung, a monster, ordered general withdrawal after success of the Incheon Landing Operation.

奇襲南侵　北傀僞軍
乘勝長驅　洛東突破
美士領官　作戰指揮
仁川上陸　敢行成功
仁川海邊　干滿克復
二日作戰　仁川奪還
首都奪還　北進契機
此邱秀峰　勝利告動
洛東防禦　熾熱攻防
戰勢易戰　北進撥阪
民族死活　韓國戰爭
此地正義　自由韓國

19

부평전투 승전기념비

위치: 인천 부평구 경원대로 1184-6 (부평아트존)

1950년 9월 15일에 인천상륙작전이 성공했다.

연합군 맥아더 사령관은 최우선 과제로 김포비행장 조기 탈환을 명했다.

미 제1해병연대와 제5해병연대, 한국해병은 제5해병 연대에 배속되었다. 17일 새벽 인천 도화동에서 출발하여 경인국도를 따라 서울로 진격했다.

부평 원통이 고개(현 : 동수역 주변)로 적 T-34 전차 6대를 앞세우고 북한군 200여 명이 진격해 왔다. 이를 사전에 포착하고 미 제5해병연대가 섬멸하여 전과를 올렸다.

맥아더 사령관은 전투 직후 현장을 시찰하고 장병을 격려했다.

부평역 남쪽에 위치한 망월산과 부평시내 시가전이 벌어지면서 많은 사상자가 발생했다. 부평전투로 김포비행장과 수도 서울수복에 최대 근거를 마련하였다. 한국의 자유 평화 수호와 인류의 평화를 위해 목숨을 바친 연합군과 한국 해병대의 젊은 용사들의 넋을 기리며 참배를 했다.

2021년 2월 21일 인천지역 참전 기념비 5곳 중 마지막을 참배하니 인천지역이 한국전쟁의 격전지가 많았다.

(1. 구송도에 인천상륙작전 기념비, 2. 자유공원에 맥아더 사령관 기념비, 3. 인천 서구 아시아드 경기장 옆에 콜롬비아 참전 기념탑, 4. 인천 수봉공원에 인천지구 승전 기념비, 5. 인천 백운역 주변 백운공원에 부평전투 승전기념비 등하불명으로 제일 늦게 참배했다.)

The Monument to victory of Bupyeong battle

Location: 1184-6, Gyeongwon-daero, Bupyeong-gu, Incheon (Bupyeong Art Zone)

On 15th September, 1950, the Incheon Landing Operation was successful. Combined Forces Commander, MacArthur, ordered the early recapture of Gimpo Airfield as his top priority.

There were U.S. 1st Marine Regiment, 5th Marine Regiment, and ROK Marine Corps which was assigned to the U.S. 5th Marine Regiment. Ealry in the morning on 17th, they departed from Dohwa-dong, Incheon and advanced to Seoul along the Gyeongin route.

To Bupyeong Wontongi pass (current: near the Dongsu

Station), More than 200 nK soldiers advanced with 6 T-34 tanks at the forefront. Friendly forces detected it in advance and made military merits by defeating the enemies. Commander

MacArthur inspected the site immediately after the battle and encouraged the soldiers.

As the street battles occurred in the Mangwol Mountain which located in the south of Bupyeong Station, and Bupyeong city, there were lots of casualties. Bupyeong battle set the condition to restore Gimpo airport and capital of Seoul.

I worshiped souls of the young soldiers of combined forces and ROK marine corps that sacrificed themselves to protect ROK's freedom, peace, and peace of mankind.

On 21st February, 2021, I visited the last monument of the five monuments to participation in Korean War in region of Incheon. There were many battlefields of the Korean War in Incheon.

(1. The monument to Incheon Landing Operation in Gusong Island, 2. Commander MacArthur Memorial in Freedom Park, 3. The monument to colombia participation in Korean War

next to Asiad Stadium in Seo-gu, Incheon, 4. The monument to Incheon District Victory at Incheon Subong Park, 5. The monument to victory of Bupyeong Battle in Baegun Park near the Baegun Station which I worshiped last because of right under my nose.)

上陸作戰　成功以後
優先果題　航場奪還
美海聯隊　配屬韓海
晨出桃花　京仁國道
破敵戰車　殲滅傀儡
元帥視察　戰鬪激勵
滿月交戰　市街戰也
根擧擴保　金浦航場
韓國和平　聯合將兵
靑年勇士　靈魂參拜

20

미 해병대 행주도강 전첩비

위치 : 경기 고양시 덕양구 행주외동 60-14

　1950년 9월 15일 인천상륙작전 성공하고 미 5해병연대는 김포 비행장 인근 개화산에 도착했다.

　한국해병은 미 연대를 엄호하고 수색대원은 강 건너 행주산 아래에 도착했다.

　산성 7부 능선까지 정찰했으나 적정 미발견하고 이상 없음 보고 후 도강이 시작되니 적이 일제사격, 박격포탄 낙하되고 적 기관총 난사하고 격렬하게 저항했다.

　20일 새벽 산성에 공격준비사격 하니 정상에 괴뢰시신 2백여+ 남기고 퇴각했다.

　한미연합 해병연대 성공 도하 했으니 최초 한강이북 교두보를 확보하게 되었고 서울 탈환에 박차를 가할 수 있게 되었다.

　2020년 9월 20일, 행주산성 초입에 위치한 한미해병대 행주도강 戰捷碑를 참배하고 진정한 감사를 올리는 신삿갓이오.

The Monument to victory of U.S. Marine Corps' crossig Haengju

Location: 60-14 Haengjuoe-dong, Deokyang-gu, Goyang-si, Gyeonggi-do

　On 15th September, 1950, Incheon Landing Operation was

successful and U.S. 5th marine regiment arrived at Gaehwa Mountain near the Gimpo airport,

ROK Marines covered U.S. Regiment and reconnaissance guys arrived at Haengju Mountain by crossing the river.

They scouted the 7-part ridge of the mountain, but they didn't find the enemies' movements. They reported "CLEAR". As the river crossing started, the enemies resisted fiercely by firing, mortars and machine guns.

At early in the morning on 20th, as friendly forces conducted preparing fires at the fortress, the enemies withdrew with leaving around 200 nK puppet bodies on the top.

As ROK-U.S. Combined Marine Corps crossed Han River successfully, the first bridgehead in the north of Han River secured by friendly forces. And it could make be possible to speed up the recapture of Seoul.

On 20th September, 2020, I, gleeman Shin, worshiped the monument to victory of U.S. Marine Corps crossing Haengju which located at the entrance of Haengju fortress and gave a sincere appreciation.

仁川上陸　作戰成功
海兵聯隊　着開花山
韓國海兵　聯隊掩護
搜索隊員　城下到着
停察始作　赤情未見
異常無也　渡江上陸
赤一諸射　落迫擊彈
赤機關銃　擊烈抵抗
晨時山城　砲擊攻擊
傀儡屍身　殘存退却
韓美海兵　成功渡河
漢江以北　確橋頭堡

위치: 서울 은평구 녹번동 은평평화공원.

1950년 9월 22일 서울 수복작전 때 은평구 녹번리 전투가 치열했다. 미 해군 윌리엄 해밀턴 쇼 대위도 같이했다.

1922년 6월 5일 한국에 온 선교사 아버지 윌리엄 얼 쇼, 한국 이름은 서위염(徐煒廉)이다.

평양에서 외아들로 태어났다. 세계 2차대전 때 해군 소위로 노르망디 상륙작전에도 참가했다. 전역 후 하버드대학 박사과정 공부 중에 한국에 전쟁이 터졌다. 부모와 친구에게 "태어난 내 조국에 전쟁이 났는데 어떻게 맘 편히 공부만 하느냐, 조국에 평화가 온 다음 공부해도 늦지 않다" 했다.

유창한 한국어로 맥아더 장군을 보좌하고 9월 15일 인천상륙작전 성공 후 해병대로 보직을 바꿨다. 수도 서울 탈환에 나섰다.

녹번리에서 북괴군의 매복조의 습격을 받아 장렬히 전사했다.

은평평화공원에 동상으로 다시 세워졌다. 태어난 한국을 위해 목숨을 바친 29세 사나이다. 한국전쟁의 영웅이다.

이 애국을 귀감으로 바로 우리가 높이 기려야 한다.

* 徐煒廉 : 서위염은 해밀턴 쇼 대위의 아버지 한국 이름.

2021년 6월 21일(월), 일 년 중 낮이 가장 긴 날, 은평구 녹번동 은평평화공원, 역촌역을 답사하고 참배했다.

The Statue of William Hamilton Shaw, U.S. Navy Lieutenant
(William Hamilton Shaw, US NAVY)

Location: Eunpyeong Peace Park in Nokbeon–dong, Eunpyeong–gu, Seoul.

On 22nd September, 1950, during the Seoul Restoration Operation, the battle of Nokbeon-ri in Eunpyeong-gu was fierce. Lieutenant William Hamilton Shaw, U.S. Navy was there.

William Earle Shaw, a missionary, Hamilton's father, who came to ROK on 5th June, 1922, and had Korean name which is Seo Wi-Yum(廉煒徐). An only son, Hamilton was born in Pyongyang.

He also participated in the Normandy landing operation as a Lieutenant Junior Grade in World War II.

After being discharged from the military, a war broke out in Korea while studying for a doctorate at Harvard University. He told his parents and friends, "How can I study comfortably. There is a war in my country where I was born? It is not too late to study after peace comes to my country."

He assisted General MacArthur with fluent Korean and

changed his position to the Marine Corps after the successful Incheon Landing Operation on 15th September. He fought to recapture Seoul. In Nokbeon-ri, he was attacked by an ambush from nK puppet Army and killed in action.

He was arose as a statue in Eunpyeong Peace Park. He is a 29-year-old man who sacrificed his life for ROK. He is a hero of the Korean War. We should be honoured with this good example of patriotism.

* Seo, Wi-Yum is the Korean name of Lieutenant Hamilton Shaw's father.

On Monday, 21st June, 2021, on the day which has longest day of the year, I visited and worshiped Eunpyeong Peace Park and Yeokchon Station in Nokbeon-dong, Eunpyeong-gu.

收復作戰　碌磠戰熾
海軍大尉　徐煒廉子
韓國宣教　父徐煒廉*
子息誕生　平壤地域
二次大戰　海軍少尉
上陸作戰　爲參戰也
轉役以後　博士受業
韓國戰爭　參加戰死
恩平公園　誕起立像
韓國英雄　愛國龜鑑

해밀턴 쇼대위(William Hamilton Shaw, LT. U.S. NAVY)

한미해병 참전비

위치: 경기 파주시 조리읍 장곡리 75-5(봉일천 변)

인천상륙작전 성공하고 수도 서울 탈환 후에 한미 해병대가 목숨을 같이한 역전의 용사들... 빗발치는 수많은 포탄으로 암석이 가루가 되고 지면이 낮아져 산의 형태가 바뀌는 피아공방이다.

모든 악조건하에 신출귀몰 닥치는 대로 쳐부수고 북진 반격 전투를 했다.

전장터에서 수많은 젊은 넋으로 산화한 해병대원, 빛나는 충혼으로 자유 수호 수호신 되어 한반도 지킨다.

2020년 9월 25일(금), 파주 조리읍 봉일천변에 있는 한·미 해병대 참전비를 답사하고, 참배하니 그날의 혼령이 말해 주는 것을 기록하는 신삿갓.

The Monument to ROK-U.S. Marine's Participation in the Korean War

Location: 75-5 Janggok-ri, Jori-eup, Paju-si, Gyeonggi-do (by Bongilcheon Stream)

After success of Incheon Landing Operation and recaptured the capital of Seoul. There were ROK and U.S. Marines who fought to the last drop of their blood together.

There were lots of shells by attack and defense operations between friendly forces and enemies which made change rocks to sands, mountain's shape and height.

Under all the bad conditions, they destroyed everything that comes and goes. They conducted a counterattack against the nK.

Countless Marines young spirits that died in honor in the Battleground became guardians of freedom with their shining loyalty and have been protecting the Korean Peninsula.

On Friday, 25th September, 2020, I visited and worshiped the monument to ROK and U.S. marines participation in Korean War which located near the Bongil Stream in Jori-eup, Paju. And I wrote what the spirits said.

上陸成功　首都奪還
韓美海兵　血盟戰士
落爆雨彈　爲巖粉析
地低變山　彼我攻防
諸惡條件　神出鬼沒
怪鬼擊破　北進反擊
戰場魂魄　海兵忠魂
爲守護神　守韓半島

23 미 제 40사단, 213 야전포병, 기적의 가평전투(자유는 공짜가 아니다)

1951년 5월 26일 밤, 가평군 화학산 아래 생사를 건 전투가 벌어졌다. 미군 213 포병야전대대 600명과 중공군 4,000명이 밤을 새우며 싸웠다.

인천상륙작전 성공으로 북한지역 압록강까지 밀고 올라갔던 국군과 UN군은 중공군 집단 참전으로 후퇴를 거듭했다.

앞에서 싸우던 국군을 위해 105mm 곡사포로 지원하던 213 포병대대는 한국군 부대가 아무런 통지도 없이 후퇴해 버리는 바람에 졸지에 고립되었다.

적을 직접 맞딱 뜨렸다.

대대(-1) 360명과 A포대 240명이 있는 미군 진지로 중공군 4,000명이 진격해 왔다. 지휘관 프랭크 댈리 중령은 포탄신관 폭발시간을 0.5초로 설정했다.

포탄이 지면에 떨어지기 전 적의 머리 위 공중에서 터졌다. 적에게 치명적 피해를 주었다.

동이 트고 나서야 총성이 잦아들었다. 중공군은 후퇴했다. 포대 레이콕스 대위는 9명씩 정찰조를 편성해 협곡을 정찰했다. 중공군 전사자는 350여 명이다. 중공군은 정찰대를 보자마자 항복했다. 생포한 적은 830여 명이다.

기적같이 213 포병대대는 전사자가 없다. 백병전까지 치렀는데 가벼운 부상자만 몇 명 있었다. '기적의 전투'다.

인도적으로 미군이 중공군 시신을 묻어 주었다. 이를 본 중공군 포로들이 고맙다고 했단다.

2020년 10월 5일 가평지역 전적지 답사 중에 북면 이곡리 카이저길 45-23. 알려지지도 않은 미군 전적비를 우연히 알았다.

한국인 최승성 씨가 사유지 1천 평을 내놓고 참전기념비를 세우고 자리를 지키고 있었다.

국가가 못하는 일을 개인이 하고 있었다. 전적지를 답사하면서 특별한 사람을 만나는 삿갓이다.

US 40th Division, 213 Field Artillery, Miracle Battle of Gapyeong(Freedom is not free.)

On the night of 26th May, 1951, a life-and-death battle took place at Hwahak Mountain in Gapyeong-gun. 600 soldiers of U.S. 213th field artillery battalion and 4,000 soldiers of Communist Chinese Army fought all night.

ROK Army and UN forces which pushed up to the Abrok river in North Korea due to the success of the Incheon landing operation, repeatedly withdrew due to the participation of army of Communist Chinese Army. The 213th field artillery battalion which supported ROK forces in the frontline by fires in front became isolated suddenly. Because ROK forces withdrew without any notices. The 213th Battalion met the enemies directly.

4,000 soldiers of Communist Chinese Army advanced to positions of U.S. Army where were main unit of artillery battalion which consisted of 360 soldiers and A battery which consisted of 240 soldiers. Commander, LTC Frank Daly preset the time fuze at half a second. The shells exploded in the air above the enemies' head before they hit the ground. The shelling inflicted mortal damages on the enemies. It was not until dawn that the gunfires died down. Communist Chinese Army retreated. Captain Ray Cox, the battery commander organized teams consisted of nine soldiers and ordered to scout the canyon. There were about 350 soldiers KIA of Communist Chinese Army. As soon as Communist Chinese Army came across the reconnaissance teams, they surrendered. About 830 soldiers of Communist Chinese Army were captured alive.

Miraculously, nobody died of the battery. There were only a few minor wounded soldiers even though they had hand to hand fights. It was a "miracle battle." Humanistically, the U.S. military buried the bodies of Communist Chinese Army. The Chinese prisoners who saw this thanked them.

On 5th October, 2020, during an exploration of the battlefield in Gapyeong, I accidentally found unknown monument to U.S. participation in the Korean War at 45-23, Kaiser-gil, Igok-ri, Buk-myeon. Choi Seung-sung, a Korean, who donated 1,000 pyeong(a unit of area=3.954 sq. yds.) of private real estate and erected the monument to participation in the Korean War was there. An individual did what the country couldn't do. I, gleeman Shin, met the special person while exploring the battlefield.

加平戰鬪　生死對結
美砲兵隊　對中共軍
仁川上陸　進出鴨綠
未報國軍　砲臺孤立
發射砲彈　信管造整
空中爆破　致命殊害
後退中共　峽谷精察
適兵死滅　生者降伏
奇蹟砲隊　無戰死者
赤屍身埋　虜言感謝

24 미 지평리 사수작전(미 23연대) ; 51년 2월 13일

위치 : 경기도 양평군 지평면 지평리, 전쟁기념관

　미 2사단 23연대와 5기병연대는 중공군 3개 사단 규모의 집중공격을 막아낸 방어전투에서 화력과 백병전으로 처절한 사투를 했다.

　적의 인해전술과 포위망 압축하고 적은 2개 연대를 추가 투입하니 기병연대는 전차 23대 돌격중대를 편성, 연결작전을 성공했다.

　끊임없는 공방전, 백병전으로 3일간 악전고투 피에 젖은 격전지에 적은 5천여 전사자 남기고 퇴각했다. 이 전투로 중공군 개입 후 적에게 패배를 처음 안겨준 전투이다.

　UN군의 첫 승전보는 역사적인 지평리 전투다.

　UN군은 재반격의 기틀을 다지고 최초로 전술적, 작전 승리였다.

　지평리 전투 이후 UN군은 패배 의식에서 벗어나고 공세

로 전환하는 승기를 잡은 전투이니 세계 자유민주주의가 공산주의를 이기는 첫 승리이며, 한국인은 이 은혜를 어찌 갚아야 하나요?

20년 7월 26일(일) 답사, 1951년 2월 13일~16일까지 일어난 일, 전사지역인 양평 지평리 미군의 전승지를 답사하고 결초보은의 은혜를 잊지 말아야 하는 우리 대한민국이다.

작전했던 산야를 답사하고 돌아보며 감사의 눈물을 보이는 신삿갓이오.

♥ 미 2사단, 23연대장 ; 폴 프리먼 대령
　미 제 1기병사단, 5연대장 ; 크롬베즈 대령
★ 중공군 제39군, 제40군, 제42군, 중공군 사령관 ; 펑더화이

The Desperate Defensive Operation of U.S. Forces in Jipyong-ri(U.S. 23rd Regiment)

Location: Jipyeong-ri, Jipyeong-myeon, Yangpyeong-gun, Gyeonggi-do, War Memorial Hall

U.S. 23rd Regiment, 2nd Infantry Division and 5th Cavalry Regiment had a desperate battle with fire power and hand to hand fights in the defensive battle which defended concentrated attacks from Communist Chinese Army.

The cavalry regiment organized a assault company with 23 tanks and succeeded link up operation. In order to against enemies' human wave tactics, tightened enveloping net and additional 2 regiments.

The enemies retreated leaving around 5,000 KIA on fierce battle place where a 3-day and night desperate struggle between both sides with continued offensive and defensive operations and hand to hand fights took place.

This was the first battle that friendly forces defeated enemies after intervention of Communist Chinese Army. UN forces delivered the first historic victorious news from historic battle of Jipyong-ri.

UN forces achieved the first victory both tactically and strategically which paved the way for launching counterattack operations.

After the victory in Jipyong-ri Battle, UN forces could get out of the complex of losing or failure and grabbed a chance to transition to offensive operation.

Furthermore, this battle was the first victory of the world liberal democracy against the communism. How could ROK people return their favor?

Exploration date was Sunday, 26th July, 2020, the battle took place between 13rd~16th Feburary, 1951, ROK people should explore the place of U.S. victory in Jipyong-ri, Yangpyeong and never forget their favor. I, gleeman Shin, visited fields and mountains where the operations were carried out and shedded tears for the immense gratitude.

♥ Col Paul L. Freeman: CDR, 23rd Rgt, 2nd Inf Div
Col Marcel G. Crombez: CDR, 5th Cav Rgt, 1st Armor Div

★ 39th Army, 40th Army, 42th Army of Communist Chinese
Army, Commander ; Péng Déhuái

美二三聯　五騎兵聯
赤三個師　集中攻擊
防禦戰鬪　凄切死鬪
人海戰術　包圍壓縮
騎兵聯隊　連結作戰
攻中共軍　包圍壓縮
惡戰苦鬪　成功防禦
赤介入後　赤初敗背
成功作戰　功勢意欲
自由民主　克共産軍
結草報恩　韓國人焉

25

미 육군 공병부대 전적비

　한국전쟁 때 미 공병부대는 최선봉에서 기동부대의 길을 개척했다. 후퇴할 때는 아군의 안전한 철수를 위해 최후에 전장을 떠났다.

　한탄강 일내는 험준한 산익과 끼아지르는 절벽이 많았디. 그래서 공병의 임무 수행이 매우 어려웠다. 한국 국민을 위해 피, 땀, 정성으로 교량과 도로를 통하여 피난민들이 자유와 평화를 얻었다.

　전후 복구와 경제발전에 큰 공헌을 했다. 한탄강 지역 험준한 지형에서 작전에 참가한 미 공병부대 용사들에게 기념비를 세웠다.

　이 은혜 늘 영원히 잊지 않겠다는 표상이다.

　2021년 3월 6일(토), 중부 전선 경기와 철원, 고석정 일대 미 육군 공병부대의 활약상을 신삿갓과 답사했다.

The Monument to U.S. Army Engineer Units

　During the Korean War, U.S. Army engineer units breached maneuver units way at the vanguard. And when friendly forces retreated, engineer units left the battlefield at last for safe withdrawal of friendly forces.

　The region of Hantan River had many rugged mountains and steep cliffs. Therefore, it was difficult for engineer units to carry out their duties.

Through bridges and roads made by blood, sweat, and sincerity for ROK people, the refugees gained freedom and peace. The bridges and roads made a great contribution to restoration and Economic Development after Korean War.

The monument was erected for the soldiers of U.S. engineer units who operated in the rugged Hantan River area. It's a sign that we won't forget.

On Saturday, 6th March, 2021, I, gleeman Shin, explored the performances of U.S. Army Engineer units in Cheorwon, in vicinity of Goseokjeong which are on the central frontline.

戰爭始終　美工兵隊
開機動隊　後安撤收
漢灘一代　山岳斷涯
臨務守行　難處地型
爲韓國人　開拓道路
獲得自和　經濟公獻
險俊地形　漢灘江邊
美工兵隊　恩惠不忘

고석정에 있는 미 공병부대 전적비
The monument to U.S. Army engineer units in Goseokjeong

26

제 187 미 공수연대 전투단 기념비

위치 : 경기도 파주시 임진강 공원 (미국군 참전 기념비와 같이 있다)

1950년 10월 20일 평양 북방 숙천과 순천지역에 3,344명이 낙하했다.

수많은 적을 사살하고 3,818명을 포로로 잡으니 북괴군의 방어선을 무산시켰다.

1951년 3월 23일 3,486명이 파주, 문산 지역에 낙하해 후퇴하는 중공군과 괴뢰군 19사단의 퇴로를 차단하고 적 136명 사살하고, 149명을 포로로 잡았다. 그 후 187 공수연대 전투단은 강원도 원주, 인제 등지에서 지상전투에도 투입했으니 이곳 미군 참전비 주변에 기념비를 세웠다.

2020년 9월 26일(토), 미 공수연대 전투비를 답사하고 고맙고 감사한 마음을 가득 담아 참배한 신삿갓이다.

참배하고 나오니 저녁하늘에 봉황이 나는 (瑞雲之 鳳凰飛也) 좋은 징조의 구름을 봤다.

The Monument to 187th U.S. Airborne Regiment Combat Team

Location: Imjin River Park in Paju, Gyeonggi-do (with the U.S. Army Memorial)

On 20th October, 1950, 3,344 soldiers parachuted in Sukcheon and Suncheon, the northern part of Pyongyang. They disrupted the line of defense of Korean People's Army(KPA) by killing a lot of enemies and capturing 3,818 prisoners.

On 23th March, 1951, after 3,486 soldiers parachuted in the Munsan, Paju area, they blocked retreat of Communist Chinese Army and nK puppet 19th Division. They killed 136 enemies and captured 149 prisoners.

After that, U.S. 187th Airborne Regiment Combat Team engaged in Wonju, Inje in Gangwon-do. So the monument was built near the monument to participation of U.S. military in Korean War.

On Saturday, 26th September, 2020, I, gleeman, explored the monument to U.S. Airborne Regiment's battle and paid tribute with gratitude.

♥ After I worshiped I could see phoenix shaped cloud in the evening sky(瑞雲之 鳳凰飛也) which means a good omen.

空輸聯隊　平壤北落
北域作戰　適死殺也
北韓傀儡　無散防築
文山落下　退路遮斷
破中共軍　破北傀軍
江原山域　地上戰鬪
此處戰團　建記念碑

27

미 공병부대 참전기념비

위치 : 서울 용산구 한강로 한강대교 북단.

1950년 6월 25일 새벽 불법 남침을 감행한 북괴군은 T-34 전차를 앞세우고 전면적인 기습공격을 했다. 남침 저지를 위해 6월 28일 부득이 한강 인도교 (현: 한강대교)를 폭파했다. 맥아더 장군의 인천상륙 성공과 함께 9월 28일 수도 서울 수복했다.

중공군의 침공으로 또다시 수도 서울을 점령당했다.

1.4 후퇴 이후, 진퇴를 거듭하던 긴박했던 시기였다. 미 공병부대는 한강에 부교와 도보교를 설치해 군사작전을 도왔다.

공산군은 1951년 6월 완전히 쫓겨났다. 미 공병부대는 한강 인도교와 철도를 복구하였다. 한국전쟁 때 보여준 미 제8군 제62공병부대 장병들의 희생과 헌신에 감사합니다.

한강대교 북단에 참전기념비가 세워졌다. 한국인은 공병 장병의 은혜를 잊을 수가 없다.

2021년 2월 22일 서울 용산역 남쪽, 이촌동 한강시민공원 한강대교 북단에 있는 미 공병부대 참전 기념비를 답사, 미군 장병의 노고에 감사하며 참배하는 신삿갓.

(★ 다리폭파: 50년 6월 27일 국군 공병감 최창식 대령 폭파준비 완료, 북괴전차 미아리 넘자, 채병덕 육군 참모총장은 6월 28일 02시 30분에 700파운드 폭약으로 폭파)

The Monument to Participation of U.S. Army Engineer Units

Location: The northern end of Han River Bridge in Hangang-ro, Yongsan-gu, Seoul.

Early in the morning on 25th June, 1950, nK puppet Army which carried out illegal invasion to ROK conducted general surprising attacks with T-34 tanks at the forefront.

In order to stop invasion from nK, friendly forces blew pedestrian bridge(current: Han River bridge) over the Han River up inevitably on 28th June.

With General MacArthur's successful landing in Incheon, Friendly forces restored the capital of Seoul on 28th September. Capital of Seoul was taken over once again by invasion of Communist Chinese army.

It was an urgent period of continuous advance and retreat after 1.4 retreat. U.S. Army engineer units helped with military operations by installing a floating bridge and a footbridge on Han River.

Communist forces were completely driven out in June 1951.

U.S. Army engineer units restored the pedestrian bridge on Han river and railway.

I appreciate for the sacrifice and dedication of soldiers of U.S. 62nd Engineer unit of 8th army in Korean War. The monument to U.S. 62nd Engineer unit's participation in Korean War was elected at the northern end of the Han river bridge.

ROK people can't forget the favor of soldiers of engineer units.

On 22nd February, 2021, I visited the monument to participation of U.S. engineer units in Korean War which is at the northern end of the Han River bridge, Han River Civic Park in Ichon-dong, south of Yongsan Station in Seoul. I worshiped while appreciating hard work of U.S. soldiers.

(★ Blowing bridge up: Colonel Choi Chang-sik, the Chief of Engineers of ROK Army, was ready to blow up on 27th June. As nK puppet tanks went over Mia-ri, Chae Byung-deok, the

Army Chief of Staffs, ordered to blow bridge up by a 700-pound
explosive at 0230(I) on 28th June)

不法南侵　奇襲攻擊
南侵沮止　爆破大橋
上陸成功　首都收復
再侵中共　再都占領
進退緊迫　軍事作戰
美工兵隊　浮橋設置
後退共産　建設再開
建人道橋　鐵橋復舊
六二工兵　犧牲精神
工兵將兵　恩惠不忘

경기도 파주시 임진각에 세워진 미국군 참전기념비

28

미 제25사단 한강 도하 전적비

위치 : 경기 남양주시 와부읍 팔당리 347-2

1951년 3월 7일 새벽 03시 30분 전차 15대, 구난전차 1대와 미 제25사단 장병이 한강 남쪽 강변에 도착했다.

공격준비사격이 시작되고 끝나자 제3대대 K중대가 단정을 타고 강을 건너기 시작했다. 중공군의 기관총 사격이 집중되었다. 07시 40분에 중대는 도하를 했다.

08시에 A전차 중대 제 3소대장 알리 중위가 1번, 2번 전차로 2분 만에 강을 건넜다. 중앙선 철도 둑에서 적들이 기관총을 쏘아 댔다. 전차가 이들의 기관총 진지를 파괴했다.

10시에 보병과 전차 협동으로 사단은 큰 피해 없이 수도 재탈환을 위한 한강 도하 작전이 마무리되었다.

수도 서울 재탈환을 위해 한강 도하를 맨 먼저 감행한 장병은 미 25

사단 용사들이다. 이들은 서울 재탈환의 결정적 발판을 마련했다.

한국민은 감사하고, 감사하며 영원히 잊을 수 없는 와부읍 도곡리 북쪽 강변 전적비에서 나는 감사 기도를 올렸다.

2021년 2월 22일, 70년 전 역사의 현장을 답사했다.

해지는 석양 강변 그날의 장병들이 이 강안으로 달려 온 것을 상상하니 나와 한국민은 참으로 미 제25사단 장병에게 큰 빚을 지고 있지만 이 사실을 잊어버리고 살고 있다.

역사를 잊은 종족은 지구상에 국가로 오랫동안 존속할 수가 없다.

The 25th U.S. Division's Monument to crossing the Han River

Location: 347-2 Paldang-ri, Wabu-eup, Namyangju-si, Gyeonggi-do

At 0330(I) on 7 March, 1951, 15×tanks, a rescue tank and soldiers from U.S. 25th Infantry Division arrived at the south riverside of Han River.

한강 도하 기념 A photo of commemoration to Han river crossing

When the preparation fire for the attack began and ended, K Company of 3rd Battalion, began to cross the river by using small boats. Communist Chinese Army's machine gunfires were concentrated. At 0740(I), the company crossed Han River.

At 0800(I) Lieutenant Ali, 3rd platoon leader of A tank company, crossed the river with number 1, 2 tanks in two minutes. The enemies fired machine guns on the banks of the Central Line railroad. Friendly tanks destroyed their machine gun positions.

At 1000(I), with infantries and tanks cooperated, the division was able to fulfilled the Han River crossing operation to recapture the capital without big damages.

The soldiers who first carried out the Han River crossing to recapture the capital of Seoul were soldiers of U.S. 25th Infantry Division. They had set the stage for recapture of Seoul. As a ROK people I will never forget with a grateful heart. I prayed for gratitude to the monument on the northern riverside of Dogok-ri, Wabu-eup.

On 22nd February, 2021, I explored the 70-year ago historial site.

At the sunset river, as I imagined that the soldiers of that day had ran into this riverside realized that ROK people are living with forgetting the big debt for soldiers of U.S. 25th Infantry

Division.

A race that forgets history cannot survive as a nation on Earth for a long time.

美軍進入　南漢山城
着晨江邊　戰車到着
攻擊射擊　短艇出發
亂射中共　輯中射擊
戰車中隊　江中進入
適機關銃　火力集中
步戰協動　渡河成功
敢行將兵　都再還基

29

미 72전차부대 참전 기념비

위치 : 경기 가평 설악 천안리 98번지

1951년 4월 24일~25일, 중공군 3개 군단이 춘계공세를 감행해 왔다.

북괴군도 합세했다. 포위공격과 파상공격으로 강력하게 공세를 이어 나갔다.

영 연방군(영국, 뉴질랜드, 호주, 캐나다)과 국군 6사단의 아군은 열세했다.

바람 앞에 등불이 되었다.

미 72전차부대가 투입, 화력을 지원하였다. 전세가 회복되고 반격이 시작되었다. 이 전투에서 탱크부대 장병이 많이 산화되었다. 호국정신이 소멸되지 않도록 기념비를 세웠다.

한국은 자유와 평화를 누리고 있다.

미국에 큰 빚을 졌으니 잊을 수가 없다.

아니, 결코, 잊어서는 안 된다.

2021년 3월 22일 경기 가평 설악 천안리 98번지에 있는 미 2사단 제 72전차부대 장병의 전적비를 답사, 참배했다.

이 전투로 반격 작전이 시작되어 UN군과 국군이 북진하여 화천의 큰 호수에서 적을 섬멸했다. 이로써 이승만 대통령은 현대판 살수대첩으로 대호를 파로호로 명명했다.

The Memorial Monument to U.S. 72nd Tank Unit

Location: 98, Seorak Cheonan−ri, Gapyeong, Gyeonggi−do

From 24th to 25th April, 1951, three corps of Communist Chinese Army launched offensive operations in spring. nK puppet Army joined as well. They conducted continuous strong offensive operations with enveloping and wave attacks. Commonwealth Forces (UK, New Zealand, Australia, Canada) and ROK 6th Division were inferior to enemies. Friendly forces became a light in front of the wind.

U.S. 72nd tank unit were deployed to support firepower.

The war situation had been restored and friendly forces began counterattack.

Many soldiers of U.S. 72nd tank unit were killed in this battle. A monument was erected to prevent the spirit of patriotism from dissipating.

Today's ROK is enjoying freedom and peace. We can't forget that owe U.S. a lot. No, we never forget that.

On 22nd March, 2021, I visited the monument to soldiers of U.S. 72nd tank unit of 2nd Infantry Division at 98 Seorak Cheonan-ri, Gapyeong, Gyeonggi-do and paid tribute them.

This battle gave UN and ROK forces opportunity to begin counterattack. And they advanced north and wiped out the enemies in big Lake in Hwacheon. For these reasons, President Lee Seong-man named this big lake as Paro lake which means modern version of Salsu Battle.

春季攻勢　中共軍也
包圍攻擊　波狀攻擊
英聯邦軍　國六師團
壞滅直前　風前燈火
戰車部隊　投入攻擊
我軍劣勢　戰勢回復
散華將兵　尊敬紀念
韓自平和　大債不忘

파로호

72탱크부대

위치 : 강원도 양구군 동면 월운리 86- 30번지

1951년 8월 18일~ 2일, 미 2사단에 국군 5사단 36연대가 배속되었다. 이곳은 한국전쟁 중에 최대 격전지, 가혹한 피의 능선 전투다.

피의 능선은 양구 동면 비아리에 있다.

주 능선이 983고지다. 능선은 남쪽에 경사도가 급하게 형성되어있다. 그래서 방어는 용이하고 공격하기 어렵다.

3개월간 전선이 교착상태 있었다. 적군은 능선 일대에 수백 개의 엄체호와 유개호를 만들었다. 아군이 발사한 포탄이 105미리 32만 여발, 155미리 포탄 9만 여발, 2.5톤 차량으로 5 천대 분량이다.

전투가 치러지는 동안 고지마다 시신이 산을 이루었다. 또한 피가 바다를 이루었다. 피아간 혈전을 증명했다.

피로써 되찾은 이 땅은 5일간의 치열한 공방전의 결과물이다.

최종적으로 아군이 승리했다.

나라와 겨레, 세계 민주 자유를 위해 산화한 옛 전우와 미 2사단 장병들의 정신을 잊지 못한다.

나는 조용히 그들에게 명복을 빈다.

자유는 그냥 얻어지는 것이 아니었다.

Freedom Is Not Free !

2021년 3월 29일 월요일, 양구 동면 월운리 86-30번지, 국도 옆 호숫가에 고요히 있는 전적비를 답사했다.

피의 능선 유래는 당시 이곳을 취재했던 성조지(The Star and Stripes) 종군기자가 전투하던 고지를 비유하여 피의 능선(♥ Blood Ridge)이라 보도 후 불리게 되었다.

미 2사단의 전투 전적비는 경기도 가평에 있다.

The Monumnet to Battle of Blood Ridge by U.S. 2nd Infantry Division

Location: 86-30 Wolun-ri, Dong-myeon, Yanggu-gun, Gangwon-do

From 18th to 22nd August, 1951, ROK 36th Regiment of 5th Division of attached to U.S. 2nd Infantry Division. This place was the biggest battleground during the Korean War, severe battle of blood ridge took place here.

The blood ridge was located in Biari, Dong-myeon, Yanggu. The main ridge is 983m height. The ridge has a steep slope to the south. So it is easy to defend but hard to attack.

The frontline was being deadlocked for three months. The enemies made hundreds of bunkers and covers.

Our artillery fired around 320,000 rounds of 105mm shells, around 90,000 rounds of 155mm shells. It was equivalent to 5,000×2.5ton vehicles.

미 2사단 피의 능선 전투 전적비

During the battle, bodies formed a mountain at every heights.

Also, blood formed the sea. That was a proof of bloody battle between friendly forces and enemies.

This land had been reclaimed with blood is the result of a fierce battle of five days. Finally friendly forces won. I can not forget the spirits of old comrades and soldiers of 2nd Infantry Division who died in honor for country and democracy freedom in the world. I pray for their repose quietly.

Freedom was not just earned.

Freedom Is Not Free ?!

On Monday, 29th March, 2021, 86-30 Wolun-ri, Dong-myeon, Yang-gu, I explored the monument that was still at the lakeshore by the route. The name of Blood Ridge originated from a report. After a military reporter of Star and Strikes news who covered this place at the time reported this ridge as ♥ Blood Ridge by comparing highlands which a battle took place.

♥ The memorial monument to battle of U.S. 2nd Infantry Division is located in Gapyeong, Gyeonggi-do.

韓國戰爭　酷擊戰地
美二師團　國配五師
戰線膠着　三個月間
建赤掩體　作有蓋壕
我軍發射　砲彈數萬
車輛五千　多量多泰
血之稜線　屍山血海
彼我之間　血戰證明
熾烈攻後　最終勝利
戰友冥福　美軍不忘

31

펀치볼* 전투 전적비(미 5개 사단 전투)

위치 : 강원 양구 동면 임당2리

1951년 8월 29일~ 0월 30일 (2개월간) 미 제2사단, 7사단, 25사단, 45사단, 미 제1해병사단의 미 5개 사단과 국군 제3사단, 제5사단, 해병 1사단의 국군 3개 사단, 합 8개 사단이 작전 한 곳이다.

북괴군은 제 3군단, 제 5군단, 북괴 1사단, 27사단, 12사단, 합 공산군 2개 군단이다.

북괴군은 고지에 방어 진지를 구축해 방어에 유리했다. 아군은 공격에 불리한 지형의 피해가 대단히 많다.

해안지역에는 모택동 고지(1,026고지), 김일성고지(924고지) 660능선, 무명 능선이 있다. 서화리 북방, 가칠봉, 무명고지 일대 6차례 공격과 방어 전투로 고지 주인이 6번이나 바뀌었다.

미 3대대는 702고지에서 북괴군과 백병전을 했다.

미군 428명이 전사했다. 부상 장병 1,000여명이 발생했다. 미군과 국군은 펀치볼 전투에서 목표지역 1,055고지와 김일성 고지, 모택동 고지를 모두 점령하고 막을 내렸다.

세계의 자유 평화를 위해 용감무쌍한 투혼을 발휘한 미군 5개 사단(미 제2사단, 7사단, 25사단, 45사단, 제1해병사단) 장병이 우리 민족을 살렸다.

님들의 흘린 피로 이 나라를 건졌다.

이 투혼을 천추만대에 전해야 한다.

*펀치볼 Punch Bowl 뜻: 미국 종군기자가 이 분지를 보고 시 양식 화채 그릇처럼 움푹 파인 모양으로 기사를 발표했다.

*해안(亥安) 뜻: 바닷가 해안(海岸)이 아니고 亥 돼지해 편 안 安이다.

옛날 이곳이 뱀이 많아서 사람 살기 불편했다. 해서 도력 깊은 스님에 해결책을 질문했다.

뱀과 돼지는 상극이니 돼지를 사다가 방목하면 된다고 했다. 그 후 돼지로 인하여 편안히 살 수 있었다. 1년 농사지어 3년을 먹고 살 수 있는 기름진 땅이다.

2021년 3월 30일(월), 강원 양구 동면 임당 2리에 있는 펀치볼 전투 전적비와 펀치볼 북편 고지에 있는 을지 전망대를 답사 참배했다.

펀치볼 지구 전투전적비

★ 이 전투에서 국군 5사단 장병 600명이 전사하고 400명이 실종되었다.

미군은 적을 2,700여 명 사살했다. 북괴군 550명을 생포했다.

5사단은 적 1,000명을 사살하고 250명을 생포했다. 이 전투로

중동부지역의 우위 확보함으로써 휴전 협상에 압박을 가해 정치적 효과를 거둘 수 있었다.

우리 대한민국은 UN군에, 특히 미국에 참으로 많은 빚을 지고 살고 있다.

참전한 장병과 산화해 하늘에 별이 된 장병을 잊으면 한국인 되기를 포기한 사람이다.

The Monument to Punch Bowl* Battle (Five U.S. Divisions)

Location: Imdang 2-ri, Dong-myeon, Yang-gu, Gangwon-do

From 29th August to 30th October, 1951(for two months), a total of 8 Divisions, U.S. 5×Divisions(2nd, 7th, 25th, 45th, 1st marine Division) and ROK 3× Divisions(3rd, 5th, 1st marine Division) conducted operations in this place.

There were 2-corps size of Communist Army which consisted of nK puppet 3rd Corps, 5th Corps, 1st Division, 27th Division, 12th Division.

nK puppet Army was advantageous for its defense by establishing defensive positions on the highlands. Friendly forces suffered a great deal of damage from the terrain unfavorable to attack.

There were Mao Zedong Highlands(1,026 heights) - Kim Il-seong Highlands(924 heights) - 660 Ridge - unknown Ridge in the coastal area.

The owner changed six times as six times of offensive and defensive operations in the northern part of Seohwa-ri, Gachil peak, and the unknown highlands.

U.S 3rd Battalion conducted hand to hand fights against nK puppet Army on 702 height. 428×U.S. soldiers were killed in action. There were about 1,000 wounded soldiers.

The Punch bowl battle ended after occupying all of 1,055, Kim Il-sung and Mao Zedong highlands which were objectives of U.S. and ROK military.

U.S. soldiers of 5 Divisions (2nd, 7th, 25th, 45th, 1st marine Divisions) who fought bravely for world freedom and peace saved our people. The blood that the soldiers shed saved this country. This fighting spirits must be conveyed forever.

* The Meaning of Punch Bowl : A U.S. war correspondent had seen the basin and published the article which depicted the basin as a hollow shaped bowl for western fruits salad.

*Meaning of the Haean: not the coast of the sea, but safe thanks to pigs. In the old days, there were many snakes here, so it was uncomfortable for people to live. So They asked the super wise monk for a solution. He said "Snakes and pigs are at odds, so you can buy pigs and graze them". After that people could live comfortably thanks to pigs. This is a fertile land which provide for three years products with just one farming.

On Monday, 30th March, 2021, I visited and worshiped the monument to Punch bowl battle in Imdang 2-ri, Dong-myeon, Yang-gu, Gangwon-do and Eulji observatory on the heights northern of Punch bowl.

★ In this battle, 600 soldiers from ROK 5th Infantry Division were killed in action, 400 soldiers were missing. U.S. Army killed more than 2,700 enemies. 550 nK puppet soldiers were captured. ROK 5th division killed 1,000 enemies and captured 250.

By securing the upper hand in the Middle East with this battle, We could achieve political effects on the armistice negotiation.

Republic of Korea, our country, owed UN forces especially U.S. a lot. If you forget the soldiers who fought in the Korean War and the soldiers who became stars in the sky, you are a person who gave up being ROK people.

美軍全力　國軍全力
亥安地域　擴保作戰
北傀集團　二個軍團
高地有利　防禦有利
攻擊不利　美軍不利
我軍不利　披害過多
亥安一代　高峯高地
六次功擊　攻防變主
美三大隊　白兵戰勝
四百戰死　一千負傷
目標地域　完全占領
將兵弗忘　恩惠不忘

32

적성리 전투 전승비 (미 10군단 지원)

위치 : 경북 문경시 동로면 적성리 승전공원.

1951년 1월 13일~16일(4일간) 문경 동로면 적성리 전투가 있었다. 미 제 10군단에 배속된 국군 특별공격대대(대대장 배동걸 소령) 300명과 북괴군 10사단(남해사단) 1개 연대 3,000명과 4일간의 전투다.

대대장은 장병들의 휴식을 위해 적성 초등학교 교실에 취침하고자 했다. 이때 2중대장(손 장래 중위)의 건의로 경찰지서 뒤편에 진지를 구축했다.

기온은 영하 15도였다. 새벽 5시 적은 꽹과리와 북을 치며 공격해 왔다. 지역 청년방위대 42명, 지서 경찰 16명이 도왔다. 3명의 미 고문관과 연락장교 하비슨 소령, 통신 하사관도 있었다.

적들은 주야간 공격을 해왔다. 적을 최단 거리 10, 20m로 끌어들여 조준사격으로 탄약을 절약했다. 진지 앞에 적의 시체들이 즐비했다.

미 통신 하사관의 무선연결로 정찰기 2대가 날아왔다. 30분 후 F-5 전투기 편대 4대가 미 고문관의 유도와 지시로 기총소사와 네이팜탄으로 적을 공격했다. 피아 보급품이 고갈되었다. 헬기 2대가 날아와서 학교 운동장에 탄약과 씨레이션을 투하하고 돌아갔다. 적의 3차 공격도 막아냈다.

적이 도주하고 난 후 전과는 적 사살 1,247명, 포로 군관 7명, 포로 사병 72명, 소총과 무기 370정, 박격포 2문이다.

아군의 손실은 전사 9명, 부상 2명, 미군 부상 2명, 민간인 4명, 경찰

전승비 A photo of the monument to victory in the battle

부상 2명, 청년방위대 전사 7명이다.

미 10군단장 알몬드 군단장님의 최고 칭찬과 격려를 받았다.

싸우고자 하는 국군과 지원한 미군, 지역 청년방위대 42명, 경찰 16명의 결사 방어로 승리했다.

2021년 9월 11일(토), 동로면 적성리에 있는 승전비와 충혼비를 답사하고 동행자 보경사 효경스님과 참배했다. 특히 16세 때 청년방위대로 참전한 현재 생존자 1명, 87세 조윤섭 어른(010-4587-4102)과 1시간 대담했다.

탄약이 떨어져 갈 때 대대장은 최후 1발은 가지고 있어야 한다고 했다.

시체를 짐승들이 마구 뜯어먹어 구덩이 파고 숫자를 세니 1,257구를 묻어 주었다.

산화하신 장병과 애국정신을 현대에 교육해야 한다고 생각하는 신 삿갓이다.

The Monument to Victory of Jeokseong—ri Battle(supported by U.S. 10th U.S. Corps)

Location: Seungjeon Park, Jeokseong—ri, Dongro—myeon, Mungyeong—si, Gyeongsangbuk—do.

From 13th to 16th January, 1951(for four days), there was a battle in Jeokseong-ri, Dongro-myeon, Mungyeong. It was a four-day battle between 300 soldiers of ROK Special Attack Battalion(commander Bae Dong-gul) which attached U.S. 10th corps and 3,000 nK puppet soldiers form the regiment of 10th(Namhae) division.

The battalion commander tried to make his soldiers took a rest and slept in the classroom of Jeokseong elementary school. At that time, positions were established behind the police station at the suggestion of 2nd company commander(Lieutenant Son Jang-rae). The temperature was 15 degrees below zero.

The enemies attacked at 0500(I) while beating kkwaenggwari(a kind of Korean traditional percussions) and drums. 42 members of the local youth defense team and 16 police officers helped. There were also three U.S. advisers, a liaison officer Major Harbison and a signal sergeant. The enemies had been attacking day and night. Friendly forces saved ammunitions by drawing the enemies in the shortest distance of 10 or 20 meters for aiming shots. There were rows of he enemy's corpses in front of the positions.

Two reconnaissance planes flew in with a radio connection from a U.S. signal sergeant. Half an hour later, four F-5 fighter squadrons attacked the enemies with gunfires and napalm bombs, guided and directed by U.S. advisers. Both friendly force and enemy's supplies ran out. Two helicopters had flew in, dropped ammunitions and MREs(Meal, Ready to Eat) on the school playground and returned. friendly forces prevented the enemies' third attack as well. The military achievements included 1,247 enemy soldiers, 7 POWs of officers, 72 POWs of private, 370 rifles and weapons, and 2 mortars.

The loss of friendly forces were nine KIA, two WIA, two U.S. WIA, four civilians and two police injured and seven KIA of young defense team.

They received the highest praise and encouragement from Commander Almond of the 10th U.S. corps. Friendly forces won the battle with ROK military which had will to fight, the U.S. military which supported, 42 members of the local youth defense team, and 16 police officers.

On Saturday, September 11, 2021, I explored the victory monument and the war memorial in Jeokseong-ri, Dongro-myeon, and paid tribute with Monk Bogyeong who was my companion. In particular, I had an hour's talk with one survivor, 87-year-old veteran Cho Yoon-seop (010-4587-4102) who participated as a youth defense team at the age of 16. When ammunitions ran out, the battalion commander said that he should have the last round. As the animals ate the bodies, friendly forces dug holes and buried the bodies. There were 1,257 bodies. I, gleeman Shin who think that the modern era should educate about the soldiers who died in honor.

聞慶赤城　特攻擊隊
三百名對　適三千名
隊員休息　學校敎室
建中隊長　陣地構築
寅時赤攻　一次攻擊
最短引距　措埠射擊
軍警民合　決死防禦
空中支援　美空應援
適三次攻　美軍支援
最後勝利　國軍萬世

문경 전투 현재 최후생존자 조윤섭 어른 87세/필자
The Last Survivor from Battle of Mungyeong /
Cho Yoon-seop, 87 years old

33

미 제1해병 항공사단 전몰용사 충령비

위치 : 포항시 남구 포항기상대 옆, 충령비 공원.

1950년 6월 25일 한국전쟁이 발생하자 7월 7일 캘리포니아주 펜들턴 기지에서 항공사단이 창설되었다.

해병대를 지원할 제1해병 항공사단(MAW : Marine Air Wing)을 장교 192명, 병사 1,358명, 전투기 60대, 정찰기 8대, 구조헬기 4대로 편성했다.

항공모함은 일본 고베항에 도착했다. 한국해역으로 이동했다.

1950년 8월 3일 전투기 8대를 발진하여 경남 진주지역 북괴군 6사단과 낙동강 창녕지역을 도하하는 북괴 4사단을 타격했다.

8월 4일 경남 고성지역으로 날아간 전투기 조종사들은 지상에 활동 중인 전술항공통제반 (TACP: Tactical Air Control Party)의 유도에 따라 작전을 수행하였다.

비포장도로를 이동하던 북괴군 행렬발견, 로켓포와 기총소사를 가했다.

해병대원들이 현장에 도착해 보니 북괴 83 기계화 보병연대 차량과 싸이드 카 100대가 파괴되었다. 주변에서 북괴군 시신 200구가 발견되었다.

9월 22일 항공사단은 인천상륙작전이 성공함에 따라 김포비행장으로 이동, 지원을 했다.

10월 26일 원산 주변 연포 비행장으로 이동했다. 중공군의 개입으로 개마고원 일대와 장진호 전투를 12월 11일까지 공격 지원을 했다.

이후 포항 비행장으로 이동하여 근접지원을 했다. 첫 출격 이래 휴전까지 127,496회의 전투비행을 했다. 근접항공지원을 39,500회 실시하고 공산군 공격을 격퇴했다.

해병사단은 436대의 항공기를 잃었다. 258명의 장병이 전사했다. 65명 실종, 174명 부상을 당했다.

우리 대한민국은 미 제1해병사단에 많은 빚을 졌다.

포항시 남구 송도동 산1번지에 그날을 증언

하는 전몰용사 충령비가 지금도 빛나고 있다.

2021년 7월 28일 포항 충령비를 답사하고 묵념했다.

길고 긴 전사를 요약해서 후손에게 알려 溫故知新*하고 싶어서 뙤약볕 36도 온도에 역사를 밟고 생각한 신삿갓이다.

*온고지신 : 옛것을 익히고 그것을 이루어 새 것을 아는 것.

The Monument to the War dead, Fallen soldiers of U.S. 1st Marine Air wings

Location: Chungnyeongbi Park, next to Pohang Meteorological Observatory in Nam-gu, Pohang.

After the Korean War broke out in 1950, the air wings was established at Pendleton Base, California, on 7th July.

The Marine Air Wings (MAW) consisted of 192 officers, 1,358 soldiers, 60 fighter jets, 8 reconnaissance planes, and 4 rescue helicopters to support the marine corps.

The aircraft carrier arrived at Kobe Port in Japan.
It moved to Korean waters.

On 3rd August, 1950, after eight fighter jets had been launched, attacked nK puppet 6th Division in Jinju, Gyeongsangnam-do and nK puppet 4th Division crossing Changnyeong area of Nakdong River.

On 4th August, fighter pilots who flew to Goseong, Gyeongsangnam-do carried out their missions in accordance with the guidance of Tactical Air Control Party(TACP) on the ground.

Rocket guns and guns fired after discovering a procession of nK puppet soldiers moving to unpaved roads. When marines arrived at the scene, they could find 100 destroyed side cars and vehicles of nK puppet 83rd Mechanized Infantry Regiment.
Around 200 bodies of the nK puppet Army were found.

On 22nd September, as the Incheon landing operation

succeeded the air wings had moved to Gimpo airport and supported friendly forces.

On 26th October, it moved to Yeonpo Airfield near Wonsan. As the Communist Chinese Army intervened, It supported attacks in the Gaema Plateau area and the Battle of Jangjin Lake until 11th December.

After that, it moved to Pohang Airfield and provided Close Air Supports(CASs). Since its first launch, it carried out 127,496 combat flights until the armistice. CASs were carried out 39,500 times and communist attacks were repelled.

The Marine Division lost 436 aircraft. 258 soldiers were killed in action. 65 soldiers were missing and 174 soldiers injured.

Republic of Korea owes a lot to the U.S. 1st Marine Division. The monument to the war dead which testified that day, is still shining at San 1, Songdo-dong, Nam-gu, Pohang.

On 28th July, 2021, I visited the monument to the war dead in Pohang and paid a silent tribute. Since I, gleeman Shin wanted to summarize the long history of Korean War and to inform descendants for Ongojishin*, explored history and thought many things at the temperature of 36 degrees in the scorching sun.

*Ongojishin: To Know the new things by learning the old things

韓國戰爭　海兵創航
航空母艦　日本到着
最初發進　武裝航空
晉州地域　打赤六師
洛東江邊　適渡河隊
爆彈投下　機銃燒射
上陸成功　金浦航場
元山移動　軟浦航場
蓋馬高原　擊中共軍
長津湖域　鎭出功擊
浦項航場　近接支援
戰術配置　浦項駐屯

34

웨버대령 원주전투 영웅

미 187공수부대 윌리엄 웨버 대위는 6·25전쟁 영웅이다.

1951년 2월 강원 원주 북방 324고지 참호전투를 이끌었다. 전략 요충시에 매복한 날 밤, 중공군이 호각과 나팔소리를 울리며 진격해 왔다. 기습공격을 한차례 격파했지만, 수백 명의 적군이 끊임없이 몰려왔다.

참호에 적군 수류탄이 날아들었다. 급히 오른손으로 잡아 밖으로 던지는 순간 폭발하여 오른 팔이 날아갔다. 계속 전투지휘를 했다.

다음 날 아침 참호에 박격포 탄이 떨어져 오른쪽 다리를 부상 당했다. 혹한에 피가 얼어 굳어 끔찍했다. 이 전투에서 중대원 42명이 전사했다. 64명이 부상 당했다. 3일간의 전투로 끝내 중공군을 몰아냈다.

20대에는 한국을 지키려 공산군과 싸웠고, 37년간 군 생활, 대령 퇴역 후에는 6 · 25 전쟁이 미국과 한국에 잊혀진 전쟁이 안 되게 싸웠다.

한국을 지키려 원주 북쪽 324고지에서 미 육군 187공수 부대의 자유와 평화위해 흘린 피의 댓가를 절대 잊어서는 안 된다.

2022년 4월 12일, 조선일보에 미국의 전쟁 영웅집안 대를 이은 한국 사랑의 딸 베스 웨버와 손녀 데인 웨버의 기사가 났다.

미국과 한국이 6·25 한국전쟁 잊지 않으려는 감동기사에 환호하는 신샀갓 입니다.(웨버 대령은 4월 9일 97세로 별세했다. 한국을 진심으로 사랑한 노병)

♥ 187 공수 특전단 기념비는 미국군 참전 기념비와 함께 문산 임진각 공원에 있다.

Colonel Webber, the Hero of Wonju battle

Captain William Webber form 187th airborne, is a hero of Korean War. In February 1951, he led the trench battle on the Hill 324 which were north of Wonju, Gangwon-do.

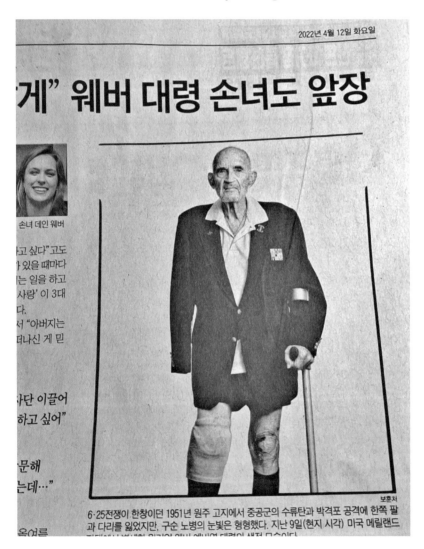

2022년 4월 12일 화요일

'게" 웨버 대령 손녀도 앞장

손녀 데인 웨버

···고 싶다"고도
··· 있을 때마다
···는 일을 하고
···사랑' 이 3대
···다.
···서 "아버지는
···떠나신 게 믿

···단 이끌어
···하고 싶어"

···문해
···는데…"

···올여름

6·25전쟁이 한창이던 1951년 원주 고지에서 중공군의 수류탄과 박격포 공격에 한쪽 팔과 다리를 잃었지만, 구순 노병의 눈빛은 형형했다. 지난 9일(현지 시각) 미국 메릴랜드

보훈처

On the night while ambushing at the strategic point, the Communist Chinese Army advanced with the whistle and trumpet sounds. A surprise attack was defeated, but hundreds of enemy troops were constantly rushing in.

The enemy grenades flew into the trench. As soon as he grabbed it with his right hand and tried to throw it out. But the grenade was exploded at his right arm. Although he injured, he continued to command and control the battle.

In the next morning, a mortar shell fell on the trench and injured his right leg. His blood was frozen in the freezing cold. it was terrible.

42 company members were killed in the battle. 64 soldiers were injured. After three days of battle, the Communist Chinese Army was finally driven out.

In his 20s, he fought against communist forces to protect ROK, and retired as a colonel after 37 years of military service, he was eager to not be forgotten Korean War across the United States and Korea.

The price of blood to protect ROK's freedom and peace of 187th U.S. Army Airborne troops on the 324th highland north of Wonju should never be forgotten.

On 12th April, 2022, the Chosun daily newspaper reported that Beth Webber, the daughter of William Webber who loves Korea form U.S. war hero family. I, gleeman Shin cheers for the touching article that the U.S. and ROK do not want to forget the Korean War. (Colonel Webber passed away on 9th April at the age of 97. The old soldier who loved ROK with all his heart)

♥ The 187th Airborne Special Forces Monument is located in Imjingak Park in Munsan along with the U.S. Army Participation Monument.

35

미, 바이든 대통령 한국전 영웅에 훈장 수여 2021. 5. 21.

94세 퍼킷 예비역 대령, 중위 때 한국전쟁 참전하여 중공군 인해전술, 청천강 전투에서 활약했다.

'명예훈상(Medal of Honor)'은 대통령 수여 최고훈장, 피로 맺은 한미 동맹 기억의 메시지다.

미 육군 특수부대인 제8레인저 중대원 51명과 한국군 9명을 이끌던 퍼킷 중위는 당시 그의 작전지역에 약 2만 5000명의 중공군이 있다는 보고를 받았다.

1950년 11월 25일 중공군 18만명이 청천강을 북진하려던 국군과 미군을 공격했다. 공포스러웠을 것이다. 무식한 인해전술이 아니었다.

당시 모택동은 한국군을 집중 공격하라고 했다.

훈련 기간, 장비 모두 부족하다는 사실을 잘 알고 있다. 청천강 오른쪽을 지키던 국군 2군단이 궤멸됐다. 주력인 미 8군이 완전 포위될 위기였지만 터키여단의 사투 덕분에 겨우 퇴각로를 확보했다.

터키군은 모자를 던져놓고 그 뒤로는 물러서지 않았다고 한다.

청천강 전투에서 1만 명 이상의 전사자를 낸 미군은 38선 이북을 포기하고 후퇴해야 했다. 남북통일의 꿈이 산산조각 났다.

71년 전 미 육군 레인져(특수부대) 중위로 한국전쟁에서 10배 넘는 중공군 병력과 맞서 싸웠던 퍼킷 중위는 6·25 전쟁 중이던 1950년 11월 청천강 일대 205 고지에서 부대원과 한국군(카투사)을 이끌고 중공군 수백 명을 물리친 공로로 이날 명예훈장을 받았다.

23세 젊은 중위였던 그는 부하들이 적의 위치를 파악할 수 있도록 세 번이나 참호 밖으로 달려 나갔다가 큰 부상을 입었다.

참전용사의 희생으로 한국이 평화를 수호하고 자유를 만끽하고 있다.

한국전쟁 때 미군은 36,574명이 전장에서 전사했다. 미국은 은혜국이다. 한국은 갚을 수 없는 빚을 미국에 지고 있다.

절대로 절대로 잊어서는 안 된다.

바이든 대통령은 중공군의 인해전술에 맞서 함께 피흘려 한국의 민주주의를 수호했던 과거를 상기시켰다.

퍼킷 전 중위는 1971년 대령으로 전역했다. 92년 육군 레인져(특수부대) 명예의 전당에 현액 됐다.

U.S. President Biden awarded a Medal to the Hero of the Korean War 2021. 5. 21.

94-year-old Colonel Puckett, a reserved officer, participated in the Korean War when he was a lieutenant and fought in the Battle of Cheongcheon River against the Communist Chinese Army's human wave tactics. The "Medal of Honor" is the highest medal awarded by the President. It is a message of memory from the ROK/U.S. blooded alliance.

Lt. Puckett who led 51 members of 8th Ranger Company which were one of the U.S. Army's special forces and 9 ROK soldiers was reported that around 25,000 soldiers of Communist Chinese Army were in his operational area at the time.

On 25th November, 1950, 180,000 soldiers of Communist Chinese Army attacked ROK and U.S. forces which were trying to advance north of the Cheongcheon River. It would have been terrifying. It wasn't ignorant human wave tactics. At that time, Mao Zeo-dong ordered to attack ROK forces intensively. He was well aware that ROK forces' training discipline and equipments were insufficient. The ROK 2nd Corps which was defending the right side of the Cheongcheon River was destroyed. The main U.S. 8th Army was on the verge of being completely surrounded, but thanks to the Türkiye brigade's struggle, it managed to secure a retreat path. It is said that the soldiers of Türkiye Army threw their hats and did not back down after that. The U.S. military which lost more than 10,000 soldiers in the Battle of Cheongcheon River had to give up north of 38th parallel area and retreat. The dream of reunification between the two Koreas were shattered. Lieutenant Puckett from U.S. Army Ranger(special forces) who fought against more than 10 times Communist Chinese Army in the Korean War 71 years ago was awarded the Medal of Honor for leading troops and ROK soldiers(KATUSA) to defeat hundreds of Communist Chinese Army at 205 highlands near the Cheongcheon River during the Korean War in November 1950. The 23-year-old young lieutenant was seriously injured when he ran out of the trench three times to find the location of enemies.

At the expense of veterans, ROK is protecting peace and enjoying freedom. During the Korean War, 36,574 U.S. soldiers

were killed in action. America is a benefactor. Korea owes the
U.S. debts that cannot be paid back. Never forget.

President Biden recalled the past that bled together against
Communist Chinese Army's human wave tactics to defend
ROK's democracy. Former Lieutenant Puckett was retired as a
colonel in 1971. He was inducted into the Army Ranger(Special
Forces) Hall of fame in 1992. The end.

한국전 영웅 훈장수여

1950년 6월, 영국은 대한민국을 돕기 위해 UN 참전국 중 두 번째로 자국의 육. 해. 공군 병력을 한국에 파병하였다.

영국해군은 인천상륙작전을 포함하여 수많은 전투에 전투자산을 투입하였으며, 2개 영국 여단은 제1영연방사단의 중추적인 역할을 하였다.

영국군이 참여한 주요 전투는 낙동강 방어전투, 박천전투, 임진강전투, 가평전투, 코만도작전, 해피벨리전투 그리고 후크고지전투 등이 있다.

In June 1950 the United Kingdom was the second UN member state to go to ROK's aids with naval, army and air force. Royal Navy assets joined the Incheon Landing and numerous other battle, and two British Army brigades played a pivotal roles the of the 1st Commonwealth Division. Battles which UK forces participated in including Nakdong River battle, Bakchon battle, Imjin River battle, Gapyeong battle, Operation Commando, Happy Valley and Hook highlands battles.

영국

United
Kingdom)

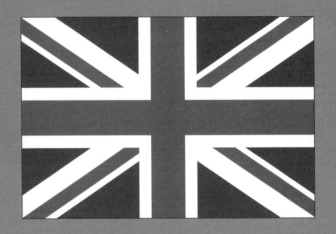

- 참전기간 (Date of Participation) : 1950. 6. 29. – 1957
- 참전규모 (Troops Provided) : 2개 보병여단(2 Infantry Brigades),
                              1개 특공대 (1 Commando Unit),
                              함정 50척(50 battle ships)
                              11개 비행중대 (11 Air squadrons)
- 참전연인원 (Total Participation) : 81,084
- 부상자 (Wounded in Action) : 2,674
- 전사자 (Killed in Action) : 1,108

영국군 참전 기념비

위치: 경기도 가평군 가평읍 신용길 4번지

(영연방: 호주, 뉴질랜드, 캐나다, 英)

1950년 6월 25일 북한 공산괴뢰 불법 남침하니 영국군은 세계평화와 자유 수호를 위해 UN군의 일원으로 지원군 중 두 번째로 많은 병력을 6월 29일에 파견했다.

참전 초기에는 낙동강 방어전에서 북괴군 제10사단을 대구 현풍지역에서 공격해 승리하고, 이어 북한지역의 박천전투(1950.10.25.), 정주전투(10.29.), 남한지역 고양지역, 송추전투(51.1.1.),
임진강 설마리전투(51.4.25.) 그로스터 대대의 옥새(포위되어 옥보석 구슬이 부서지는 고통전투), 가평전투 등으로 빛나는 투혼을 발휘하며 승리했다.
영국군은 연인원 56,000여 명 참전하고, 그중에 1,109명이 전사했으며, 부상 2,674명의 피해를 입었다. 특히 가평전투는 한국의 자유와 평화, 민주주의를 위해 용감히 싸운 영연방 4개국의 참전용사에게 고개 숙여 깊은 감사드린다.
대한민국은 영국에 갚을 수 없는 은혜를 입었다.
영원토록 영국에 빚진 나라다. 희생한 장병들의 투혼을 어찌 잊으랴!

2020년 10월 6일 火, 천고마비 한국의 가을하늘을 만끽하면서 경기 가평읍에 있는 영국군 참전비를 답사하며 참배를 하는 신삿갓.

The Monument to UK forces' Participation in the Korean War

Location: 4, Sinyong-gil, Gapyeong-eup, Gapyeong-gun, Gyeonggi-do

(Commonwealth: Australia, New Zealand, Canada, UK.)

On 25th June, 1950, when the nK communist forces invaded ROK, UK sent the 2nd largest forces after the U.S. on 29th June the same year. They were a part of the UN forces in order to protect peace and freedom in the world.

At the early stage of participation of war, they defeated the nK puppet 10th army at Hyeopung area in Daegu, and succeeded in the battles of Bakchun(Oct 25, 1950) and Jeongju(Oct 29, 1950) in nK area, Goyang, and Songchu(Jan 11, 1951) in ROK area.

The Gloster battalion succeeded in the Seolmari battle(April 25, 1951), OKsae battle(painful battle as much as jewellery got broken by surround) on the Imjin River and

then Gapyeong battle with an indomitable spirit.

A total 56,000 UK soldiers participated in the war, among whom there were 1,109 KIA and 2,674 wounded.

Especially, I bowed to the soldiers of the British commonwealth 4 nations who fought and sacrificed themselves for peace and democracy of ROK.

ROK people owes irreparable debts to the United Kingdom and her sacrifice.

We shall never forget their sacrifice and indomitable spirits!

On Tuesday 26th Oct, 2020, I, gleeman Shin who came and paid homage at an autumn day when the sky was blue with no clouds and harvest was plentiful, at the UK Participant Monument located in Gapyeong.

北韓傀儡　不法南侵
英軍參戰　軍力急派
世界平和　自由守護
韓國戰爭　犧牲多大
參戰初期　防洛東江
北域戰鬪　南域戰鬪
戰雪馬里　玉碎投魂
防中共軍　遲連勝利

영국군 참전기념비

加坪戰鬪　駐英聯邦
自由守護　韓國平和
參戰勇士　不知名也
犧牲將兵　千秋忘焉

02 임진강 전투
(영국 29여단, 글로스터 대대)

위치 : 경기 파주시 적성면 구읍리 112 (영국군 설마리 전투추모공원)

1951년 4월 초 UN군은 캔사스 선(Kansas Line: 임진강- 화천-양양 – 남애리)으로 진출하여 방어선을 구축하고 있었다.

중공군은 서부전선에서 유엔군을 포위 섬멸하고 서울을 재점령하기 위해 1차 춘계공세를 준비했다. 22일부터 화천군 사창리, 임진강 연천 일대의 유엔군의 진지를 공격했다.

영국군 제 29여단 예하 글로스터 대대는 22일 적성면 구읍리 일대 임진강 남안 있었다.

이날 22시경 중공군 1개 연대가 임진강을 건너와 대대를 공격했다. 중과부적으로 대대는 설마리로 철수했다. 다음날 235고지, 설마리고 지, 314고지에서 방어진지를 구축했다.

23일 자정을 기해 중공군 제187사단이 집중공격을 해왔다. 이튿날 새벽에 대대는 퇴로를 차단당한 채 포위되고 말았다.

24일 필리핀 제10대대가 글로스터 대대 구출작전을 폈다. 하지만 두 번의 구출작전은 실패했다. 이에 제29여단장 브로디(Tom Brodie) 준 장은 글로스터 대대장에게 포위망을 뚫고 철수할 것을 명령했다.

글로스터 대대는 중공군 3개 사단의 파상적인 공격을 수차례 격퇴 시켰지만 탄약부족으로 전투 한계선에 이르고 있었다. 대대장은 부상 자와 함께 고지에 남아 있었다. 각 중대장들에게 철수하라고 명령했 다. 따라서 후방으로 철수하기 시작했다. 하지만 중공군의 집중사격을 받고 전사하거나 포로가 되었다.

글로스터 대대의 선전으로 중공군 제63군 3개 사단 4만 2천명이 설

마리에서 3일간 발이 묶여 진격하지 못했다. 그로 인해 중공군은 미 제24사단과 제25사단을 포위하려던 계획을 달성하지 못했고 중공군의 대공세는 실패로 끝났다.

중공군 3개 사단이 임진강 도강, 글로스터 연대는 '18대 1'로 싸운 영국군은 맞붙었다. 그 용맹의 출발점은 자유수호의 의지였다.
3일간의 결전에 UN군 재편 시간을 주고 서울침공 저지하는데 공헌하고 계획을 변경케 했고 자유민주주의를 지키기 위해 생소한 나라 감악산 북방 설마리 산야가 피범벅이 되었다.
역사를 잊어버린 민족, 은혜를 잊은 국민들은 영국에 빚진 대한민국 국민들이다.

20년 6월 5일(금), 6 · 25 지원군을 답사 하면서 1951년 4월 22일 ~25일까지 전투상황, 파주, 임진강 주변을 경유 설마리 영국군 추모공원에 들렀다.   이 땅이 피범벅 된 역사의 현장을 숨죽이며 살펴보다가 참으로 우리 대한민국은 영국에 빚진 민족이라고 생각하며 산야를 유람하는 신삿갓이오. (59명 전사, 526명 포로, 180명 부상, 수용소 사망 34명)

♥ 영국은 6 · 25 전쟁 때 16개 참전국 중 2번째로 많은 병력을 지원, 한국 전쟁 중 1,109명 전사, 2,674명이 부상을 당했다.
♥ 지휘관은 후방 포병에게 "내 머리에 포탄을 쏴라!"라고 지원 요청한 대대장, 칸 중령이다. 임진강 전투는 영국군 5700여 명이 3만여 명의 중공군 남하를 막아 서울 침공을 저지했다.

The Battle of Imjin river
(British Gloster Battalion of 29th Brigade)

Location: 112 Gupeup-ri, Jeokseong-myeon, Paju-si, Gyeonggi-do (Seolmari Battle Memorial Park for British Army)

In early April 1951, UN forces had advanced to Kansas

Line(Imjin River - Hwacheon - Yangyang - Namae-ri) and established the defense line on the Kansas Line. The Communist Chinese Army prepared the first spring offensive to surround and annihilate the UN forces on the western frontline and to re-occupy Seoul. Starting from the 22nd, they attacked the UN forces' positions in Sachang-ri, Hwacheon-gun, Yeoncheon IVO Imjin River.

Gloster battalion of the 29th brigade of the British Army was on the south bank of the Imjin River in Gueup-ri, Jeokseong-myeon. Around 2200(I) on the day, a regiment of the Communist Chinese Army crossed the Imjin river and attacked the battalion.

Due to outnumbered the battalion had to withdraw to Seolma-ri. The next day, they established defensive positions at Hill 235, Hill of Seolma-ri and Hill 314. As of midnight on 23rd, 187th division of the Communist Chinese Army carried out intensive attacks. The battalion was surrounded with blocked retreating ways at dawn on the following day.

On 24th, the 10th battalion of the Philippines Army conducted rescue operations for Gloster Battalion. However, two rescue operations failed. Brigadier General Tom Brodie of the 29th Brigade ordered commander of Gloster Battalion to withdraw through the siege.

The Gloster Battalion repelled several catastrophic attacks from three divisions of the Communist Chinese Army, but it was reaching the limit of the battle due to lack of ammunitions. The battalion commander remained on the highlands with the wounded. Each company commander was ordered to withdraw. Accordingly, they began to withdraw to the rear. However, they were killed or taken prisoner after being heavily shots by Communist Chinese Army.

Due to the fight well of the Gloster Battalion, 42,000 soldiers of three divisions of the 63rd Army from Communist Chinese Army were unable to advance in Seolma-ri for three days. As a result, the plan to surround the U.S. 24th and 25th divisions failed, and Communist Chinese Army's grand offensive ended in failure.

Three divisions of Communist Chinese Army which crossed Imjin River and Gloster Battalion fought "18 to 1". Its bravery started from the will to defend freedom. The three-day battle gave time to reorganize the UN forces, contributed to blocking the invasion of Seoul, and caused them to change enemy's plans, and the unfamiliar country of Mt. Gamak, northern Seolma-ri, was covered in blood to protect liberal democracy. The people who forgot history and the people who forgot favor are the people of the Republic of Korea who owes to British.

On 5th June(Fri), 2020, While I explored memorial places of UN forces, I visited British Military Memorial Park by passing by the combat situations from 22nd to 25th April, 1951, Paju, and the Imjin River. As I took a breathless look at the scene of history in which this land was covered in blood, I, gleeman Shin who tours the mountains and fields thinking that the Republic of Korea is a nation owed to Britain. (59 soldiers, 526 prisoners, 180 wounded, and 34 killed in camps)

♥ Britain supported the second-largest number of troops among the 16 nations participating in the Korean War, with 1,109 killed and 2,674 wounded during the Korean War.

♥ Commander was Lieutenant Colonel Khan, who requested assistance from the rear artillery by saying, "Shoot shells on my head!" In the Battle of the Imjin River, as around 5,700 British soldiers blocked 30,000 soldiers of Communist Chinese Army advancing southward, they prevented the invasion of Seoul.

赤三個師　英待防禦
十八對一　苦群憤鬪
勇猛出發　自由守護
三日決戰　後方改編
首都抵止　赤劃變更
自由民主　爲韓國人
北方山野　血土浸紋
忘歷史民　忘恩惠國
債權英國　債務韓國

03

파주 설마리 까마귀 떼

1951년 4월 22일~25일. 70년 전 3일간 임진강을 도강한 중공군 3개 사단에영국 글로스터 1대대는 18대 1의 수적 열세에 밀리지 않았다.

임진강 전부에서 싸운 영국군의 그 용맹의 출발점은 자유 수호 의지로 대한민국이 생환했다.

70년 전 그날 자신의 목숨을 던진 부하 장병들은 전사하고, 부상당하고, 포로가 되었다. 그 영혼이 까마귀로 환생되어 원한의 통곡소리 머리위로 고함치며 나는데 모든 한국인들이여! 휴전중이라고 자각하라네.

21년 2월 28일. 지난해 5월 영국군 설마리 전적비를 답사 후 두 번째다.

도착하자 산곡에 까마귀 소리 요란하더니 참배하는 대대장 칸 중령 십자가 기념비 주변을 날며 소리친다.

요상하고 특이한 일이다. 참배하고 나오니 고요하다.

전사자 영웅들의 영혼이 까마귀로 환생했다고 역사를 잊은 민족에서 실천하는 국민 되기를 소망하는 신삿갓이오.

(♡고국 영국으로부터 5,000마일(8,000여km) 떨어진 곳에 동맹의 부름 받고 달려왔다. 전사 59명, 포로 526명, 수용소 사망 34명, 탈출 67명 성공)

A Flock of Crows at Seolma-ri in Paju

From 22nd to 25th April, 1951. The three divisions of Communist Chinese Army crossed the Imjin River for three days 70 years ago.

The UK 1st Battalion, Gloster, was not outnumbered by 18 to 1.
The starting point of the British bravery in the Battle of the Imjin River because The Republic of Korea's will to protect freedom.

70 years ago on that day, the soldiers who threw their lives were killed, injured, taken prisoner. Their souls were reincarnated as crows

The wailing of resentment was flying, shouting over my head over head. All ROK people! They want you to realize that you are in the armistice.

Today is 28th February, 2021. This is second time to be here after exploring the Battle Monument to the British Army in May last year. When I arrived the crows were screaming in the mountains. They were flying and yelling around the memorial cross to the battalion

commander LTC Khan. It's weird and unusual. It was quiet after visiting the monument. I think that the souls of the fallen heroes are reincarnated as crows. I, gleeman Shin who wish to become a citizen who practices in a nation that has forgotten history.

(♡ They ran 5,000 miles (8,000 km) away from his home country of England under the call of the alliance. 59 KIA, 34 died in the camp, 67 escaped successfully among the 526 prisoners)

英國大隊　臨津戰鬪
數積劣勢　一八對一
勇猛英軍　自由守護
戰七十前　生還韓國
部下將兵　戰死傷捕
靈魂換生　烏群再活
痛曲解怨　高聲飛行
諸痛韓人　覺休戰中

04

영국군 가평전투(영국군 27여단)

위치 : 경기도 가평군 가평읍 신용길 4.

1951년 4월 19일 영연방 제 27여단은 강원 사창리 일대에서 진지를 국군 6사단 19연대에 인계하고 가평으로 이동하였다.

영국 27여단은 가평천으로 집결했다. 여단장은 대대를 북면 수덕산 고지에 배치했다. 캐나다 PPCLI 대대를 이곡리 고지에 배치하고, 호주 대대를 죽둔리 504고지에 배치했다.

4월 24일 새벽 1시 30분경 중공군이 호주 대대를 공격하기 시작했다. 호주 대대 B중대가 죽둔리- 골말 간 좁은 길을 따라 능선에 배치되어 있었다.

미 제72 전차대대가 B중대를 지원하기 위해 출동했다가 보급을 위해 죽둔리 후방으로 이동했다. 그 사이에 중공군이 B중대 우측을 돌아 A, C, D중대를 공격했다. 전투는 새벽까지 이어졌고 적은 대대본부와 가평을 감제할 수 있는 고지를 점령했다. 이후 중공군의 공격이 하루종일 되풀이되었다.

18시경 미 제1기병사단 제5연대가 가평으로 급파되었다.

캐나다군 대대와 미들섹스 대대 후방으로 나누어 배치되었다.

얼마 후 중공군 1개 중대가 B중대로 공격해 들어 왔다. 집중사격으로 격퇴시켰다. 23시경 적의 공격이 재개 되었다. 6소대 병사들은 철수했다가 역습을 감행하여 진지를 탈환했다. 캐나다 대대는 81미리 박격포와 50미리 기관포로 적의 침투지역을 강타하여 중공군에게 막대한 피해를 입혔다.

미들섹스 대대도 공격을 당했지만 뉴질랜드군 제 16포병대대 지원으로 격퇴시켰다.

호주 대대는 전사 32명, 부상 59명, 포로 3명의 인명피해가 발생했다. 캐나다 대대는 10명이 전사하고 23명이 부상을 당했다. 반면 중공군은 500여 명이 전사하는 피해를 입었다.

영국군은 연인원 56,000여 명이 참전했다. 그중에 1108명이 전사하고 2,674명이 부상을 당했다. 179명이 실종되었고 977명이 포로가 되었다.

영국군 전사자 중 885명은 부산 유엔기념 공원에 묻혀있다.

Battle of Gapyeong, British Army (27th Brigade)

Location: 4, Sinyong-gil, Gapyeong-eup, Gapyeong-gun, Gyeonggi-do.

On 19th April, 1951, the 27th Brigade of Commonwealth handed over its positions to the ROK 19th Regiment of 6th division in Sachang-ri, Gangwon-do, and moved to Gapyeong. The British 27th Brigade gathered in Gapyeong Stream. The brigade commander deployed the battalion to the highlands of Sudeok mountain in Buk-myeon. The Canadian PPCLI Battalion was deployed at the Igok-ri Highlands, and the Australian Battalion was deployed at the 504 Jukdun-ri Highlands.

At around 0130(I) on 24th April, Communist Chinese Army began attacking the Australian Battalion. Company B of the Australian Battalion was stationed on the ridge along the narrow road between Jukdunli and Golmal. The 72nd U.S. tank battalion was dispatched to support Company B, and moved to the rear of Jukdun-ri for sustainment. In the meantime, the Communist Chinese Army turned to the right of Company B and attacked Company A, C, and D. The fighting continued until dawn, and the enemies occupied the battalion headquarters and the highlands where Gapyeong could be controlled. Since then, Communist Chinese Army attacks had been repeated throughout the day.

Around 1800(I), the 5th Regiment of 1st U.S. Cavalry Division was dispatched to Gapyeong. It was divided and deployed in the rear of the Canadian Army battalion and the Middlesex Battalion. Soon after, a company of Communist Chinese Army attacked Company B. They were repelled with concentrated fire. The enemy's attacks resumed around 2300(I). The soldiers of 6th platoon withdrew and returned the positions with counterattacks. The Canadian Battalion struck the enemy's infiltration area with 81mm mortars and 50mm cannons, causing heavy losses to the Communist Chinese Army. The Middlesex Battalion was also attacked, but Communist Chinese Army was repelled by the support of the 16th New Zealand Artillery Battalion.

The Australian Battalion suffered 32 casualties, 59 injuries and 3 prisoners. The Canadian Battalion was killed 10 soldiers and wounded 23. On the other hand, more than 500 Chinese soldiers were killed.

More than 56,000 British soldiers participated in the war. Among them, 1,108 were killed and 2,674 were injured. 179 people were missing and 977 were taken prisoner. 885 British soldiers are buried in the UN Memorial Park in Busan

네덜란드는 미국, 영국, 호주에 이어 네 번째로 한국에 군대를 파병하였다. 유엔 안전보장 이사회의 결의에 의해 먼저 해군 구축함 1척을 파견하였고, 이후 총 6척의 함정을 파견하여 미 극동해군과 함께 해상작전을 수행하였다. 한국의 전황이 악화되자 네덜란드는 보병 1개 대대를 더 파병하였다.

보병대대는 1950년 11월 23일 부산에 도착하여 11월 말에 전방으로 이동한 후 미 제2사단에 배속되어 작전 활동에 들어갔다.

전쟁 동안 수행한 주요 전투는 횡성전투와 인제전투이다.

The Netherlands was the fourth country which sent troops to ROK after the US, UK and AUS. In respond to the UN security council resolution, Netherlands had dispatched a destroyer after that dispatched a total of six naval ships to conduct maritime operations with the U.S. Far East Navy. As the ROK's war situation was getting worse, Netherlands dispatched another Infantry Battalion additionally.

On 23rd November, 1950, the Infantry Battalion had arrived in Busan and moved forward on the end of November. then was assigned to the US 2nd Infantry Division to conduct operations. During the war their major battles were Hoengsong and Inje battle.

네덜란드

Netherlands

- 참전기간 (Date of Participation) : 1950. 7. 16 ~ 1955. 1
- 참전규모 (Troops Provided) : 1개 보병대대 (1 Infantry Battalion), 함정 6척 (6 Ships)
- 참전연인원 (Total Participants) : 5,322
- 부상자 (Wounded in Action) : 645
- 전사자 (Killed in Action) 124

01

네덜란드군 참전 기념비

위치 : 강원도 횡성군 우천면 한우로 우항 2길 3.

네덜란드는 2차 세계대전 직후 전쟁의 상흔이 아물지 않았다.

1950년 6월 25일 북한괴뢰가 불법 남침했다. 공산주의와 싸우고 자유를 지킬 전쟁으로 한국전쟁에 파병을 결정했다.

네덜란드는 육군과 해군을 파병했다.

육군은 11월 23일 부산에 도착 후 참전 초기에 미 제2사단 38연대에 배속되어 충주로 이동했다. 해군은 50년 7월 19일 서해안 미국 지원 중대에 도착 후 활동했다.

원주전투(1951. 1. 13) 횡성전투(51. 2. 6) 중공군과 삼마치 전투와 횡성 읍내전, 홍천 북방에 위치한 가리산 전투(51. 5. 14), 인제전투(51. 5. 27) 도솔산에서 백병전을 펼쳤다.

네덜란드의 파병군, 오렌지 공의 억센 후예들은 충정과 용기로 붉은 공산침략자와 싸웠다.

네덜란드는 한국전쟁 때 4,748명 파병하여 연인원 5,322명이 참전했다. 그중에 122명 전사, 381명 전상, 3명 실종, 264명 비전투부상 등으로 총 768명의 피해를 입었다.

과거에는 네덜란드가 한국을 도왔다. 이제는 한국이 네덜란드를 도와야한다. 대한민국은 네덜란드를 기억합니다.

그들은 우리 한국의 영웅입니다.

♡ 네덜란드 국을 한자는 화란 和蘭으로 표시한다.

2020년 11월 16일 월, 횡성에 있는 네덜란드 참전국 기념비를 답사했다.

기념비 주변을 노인 10명이 청소하고 있었다. 보기가 참 좋았다. 횡성 읍내 전투에서 중공군과 전투에서 지휘관 오우덴 중령을 잃었다.

어르신들의 추모하는 느낌이 들었다. 이곳에서 횡성군민의 6·25 전사자 기념비도 함께 답사하는 신삿갓이다.

The Monument to Netherlands forces' Participation in the Korean War

Location: 3 Woohang 2-gil, Hanwoo-ro, Ucheon-myeon, Hoengseong-gun, Gangwon-do.

The war scars of World War II of Netherlands were not yet closed up. The nK communist regime launched invasion to ROK on 25th June, 1950.

Netherlands decided to dispatch forces to the Korean War to defend the freedom of my country ROK by fighting against the nK communist.

Netherlands sent army and navy. The army had arriv

ed on 23rd November, 1950, at Busan port and had been attach
ed to 38th regiment of US 2nd Infantry Division and then mov
ed to Chungju.

On 19th July, 1950, the navy had arrived to the support group
of US navy in West coast of ROK and began operations together
with US navy.

Netherlands army conducted hand to hand fights against
Communist Chinese Army in the battles of Wonju(1951. 1. 13.),
Hoengseong(51. 2. 6.), Samachi, Hoengseong town, Mt. Gari(51.
5. 14.) in the north of Hongcheon and Mt. Dosol in Injae(1951. 5.
27.).

Netherlands soldiers who were strong and tough descendants
of orange fought with the heartfelt loyalty and courage, against
the red communist aggressors.

Netherlands dispatched 4848 soldiers and among them KIA
were 122, wounded 381, missing 3 and noncombatant wounded
were 264.

During the Korean war Netherlands helped ROK, and
now ROK ought to help back Netherlands. ROK remembers
Netherlands.

All the soldiers of Netherlands who fought for my country are
heroes of ROK.

♡ We write the country name of Netherlands as 和蘭 in Chinese characters.

On 16th November(Mon), 2020, I, gleeman Shin, visited the Korean war monument to the Armed Forces of Netherlands in Heongseong.

Around 10 senior citizens were cleaning the memorial site, It looked very good to me. Lt. colonel Ouden, the battalion commander, lost his life while fighting against Communist Chinese Army at the Hoengseong town battle. The senior citizens who were cleaning the monument seemed to worship the sacrificed soldiers for the peace and freedom of ROK.

I, gleeman Shin, also visited the 6・25 Memorial site to persons killed in Hoengseong during the Korean War.

和蘭之國　大戰直後
北韓傀儡　不法南侵
戰共産軍　爲自由國
韓國戰爭　派兵結定
派陸海軍　釜山到着
參戰初期　美軍配屬
原州戰鬪　橫城戰鬪
加里戰鬪　麟蹄戰鬪
韓國平和　恩惠之國
過去助韓　今助和蘭

02

오우덴 중령 현충비(네덜란드 대대장)

위치 : 강원도 횡성군 읍하리 40.

1951년 2월 12일~13일, 화란 대대는 미 38연대를 따라 진격했다. 두 꺼비 강 북쪽 지역에 배치 완료했다.

11일 밤 중공군 제 39, 제 40, 제 42, 제 66집단군이 횡성 축선으로 공격했다. 홍천 관문 삼마치 고개에서 전투가 벌어졌다.

12일 미군과 한국군이 철수했다.

중공군이 후방까지 침투했다. 화란 대대 지휘부가 포위되었다. 수류 탄이 터지고 교전했다.

아군 철수를 끝까지 엄호한 화란군이다. 횡성전투에서 대대장과 인 사장교를 비롯해 17명이 전사했다. 37명의 부상자도 발생했다. 횡성 비행장에 와서 재정비했다.

2021년 3월 30일, 횡성읍 읍하리 40번지, 네덜란드 참전 기념비를 답사한 날 읍하리에서 기념비를 찾았다. 못 봤다. 두 번째 가서 찾았다.

대한민국의 자유와 평화를 위하여 과감히 싸운 화란장병의 영령을 추모하며 오랫동안 참배를 했다.

The Memorial Monument to Lieutenant Colonel Ouden (Dutch Battalion Commander)

Location: 40, Eupha-ri, Hoengseong-gun, Gangwon-do.

On 12th~13th February, 1951, the Hwaran(Dutch) Battalion advanced along the U.S. 38th Regiment. They completed deployment in the northern part of the Dukubi(toad) river.

On the night, the 11th, 39th, 40th, 42nd, and 66th army of Communist Chinese Army attacked along the Heongseong axis. A battle broke out at Sammachi Pass, the gateway to Hongcheon. The U.S. and ROK troops withdrew on 12th.

The Communist Chinese Army penetrated into the rear. The command of the Hwaran(Dutch) battalion was surrounded. The grenades exploded and they engaged.

It was the Dutch Army, which was covered until the end of ROK forces' withdrawal. 17 soldiers were killed in the Battle of Hoengseong, including battalion commander and personnel officer. There were also 37 injuries. They moved to Hoengseong airport and reorganized.

On 30th March, 2021, I found the monument at 40, Euphari, Hoengseong-eup when I visited the monument to Dutch participation in the Korean War. I could find out for my second time visit. I paid a long tribute to Dutch soldiers who fought boldly for the freedom and peace of the Republic of Korea.

和蘭大隊　橫城北方
配置完了　蟾江地域
洪川關門　交戰中共
橫城攻擊　美軍撤收
交戰現場　包圍指揮
爆手榴彈　戰死多數
美韓撤收　最終奄護
橫城戰鬪　英靈追慕

네덜란드 오 중령 기념비

1951년 1월 10일 ~ 2월 28일(50 여일) 전략적 요충지 원주지역이다.
미 제2사단, 미 제1 해병사단, 프랑스대대, 네덜란드 대대, 국군 제3,
제6, 제8사단이 작전했다.

중공군 제37군, 북한 괴뢰 5군단, 혼성부대, 제2군단, 제2, 제9, 제
10, 제31사단과의 공방전이다

적군의 공격으로 미 2사단은 원주지역으로 철수하는 아군을 엄호했
다. 제37포병대대의 지원받았다. 괴뢰군 남하를 저지했다. 포병은 약
3천 톤의 포탄을 퍼부었다. 북한 괴뢰군에게 치명타를 가했다

미 23연대와 배속된 프랑스 대대는 학성동 야산을 점령했다. 미 38
연대는 배속된 네덜란드 대대와 소초면에 진지를 구축했다.

포병대대는 진출한 적과 백병전을 했다. 진지를 고수했다. 괴뢰군은
600 여구의 시신을 남기고 퇴각했다.

미 23연대의 총공격으로 적을 1천여 명 사살했다. 미 38연대는 총
공격으로 종심을 확보했다.

잔적 북괴 선전부대는 해병 사단에 의해 소탕됨으로써 천지를 흔들
던 포성이 잠들고 비 오듯 쏟아지는 총탄도 사라졌다.

원주지역에서의 님들의 빛나는 충성과 용감무쌍함을 후손들은 알아
야 한다.

UN군 미 10군과 네덜란드군과 프랑스군의 세계의 자유와 평화를
위해 흘린 피 값을 한국인은 잊어서는 안 된다.

2021년 3월 30일 원주시 태장 2동 1667번지에 위치한 원주지역 전투 전적비를 답사했다. 역사를 잊으면 그 역사 반복한다.

The Monument to Battle of Wonju District (Netherlands Army)
(U.S. 2nd Division, Netherlands Army, French Army)

1951 10th January ~ 28th Feburary (50 days) Wonju was key points of strategy. U.S. 2nd Marine Division, U.S. 1st Marine Division, French Battalion, Dutch Battalion, ROK 3rd, 5th, 6th and 8th Divisions conducted operations.

Friendly forces fought against 37th army of Communist Chinese Army, nK puppet 5th Corps, mixed unit, 2nd Corps, 2nd, 9th, 10th, and 31st divisions.

The U.S. 2nd Infantry Division covered friendly forces' withdrawal to the Wonju area. The 37th Artillery Battalion supported by fire. They blocked the nK puppet's southward movement. The artillery fired about 3,000 tons of shells. nK puppet troops had been fatally hit.

The U.S. 23rd Regiment and the French Battalion which were attached to the U.S. 23rd Regiment occupied the mountain in Hakseong-dong. The U.S. 38th Regiment and dispatched Netherlands Battalion established positions in Socho-myeon.

The artille ry conducted hand to hand fights against the advancing enemies. They retained the positions. The puppet troops retreated, lea ving around 600 bodies be hind.

The U.S. 23rd Regime nt's general attack killed

more than 1,000 enemies. The U.S. 38th Regiment secured dep th with a general attack.

As nK propaganda unit, the remnants of nK puppet Army, were wiped out by the marine division, sound of artillery fire that shaking the sky and earth and bullets like rainfall were disappeared.

Descendants should know that the glorious loyalty and

bravery of the soldiers in Wonju. ROK people should not forget that the U.S. 10th corps, the Dutch and French troops of U.N. forces shed blood for world freedom and peace.

On 30th March, 2021, I explored the monument of battlefield in Wonju at 1667, Taejang 2-dong, Wonju-si. If you forgot history, we might repeat it.

戰略要地　原州地區
聯合軍集　佛蘭和蘭
中共軍集　傀儡軍團
混姓部隊　攻防戰鬪
因赤攻擊　撤收奄護
砲兵指援　南下抵止
正面攻擊　展白兵戰
砲擊攻擊　破騎馬隊
敵掃蕩戰　海兵師團
將兵弗忘　恩惠不忘

캐나다는 2만 6천명 이상의 용사가 유엔의 일원으로 극동 지역의 6.25 한국전쟁 때 참전하였다. 캐나다 군인들은 가평전투와 355고지와 후크고지전투 등에서 용감하게 싸웠다.

왕립 캐나다 해군의 구축함들은 한반도 해안에서 순찰임무를 수행하였으며, 왕립 캐나다 공군은 태평양을 건너며 공수임무를 수행하였다.

More than 26,000 Canadians served with United Nations force in the Far East during the Korean War. Canadian soldies saw heavy action in fighting at places like Kapyong, Hill 355 and the Hook. Royal Canadian Navy destroyers also patrolled the waters off the Korean Peninsula and Royal Canadian Air Force transport planes flew supply runs across the Pacific Ocean.

On 29th July, 1950, in accordance with the UN resolution, France deployed a naval ship to POK to participate in Incheon landing operation. On 29th November, a French Infantry Battalion which landed in Busan was attached U.S. 23rd Infantry Regiment and participated in Battles of Twin Tunnel, Jipyeong-ri, Heartbreak Ridge, Wonju, Puchaeteul, Inje, Iron triangle, T-Bone, Arrow-Head, Songkok and Chungasan.

캐나다

Canada

- 참전기간 (Date of Participation) : 1950. 7. 25 ~ 1957. 6
- 참전규모 (Troops Provided) : 1 개 보병여단(1 Infantry Brigade), 함정 8척 (8 Ships),
  1개공수 비행 대대(1 Transport Squadron).
- 참전연인원 (Total Participants) : 26,791
- 부상자 (Wounded in Action) : 1,212
- 전사자 (Killed in Action) : 516

캐나다군 전투 기념비

위치: 경기도 가평군 북면 이곡리.

1950년 6월 25일 북한 공산군이 불법 남침했다. 캐나다는 한국에 육해공군을 인구비례 가장 많은 병력을 파견했다.

안녕과 세계평화 위하여 UN군 일원으로 긴급하게 해군과 공군을 파견했다. 육군 PPCLI* 파트리카 공주연대를 부산에 파견했다.

초기작전은 삼량진지역 북괴군 소탕작전 시작으로 여주, 가평전투 (1951. 4. 24), 운천 자일리전투(1951.5.6), 코만도작전(51.7.28 : 임진강 ~264고지), 연천 고왕산전투(52. 10.23), 나부리 고지쟁탈전(53. 5) 개성북방까지 진출하는 빛나는 투혼을 발휘했다.

캐나다군은 연인원 29,940명 참전했다. 그중에 516명 전사하고, 1,255명 부상을 입었다. 특히 가평 북면 전투에서는 한국의 자유 평화, 민주주의를 위해서 젊음을 바친 장병의 희생에 영원히 잊을 수 없습니다.

*PPCLI : 파트리카 공주의 캐나다연대 제2대대, Princess Patticia' s Canadian Light infantry, 918명.

2020년 10월 15일 , 가평군 북면 이곡리에 소재한 캐나다군의 전투 기념비를 답사하고, 참배하며 감사와 빛나는 영혼위해 기원하는 신삿갓.

The Monument to the Battle of the Canadian Forces

Location: Igok–ri, Buk–myeon, Gapyeong–gun, Gyeonggi–do.

On June 25, 1950, the North Korean Communist Army illegally Invaded South Korea. Canada returned to Korea, sending a large number of troops from their Army, Navy and Air Force.

For the sake of peace and well-being, the United Nations Army's navy and the air force was dispatched. Army PPCLI* (Princess Patricia's Canadian Light Infantry) was sent to fight in Busan.

The initial operation was the start of the Northern Government's sweep of Samryangjin, Battle of Yeoju and Gapyeong (April 24, 1951) and Battle of Xili in Uncheon (1951).

Operation Komando, Imjingang River to,
Battle of Yeoncheon Gowangsan Mountain, Battle of Naburi Highlands,
Canada showed its brilliant fighting spirit, advancing to the northern part of Kaesong.

Canadian forces sent 29,940 men into battle. Among them 516 people were killed in action and 1,255 were injured.

Especially in the Battle of Gapyeong, fighting for Korea's free peace, at the sacrifice of a soldiers who dedicated their youth to democracy, I will never forget it.

*PPCLI: Princess Patricia's Canadian Light Infantry, 2nd Battalion, Princess Patricia's Canadian Light infantry, 918.

October 15th, 2020. Located in Igok-ri, Buk-myeon, Gapyeong-gun, you can visit Canadian combat monuments.

(Canadian troops were the 5th largest number of participating countries)

北韓傀儡　不法南侵
貴國參戰　派陸海空
世界平和　自由守護
韓國戰爭　崇高犧牲
參戰初期　急派海空
派公主軍　遣着釜山
驪州戰鬪　加坪戰鬪
防臨津江　高旺戰鬪
自由守護　韓國平和

1950년 7월 29일, 프랑스는 유엔 안전보장이사회 결의안에 의거하여 한국에 해군 함정을 보내 인천상륙작전에 참가하였다.

11월 29일 한국에 도착한 프랑스 보병대대는 미 제2사단 23보병연대에 배속되어 쌍터널, 지평리, 단장의 능선, 원주, 부채뜰, 인제, 철의 삼각지대, 티-본 (T-Bone)고지, 화살머리, 송곡, 충아산 전투에 참전하였다.

Le 29 juillet 1950, la France a envoyé un navire de marine en Corée du Sud sur la base d'une résolution du Conseil de sécurité des Nations Unies pour participer à l'opération d'atterrissage d'Incheon. Arrivé en Corée le 29 novembre, le bataillon d'infanterie français a été affecté au 23e régiment d'infanterie de la 2e division américaine et a participé à la bataille de Ssang Tunnel, Jipyeong-ri, la crête de Danjang, Wonju, Fan Garden, Inje, Triangle de Fer, T-Bone, Arrowhead, Songgok et Chungasan.

On 29th July, 1950, in accordance with the UN resolution, France deployed a naval ship to POK to participate in Incheon landing operation. On 29th November, a French Infantry Battalion which landed in Busan was attached U.S. 23rd Infantry Regiment and participated in Battles of Twin Tunnel, Jipyeong-ri, Heartbreak Ridge, Wonju, Puchaeteul, Inje, Iron triangle, T-Bone, Arrow-Head, Songkok and Chungasan.

프랑스

French Republic

- ■ 참전기간 (Date of Participation) ; 1950. 7. 22. – 1965. 6
- ■ 참전규모 (Troops Previded) : 1개 보병대대(1 Infantry Battalion), 함정 1척 (1 Battle Ship)
- ■ 참전연인원 (Total Participants) : 3,421
- ■ 부상자 (Wounded in Action) : 1,008
- ■ 전사자 (Killed in Action) : 269
- ■ Date de participation : 1950 . 22.– 1965 . 6
- ■ Taille de la guerre : 1 bataillon d'infanterie (1 Infantry Bataille), Un piège (1 Ship)
- ■ Nombre total de participants: 3,421
- ■ Blessés: 1,008
- ■ Mort (en action) : 269

01

프랑스군 참전 기념비

위치: 수원시 장안구 파장동 31-2 번지

‘불가능은 없다’ 는 신념을 가진 나폴레옹 후예들!

세계평화와 한국의 자유민주주의 위해서 왔다.

1950년 11월 29일 부산에 도착해서 수원에 집결, 미 제 2사단에 배속된 후에

원주 쌍터널 전투(1951. 1. 31~2. 2)

양평 지평리 전투(1951. 2. 13~15)

양구 단장, 창자가 끊어지는 아픔 능선(9. 13~10. 13)

백마고지 서쪽지역인 화살머리 전투(1952. 10. 6~10)

중공군이 새벽부터 5시간 동안 화살고지에 1천 발 이상의 포탄을 쏘았다. 그 후 나팔 불며 파상공격 했다.

용감한 프랑스군은 결사적 방어로 그들을 무산시켰다.

전장 정리 들어간 부대는 북쪽 경사면 전초기지에서 중공군 600여구 시신을 발견했다.

한국전에 참전한 프랑스군은 연인원 3,421명, 그중에 288명 전사, 7명이 실종되었으니 한국은 프랑스에 천년만년 은혜를 어찌 잊으랴?

2020년 9월 21일 月, 수원 파장동에 있는 프랑스군 참전 기념비를 답사하고 참배하는 신삿갓.

Mémorial de l'armée française

Emplacement : 31-2 Pajang-dong, Jangan-gu, Suwon.

' Les descendants napoléoniens qui croient que " rien n'est impossible " !
Je suis venu pour la paix mondiale et la démocratie libérale de la Corée.

Je suis arrivé à Busan le 29 novembre 1950
Après s'être rallié à Suwon et avoir été affecté à la 2e division américaine,

Bataille du tunnel de Wonju (31-22 janvier 1951)
Bataille de Yangpyeong-ri (13-15 février 1951)
Le chef Yanggu, la crête douloureuse où les intestins se brisent (9.13-10.13)

Bataille de la tête de flèche à l'ouest de l'Annonciation (1952.10.6-10)
Plus d'un millier de tirs sur la pointe de la flèche pendant cinq heures à partir de l'aube.
J'ai tiré un obus. Puis j'ai soufflé et j'ai fait une vague.

Les braves troupes françaises les ont vaincus par une défense associative.

Les unités qui ont été réorganisées sur le champ de bataille sont situées sur l'avant-poste de la pente nord,

Plus de 600 corps de l'armée de l'air chinoise ont été retrouvés.

Les Français qui ont participé à la guerre de Corée avaient 3 421 hommes, 288 d'entre eux ont été tués, 7 disparus,

Comment la Corée oublie-t-elle la grâce de mille ans de la France?

21 septembre 2020. 月, le monument aux morts de l'armée française à Pajang-dong, Suwon

Un gentleman en quête et en visite.

The Monument to French Forces's participation in the Korean War

Location: 31–2 Pajeong–dong, Jangan–gu, Suwon

French soldiers were courageous and powerful as if they were the soldiers of Napoleon whose motto was "Nothing is impossible." They came to fight for peace and democracy in ROK. On 29th November, 1950, they had arrived at Busan and assembled in Suwon. And then they were attached the US army 2ID, and later for battle.

From then on, they participated in the battles; the Twin-tunnel in Wonju(31st Jan to 2nd Feb, 1951), Jipyeoni, Yangpeong(13th Feb to 15th, 1951), Danjang in Yanggu(13th Sept to 13th Oct the same year) * Danjang means the pain of cutting off intestines.

And in the battle of the Arrowhead(6th to 10th Jun, 1952), west of the White Horse ridge, the Communist Chinese Army bombarded with more than a thousand shells, and launched a series of attacks with numerous soldiers for 5 hours from dawn. But the French soldiers defeated them with decisive courage. Later, the French Army found 600 bodies of the Communist Chinese Army at the north of their outposts.

France sent 3421 soldiers, among which 288 were dead and 7 were missing.

We shall never forget their sacrifice and indomitable spirits! ROK people owes irreparable debt to France and her brave soldiers.

On 21st September, 2020, I, gleeman Shin visited and paid homage at the monument to French Army in Pajan-dong, Suwon.

無不可能　信念後裔
世界平和　韓國自由
釜山到着　水原集結
原州地坪　斷腸戰鬪
傀中共軍　矢頭高地
爆雨砲彈　波狀攻擊
決死防禦　攻擊無散
高貴靈魂　韓地生息
國佛蘭西　結草報恩
犧牲將兵　長久紀憶

프랑스 참전기념비 A photo of the monument to participation of France

02

프랑스 지평리 전투 기념비

위치: 경기도 양평군 지평면 곡수리 60 (지평리전투 기념관)

하늘이 내린 프랑스 전설의 용장 육군중장이 중령으로 강등해서 세계자유를 위해 한국에 왔다. 프랑스 대대장으로 대대원과 지평리 산악에 미 23연대의 일원이 되었다.

중공군 3개 사단과 미 2개 연대와 공방전과 백병전으로 3일간의 악전고투, 적은 전사자 5천 명 남기고 퇴각했다.

승리한 후 몽 중령은 귀국하고 장군 계급을 회복해 10년 지난 후에 생을 마감, 대통령 샤를 드골이 울면서 직접 장례를 치렀다.

프랑스에게 빚을 진 대한민국은 영원히 갚을 수 없는 채무국이 되었다네.

20년 7월 26일 양평 지평리 프랑스군의 전승지를 답사하고 결초보은의 은혜를 잊지 말아야 하는 우리 처지와 한국정부 처신이 6·25 영웅 백선엽 장군 서거를 돌아보며 한탄하는 신삿갓이오.

Monument à la bataille de Jipyeong-ri en France

Localisation: Goksu-ri 60 (Jipyeong-ri Battle Hall) à Jipyeong-myeon, Yangpyeong-gun, Gye

Le lieutenant-général de l'armée, le légendaire dragueur

français du ciel,

Il a été rétrogradé au lieutenant-colonel et est venu en Corée pour la liberté mondiale.

Chef de bataillon français, membre du bataillon et de la montagne de Jipyeong-ri

Il est devenu membre du 23e régiment des États-Unis.

Trois divisions de l'armée chinoise, deux régiments américains, une bataille aérienne et une guerre blanche.

Trois jours de lutte acharnée, l'ennemi s'est retiré, laissant 5000 morts.

Après sa victoire, le lieutenant-colonel Mong est rentré chez lui, a retrouvé son général et est mort dix ans plus tard.

Le président Charles de Gaulle pleurait et organisait lui-même des funérailles.

La Corée du Sud, qui doit à la France une dette irrémédiable,

C'est devenu un pays débiteur.

Le 20 juillet, le 26 juillet, l'armée française de Yangpyeong Jipyeongpyeong-ri.

Nous ne devons pas oublier la grâce de l'exploration et de la générosité.

Le général Baek Sun-yeop, le héros de 6,25 ans, est mort.

Un gentleman se retourne et se lamente.

The Monument to French Army in Battle of Gipyeong-ri

A legendary brave General French LTG R Monclar who might have been sent by heaven, came over to ROK for world peace, having demoted his rank to LTC.

He, as the French battalion commander, became one of a team member of the 23rd U.S regiment at the mountain in Gipyeong-ri battle area.

A 3-day and night desperate offensive and defensive battle, and hand to hand fights, between 3 Chinese Divisions and 2 U.S. Regiment, made the enemy(Chinese army) retreat leaving 5,000 KIA.

After the victory in the Korean war, LTC R Monclar returned home and recovered his previous rank LT general, and passed away 10 years thereafter. The funeral service for him was held by the then president Charles De Gaulle with tears dropping.

For his great favor, there is, forever and ever, no way the Republic Of Korea could repay France.

On Sunday, July 26, 2020, I, gleeman Shin who is lamenting over the death of General Baek, Seon Yeop, the 6 · 25 Korea war hero, after visiting a war victory site Gipyeong-ri, Yangpyeong, where French warriors fought over bravely and fiercely for my country ROK, for which, how ROK could forget the big gratitude that we owe the French Army.

天賜佛將　傳說勇將
中領降等　爲世自由
佛軍大隊　地坪山岳
美二三聯　參可一隊
攻中共軍　攻防白兵
惡戰苦鬪　成功防禦
夢泰*中領　歸回將軍
十年後終　葬大統領
佛蘭西債　大韓民國
永遠不死　債務國也

*夢泰將軍: 몽태장군,
　= 몽클라르 장군, 꿈몽, 클태. 꿈이 큰 장수라는 뜻.
*General Montae,
　= General Montclar, Mon(dream), tae(big). The meaning is
　general who has a big dream.

03

프랑스 몽클라르 장군의 마지막 사명

6·25 당시 몽클라르 장군에 대한 얘기를 들었다.

내용이 궁금했다. 경기도 양평 지평리를 직접 찾아가 기념관과 기념일을 볼 수 있었다.

공산군이 남침으로 6·25 전쟁이 발발했을 때 프랑스는 유엔 안보리 상임이사국 5개국 중 하나였으나 제2차 세계대전 이후 국내 사정으로 전투 병력을 보낼 여유가 없었단다. 그 실정을 알게 된 몽클라르는 전국을 누비고 다니면서 자신과 같이 한 전쟁의 참전할 지원병을 모집했다.

전투 경험이 풍부하고 그를 존경했던 600명이 동참했다. 대대 병력이 마련된 것이다.

그런데 문제가 생겼다. 장군(중장)이 대대를 지휘한다는 것은 당시 관례상 허용되지 않았다. 몽클라르 장군은 중령 계급장을 기꺼이 자청했다. 그리고 만삭인 아내를 설득했다. 무릎을 꿇고 "군인으로서의 마지막 사명과 명예를 위해 허락해 달라"고 용서를 구했다. 아내는 아버지 없는 아이가 되지 않기를 바라면서 남편을 한반도 전쟁터로 떠나보냈다.

장군은 그때 58세였다. 그렇게 출정한 프랑스 대대는 미 보병사단 23연대에 합류해 양평 지평리를 방어하는 책임을 맡게 되었다. 그 요충지를 돌파하려는 중공군 3개 사단 병력은 지평리 산악지역을 포위하고 총공격을 개시했다. 그것이 전쟁 역사에 기록된 지평리 전투였다.

1951년 2월 13일부터 15일에 걸친 치열한 혈전이었다. 지평리 전선을 사수하라는 명령을 받은 미군과 프랑스군은 그 전투에서 기적처럼 승리했다.

전사 52명 실종 42명 희생자가 생겼으나 중공군은 전사자 약 5,000명을 남기고 퇴각했다. 미 공군의 폭격 등 외부 지원이 있었으나 1개 연대가 3개 사단의 협공을 방어한 전투는 상상하기 어려운 전과였다.

중공군에 밀리던 UN군은 자신감을 회복했다.

휴전과 더불어 귀국한 몽클라르 장군은 10년 후에 군사 기념시설인 앵발리드 관리 사령관으로 여생을 마쳤다. 그 기념관은 나폴레옹의 묘소이기도 해 국가적 영광을 상징하는 명소이다.

몽클라르 장군은 1964년 6월 3일 세상을 떠났다. 그의 유해는 앵발리드 안에 있는 성당 지하에 안장되었다.

당시 프랑스 대통령 샤를 드골이 직접 장례식을 집행했다.

대통령이 눈물을 흘리면서 고인의 숭고한 군인정신과 자유를 위한 생애를 국가적 예를 갖추어 추모했다.

La dernière mission du général français Montclair

J'ai entendu parler du général Monclar à l'époque. J'étais curieux du contenu. J'ai pu visiter Jipyeong-ri, Yangpyeong-do, et voir le mémorial et l'anniversaire. Lorsque la guerre de 6 • 25 a éclaté à cause de l'invasion du Sud par l'armée communiste, la France était cinq membres permanents du Conseil de sécurité de l'ONU, mais après la Seconde Guerre mondiale, elle ne pouvait pas se permettre d'envoyer des troupes de combat pour des raisons domestiques. Après avoir appris la situation, Monclar a voyagé dans tout le pays et a recruté des volontaires pour participer à la guerre de Corée comme lui. 600 personnes qui avaient une grande expérience de combat et qui l'admiraient se sont jointes. Une force de bataillon a été mise en place. Mais il y a un problème.

Il n'était pas d'usage à l'époque qu'un général (lieutenant-général) commande un bataillon. Le général Montclair s'est porté volontaire pour le grade de lieutenant-colonel. Et j'ai convaincre ma femme de tout faire. Je me suis agenouillé et j'ai demandé pardon en disant "Donnez-moi votre permission pour votre dernière mission et votre honneur en tant que soldat". La femme a envoyé son mari sur le champ de bataille de la péninsule coréenne dans l'espoir de ne pas être un enfant sans père. Le général avait alors 58 ans.

Le bataillon français ainsi formé a rejoint le 23e régiment de la division d'infanterie américaine pour défendre Yangpyeong-ri. Les trois divisions de l'armée de l'air chinoise qui ont essayé de traverser le point clé ont encerclé la région montagneuse de Jipyeong-ri et lancé une attaque générale. C'était la bataille de Jipyeong-ri inscrite dans l'histoire de la guerre. C'était une bataille sanglante qui dura 15 jours à partir du 13 février 1951. Les troupes américaines et françaises, qui ont reçu l'ordre de défendre le front de Jipyeong-ri, ont miraculeusement gagné la bataille. 52 morts ont disparu et 42 victimes, mais l'armée de l'air chinoise s'est retirée, laissant environ 5 000 morts. Bien qu'il y ait eu un soutien extérieur, comme les bombardements de l'armée de l'air américaine, il était difficile d'imaginer une bataille où un régiment défendait la collaboration de trois divisions. L'armée de l'ONU, qui a été repoussée par l'armée chinoise, a retrouvé confiance.

Le général Monclar, rentré chez lui avec la trêve, a terminé le reste de sa vie dix ans plus tard en tant que commandant de la direction des Invalides, un établissement commémoratif militaire. Le mémorial est aussi la tombe de Napoléon et une attraction qui symbolise la gloire nationale. Le général Munklar est décédé le 3 juin 1964. Ses restes ont été enterrés dans le sous-sol de la cathédrale dans les Invalides. Le président français de l'époque, Charles de Gaulle, a lui-même exécuté les funérailles. En pleurant les larmes du président, il a commémoré le noble esprit militaire et la vie du défunt pour la liberté avec des exemples nationaux. fin

The last mission of French General Montclar

I heard about General Montclar at the time of Korean War I was curious about the contents. I was able to visit Jipyeong-ri, Yangpyeong, Gyeonggi-do, and see the memorial hall and anniversary. France was five permanent members of the UN Security Council when the Communist Army Invasion from North Korea and broke out Korean War, but France could not afford to send combat troops due to domestic circumstances after World War II. Upon learning of the situation, Montclar traveled around the country and recruited volunteers to participate in the Korean War like himself. 600 people who had extensive combat experience and respected Montclar participated. A battalion of troops has been established. But there was a problem.

It was not customary at the time for a general to command the battalion. General Montclar willingly volunteered for the rank of lieutenant colonel. And he persuaded his late wife. On his knees, he asked for understanding, saying, "Please allow me for my last mission and honor as a soldier." The wife sent her husband to the Korean Peninsula battlefield, hoping not to make her kids who don't have father. The general was 58 years old at the time.

The French Battalion joined the 23rd Regiment of the U.S. Infantry Division and was in charge of defending Jipyeong-ri, Yangpyeong. Three Chinese divisions trying to break through the key point surrounded the mountainous area of Jipyeong-ri and launched a general attack. That was the Battle of Jipyeong-ri recorded in the history of the war. It was a fierce bloody battle from 13th to 15th February, 1951. The U.S. and French forces, ordered to defend the Jipyeong-ri frontline, miraculously won the battle. 52 soldiers were killed 42 missing, but the Communist Chinese Army retreated, leaving about 5,000 dead. Although there was external support, such as bombing by the U.S. Air Force, the battle in which one Regiment defended the three Divisions was a difficult millitary achievements to imagine. The UN forces, which had been pushed back by Communist Chinese Army, regained confidence.

Returning home with the ceasefire, General Montclar ended the rest of his life 10 years later as commander of the management of Angbalid, a military memorial facility. The memorial hall is also Napoleon's graveyard, a landmark symbolizing national glory. General Munklar died on 3rd June, 1964. His remains were buried in the basement of the cathedral in Anvalid. At that time, French President Charles de Gaulle personally conducted the funeral. While shedding tears of the president, he commemorated the deceased's noble military spirits and life for freedom with national examples. The end.

몽클라르 중령 (1892~1964)
프랑스

· 프랑스대대장
· 1, 2차 세계대전을 참전하고 중장까지 진급
· 한국전 참전을 위해 스스로 중령으로 강등하여
  6·25전쟁 참전

"계급은 중요하지 않다.
곧 태어날 자식에게 유엔군의 일원으로 평화를 위해
참전했다는 긍지를 물려주고 싶다."

몽태장군 사진 A photo of general Montclar

04

군의관, 줄 장루이 소령 동상 (프랑스군)

위치: 강원 홍천군 두촌면 장남1리 219번지

1951년 5월 8일, 프랑스 줄 장루이 소령은 홍천 두촌에서 전투를 했다.

그는 34세 꽃다운 나이에 하늘에 별이 되었다.

프랑스군은 미 23연대에 배속되어 홍천 방면으로 북진했다. 4월 5일에는 38선을 넘어 화천으로 진입했다. 전쟁의 와중에도 주민들의 치료까지 끝까지 맡아 주었다. 이 땅에 인도주의 정신을 길이 남겼다.

그의 거룩한 정신을 오랫동안 후세에 남기기로 했다. 전사한 현장에 군의관 동상 앞에서 오랫동안 참배를 했다.

2021년 3월 30일 강원 홍천군 두촌면 장남1리 219번지에 있는 프랑스 군의관 동상을 답사하고 참배했다.

한·불 수교 100주년 맞아 그의 거룩한 정신을 새겼다.

한국은 자유진영에 참 많은 빚을 졌다. 특히 한국전쟁 때 파병한 16개국에 대해서는 잊지 말고 은혜를 갚아야 한다.

Le médecin militaire, statue du major Jules Jean-Louis (France)

Localisation : 219 Jangnam 1-ri, Duchon-myeon, Hongcheon-gun, Gangwon-do

Le 8 mai 1951, le major français Jules Jean-Louis à Duchon, à Hongcheon,

Il a combattu. Il est devenu une étoile dans le ciel à 34 ans.

Les Français ont été affectés au 23e Régiment des États-Unis et se sont dirigés vers le nord vers Hongcheon.

4. Le 5, il a franchi le 38e parallèle et est entré à Kyeong.

Au milieu de la guerre, il a même pris en charge le traitement des résidents jusqu'

L'esprit humanitaire a été laissé sur cette terre.

Il a décidé de laisser son esprit saint à la postérité pendant longtemps.

devant la figure d'un médecin militaire sur la scène de la mort,

J'ai vénéré pendant longtemps.

Le 30 mars 2021, à 219 Jangnam 1-ri, Duchon-myeon, Hongcheon-gun, Gangwon-do.

J'ai visité et rendu visite à un médecin militaire français. relations diplomatiques entre la Corée et le bouddhisme

À l'occasion du centenaire, il a compté son saint esprit. La Corée du Sud est devenue très endettée par le camp libéral. surtout pendant la guerre de Corée.

Nous ne devons pas oublier les 16 pays qui ont envoyé des troupes et nous devons vous remercier.

The Statue of Army Surgeon, Major Zul Zhanglui (French military)

Location: 219, Jangnam 1-ri, Duchon-myeon, Hongcheon-gun, Gangwon-do

1951. On 8th May, Major Zul Zhanglui of France, fought at Duchon, Hongcheon. He became a star in the sky at the age of 34.

The French forces were attached to the U.S. 23rd regiment and advanced north toward Hongcheon. On 5th April, they crossed the 38th line and entered Hwacheon. Even in the midst of the war, he even took care of the residents until the end. He left humanitarian spirit on this land forever.

I decided to retain his holy spirit for a long time.
In the presence of an Army Surgeon at the scene of his death, I paid a long visit to the shrine.

On 30th March, 2021, at 219, Jangnam 1-ri, Duchon-myeon, Hongcheon-gun, Gangwon-do. I visited and paid tribute to a French Army Surgeon. On the 100th anniversary of ROK and France diplomatic relations. I established his holy spirit. ROK owes so much to the liberal camp. Especially during the Korean War. Don't forget to return the favor to the 16 nations that sent troops.

醫務隊長　洪川戰鬪
似花壯烈　散華星天
美聯配屬　佛蘭西軍
洪川方面　北進繼屬
越三八線　華川進入
戰爭中也　住民治療
大韓民國　自由守護
此地人道　精神永遠

불 장루이 소령 Major Zul Zhanglui of France

프랑스군 지평리 지구 전투 기념비

위치 : 경기도 양평군 지평면 지평리 (지평리전투 기념관)

1951년 2월 13일~15일(3일간) 프랑스군은 미 23연대에 배속되었다. 지평리 서쪽 분지에 방어 진지를 구축했다.

중공군 제115, 제116사단, 차출된 4개 연대에 프랑스군은 포위되고 말았다.

13일 밤 포위망이 좁혀져 왔다. 대대 전초진지에서 전투가 벌어졌다. 일진일퇴 혼전이다. 날이 밝자 적은 물러났다.

14일 밤 적은 나팔 불고 돌격해 왔다. 기관총과 수류탄으로 반격했다.

진지주변에 박격포탄이 떨어졌다. 포격전이 시작되었다.

14일 밤 재차 공격이 시작되었다. 방어 진지가 일부 피탈되었다. 야간 혈전이 되었다. 진지방어 성공했다.

프랑스 대대는 몽클라르 지휘하에 3일간의 혈전으로 방어 진지를 지켜냈다.

프랑스군은 세계 자유 평화와 한국민의 자유를 위해 제 목숨을 던졌다. 숭고한 정신은 한국을 피로 수호했다.

프랑스군의 뜻을 기려 한·불 양국은 혈맹관계가 되었다. 한국은 프랑스군의 헌신을 잊을 수 없다.

2021년 4월 12일 비 오는 날, 양평군 지평리역에 갔다.

역 주변에 있는 지평리 전투 기념비를 비를 맞고 답사하고 참배했다.

Monument commémoratif de la bataille du district de Jipyeongri

Localisation : Jipyeong−ri, Jipyeong−myeon, Yangpyeong−gun, Gyeonggi−do (Mémorial de la)

du 13 février 1951 au 15 mars (pendant trois jours), l'armée française s'est rendue au 23e régiment des États-Unis

Affecté. Un camp de défense a été construit dans le bassin ouest de Jipyeong-ri.

Les Français ont été encerclés par les 115e et 116e divisions de l'armée de l'air chinoise et les 4 régiments détachés.

Le siège s'est resserré dans la nuit du 13. La bataille à l'avant-

poste du bataillon

Ça s'est passé. C'est un combat acharné. À l'aube, l'ennemi s'est retiré.

Dans la nuit du 14, l'ennemi s'est précipité. Ils ont riposté avec des mitrailleuses et des grenades. Des obus de mortier sont tombés autour de Jijin.

La bataille d'artillerie a commencé.

L'attaque a recommencé dans la nuit du 14. une position défensive.

C'est fait. C'est devenu un caillot de sang de nuit. J'ai réussi la langue de l'épicéa.

Le bataillon de France a passé trois jours sous le commandement de Montclair.

Il a défendu la position défensive.

L'armée française s'est engagée pour la paix mondiale et la liberté des Coréens

J'ai jeté ma vie. L'esprit noble a défendu la Corée avec du sang.

C'est devenu une alliance sanglante entre les deux pays en l'honneur de la volonté de l'armée française.

La Corée du Sud ne peut oublier le dévouement de l'armée française.

Le 12 avril 2021, un jour de pluie, je suis allé à la gare de

Jipyeong-ri, Yangpyeong-gun. Le monument commémoratif de la bataille de Jipyeong-ri autour de la gare a été visité et vénéré sous la pluie.

The Monument to Battle of French Army Jipyeong-ri District

13th to 15th February, 1951(for three days) French troops were attached the U.S. 23rd Regiment. Defensive positions were established in the western basin of Jipyeong-ri.

The 115th and 116th Divisions of the Chinese Communist Party, and the four Regiments that were dispatched, surrounded French troops.

The siege narrowed on the night of 13th. Combat happened at the Battalion's outpost. It's a hell of a fight. At daybreak the enemies retreated.

On the night of 14th, the enemies blew trumpets and charged. Friendly forces fought back with machine guns and grenades. Mortar shells fell around the positions. The artillery battle began.

The attack began again on the night of 14th. Some of the defensive positions have been hijacked. It was a desperate fight. Friendly forces succeeded in defending.

The French Battalion, under command of Montclar, suffered a three-day desperate fights and defended the defensive positions.

The French Army threw their lives working for the freedom of the world and the freedom of the ROK people. The sublime spirits defended ROK with blood.

It became a blood alliance between France and ROK to honor the will of the French Army. ROK cannot forget the dedication of the French Army.

On 12th April, 2021, I went to Jipyeong-ri Station in Yangpyeong-gun on rainy day. I explored and paid tribute to the Jipyeong-ri Battle Monument near the station in the rain.

美聯配屬　陣地具築
中共軍攻　包圍佛軍
一進一退　混戰係屬
圓形陣地　落搏擊彈
波狀攻擊　一部彼奪
三日血戰　陣地防禦
佛軍犧牲　世界自平
韓佛血盟　不可忘也

지평리역 A Photo of Jipyeong—ri Station

프랑스 센 강변 6·25 전쟁 기념비 제막

프랑스 정부, 참전 글귀만 있던 비석에 프랑스군 268명, 한국군 24명 새겨 참전국 중 전사자 비율 가장 높다.

양국 모두 서로를 잊지 않을 것이다.

프랑스 국방부가 1950년부터 53년까지 한국 강원도 일대 전선 등에서 전사한 참전용사 292명의 이름을 새긴 동판을 한국전쟁 참전기념비에 붙이는 제막식이 있었다.

프랑스군은 6·25 전쟁에 약 3,500명이 참전했으며 파병 장병 대비 전사자 비율이 7%로 당시 참전한 외국 군대 중 가장 높다.

전쟁 당시 프랑스군이 치른 가장 치열한 전투였던 '단장의 능선전투'다.

이날 제막식에는 6·25 전쟁 당시 지휘했던 랄프 몽클라르 장군의 아들 롤랑 몽클라르 씨도 참석했다.

한국을 잊지 못해 집에 태극기를 걸어두고 살았던 베나르 참전용사는 2015년 별세할 때 한국 땅에 묻어 달라는 유언을 남겼다.

프랑스 보훈장관은 프랑스군이 6·25 전쟁에 참전한 것은 프랑스 영토와 국익을 위한 것이 아니라 UN 주도하에 평화를 지키기 위한 것으로 역사에 매우 특별한 일이라고 했다.

한국은 프랑스에 잊지 못할 은혜의 나라다.

프랑스군의 참전용사들의 희생 때문에 한국의 평화를 수호하고 발전할 수 있었다.

한국은 갚을 수 없는 빚을 프랑스에 지고 있다.

절대로 절대로 잊어서는 안 된다.

Inauguration du monument de la guerre de 6 · 25 sur les bords de la Seine en France

2021. 5. 18.

Le gouvernement français a inscrit 268 soldats français et 24 soldats sud-coréens sur la pierre tombale qui n'avait que des inscriptions de guerre, ce qui en fait la plus forte proportion de morts parmi les anciens combattants. Les deux pays ne s'oublieront pas.

Il y a eu une cérémonie où le ministère français de la Défense a inscrit une plaque de bronze portant les noms de 292 anciens combattants morts sur le front dans la province de Gangwon, en Corée du Sud, de 1950 à 53. L'armée française a participé à la guerre de Corée, avec environ 3 500 personnes et 7% des morts par rapport aux soldats envoyés, le plus haut parmi les troupes étrangères qui ont participé à l'époque. C'est la bataille de la crête du général, la bataille la plus féroce que l'armée française ait menée pendant la guerre.

Roland Monclar, fils du général Ralph Monclar, commandant pendant la guerre de Corée, a également assisté à la cérémonie d'inauguration. Le vétéran Benar, qui n'a pas pu oublier la Corée, a laissé un testament pour enterrer le drapeau coréen à sa mort en 2015.

Le ministre français des Anciens Combattants a déclaré que la participation des Français à la guerre de 6 · 25 n'était pas pour le territoire français et l'intérêt national, mais pour préserver la paix sous l'égide de l'ONU, ce qui est très spécial pour l'histoire.

La Corée est un pays de grâce inoubliable pour la France. Les sacrifices des anciens combattants de l'armée française ont permis de défendre et de développer la paix en Corée. La Corée du Sud a une dette irréparable envers la France. Il ne faut jamais oublier. C'est fini.

The Unveiling of the 6 · 25 War Memorial on the Seine Riverside in France

2021. 5. 18.

The French government carved 268 French soldiers and 24 ROK soldiers on a monument that only had words to participate in the war. It's the highest percentage of dead among participating nations. Both countries will not forget each other.

The French Ministry of National Defense put the copper plate engraved with the names of 292 veterans who died on the front lines of Gangwon-do, ROK, from 1950 to 53 on the monument to participate in the Korean War. About 3,500 French soldiers

participated in the Korean War, and the ratio of dead to dispatched soldiers was 7%, the highest ratio among foreign troops who participated at that time. It was the Battle of the heart break ridge, the fiercest battle fought by French troops during the war.

Roland Montclar, son of General Ralph Montclar, who commanded during the Korean War, also attended the unveiling ceremony. Veteran Benard, who lived with the Korean flag hanging at home because he could not forget Korea, left a will to bury him on Korean soil when he died in 2015.

프랑스 센강변 6.25한국전쟁 참전기념비

The French Minister of Veterans Affairs said the French military's participation in the Korean War was not for French territory and national interests, but for the protection of peace under the leadership of the United Nations, which is very special to history.

ROK is a country which has unforgettable favor of France. Because of the sacrifices of the French military veterans, we were able to defend and develop peace in ROK. ROK owes France an irredeemable debts. Never forget. The end.

필리핀은 미국, 영국에 이어 지상 전투부대를 한국에 파병한 최초의 아시아 국가이다.

1950년 9월 19일 필리핀 전투부대(PEFTOK)의 다섯 전투부대(BCT) 중의 첫 번째가 부산에 도착하였다.

필리핀 병사들은 율동 전투, 아스날고지 전투, 이리고지 전투에서 용감하게 한국을 위해서 싸웠다.

The Philippines was the first Asian nation to send a ground forces to ROK, following U.S. and U.K. The first of the five Battalion Combat Teams(BCT) of the Philippine Expeditionary Forces to Korea (PEFTOK) landed in Busan on 19th September, 1950. The Philippine soldiers gallantly fought for ROK in the Battle of Yuldong, Battle of Arsenal Hill, and the Battle of Eerie Hill.

필리핀

Philippines

- 참전기간 (Date of Participation) : 1950. 9. 19 ~ 1955. 5
- 참전규모 (Troops Provided) : 1개 대대전투단(1 Battalion Combat team)
- 참전연인원 (Total Participants) : 7,420
- 부상자 (Wounded in Action) : 313
- 전사자 (Killed in Action) : 113

01

필리핀군 참전 기념비

위치 : 경기 고양시 덕양구 대양로 5 (관산동)

필리핀은 자유 민주주의를 지키기 위해 한 치의 망설임 없이 한국전쟁 파병을 결정했다.

연천 율동전투에서 중공군에 포위된 상태에서 공세를 막아내어 미 3사단 성공적으로 철수시키고 철원전투에서 중공군 전초를 9번 교전하고 6번의 백병전을 치렀다.

전쟁 중 혈전 속에 서로 옆에서 피 흘린 혈맹형제 양국의 번영과 한국은 갚을 수 없는 큰 빚을 지고 있다.

2020년 9월 19일, 관산동 소재 참전 기념탑을 참배 했다.

1950년 9월 19일 미국, 영국 다음으로 7,420명을 파병해서 그중 488명이 고귀한 영혼이 되었다.

♥ 당시 참전한 피델 라모스 소대장이 고국으로 돌아가 참모총장과 국방장관을 거쳐 12대 필리핀 라모스 대통령이 되었다.

The Monument to Philippine Army's Participation in the Korean War

Location : Daeyang-ro 5, Deokyang-gu, Goyang-si, Gyeonggi-do (Gwansan-dong)

Philippines decided to dispatch her military forces without any hesitation for defence of the liberal democracy of ROK.

In Yuldong battle, As Philippine forces defeated Communist Chinese Army U.S. 3rd Infantry Division which was enveloped to withdraw successfully.

Also at Cheolwon battle, Philippine forces encountered 9 times with the Chinese outposts and conducted hand to hand fights 6 times with them.

There were prosperity in the both bloody countries in the Korean War. ROK owes Philippines big debts which can't return.

On 19th September, 2020, I visited the war Memorial to Philippines forces located at Kwansan-dong.
Philippines the 3rd nation following by U.S. and U.K. that dispatched total 7,420 soldiers to Korean War, among which 488 soldiers became the souls of immortality.

(♥ After the Korean War, former platoon leader Fidel V. Ramos, who participated in the Korean War, had became chief of staffs Army, ministry of defence and became the 12th president of Philippines finally)

自由民主　守護爲也
一寸無忘　派兵韓國
栗洞戰鬪　包圍狀態
攻勢防禦　成功美撤
鐵原戰鬪　戰哨中共
九回交戰　六回白兵
戰爭血戰　血盟兄弟
兩國繁榮　債負韓國

252

02

필리핀군 율동전투 전적비

위치 : 경기도 연천군 연천읍 상1리.

1951년 4월 22일-23일, 필리핀 제10대대장 Dionisio S. Ojeda 중령은 연천 상리 율동마을 야산에 진지를 구축했다.

새벽 1시경 중공군 1개 대대가 B중대, 예비대 C중대, 특수중대로 집중 공격해왔다. 제10대대는 행정요원까지도 전투에 가담한 끝에 적을 어렵게 격퇴했다.

특수중대장 얍 대위는 선두에서 고지로 돌진했다. 뒤따르는 소대원도 돌진했다. 이때 전방에서 날아온 적의 총탄에 중대장이 맞았다.

이 율동전투 결과로 500여명의 중공군 사상자 발생했다.

제10대대는 12명 전사, 38명 부상, 실종 6명의 피해를 입었다.

한국의 자유와 평화를 수호하기 위해 참전한 필리핀군이 가장 치열한 전투를 벌인 곳이다.

자신의 목숨을 던져 한국인의 생명을 살린 진짜 영웅들이다. 이 은혜를 잊을 수 없는 곳에서 영웅들에게 참배를 했다.

2021년 3월 6일, 경기 연천읍 상리 460-1에 있는 한국전쟁 70주년에 70년 만에 연천 상리 야산지역 밤나무 골(栗洞)에 필리핀군과 중공군의 격전지 야산에서 그날의 전투상황을 눈에 그려보는 신삿갓이다.

♥ 한국전쟁에 필리핀군은 7,148명 참전하고

전사 112명, 부상 299명, 실종 16명의 전상자 발생

♡ UN군 병사의 눈으로 우리 자신을 바라보니 한국전쟁 때 많은 연합군 장병들이 전사했다.

한국이 파견국 16개 나라에 큰 빚을 지고 있는 것을 모르는 듯하다. (학교에서 가르치지 않아서)

The Monument to Philippine Army's Yuldong Battle

Location: Sang 1-ri, Yeoncheon-eup, Yeoncheon-gun, Gyeonggi-do.

22nd-23rd April, 1951, commander of 10th Battalion, Lieutenant Colonel Dionisio S. Ojeda established positions on the hill in Yuldong Village, Sang-ri, Yeoncheon.

At around 0100(I), a battalion of Communist Chinese Army attacked intensively with Company B, Reserved Company C, and Special Company. The 10th Battalion defeated enemies barely even had administrative personnel participated in the battle.

Special Company commander, Yap rushed to the high ground.
The following members of platoon also rushed. The company commander was shot by an enemy bullet which came form opposite.

This battle resulted in the casualties of more than 500

Communist Chinese Army. 12 soldiers KIA, 38 WIA and 6 missing of the 10th Battalion.

This place where Philippine troops fought most fiercely to protect ROK's freedom and peace. They are real heroes who saved the lives of Koreans by throwing their lives. I paid tribute to the heroes in the place where I could not forget this favor.

On 6th March, 2021, at 460-1, Sang-ri, Yeoncheon-eup, Gyeonggi-do.
On the 70th anniversary of the Korean War, for the first time in 70 years. I, gleeman Shin, depicts the battle situation of the day in the battlefield of the Philippine and Communist Chinese Army in Bamnamu Valley, Yeoncheon Sangri Hill.

(♥ 7,148 Filipino soldiers participated in the Korean War among them 112 KIA, 299 WIA, 16 missing)

♡ Looking at ourselves with the eyes of soldiers of UN forces. Many soldiers were killed in the Korean War.
Koreans seem like that they don't know that ROK owes big debts to 16 dispatched nations. (Because teachers didn't teach about it at the school)

守護自平　爲韓國人
對中共軍　栗洞戰鬪
赤三庚攻　群中共軍
諸總力戰　擊退成功
特殊中隊　先頭突進
適彈命中　中隊長也
戰死將兵　韓國英雄
韓國平和　恩惠不忘

필리핀 율동 전적비
A photo of memorial to Philippine forces in the Yuldong battle

호주는 미국과 영국에 이어 세 번째로 한국에 군대를 파견하였고, 육, 해, 공군 모두 참전하였다.

유엔 안전보장 이사회의 한국원조 결의에 따라 곧바로 2척의 함정과 1개 비행대대를 파견하였고, 9월 27일에는 보병 1개 대대를 파병하였다.

전쟁 기간 해군은 항공모함 1척, 구축함 2척, 프리킷트함 1척, 수준의 전력을 유지하면서 해상작전을 실시하였다.

전쟁 동안 수행한 주요 전투는 마량산 전투, 애플오차드 전투, 구진 전투, 청주 전투, 사미천 전투, 박천 전투, 가평 전투이다.

Australia was the third nation following the US and UK to send troops to ROK. Australia sent ground, naval and air force to ROK. When the United Nations Security Council passed resolutions to support ROK, Australia promptly complied and deployed two battle ships and one fighter squadron. Then on 27th September, the Australian government dispatched an infantry battalion. During the Korean War, Australia naval forces conducted maritime operation with keeping the following strength level; 1 aircraft carrier, 2 destroyers, 1 frigate. Its major battles include the battles of Mt. Maryang, Apple Orchard, Kujin, Cheongju, Samicheon, Bakcheon and Gapyeong.

호주

Australia

- 참전기간 (Date of Participation) : 1950. 6. 29 ~ 1957. 8
- 참전규모 (Troops Provided) : 3개 보병대대(3 Infantry Battalions), 함정 9척 (9 Ships),
  1개 전투비행대대(1 Fighter Squadron),
  1개 수송기 대대 (1 Tranporter Squadron),
  1개 정비 대대(1 Maintenance Battalion),
  1개 기병대대 (1 Cavalry Battalion)
- 참전연인원 (Total Participants) : 18,000
- 부상자 (Wounded in Action) : 1,216
- 전사자 (Killed in Action) : 340

호주군 전투 기념비

위치 : 경기도 가평군 북면 목동리, 호주, 뉴질랜드 참전공원.

1950년 6월 25일 북한괴뢰 집단이 불법 남침했다.

오스트레일리아군은 한국의 안녕과 세계평화를 위해 UN군의 일원으로 한국전에 파병되었다.

육군은 9월 27일 부산에 도착하여 영연방 제27여단에 배속되었다.

해군은 7월 1일 한국해역에서 활동을 시작했다.

공군은 6월 30일 한국에 도착해 미 제 공군에 배속되었다.

최초 호주군은 경북 김천지역 북괴군 1만여 명을 소탕했다. 그 후 성주군으로 이동, 영연방 제27여단에 배속되었다.

북한지역 사리원전투(50.10.16.)에서 북괴군 3,200명을 포로로 잡았다. 황해도 봉산 영유리(10. 20.) 전투에서 적 240명을 생포했다.

박천 전투(10. 30.) 중공군과 첫 전투에서 백병전을 했다. 가평 전투(51: 4. 19.) 중공군의 제118사단이 한국군 제6사단의 화천군 사창리를 돌파했다. 가평을 점령 후 남하하여 수도 서울을 점령하려는 중공군을 호주군이 성공적으로 방어했다. 중공군의 4월 대공세는 실패했다.

호주군은 한국전쟁 중에 연인원 17,164명이 참전했다.

한국의 자유와 평화를 위해 340명이 전사했다. 1,230명이 부상을 입었다.

호주의 도움으로 한국은 구사일생으로 위기를 모면했다. 오늘의 대한민국을 있게 했다.

우리는 호주가 은인국임을 결코 잊지않고 있습니다.

2020년 10월 15일 가평군 북면 목동리, 호주군이 승리한 지역에 위치한 참전 기념비에서 늦은 점심으로 햇반 전투식량을 익혀 먹으면서 호주군의 혼령들과 밥을 나누어 취식하며 눈물 젖은 밥을 먹은 신삿갓이다.

The Monument to Australian Forces' participation in the Korean War

Location : Mokdong-ri, Buk-myeon, Gapyeong-gun, Gyeonggi-do, Australia, and New Zealand Participation Park.

On 25th June, 1950, nK puppet communist regime committed an illegal attack to ROK. Australian forces were dispatched as a part of UN forces to ROK for the peace of ROK and the world.

On 27th September, Australian Army had arrived at Busan and was attached to the 27th Commonwealth Brigade. And then On 1st July, Australian naval forces began to conduct operations on the Korean waters. On 30th June, Australian Air Forces had arrived and were attached to the US 5th Air Forces.

At the initial operations, Australian forces mopped up about 10 thousand nK communist soldiers in the Kimcheon area. Thereafter moved to Seongju-gun and were attached to the 27 commonwealth Brigade. In Sariweon battle(16th Oct, 1950) in nK area, Australian forces caught 3,200 nK soldiers as POWs and also in Young-yu-ri battle(20th Oct, 1950) in Bongsan,

Hwanghae-do, caught 240 enemy soldiers alive.

In Bakcheon battle(30th Oct.), Australian Army had hand to hand fights against soldiers of Communist Chinese Army. In Gapyeong battle(19th April, 1951), Chinese 118 Division penetrated Sachang-ri, Hwacheon-gun(that was operation area of ROK 6th Division). Australian Army successfully defended the hinese 118 Division(entry forces) of Communist Chinese Army whose plan was to occupy Gapyeong area and advance southward to take up Seoul, the capital of ROK. This successful defense of Australian Army made the April large attack of Communist Chinese Army end in failure.

Total of 17,615 Australian Armed Forces participated in Korean war, among which 340 soldiers KIA and 1,230 soldiers WIA for the peace and freedom of ROK. With the favor of your country, ROK narrowly escaped the crisis. Australia, Your country, made today's Republic of Korea. We never forget that Australia is a savoir nation.

On 15th October, 2020, I shared instant rice MRE(Meal Ready to Eat) for late lunch with Australian spirits and ate tearful rice while at the war memorial located in Mokdong-ri, Buk-myeon, Gapyeong-gun, where the Australian army won the battle.

北韓傀儡　不法南侵
濠州參戰　派陸海空
陸着釜山　英聯配屬
海韓域作　空軍配屬
最初戰鬪　金泉地域
北傀軍滅　消蕩作戰
沙里院戰　多捕獲得
鳳山戰戰　博川戰鬪
加平戰鬪　防中共軍
適首都進　遮斷成功
自由守護　韓國平和
求死一生　恩人之國

튀르키예는 유엔 안전보장 이사회의 결의에 따라 한국에 육군 1개 여단을 파병하였다.

여단 내에는 보병을 비롯하여 보병, 포병, 공병, 수송, 통신, 의무, 병기부대들이 포함되어 독립전투를 수행할 수 있는 전투 편성을 갖추고 있었다.

터키여단은 자신들의 사상자에 비해 적에게 10배의 사상자를 낸 전과를 올려 유엔군의 사기를 높였다.

전쟁 동안 수행한 주요 전투는 김량장 전투와 네바다 전초전이다.

Türkiye fully supported the UN resolutions by sending a Army brigade The brigade could carry out an independent combat because it consisted of infantry, artillery, engineer, transportation, communications, medical and ordnance units. The brigade inflicted ten times more casualties to the enemy than their own and boosted the morale of the UN force. Its major battles include the battle of Gimyangjang and battle of Nevada outpost.

- 참전기간 (Date of participation) : 1950. 10. 18 – 1971. 6
- 참전규모 (Troops Provided) : 1 개 보병여단 (1 Infantry Brigade)
- 참전연인원 (Total Participants) : 21,212
- 부상자 (Wounded in Action) : 1,155
- 전사자 (Killed in Action) : 891

튀르키예

Republic of Türkiye

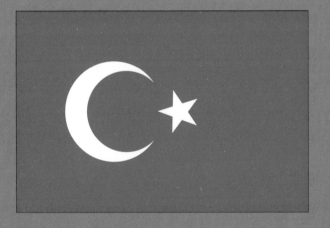

Türkiye, BM Güvenlik Konseyi'nin karar ı uyar ı nca Kore'ye piyade, topçu, mühendis, ulaşt ı rma, haberleşme görev ve silah birliklerinden oluşan bir tugay gönderdi ve bağ ı ms ı z muharebeler yapabilecek muharebe teşkilat ı na sahipti. Türk tugay ı , düşmana kendi zayiat ı n ı n 10 kat ı n ı vererek BM güçlerinin moralini yükseltti. Savaş s ı ras ı nda yap ı lan ana muharebeler Kimryangjang Savaş ı ve Nevada karakoluydu.

01

튀르키예군 참전 기념비

위치 : 경기도 용인시 기흥구 동백동 산 16

BC 2333년부터 AD 108 년까지 고조선의 형제국이었다. 아시아 대륙 서쪽 끝까지 갔다.

1950년 6월 25일 북한 공산 집단이 불법 기습 남침했다.

튀르키예공화국은 10월 17일 참전해서 휴전까지 함께했다. 많은 공적을 올렸다.

부산에 도착해 대구로 이동했다.

미 제9군단에 배속, 11월 초순부터 서부전선 평북 개천 군우리 전투(50. 11.), 수원 북방 수리산 전투(51. 1. 30), 와이오밍(Wyoming : 연천~와수리~ 화천저수지(4. 5.), 마지막 고랑포 전투에서 적 3,000명을 사살하고 5명도 생포했다.

특히 용인 김량장동 전투(1951. 1. 25~27)에서 터키군의 용감한 백병전은 UPI 기자에 의해 승전이 전 세계에 보도 되었다. 해서 미국대통령과 한국 이승만 대통령의 부대 표창도 받았다.

티르키예군은 한국전쟁 중에 연인원 14,936명이 참전했다.

한국의 자유 평화를 위해 침략자와 싸우며 형제국을 위해 전상자 3,064명이 고귀한 혼령이 되었다. 형제를 위하여 목숨을 바치면 이보다 큰 사랑이 없는데 한국인은 이 사랑을 어찌 갚으리오.

2020년 10월 20일, 용인시 영동고속도로 마성나들목, 원주 가는 남쪽에 위치한 터키군 참전 기념비를 답사하고 참배를 했다.

고조선, 단군조선의 형제국 참배에 감개 무량한 신삿갓입니다.

♥ 이스탄불 완전 정복하던 밤, Mehmet 황제가 밤하늘 보니
초승달과 별이 반짝반짝 반겨주어서 國旗에 초승달과 별이 빛나는
국기다.

自紀元前 至紀元後
極西大陸 兄弟之國
北韓傀儡 不法南侵
貴國參戰 世界平和
釜山到着 美軍培屬
西部戰線 平北戰鬪
水原戰鬪 高浪浦戰
龍仁戰鬪 貴國將兵
白兵戰爭 世界報導
韓美統領 部隊表彰
自由守護 韓國平和
犧牲將兵 愛韓忘焉

The Monument to Türkiye forces' Participation in the Korean War

Location: San 16, Dongbaek-dong, Giheung-gu, Yongin-si, Gyeonggi-do

Old Türkiye was a brother country of the Gojoseon from BC 2333 to AD 108. This County went as far as the west end of the Asian continent.

On 25th June, 1950, nK communist regime launched an illegal surprise invasion into ROK. Türkiye had participated in the Korean war and stayed in ROK until the armistice was made, during which period Türkiye made many contributions.

The Türkiye forces had arrived at Busan and moved to Daegu. And then were attached to the US 9th Corps. From the early November, Türkiye forces participated in below battles and the forces killed 3,000 enemies and caught 5 POWs

Gunu-ri battle (November 1950) in the west frontline, at Gaecheon, Pyeongbuk province, Surisan battle(30th January, 1951) north of Suwon. At Wyoming battle (Yeoncheon~Wasu-ri~Hwacheon reservoir, 5th April), and at the last battle of Gorangpo.

Especially Türkiye forces' victory news of the gallant hand-to-hand fights (on 25th-27th Jan, 1950) against the enemies at Gimryangjang-dong was reported all over the world by the

UPI war correspondent, and Türkiye forces were awarded a presidential unit citations by then presidents of US and ROK (Lee, Seong Man).

Türkiye dispatched 14,936 soldiers. The 3,064 soldiers died and became honorable souls while fighting against to protect freedom and peace of ROK. There is no greater love than devoting his life for his brother nation. How could Koreans pay back their love of this.

On 20th October, 2020, I, gleeman Shin visited the Korean war Memorial devoted to the Türkiye souls which was set up close to the Maseong interchange of Youngdong expressway in Yongin city, the way to Wonju.

I, gleeman Shin, was moved deeply by worshipping the souls of our brother country which connected each other from the first state Gojoseon, Dangun Joseon of Korea.

♥ In the night, Türkiye emperor Mehmet Estanbul completely. The shining crescent and stars welcomed him. So there are crescent and stars on the Türkiye national flag Turkish flag.

02
튀르키예 여단의 사투로 퇴각로 확보

94세 퍼킷 예비역 대령, 중위 때 한국전쟁에 참전하여 중공군 인해전술에 맞서 청천강 전투에서 활약을 했다.

내동령이 수여하는 최고 훈장인 '명예훈장(Medal of Honor)'을 받았다, 피로 맺은 한미 동맹을 기억하는 메시지다.

미 육군 특수부대인 제8레인저 중대원 51명과 한국군 9명을 이끌던 퍼킷 중위는 당시 그의 작전 구역에 약 2만 5000명의 중공군이 있다는 보고를 받았다.

1950년 11월 25일 중공군 18만명이 청천강을 북진하려던 국군과 미군을 공격했다. 공포스러웠을 것이다. 무식한 인해전술이 아니었다.

당시 모택동은 한국군을 집중 공격하라고 지시를 했다. 훈련 기간, 장비 모두 부족하다는 사실을 잘 알고 있었다. 청천강 오른쪽을 지키던 국군 2군단에 중공군은 궤멸됐다. 주력인 미 8군이 완전 포위될 위기였지만 터키여단의 사투 덕분에 겨우 퇴각로를 확보했다. 터키군은 모자를 던져놓고 그 뒤로는 물러서지 않았다고 한다.

청천강 전투에서 1만명 이상 전사자를 낸 미군은 38선 이북을 포기하고 후퇴해야 했다. 남북통일의 꿈이 산산조각났다.

71년 전 미 육군 레인 (특수부대) 중위로 한국전쟁에서 10배 넘는 중공군 병력과 맞서 싸웠던 퍼킷 중위는 6·25 전쟁 중이던 1950년 11월 청천강 일대 205고지에서 부대원과 한국군(카투사)을 이끌고 중공군 수백 명을 물리친 공로로 이날 명예훈장을 받았다.

23세 젊은 중위였던 그는 부하들이 적의 위치를 파악할 수 있도록 세 번이나 참호 밖으로 달려 나갔다가 그는 큰 부상을 입었다.

참전용사의 희생으로 지금 한국은 평화를 수호하고 자유를 만끽하고 있다.

퍼킷 전 중위는 1971년 대령으로 전역했다. 92년 육군 레인져 (특수부대) 명예의 전당에 헌액됐다.

Securing the Retreat Path with of Desperate Struggle of Türkiye Brigade

2012. 5. 21.

Colonel Puckett, 94 years old, reserved officer, fought in the Korean War when he was a lieutenant. At the time he fought against Communist Chinese Army's human wave tactics in the Cheongcheon river battle. He was awarded "Medal of Honor" the President's highest medal, It is a message that remember blood ROK/US alliance.

Lieutenant Puckett, who led 51 members of the 8th Ranger Company, a U.S. Army special forces unit, and 9 ROK soldiers was reported to have about 25,000 Communist Chinese Army in his operational area at the time. It might be horrible. Because it was not ignorance hunan wave tatics. At the time, Mao Jeo dong ordered intensive attacks on ROK.

On 25th November, 1950, 180,000 soldiers of Communist Chinese Army attacked ROK and U.S. troops who were trying to advance north of the Cheongcheon River. He was well aware that both the training period and equipments were insufficient. The Communist Chinese Army was destroyed by the ROK 2nd

Corps, which was guarding the right side of the Cheongcheon River. The U.S. 8th Army, main force, was on the verge of being completely enveloped, but thanks to the Türkiye brigade's struggle, it managed to secure a retreat path. There are stories that the Türkiye Army threw its hat and did not step back after that. The U.S. military, which killed more than 10,000 soldiers in the Battle of the Cheongcheon River, had to give up its 38th parallel north and retreat. The dream of reunification between the two Koreas had been shattered.

Puckett, a U.S. Army Ranger(special forces) lieutenant who fought against more than 10 times the Communist Chinese Army in the Korean War 71 years ago, was awarded the Medal of Honor for leading his soldiers and ROK soldiers(KATUSA, Korean Augmentation To the US Army) to defeat hundreds of Communist Chinese Army at 205 Hill in the Cheongcheon River during the Korean War in November 1950. The 23-year-old young lieutenant ran out of the trench three times to let his soldiers know the location of the enemies, and he was seriously injured.

At the expense of veterans, ROK can defend peace and enjoy freedom right now. During the Korean War, 36,574 U.S. soldiers were killed on the battlefield. The United States is a benefactor to ROK. ROK owes the U.S. a debt that cannot be paid back. You must never forget.

President Biden recalled the past when the Chinese army

bled together against human wave tactics Communist Chinese Army to defend democracy in ROK. Former Lieutenant Puckett was discharged as a colonel in 1971. In 1992, he was inducted into the Army Ranger (Special Forces) Hall of fame. The end.

터키는 현재 아세아 대륙의 서쪽에 위치한 국가로, 터키와 한국은 과거 고조선 시대(BC 2333~AD 108)부터 같은 형제국으로서의 연이 있다.

Türkiye, mevcut Asya kıtasının batı kesiminde yer alan bir ülkedir ve Türkiye ve Kore, Gojoseon döneminden (MÖ 2333 - MS 108) beri kardeş ülke olarak bir ilişkiye sahiptir.

1950년 6월 25일 북한 공산군은 남침했다.
튀르키예 공화국은 1950년 10월 17일에 참전해서 휴전까지 함께 참여했다. 튀르키예군은 한국 전쟁에서 많은 공적을 올렸다.

Kuzey Kore komünist güçleri 25 Haziran 1950'de Güney Kore'yi işgal etti. Türkiye Cumhuriyeti ise 17 Ekim 1950'de Kore savaşına katıldı ve mütarekeye kadar savaşta yer aldı. Türk ordusu Kore Savaşı'nda bulunduğu sürece birçok başarıya imza attı.

부산에 도착해 대구로 이동했다. 미 제 9군단에 배속, 11월 초순부터 서부전선 평북 개천 군우리 전투(50. 11.), 용인 김량장동 전투(51. 1. 26) 수원 북방 수리산 전투(51. 1. 30), 와이오밍(Wyoming : 연천~와수리~화천저수지(4. 5), 마지막 고랑포 전투에서 적 3,000명을 사살하고 5명을 생포했다.

Türk ordusu önce Busan'a ard ı ndan Daegu'ya hareket etti.
Türk ordusu ABD 9. Kolordusu'na konuşland ı r ı ld ı . Kas ı m
1950'nin başlar ı ndan itibaren Bat ı Cephesinde Gunuri
(Kas ı m 1950), Yongin ve Gimryangjangdong muharebelerine
(26 Ocak 1951); Suwon'un kuzey kesiminde Surisan Muharebesi
(30 Ocak 1951) ve Wyoming Muharebesi'ne (Yeoncheon-
Wasuri-Hwacheon / 5 Nisan 1951), son olarak ise Goryangpo
Muharebesi'ne kat ı larak düşman saflar ı ndan 3000 askeri
yenmiş ve 5 kişiyi de esir alm ı şt ı r.

특히 용인 김량장동 전투(1951. 1. 25 ~ 27) 튀르키예군의 용감한 백
병전은 UPI 기자에 의해 승전이 전 세계에 보도 되었다. 해서 미국 대
통령과 한국 이승만 대통령의 부대 표창을 받았다.

Özellikle Yongin'deki Gimryangjangdong Muharebesi'nde
(27 Ocak 1951) Türk ordusunun cesaret dolu göğüs göğüse
mücadelesi UPI muhabirleri taraf ı ndan rapor edilmiş ve
dünya çap ı nda yank ı uyand ı rm ı şt ı r. Türk ordusu bu
sayede ABD başkan ı ve Güney Kore Devlet Başkan ı Syngman
Rhee'den bir takdirname alm ı şt ı r.

튀르키예군은 한국전쟁 당시 참전국 중 네 번째로 많은 2만 1,500명
을 파병했다. 그중에 966명이 전사하고 1,155명이 부상당했다. 그들은
한국 군인들과 어깨를 나란히 하며 싸웠고, 싸우다 죽어 한국의 아들
이 되었다.

Kore Savaş ı s ı ras ı nda Türk ordusu, gönderdiği 21.500 asker ile savaşa kat ı lan ülkeler aras ı nda dördüncü büyük orduyu meydana getirmiştir. Bunlardan 966's ı hayat ı n ı kaybetmiş ve 1.155'i ise yaralanm ı şt ı r. Koreli askerlerle omuz omuza savaş ı rken can veren Türk askerleri art ı k Kore'nin oğullar ı olmuşlard ı r.

한국의 자유 평화를 위해 침략자와 싸우며 형제국을 위해 전상자는 고귀한 혼령이 되었다. 형제국을 위하여 목숨을 바치면 이보다 큰 사랑이 없는데 한국인은 이 사랑을 어찌 갚으리오.

Kore'de özgürlük ve bar ı ş için düşmana karş ı savaşan Türk askerleri, kardeşlik için mücadele veren asil ruhlar haline gelmişlerdir. Kardeş için can verdiren yüce sevginin bir örneğidir bu. Koreliler bu ulu sevginin karş ı l ı ğ ı n ı nas ı l verebilir?

2020년 10월 20일, 용인시 영동고속도로 마성나들목, 원주가는 남쪽에 위치한 튀르키예군 참전 기념비를 답사하고 참배를 했다.

20 Ekim 2020'de Yeongdong otoyolu üzerindeki Masong kavşağ ı nda Wonju'nun güneyinde bulunan Türk ordusu Kore Savaş ı 'na Kat ı l ı m An ı t ı 'n ı ziyaret ettik.

★ 에르도안 튀르키예 대통령은 6·25 전쟁 70주년, 영상 메세지를 통해 순교자들에게 자비와 감사를 표한다. 한국 땅의 영원한 휴식처에 나란히 누워 있는 영웅들의 성스러운 기억에 경의를 표했다.

★Türkiye Cumhuriyeti'nin Cumhurbaşkanı Erdoğan, Kore Savaşı'nın 70. yıl dönümünde bir video mesaj ile şehitlere rahmet ve minnetlerini dile getirmiş ve Kore toprağında hayata gözlerini yuman Türk kahramanlarını saygıyla anmıştır.

☆ 에르신 에르친 주한 튀르키예 대사는 6·25 전쟁이 끝난 뒤에도 튀르키예는 한국인을 가족처럼 지켰다고 했다.

☆Türkiye'nin Kore büyükelçisi Ersin Erçin, Kore Savaşı'nın ardından imzalanan ateşkesten sonra da Korelilerin Türkler için bir aile gibi görülmeye devam ettiğini söyledi.

♥이스탄불 완전 정복하던 밤, Mehmet 황제가 밤하늘을 보니 초승달과 별이 반짝반짝 반겨주어서 國旗에 초승달과 별이 빛나는 국기다.

♥İstanbul'un fethedildiği gece, Fatih Sultan Mehmet gökyüzüne bakmış. Hilal ve yıldızlar parıldıyormuş. İşte Türklerin ulusal bayrağının üstünde de hilal ve yıldız öyle parlamaktadır.

미국의 바이든 대통령 한국전 영웅에 훈장 수여

ABD Başkanı Biden, Kore Savaşı kahramanına madalya verdi.

94세 퍼킷예비역 대령, 중위 때 한국 전쟁에 참여하여 특히 중공군

276

인해전술, 청천강 전투에서 활약했다. 명예훈장은 대통령 수여 최고훈장이며, 피로 맺은 한국과 미국의 동맹 기억의 메시지다.

94 yaşındaki Albay Puckett, Kore Savaşı'na teğmen olarak katılmıştı. Puckett, özellikle Çin ordusunun taktiklerine karşı Cheongcheon Nehri Muharebesi'nde yüz yüze çarpıştı. Bu Onur Madalyası, başkanı tarafından verilen en yüksek madalyadır ve Kore ile Amerika Birleşik Devletleri arasında kanla yapılan ittifakın bir hatırasıdır.

미 육군 특수 부대의 제8레인저 중대원 51명과 한국군 9명을 이끌었던 퍼킷 중위는 당시 그의 작전 구역에 약 2만 5천명의 중공군이 있다는 보고를 받았다.

ABD Ordusu Özel Kuvvetleri'nde 8'inci Ordu Muhafız Bölüğü'nün 51 üyesi ve dokuz Güney Koreli'nin başında bulunan Teğmen Puckett'ın bahsi geçen dönemdeki faaliyet bölgesinde yaklaşık 25.000 Çin askerinin bulunduğu bildirilmiştir.

1950년 11월 25일 중공군 18만 명이 청천강을 북진하려던 국군과 미군을 공격했다. 당시 모택동은 한국군을 집중 공격하라 했다. 모택동은 국군에게 훈련 기간, 장비 모두 부족했다는 사실을 잘 알고 있었다. 청천강 오른쪽을 지키던 국군 2군단이 궤멸됐다. 주력인 미 8군이 완전 포위될 위기였으나, 터키 여단의 사투 덕분에 겨우 퇴각로를 확보했다. 튀르키예군은 모자를 던져놓고 그 뒤로는 물러서지 않았다고 한다.
청천강 전투에서 1만 명 이상의 전사자를 낸 미군은 38선 이북을 포기하고 후퇴해야만 했다. 남북통일의 꿈이 산산조각 났다.

25 Kas ı m 1950'de 180.000 Çinli asker, Cheongcheon Nehri boyunca kuzeye doğru hareket eden ROK ve ABD kuvvetlerine sald ı rm ı şt ı r. O s ı rada Mao Zedong, Kore ordusuna yoğun taarruz emri verir. Mao, Güney Kore ordusunun hem eğitim disiplininden hem de teçhizattan yoksun olduğunun çok iyi fark ı ndayd ı . Cheongcheon Nehri'nin sağ taraf ı n ı koruyan 2. ROK Kolordusu yok edilmişti. Ana kuvvet olan ABD 8. Ordusu tamamen kuşat ı lman ı n eşiğindeydi, ancak Türk Tugay ı 'n ı n mücadelesi sayesinde güçlükle de olsa geri çekilme sağland ı . Türk ordusunun şapkay ı yere att ı ğ ı ve bundan sonra da geri ad ı m atmad ı ğ ı söylenmektedir. Cheongcheon Nehri Muharebesi'nde, ABD Ordusu pes etmek ve 38. paralelin güneyine çekilmek zorunda kalm ı ş, Kuzey ve Güney Kore'nin yeniden birleşme hayali ise paramparça olmuştur.

71년전 미 육군 특수 부대 중위로 한국전쟁에서 10배 넘는 중공군 병력에 맞서 싸웠던 퍼킷 중위는 6 · 25전쟁 중이던 1950년 11월 청천강 일대 205고지에서 부대원과 한국군을 이끌고 중공군 수백 명을 물리친 공로로 명예 훈장을 받았다.

71 y ı l önce, Kas ı m 1950'de Kore Savaş ı s ı ras ı nda, ABD Ordusu Özel Kuvvetleri'nde görev alan Teğmen Puckett, Tepe 205'te kendi birliklerine ve Kore birliklerine liderlik ettiği ve yüzlerce Çinli askeri mağlup ettiği için Onur Madalyas ı ile ödüllendirilmiştir.

23세의 젊은 중위였던 그는 부하들이 적의 위치를 파악할 수 있도록 세 번이나 참호 밖으로 달려 나갔는데, 이로 인해 그는 큰 부상을 입었다. 참전용사의 희생으로 한국이 평화를 수호하고 자유를 되찾았다. 한국 전쟁 때 미군은 36,574명이 전장에서 전사했다. 미국은 은혜국이다. 한국은 갚을 수 없는 빚을 미국에 지고 있다. 이를 절대로 잊어서는 안 된다.

23 yaşında genç bir teğmen, askerlerinin düşmanın yerini belirlemesine yardım etmek için üç kez siperden çıkmış ve bu da ciddi yaralanmalara neden olmuştur. Gazilerin fedakârlıkları sayesinde Kore barışı savunulmuş ve Kore özgürlüğünü yeniden kazanmıştır. Kore Savaşı sırasında, savaş alanında 36.574 Amerikalı hayatını kaybetmiştir. Amerika, bir lütuf ülkesidir. Kore'nin ABD'ye ödenemez bir borcu vardır ve bu asla unutulmamalıdır.

바이든 대통령은 중공군의 인해전술에 맞서 함께 피 흘려 한국의 민주주의를 수호했던 과거를 상기시켰다. 퍼킷 전 중위는 1971년 대령으로 전역했다. 92년 육군 특수 부대 명예의 전당에 현액 되었다. 끝.

Başkan Biden, Çin ordusunun taktiklerine karşı birlikte kan dökerek Güney Kore demokrasisini savunmanın tarihini hatırlatmıştır. Eski Teğmen Puckett, 1971'de albay olarak emekli olmuştur. 1992'de Ordu Özel Kuvvetler Onur Listesi'ne girmiştir. Son.

태국은 아시아 국가들 중 가장 먼저 유엔의 한국지원에 호응해 지원의사를 표명하였다.

6·25 한국전쟁 발발 5일 후인 6월 30일 쌀 4만 톤을 제공하는 것으로 유엔안전보장 이사회의 결의에 지지를 보냈다.

태국은 1개 대대의 육군병력 이외에도 프리깃트함 3척과 왕립 타이공군의 C-47 수송기를 보내는 등 육, 해, 공군을 모두 파견했다. 태국군은 포크찹 고지 방어에서 3차에 걸친 중공군의 공격을 백병전으로 격퇴함으로써 '작은 호랑이' 라는 애칭을 얻기도 하였다.

The Kingdom of Thailand was the first Asian nation to express the support in response to the UN's decision. On 30th June, five days after the outbreak of the war. Thailand supported the UN resolutions by providing 40,000 tons of rice. Thailand sent a Infantry Battalion, naval and air forces to ROK with 3 frigate and C-47 aircraft of the Royal Thai Air Force. Thai troops earned the nickname of 'Little Tigers', as they defeated three strikes by Communist Chinese Army on the Pork chop Hill.

- 참전기간 (Date of Participation) : 1950. 11. 7 – 1972. 6
- 참전규모 (Troops Provided) : 1개 보병대대 (1 Infantry Battalion)
  함정 5척(5 Ships),
  1개 수송기편대(1 Transport Formation)
- 참전연인원 (Total Participants) : 6,326
- 부상자 (Wounded in Action) : 1,139
- 전사자 (Killed in Action) : 129

태국

Thailand

ชื่อเรื่อง อนุสาวรีย์ การเข้าร่วมรบของกองทัพไทย

อนุสาวรีย์ การเข้าร่วมรบของกองทัพไทย

เมื่อวันที่25 มิถุนายน พ.ศ.2493 เวลา 04.00น.ระหว่างที่เกาหลีเหนือรุกรานเกาหลีใต้อย่างผิดกฎหมาย

กองทัพไทยส่งทีมสนับสนุนทางบก ทางทะเล ทางอากาศ และทางการแพทย์ไปยังสงครามเกาหลี

เมื่อวันที่ 28 เดือนพฤศจิกายน พ.ศ. 2493 เขาได้รับมอบหมายให้เป็นกองพลที่29ของกองทัพอังกฤษ

กองทัพไทยได้ย้ายไปเปียงยาง เมื่อวันที่3 เดือนมกราคม พ.ศ.2494 การรบครั้งแรกเป็นการจู่โจมกองกำลังจีน

โดยไม่ทันตั้งตัว

การต่อสู้ ของยอนชอนยูลดง(31.7.2494) การต่อสู้ที่ โพคชบ ทงทูซ่อน (22.1.2495)

234ที่เรียกว่าโพคชบเพราะมีลักษณะคล้ายซี่โครงหมู

ยุทธการที่ฮิมฮวาโกจิ (13.7.2496) กองทัพจีนเอาชนะและปกป้องศัตรูในการต่อสู้ประชิดตัว

จำนวนทหารไทย 12,845นาย เสียชีวิต 129ราย บาดเจ็บ 1,139ราย และสูญหาย 5ราย เหยื่อการต่อสู้ทั้งหมด
1,296คน หลั่งเลือด หยากเหนือ และนำตาเพื่ออิสรภาพและสันติภาพในเกาหลี เขาเหล่านั้นเป็นวีรบุรุษ

ราชอาณาจักรไทยได้ช่วยเหลือประเทศเกาหลี อนุสาวรีย์แห่งความสง่างามถูกสร้างขึ้นที่กองทหารรกษาการณ์สุดท้
ายของ กองทัพไทยที่ต่อสู้ เพื่อเสรีภาพและสันติภาพของเกาหลี เป็นที่ที่พระมหากษัตริย์ไทยได้เคยเสด็จมาเยือน

ตั้งอยู่ที่ มุนอมรี ยองบุกเมียน โพชอน เมื่อวันที่ 2 เดือนพฤศจิกายน พ.ศ.2563
ฉนเดินขึ้นบนไดไปหาอนุสาวรีย์ทหารผ่านศึก ราวกับว่าพี่ชายของฉนเสียชีวิต นำตาไหลพรากไม่ช้าก็คร่าครวญ
นี่เป็นหวครั้งที่15 จากทั้งหมด16ประเทศ และไม่เคยมือะไรแบบนี้มาก่อน บางทีชาติก่อนฉนอาจใช้ ชีวิตแบบคนไทย
พออกจากที่นนนำตาก็หยุดลง

ประเทศไทย

ประเทศไทยเป็นประเทศแรกในเอเชียที่ตอบสนองต่อความช่วยเหลือของสหประชาชาติต่อเกาหลี และแสดงเจตจำนงที่
จะสนบสนุน เมื่อวันที่30 เดือนมิถุนายน 5วนหลังจากเกิดสงครามเกาหลีขึ้น 6 · 25สงครามเกาหลีได้มีการสนบสนุน
ของคณะรัฐมนตรีความมั่นคงแห่งสหประชาชาติด้วยการจดข้าวสารจำนวน40,000ตน นอกจากกำลงพลของกอง
ทพบก หนึ่งกองทหนแล้ว ประเทศไทยยงส่งกำลงทางบก ทางทะเล และทางอากาศทั้งหมด รวมทั้ง เรือรบสามลำ
เครื่องบินขนส่ง

C—47 ของกองทัพอากาศไทยอีก1ลำ

กองทัพไทยปกป้องที่โพคชบโกจิ

태국군 참전 기념비

위치 : 포천 영북면 문암리, 태국군 참전기념 공원.

1950년 6월 25일 04시 북괴군의 불법 남침 시에 태국군은 육, 해, 공군 및 의료지원반까지 한국전에 파견했다.

1950년 11월 28일, 영국군 29여단에 배속되었다.

태국군은 평양으로 이동했다.

51년 1월 3일 최초전투는 중공군을 기습공격했다.

연천율동전투(51. 7. 31), 동두천 포크찹 전투(52. 1. 22) 234고지가 돼지 갈비뼈를 닮아서 포크찹이라 불렀다. 김화고지 전투(53. 7.13) 중공군을 백병전으로 무찌르고 승리하고 방어했다.

태국군은 연인원 12,845명이 참전했다. 전사자 129명, 부상자 1,139명 실종 5명이다. 총 합계 전투 피해자 1,296명이 한국의 자유와 평화를 위해 피, 땀, 눈물을 흘렸다. 이들은 영웅이다.

태국은 한국에 은혜를 베풀었다.

한국의 자유, 평화를 위해 싸운 태국군의 최후주둔지에 은혜의 기념탑을 세웠다. 태국국왕이 다녀간 곳이다.

2020년 11월 2일, 포천 영북면 문암리에 있다.

참전 기념비를 찾아 계단을 올라섰다. 친형제가 전사한 듯 했다. 눈물이 흐르더니 이내 통곡으로 변했다.

16개국 중 답사 15번째인데 이런 일은 없었다.

아마 나의 전생이 태국인으로 산 것 같았다. 자리를 뜨니 눈물이 그쳤다.

The Monument to Thai forces' Participation in the Korean War

Location: Munam—ri, Yeongbuk—myeon, Pocheon, Thai Army War Memorial Park.

Thailand dispatched Army, Naval, Air Forces, and even Medical Support Team to Korean War when nK committed the illegal invasion to ROK, my country at 0400(I), 25 June, 1950.

On 28th November, 1950, Thailand Forces had been attached to the British 29th brigade and moved to Pyeongyang. Thailand Forces surprised Communist Chinese Army as their first battle on 3rd January, 1951.

Also, they participated in Yuldong battle(31st July, 1951) in Yeoncheon and Pork chop hill battle(22nd January, 1952), Dongducheon. The origin of the name of Pork chop(234 hights) Hill was that it looked like 'Pork chop'.

At Kimhwa hill battle (13rd July, 1953), they carried out hand to hand fights against Communist Chinese Army successfully and conducted a successful defense.

Total 12,854 Thailand soldiers participated in Korean war among which 129 KIA, 1,139 WIA and Missing 5. They are heroes who shed blood, sweat and tears for the freedom and peace of ROK.

Thailand conferred benefits upon my country ROK and monument of gratitude was set up at their last post here in Munam-ri, Yeongbuk-myeon, Pocheon-gun where the place the king of Thailand visited.

On 2nd November, 2020, When I, gleeman Shin, stepped up in front of the monument to the Armed Forces of Thailand and felt as if my siblings had passed away. I could not hold my tears and wailed loudly. This was my 15th monument of 16 nations' monuments that I visited. It was the first time that made me wail loudly like this. I wonder I might have lived as a Thai person in the previous life. My teardrops stopped when I left the monument.

北韓傀儡　不法南侵
派太國軍　遣陸海空
配續英國　平壤進入
最初戰鬪　寄襲中共
栗洞戰鬪　東豆川鬪
白兵戰開　最後勝利
金化戰鬪　防中共軍
韓自平和　恩惠之國

남아프리카공화국은 아프리카 국가 중 최초로 한국에 공군부대를 파병했다. 지리적 여건으로 인하여 지상군 파병이 어렵게 되자 공군만을 파병하게 되었다.

1950년 11월 '하늘을 나는 치타'로 불리던 제2전투비행대대는 미군으로부터 F-51 무스탕전투기 16대를 인수받아 공중작전에 투입되었다.

남아프리카 공군부대는 미 공군에 배속되어 후방차단 작전과 폭격작전을 수행하였다. 전쟁 동안 수행한 주요전투는 스트랭글 폭격작전과 강압작전이다.

The Republic of South Africa was the first African country to dispatch Air Force to ROK. South Africa sent an air force unit instead of the ground troops because of its distance to Korea. In November, 1950, the South Africa Air Force's 2nd Fighter Squadron as known as 'Flying Cheetahs' took over 16 Mustang aircraft from the US and conducted its air operations. Republic of South Africa Air Force provided air support for the ground operations and conducting the rear area interdiction operations. Its major battles include the strangle bombing operation and coercion operation.

남아프리카공화국

Republic of South Africa

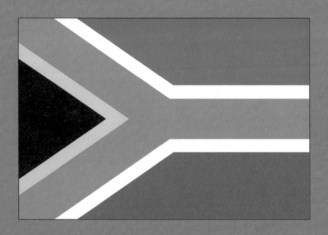

- ■ 참전기간 (Date of participation) : 1950. 11. 16 – 1953. 10
- ■ 참전규모 (Troops Provided) : 1개 전투비행대대 (1 Fighter Squadron)
- ■ 참전연인원 (Total Participants) : 826
- ■ 부상자 (Wounded in Action) : 0
- ■ 전사자 (Killed in Action) : 37

남아프리카공화국 참전 기념비

위치 : 경기도 평택시 용이동. 남아프리카 공화국 기념공원.

인류의 고향은 아프리카다.

남아공은 아프리카의 기준점, 중심이고 대륙 전체를 받쳐준다. 인류에게 희망을 주는 나라, 남아프리카 공화국은 희망봉을 가지고 있다.

1950년 6월 25일 북한 괴뢰군이 한국을 불법 남침했다. 귀국은 공군을 파견했다, 미 공군에 배속되었다.

초기전투에는 미 공군과 함께 북한 청천강 이북지역으로 출격하여 집결지와 보급소를 폭격했다.

교살 작전(1951. 8. 18) 북한 중서부지역 철교, 교량, 보급품, 수송차량을 폭격했다.

차단 작전(52. 2. 25) 정주와 군우리 일대 적 MIG-15기와 공중전을 전개하여 적기를 격추시키기도 했다.

강압 작전(52. 6. 23) 북한지역 수력발전소, 군수품 공장, 보급품 기지를 폭격했다.

초계비행(53. 1. 2) 압록강 지역에 진출하여 초계 정찰, 아군 폭격기의 엄호와 초계비행을 했다.

아프리카 공화국은 공군을 파견하여 한국민의 자유를 지켰으며, 대한민국 평화를 선물했으니 한국의 은혜국가이다.

남아공의 비행대대는 405회 출격하여 적 전차 44대, 야포 221문, 차량 891대, 교량 152개를 파괴했다.

남아공 공군의 한국전쟁 참여인원 826명 중에서 조종사 23명, 전투지원병 2명이 전사했다. 또 조종사 11명이 실종되었다. 또 포로는 8명 있었는데 휴전 이후 포로교환 때 복귀했다.

2020년 12월 1일 화, 평택시 용이동에 위치한 남아공 참전 기념비를 답사했다.
한국전쟁 당시 우리는 전투기가 1대도 없었는데 남아공은 그 당시, 세계 2차 대전시 전투기 조종사들이어서 전투 참전 경험이 풍부했다.
부러워하는 신삿갓이다.

The Monument to Republic of South Africa's Participation in the Korean War

Location: Yongyi-dong, Pyeongtaek-si, Gyeonggi-do, South Africa Memorial Park.

The homeland of human being is Africa. Republic of South Africa is the center, which prop up the whole Africa continent with. The country that gives hope to human being, which has the cape of good hope.

On 25th June, 1950, nK communist troops launched illegal invasion into ROK. Republic of South Africa sent Air Forces to ROK and it was attached to U.S. Air Force.

At the early stage of war, Republic of South Africa squadron carried out sorties with U.S. Air Force above the north of the Cheongcheon River, bombing enemy's assembly areas and supply points.

During the strangulation operation(18th August, 1951) : Republic of South African Squadron bombed the steel bridges, military supplies, and transportation vehicles of the enemy.

During the air interdiction operation(25th February, 1952) : Republic of South African Squadron also shot down MIG-15 enemy's fighter jets by air combats over the areas of Jeongju and Gunu-ri.

During the coercive operation(23rd June, 1952): Republic of South Africa Squadron bombed the hydroelectric power plants, military supplies plants, and supplies points in the northern area. During the air patrol operation(2nd January, 1953): Republic of South Africa Squadron advanced into the area of the Amnok River, performed patrol recce, covered friendly bombers and flew air patrols.

Your country kept the freedom of ROK by sending Air Force.

Since your country presented freedom to ROK, you are our benefactor and we are greatly indebted to your country.

Republic of South Africa Squadron made a record of 12,405 sorties, destroying enemy's 44 tanks, 221 field guns, 891 vehicles and 152 bridges.

The total number of Air Force detached to Korean War was 826 soldiers, among which 23 pilots and 2 combat support soldiers KIA, and 11 pilots were missing.

Also 8 became POWs and they returned during the exchange of POWs after ceasefire.

On Tuesday, 1st December, 2020, I, gleeman Shin, visited to the Korean War monument devoted to the forces of Republic of South Africa, which was located at Yongyi-dong, Pyeongtaek city.

During the Korean War, ROK owned no fighter jets, but Republic of South Africa had many fighter jet pilots of which had a lot of fighting experience during World War ll. I envy this a lot.

人類故鄕　貴國中心
希望國家　國喜望峰

北韓傀儡　不法南侵
空軍派遣　美空配屬

初期戰鬪　淸川以北
爆集結地　破壞補給

絞殺作戰　遮斷作戰
强壓作戰　哨戒飛行

貴國派遣　韓民獲自
韓國平和　恩惠之國

그리스는 6 · 25 한국 전쟁에 참전하여 보병 1개 대대와 7대의 C-47 다고타 항공기로 구성된 공군 1개 공수비행 대대를 파병하였다.

공수비행 대대는 장진호 전투를 지원하였으며, 총 2,916회의 임무를 수행하였다.

그리스군은 미 해병 사단을 직접 지원하여 전 · 사상자를 후방지역으로 후송하는 중요한 역할을 담당하였다. 전쟁 중 수행한 또 다른 주요 전투는 노리고지 전투와 북정령 전투이다.

Greece participated in the Korea War. And dispatched 1 battalion and 1 Air Force squadron which consisted of 7 C-47 Dakota aircraft. The squadron supported the battle of the Jangjin lake and executed a total of 2,916 missions. Greek forces provided direct support to the US Marine Division and played an important role in evacuating casualties to the rear area. Other major battles which they conducted during the Korean War include the battles of Nori hill and Bukjeongryeong.

그리스

Greece

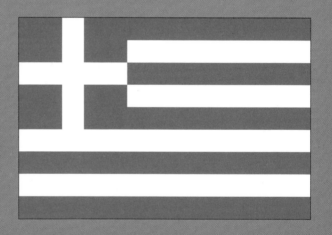

- 참전기간 (Date of Participation) : 1950. 12. 9 - 1955. 12
- 참전규모 (Troops Provided) : 1개 보병 대대(1 Infantry Battalion)
  1개 공수 비행대대(1 Transport Squadron), 7×C-47
- 참전연인원 (Total Participants) : 10,255
- 부상자 (Wounded in Action) : 617
- 전사자 (Killed in Action) : 187

그리스군 참전 기념비

위치 : 경기도 여주시 가남읍 여주남로 722 (여주휴게소 내부),
　　　　장차 여주시 영월공원으로 이전계획.

　그리스국은 문명의 요람국이다.
　문명의 영원한 가치를 지켜온 신전국가다.
　1950년 6월 25일 북한 괴뢰가 불법 남침해오자 UN 파병 요청을 받고 자유 수호를 위해 흔쾌히 승낙했다. 한국에 육군과 공군을 파병했다.
　참전 초기 50년 12월 13일에 수원으로 이동, 미 제1기병사단 5연대에 배속되어 충주지역 북한군 패잔병 소탕 작전을 수행했다.
이천전투(1951. 1. 25) 중공군 대부대와 전투해서 적 800명을 사살했다.
리퍼작전(51. 3. 7) (임진강 _전곡 _ 화천 _ 양양)
연천전투(51. 10. 3) 코만도 작전했다.
철원전투(53. 6. 10) 철원 북방 미륵동 420 해리 고지, 중공군과 백병전 승리했다.
　그리스의 한국전쟁 참전 인원은 5,532명과 8명의 여성 간호장교가 있었다.
그리스는 1955년 철수할 때까지 연인원 10,184(공군 397명)명이 참전하였으며 전사 186명, 부상 610명, 실종 2명, 총 741명의 인명 피해를 입었다.
　대한민국은 한국의 자유와 세계 평화 위해서 도와준 그리스를 그리스를 영원히 기억하겠습니다.
정의를 위해 몸 바친 고귀한 생명과 영혼은 한국인의 영웅입니다.
　그리스는 은혜의 나라다.

　2020년 11월 23일 월, 그리스군 참전 기념비는 원주 가는 여주 휴게소에 현재 위치한다. 장차 여주시 영월공원으로 이전 예정이다.
　그리스 참전 기념비를 답사하면서 고대국가의 정체성에 대한 많은 느낌을 받았다. 은혜국을 위해 오랫동안 묵념한 신삿갓이다.

The Monument to Greek forces' Participation in the Korean War

Location: 722 Yeoju Nam-ro, Ganam-eup, Yeoju-si, Gyeonggi-do (inside of Yeoju Rest Area), Plans to relocate to Yeongwol Park in Yeoju City in the future.

Greece is cradle nation of civilization. And it's a shrine nation which has been defending the value of civilization since ancient times.

On 25th June, 1950, nK regime launched an illegal aggression against the Republic of Korea. Greece willingly accepted the request of the UN for protection of freedom and dispatched Army and Air Force.

On 13th December, 1950, at the early stage Greek forces moved to Suwon and were attached US 1st Calvary Division. And then they were attached the 5th Regiment of 1st Calvary Division and conducted the clear operation against the remnant enemy forces in Chungju area.

At the Icheon battle (1951. 1. 25.), GEF(Greece Expeditisonary Force) killed 800 enemy soldiers against numerous Communist Chinese Army.

Greek forces also participated in the operation Ripper(51. 3. 7.) (Imjin river – Jeongok – Hwacheon – Yangyang), Yeoncheon battle(51. 10. 3.) Commondo operation and Cheolweon battle(53. 6. 10.) They won the successful hand-to-hand fights against soldiers of Communist Chinese Army at hill 420(Hill Harry) in Mireukdong north Cheolweon.

The number of Greek participants were 5532 soldiers and 8 woman military nursing and among them there were 186 KIA, 610 wounded and 2 missing, total 741 casualties.

Greece helped keep the freedom of ROK and the world peace. ROK will never forget Greece. Those souls who sacrificed their lives for the justice are the heroes of the people of ROK. Greece is the nation of gratitude to Republic of Korea.

On 23rd November, 2020, The monument to Greek participation in the Korean War is lacated in the Yeoju resting area on the way to Wonju. It wll be moved to Yeongwol park in Yeoju. I felt the identify of an ancient nation as I explored the monument. I, gleeman Shin, paid a long silent tribute for the favor of Greece.

文明搖籃　自由守護
北韓傀儡　不法南侵
派兵要請　卽時承諾
韓國派兵　遣陸空軍
參戰初期　水原移動
美軍配屬　傀儡掃蕩
利川戰鬪　華川戰鬪
漣川戰鬪　鐵原戰鬪
貴國派軍　韓民獲自
韓國平和　恩惠之國

한국 6 · 25 전쟁 참전 떠나는 아들에게 작별말을 건네는 그리스 어느 어머니 모습 어머니
의 날에 심금울린 사진 1장.
A Greek mother who give a last farewell to her son leaving for Korean War. A touching
photo on Mother's day.

뉴질랜드는 6·25 한국전쟁에 영연방 연합군의 일원으로 육군과 해군을 파병하였다.

뉴질랜드는 1950년 7월, 유엔안전보장 이사회의 결의에 따라 2척의 호위함을 급파하였고, 같은 해 12월에는 포병, 수송, 공병, 통신부대 병력 약 1,000여 명의 육군을 파견하여 유엔군 작전에 이바지하였다.

뉴질랜드군은 6·25 전쟁 당시 가평 전투와 고왕산 전투 등의 주요전투에서 많은 활약을 하였다.

New Zealand sent ground and naval forces to ROK as part of British Commonwealth forces. In July 1950, New Zealand dispatched two frigate rapidly in accordance with the UN Security Council Resolutions. And then in December, New Zealand had sent around 1,000 soldiers of ground forces which consisted of artillery, transport, engineering and communications units and contributed UN forces' operations. Its major battles include the battle of Gapyeong and battle of Mt. Gowang.

뉴질랜드

New Zealand

- 참전기간 (Date of Participation) : 1950. 8. 1 ~ 1957. 7. 27
- 참전규모 (Troops Provided) : 1개 포병연대 (1 Artillery Regiment),
  함정 6척 (6 Ships)
- 참전연인원 (Total Participants) : 6,000
- 부상자 (Wounded in Action) : 81
- 전사자 (Killed in Action) : 45

01 뉴질랜드군 참전 기념비

위치 : 경기도 가평군 북면 목동리, 호주, 뉴질랜드 참전공원.

1950년 6월 25일 북한 괴뢰집단의 불법 남침하자 뉴질랜드는 한국의 안녕과 세계평화를 위해 UN군의 일원으로 파병 했다.

뉴질랜드는 한국보다 인구가 10배나 적은 나라다. 그럼에도 불구하고 육군과 해군을 1천명이나 파병했다.

육군 제16포병 연대는 1950년 12월 31에 부산에 도착한 105mm 포병부대로 영연방 제27여단에 배속되었다.

뉴질랜드 해군은 1950년 7월 3일 한국해역에 도착, 미 극동해군에 배속되어 작전수행을 했다.

뉴질랜드군은 재반격 작전(1951. 1. 20.)을 위해 장호원으로 이동, 캐나다군과 호주군을 지원하기 위해 남한강을 도강하여 양평 양동면으로의 진출을 지원했다. 그 후 가평 전투(51. 4. 22), 연천 마량산 전투(51. 10월초). 고왕산 전투(52. 10. 23), 후크고지 전투, 연천 두현리 (53. 4. 9)에서 중공군을 격퇴하고 1953년 6월 25일에는 한국군 제 1사단을 지원했다.

뉴질랜드군은 한국전쟁에 연인원 5,144명을 파병했다. 45명이 전사하고, 81명이 부상 당했다. 뉴질랜드군의 도움으로 한국은 구사일생 위기를 모면하고 오늘의 대한민국을 있게 했다. 파멸로 가는 한국전쟁 때 뉴질랜드의 은혜를 결코 잊을 수 없습니다.

감사합니다.

2020년 10월 15일 가평 북면 목동리 격전장에서 뉴질랜드
참전 기념비를 답사하고, 참배하는 신삿갓 입니다.
(★3,794명 참전해 103명 전사 및 부상
ㅡ필립터너 뉴질랜드 대사, 조선일보 2020.12.10일)
♥ "비바람 치던 바다는 6·25 때 부른 마리오족 노래"

The Monument to New Zealand Forces' participation in the Korean War

Location : Mokdong-ri, Buk-myeon, Gapyeong-gun, Gyeonggi-do, Australia, and New Zealand Participation Park.

On 25th June, 1950, nK communist regime made an illegal invasion to ROK. New zealand, your country, as a part of UN forces dispatched military forces to the Korean War for the peace of ROK and the world. Your country was a nation whose population is 10 times as less as that of ROK. In spite of that situation, Your country dispatched as much as 10,000 soldiers; Army and Navy.

Your 16th artillery regiment was 105mm unit which had arrived on 31st December, 1950 and attached to the 27th Commonwealth Brigade. And your navy troop had arrived on 3rd July, 1950 at Korean waters and performed maritime operations after attached to US Far East Navy.

Your forces had moved to Janghoweon for re-counterattack (20th January, 1951) and crossed the Namhan River to support the troops of Canadian and Australian for them to advance to Yangdong-myeon, Yangpeong.

Afterward, your troops fought in battles at Gapyeong (22nd April, 1951), Mt. Marang(early October, 1951), Mt. Gowang(23rd Oct, 1952), and Hook hill battle: Duhyun-ri, Yeoncheon (10th April, 1953), repelled Communist Chinese Army attacks on 3rd May.
On 25th June, 1953, they supported ROK 1st Division.

New Zealand dispatched 5,144 soldiers to the Korean War, among which of them 45 KIA and 81 WIA.

With your country's help, ROK escaped from a big crisis by the skin of its teeth and let be today's ROK

ROK people never forget your country New Zealand's gratitude when ROK was on the way of destruction.
Thank you New Zealand.

On 20th October, 2020, I, gleeman Shin, visited the Korean war Memorial to New Zealand Forces and worshiped.
(★3,794 soldiers participated in the war, 103 killed and/or injured)
- Philip Turner, New Zealand Ambassador, Chosun Daily News on 10th December, 2020)
♥ "The song of Sea of Rain and Wind was that Mario people sang during the Korean War"

北韓傀儡　不法南侵
貴國參戰　派兵海陸
陸砲着釜　英聯配屬
海軍韓域　美軍配屬
反擊作戰　進長湖院
渡南韓江　進出楊平
陽坪戰鬪　砲射支援
適首都進　遮斷成功
自由守護　韓國平和
九死一生　恩惠之國

벨기에는 룩셈부르크와 함께 보병대대를 구성하였다.

1951년 1월 31일, 부산에 도착한 전투 대대는 미 제3사단 예하의 영국군에 배속되었다. 벨기에 부대는 보급로 확보작전과 최전선 작전에 참가하며 적군의 남하를 저지하였으며 금굴산 진지를 확보하였다.

Belgium established an infantry battalion together with Luxemburg. The unit arrived Busan on 31st January, 1951. and was attached to the British forces that belong to the US 3rd infantry division. The Belgian battalion participated in securing supply routes and in frontline operations thus preventing the enemies' advancement to the South and securing the Mt. Geumgul positions.

- 참전기간 (Date of participation) : 1951. 1. 31 ～ 1955. 6
- 첨전규모 (Troops Provided) ; 1 개 보병대대 (1 Infantry Battalion)
- 참전연인원 (Total Participants) : 3,498명
- 부상자 (Wounded in Action) : 336명
- 전사자 (Killed in Action) : 106명

벨기에

Kingdom of
Belgium

01

벨기에 참전 기념비

위치 : 경기 동두천시 상봉암동 130번지

1950년 6월 25일 북한 괴뢰 집단이 불법 남침했다.

벨기에는 한국전쟁 참전을 결정했다. 이유는 침략당한 국가들 간의 연대를 보여 주고 싶었다.

뉴질랜드 역시 세계대전 당시 침략당한 역사를 갖고있어 뉴질랜드 국민들 역시 한국에 연민을 느꼈기 때문인지도 모르겠다.

뉴질랜드군 부대는 1950년 10월 1일 벨기에와 룩셈부르크와 대대 A 중대에 배속되어 베네룩스 대대가 되었다.

그리고 양국은 3월에 영연방 제 29연대 배속되어. 임진강 전투, 금 굴산 전투 (1951. 4. 22.), 금화 전투, 학당리 전투(51. 10. 10), 철원 김 화 잣골 전투(53. 1. 20)에서 중공군과 전투를 했다.

벨기에는 한국전쟁에 연인원 3,498명이 참여하여, 99명이 전사하였 다.

뉴질랜드의 값진 희생이 한국에 큰 가르침이 되었고 대한민국 평화 를 지킨 이 은혜를 한국인은 영원히 잊을 수가 없다.

2020년 10월 25일, 경기 동두천시 상봉암동 130번지에 위치한 벨기 에 참전 기념비를 답사하고 참배했다.

한국을 위해 파병한 이 두 나라가 있었기에 현재의 대한민국이 있 다.

깊은 감사를 표시한 신삿갓입니다.

The Monument to Belgium Participation in the Korean War

Location: 130 Sangbongam-dong, Dongducheon-si, Gyeonggi-do

On 25th June, 1950, nK puppet Army launched illegal invasion into ROK.

Belgium decided to dispatch her forces to the Korean War, with the reason showing joint spirit as a nation which has many historical experiences that had been invaded.

Belgium also had been invaded from other countries during the World War. So her people had the sympathy for the ROK which was invaded illegally from the Communist nK puppet Army.

On 1st October, 1950, Luxembourg forces was attached to Belgium forces, and named Beneluks Battalion.

In March the same year, the Beneluks battalion was attached to the 29th British Commonwealth Regiment and fought against the Communist Chinese Army in the following areas:
Imjin river battle, Mt. Gumgul Battle(22nd April, 1951), Kumhwa battle, Hakdang-ri battle (10th October, 1951), and Jatgol battle(20th January, 1953), Gimhwa, Cheolweon.

During Korean War a total of 3,498 soldiers of Belgium forces participated and among which KIA were 99.

The sacrifices of Belgian risking neck and limb was a great teaching to ROK. We, Koreans never forget this gratitude of Belgium that kept the peace of ROK.

On 25th October, 2020, I, gleeman Shin visited and paid respects to the monument to the armed forces of Belgium and Luxembourg.

There being the two nations who had deep compassion, here at present exist Republic of Korea. How could I express my gratitude for the sacrifices of the souls here.

北韓傀儡　不法南侵
貴國參戰　派兵陸軍
參戰理由　理由無哉
侵當國家　連代視觀
貴國亦是　世界大戰
國土侵入　憐憫同一
兩國聯合　大隊統合
英聯邦培　臨津戰鬪
金窟戰鬪　金化戰鬪
韓國平和　恩惠之國

벨기에 , 룩셈부르크 참전기념비

벨기에와 룩셈부르크는 벨기에/룩셈부르크 전투대대를 통합으로 구성하여 대한민국에 파병하였다.

1951년 1월 31일, 부산에 도착한 전투대대는 보급로를 확보하기 위한 작전에 처음으로 투입되었다.

초기 영국 29여단에 배속된 룩셈브르크 부대는 이후 수원으로 이동하여 미 제3사단에 배속되어 최전방 작전에 참가하였다.

룩셈부르크 부대가 참전한 주요 전투는 임진강 전투, 학당리 전투, 철원 전투 등이다.

Belgium and Luxembourg had established a combined infantry Belgian/Luxebourg Battalion and sent them to ROK. The battalion arrived in Busan on 31st January, 1951. and conducted security operations for the supply routes for the first time. Initially attached to the British 29th brigade and then the Luxembourg troops moved to Suwon to be attached the US 3rd Division and took part in frontline operations later. Their major battles in Korean War include the battle of Imjin, Hakdang-ri, and Cheorwon.

룩셈부르크

Luxembourg

- ■ 참전기간 (Date of Participation) : 1951. 1. 31 ~ 1953. 1
- ■ 참전규모 (Troops Provided) : 2 개 보병소대 (2 Infantry Platoons)
- ■ 참전연인원 (Total Participants) : 85
- ■ 부상자 (Wounder in Action) : 17
- ■ 전사자 (Killed in Action) : 2

01

룩셈부르크 참전 기념비

위치 : 경기 동두천시 상봉암동 130번지

1950년 6월 25일 북한 괴뢰집단이 불법 남침하자, 룩셈부르크는 한국전쟁 참전을 결정했다. 그 이유 중 하나는 제2차 세계대전 때 독일에 침략당하였다가 우방국 도움으로 해방되어 자유를 얻었기 때문인지도 모른다.

인구 대비 최다병력 100명을 파병하고 UN 참전국과 함께 한국의 자유를 지키려 싸웠다. 그 후 파병부대는 1950년 10월 1일 벨기에와 룩셈부르크와 대대 A중대에 배속되어 베네룩스 대대가 되었다.

양국은 3월에 영연방 제29연대 배속되어 임진강 전투, 금굴산 전투 (1951. 4. 22.), 금화 전투, 학당리 전투(51. 10. 10), 철원 김화 잣골 전투로 (53. 1. 20) 중공군과 전투를 했다.

룩셈부르크 부대는 연인원 110명 중 15명이 전사하거나 부상 당했다.

룩셈부르크군의 고귀한 희생이 한국에 큰 가르침이 되었다.

대한민국 평화를 지킨 이 은혜를 잊을 수가 없습니다.

2020년 10월 25일, 경기 동두천시 상봉암동 130번지에 위치한 룩셈부르크 참전기념비를 답사하고, 참배했다.

연민으로 한국을 위해 파병한 룩셈부르크가 있었기에 현재의 대한민국이 있다.

깊은 감사를 표시한 신삿갓입니다.

The Monument to Luxembourg's Participation in the Korean War

Location: 130 Sangbongam-dong, Dongducheon-si, Gyeonggi-do

On 25th June, 1950, nK communist regime illegally invaded ROK.
Luxembourg decided to participate in the Korean War.

The reason why that Luxembourg also had the experience of invasion from Germany during World War ll and was liberated from them by the help of the friendly allied nations and regained freedom.

Her dispatched soldiers was attached to the A company of Belgium battalion and which battalion was named Benelux battalion.

Luxembourg dispatched 100 soldiers, the most number among the participated countries, comparing the population with that of other participated countries in Korean War, to fight as an equal nation of UN participated nations, for defence of freedom of ROK.

The two countries attached the 29th Regiment of Commonwealth in March. They fought against the Communist Chinese Army in the Battles of the Imjin River, Mt.

Geumgul(1951.4.22.), Geumhwa, Hakdang-ri(51. 10. 10) and Cheorwon Kimhwa Jatgol Battle(53. 1. 20.)

The Luxembourg unit had 110 soldiers among them 15 soldiers killed in action or wounded in action. The sacrifice of Luxembourg became a great lesson for ROK. I can't forget this favor of keeping the peace of the Republic of Korea.

On 25th October, 2020, at 130 Sangbongam-dong, Dongducheon-si, Gyeonggi-do, I visited Luxembourg's war memorial and worshiped.

There is the present Republic of Korea because there was Luxembourg that sent troops for ROK with compassion. I am a gleeman Shin who express deep gratitude.

北韓傀儡　不法南侵
貴國參戰　派兵陸軍
參戰理由　獨侵自國
侵當國家　連代視觀
貴國亦是　世界大戰
國土侵入　憐憫同一
英聯邦培　臨津戰鬪
韓國平和　恩惠之國

룩셈부르크 참전기념비

에티오피아는 아프리카 대륙에서 지상군을 파견한 유일한 나라였다.

집단안보라는 신념을 위해 1950년 7월 유엔 안전보장 이사회의 결의에 지지를 발표했고, 8월에 물자를 지원하고 파병을 결정하였다.

에티오피아의 각뉴(Kagnew) 대대는 1951년 5월 미 제7사단에 배속되어 계속 운용되었다.

6·25 한국 전쟁기간 동안 적극산 전투, 화천지구 전투, 양구부근 전투 등 250여 차례에 달하는 전투를 수행하며 대부분 승리하는 전과를 이루었다.

Ethiopia was the only nation in the Africa continent that dispatched ground force to ROK. In July 1950, Ethiopia announced the support the UN resolutions for the belief of collective security and decided to send the supplies with troop on August, Kagnew Battalion of the Ethiopia was attached to the US 7th Division and its major battles indude the battle of Mt. jeokgeun, Hawcheon, Yanggu. They won the most of 250 battles.

에티오피아

Ethiopia

- 참전기간 (Date of Participation) : 1951. 5. 6 – 1965. 1
- 참전규모 (Troops Provided) : 1 개 보병대대 (1 Infantry Battalion)
- 참전연인원 (Total Participants) : 3,518
- 부상자 (Wounded in Action) : 536
- 전사자 (Killed in Action) : 122

에티오피아 참전 기념비

위치 : 강원도 춘천시 이디오피아길1

1950년 6월 25일 북한괴뢰 집단이 불법 남침했다.

UN이 한국에 군사지원을 요청했다. 이때 이니오피아 하일레 셀리시에(Haile Selassie) 황제는 한국의 자유를 위해 지상군 파병을 결정했다. 이디오피아 파병군대는 황실 근위병이 근간이 되었으며. 각뉴대대(Kagnew. B : 격파부대)로 명했다.

1951년 4월 16일 지부티(Djibouti) 항구를 출발 5월 7일에 부산에 도착했다.

제1 각뉴 부대는 1951년 7월 11일 가평으로 이동했다. 미 7사단 32연대 4대대에 배속되어. 화천 전투(52. 8. 9), 철원 전투(52. 10. 4), 군북면 중공군과 전투, 상감령 전투 연천 전투(53. 5. 15)에서 중공군을 백병전으로 물리쳤다.

이디오피아군은 각뉴 부대 5차 파병까지 258차례 전투를 치루며 단 1차례도 지지 않고 불패신화를 남겼다.

참전 인원 6,037명 가운데 122명이 전사하고 536명이 부상을 당했다. 단 1명의 실종과 포로가 없는 용맹을 자랑했다.

이디오피아군은 한국의 평화와 자유를 지킨 은혜국이다.

♥ 1968년 5월 19일 한국을 방문한 이디오피아 황제가 참전 기념탑을 참배한 후 기념식수를 했다.

2020년 11월 9일 월요일, 강원 춘천시 근화동에 위치한 이디오피아국 참전 기념비를 답사했다.

1977년 5월, 제 27보병사단 항공부대에 첫 부임하면서 춘천 샘밭 육군 비행장 R-307에 조종사로 근무할 때 생각없이 휴식장소, 약속장소로만 생각했던 곳이다. 전적비에서 우방국의 핏값으로 대한민국의 자유와 평화를 지켜준 에티오피아를 생각하고 감사는 신삿갓입니다.

The Monument to Ethiopia's Participation in the Korean War

Location: Ethiopia-gil 1, Chuncheon-si, Gangwon-do

On 25th June, 1950, a group of North Korean puppets invaded the ROK illegally. The UN has asked for military assistance to the ROK. At that time, Emperor Haile Selassie decided to send ground troop for freedom of ROK. The imperial guards was a mother troop of dispatched troop. It was named for the Kagnew Battalion(destroying troop). On 16th April, 1951, it left Djibouti Port and arrived in Busan on 7th May.

The 1st Kangnew Unit moved to Gapyeong on 11th July, 1951. It attached 4th Battalion, 32nd Regiment, 7th U.S. Division. It defeated Communist Chinese Army with hand to hand fights in the Battles of Hwacheon (52. 8. 9.), Cheorwon (52. 10. 4.), Gunbuk-myeon, and Yeoncheon (53. 5. 15.).

Kagnew unit fought 258 battles until the 5th dispatching. And it left myth of defeat without losing a single time.

Of the 6,037 soldiers, 122 were killed and 536 were wounded. It boasted only one missing and prisoner-free bravery.

I can't forget my return to Ethiopia as a nation of favor that protected Korea's peace and freedom.

♥ After visiting the Ethiopian Emperor's Memorial Tower on 19th May, 1968, he planted a commemorative tree.

On Monday, 9th November, 2020, I explored the Ethiopian War Memorial located in Geunhwa-dong, Chuncheon-si, Gangwon-do. When I was first appointed as an aviation pilot of the 27th Infantry Division in May 1977, I thought of it as a resting place or an appointment place when I worked as a pilot at Chuncheon Sambat Army Airfield R-307. I am grateful to Ethiopia for protecting the freedom and peace of the Republic of Korea with the cost of blood.

北韓傀儡　不法南侵
派兵要請　黃帝允許
黃室近衛　擊破部隊
釜山到着　加平移動
華川戰鬪　鐵原戰鬪
漣川戰鬪　白兵戰也
貴國派軍　不敗神化
韓國平和　恩惠之國

콜롬비아는 남아메리카 대륙에서 유일하게 한국에 군대를 파병하였으며, 육군과 해군을 지원하였다.

콜롬비아는 유엔 안전보장이사회의 결의에 따라 프리깃함 1척과 보병 1개 대대를 파병하였다.

1951년 6월 15일 콜롬비아 대대가 부산에 도착함으로써 콜롬비아는 유엔 참전국 중 마지막으로 전투부대를 파병한 국가가 되었다. 콜롬비아 보병 대대는 미 24사단에 배속되어 작전에 투입되었으며, 전쟁 동안 수행한 주요 전투는 강원도 금성진격 전투, 김화 400고지, 불모 고지 전투이다.

Colombia was the only nation in Latin America that dispatched troops to ROK. Colombia send ground and naval forces to ROK. Complying with the UN Security Council Resolutions, Colombia sent one Infantry Battalion and one frigate. The Colombia Battalion arrived in Busan on June 15. 1951. Colombia was the last UN member nation to dispatch a combat unit to ROK. The Colombia Battalion was put to combat missions attached to the U.S. 24th Division and their major battles include the battle of Geumseong, Hill 400 of Gimhwa and hill battle sterile.

- 참전기간 (Date of Participation) : 1951. 5. 8 - 1955. 10.
- 참전규모 (Troops Provided) : 1 개 보병대대(1 Infantry Battalion)
  함정 1척 (1 Ship)
- 참전연인원 (Total Participants) : 5,100
- 부상자 (Wounded in Action) : 448
- 전사자 (Killed in Action) : 213

Republic of Colombia

Colombia fue el único país de América del Sur que envió tropas a Corea y apoyó al ejército y la marina.

Colombia envió 1 fragata y 1 batallón de infantería de acuerdo con la resolución del Consejo de Seguridad de la ONU.

El batallón Colombia llegó a Busan el 15 de junio de 1951. Colombia fue la última nación miembro de la ONU en enviar una unidad de combate a Corea.

El Batallón de Infantería de Colombia se adjuntó a la División 24 de los EE. UU. y se puso en funcionamiento, y las principales batallas que se libraron durante la guerra fueron la batalla de Geumseong, la Colina 400 de Gimhwa y la Batalla de la Colina de Bulmo.

- Período de participación en la guerra : 1951. 5. 8 – 1955. 10.
- Número de personas que fueron a la guerra : 1 batallón de infantería,
                                            1 barco de guerra
- Numero de veteranos de guerra / año : 5,100
- Número de soldados herido : 448
- Muerto en acción : 213

01

콜롬비아 參戰記念塔

위치 : 인천시 서구 연희동 213-7

남미대륙의 큰 눈동자인 콜롬비아가 한국을 바라보니 세기의 큰불이 일어난 것을 알았다. 보병 1개 대대 병력과 프리킷트함 1척을 가지고 한반도로 달려와 불을 끄기 시작했다.

1951년 4월부터 1955년 10월까지 금성지구 전투에서 세계 자유 대한민국을 위하여 611명 전사했으니, 얼굴도 모르고 누군지도 모르는 미래의 친구를 위해 살신성인 실천한 보은의 이 은혜를 갚을 길 없다오.

콜롬비아는 6·25 때 중남미에서 유일하게 전투 부대를 보냈다.

당시 연인원 5,100명이 참전했다. 213명의 전사자와 448명이 부상을 당했다.

69년 만에 두 노병이 한국을 찾았다.

한국전 참전 용사 회장 예르모 로드리게스 구만 92세와 알바로 로사노 차리 씨 87세가 2021년 8월 24일 철원 전망대를 방문하였다.

1952년 1월 당시 그들 중 구스만은 파견대 소대장으로 1952년 12월에 차리 씨는 육군 병사로 참전하였다.

20년 7월 8일 수요일, 인천 서구 경명공원 주변에 위치한 6·25 참전국 기념탑을 답사하는 신삿갓이라네.

The Monument to Colombia's Participation in the Korean War

Location: 213-7, Yeonhui-dong, Seo-gu, Incheon

Waking eyes from the South American continent discovered a big fire had just broken out upon the Korean peninsula.

Rushing to the scene of fire Republic of Korea over the ocean with 1 infantry battalion and 1 naval ship christened 'Freekit', They began to fight to put out the fire bravely and fiercely against the communist nK at the battle in Kumseong area (April 1951- October 1955), and from which it suffered the casualty of KIA 611.

With what to them could we return this unforgettable great and grateful favor of their sacrifices given free of charge to the unknown future friends.

On Wed, July 2020, I, gleeman Shin visited the monument to participated nations in Korean War which located nearby the Kyeong-Myeong park in Seo-Gu, Incheon.

Cuando los grandes ojos del continente
sudamericano miraban a Corea
Esos ojos sabían que se había producido
el gran incendio del siglo.
Con 1 batallón de infantería y 1 buque fragata

Corrieron a la península de Corea
y comenzaron a apagar las luces.
De abril de 1951 a octubre de 1955

En la batalla del distrito de Geumseong
Por la libertad mundial y Corea
611 soldados murieron.
Para futuros amigos que no conocen sus caras
y no saben quiénes son.
No hay forma de devolver la bondad que
practiqué como un santo viviente.
Colombia fue el único país de América
Latina en enviar tropas de combate a las 6 · 25.
En ese momento, 5.100 personas participaron en la guerra.
Durante la guerra murieron 213 personas y 448 resultaron heridas.
Después de 69 años, los dos veteranos visitaron Corea.
Dos de los veteranos de la Guerra de Corea, Yermo Rodríguez Guman (92) y Álvaro Rosano Chari (87), visitaron la plataforma de observación de Cheorwon el 24 de agosto de 2021.

En enero de 1952, Guzmán era comandante de pelotón de la unidad de destacamento y en diciembre de 1952, el Sr. Chari participó en la guerra como soldado del ejército.

南美大陸　泰目照韓
世紀放火　認知確認
步兵大隊　戰鬪艦携
走韓半島　消火作業
始五一年　終五五年
爲韓國民　戰死六百
誰顔未知　爲未來親
殺身聖人　結草報恩

♥위치: 인천 서구 연희동 213- 콜롬비아 전적비
♥Location: 213 Yeonhui-dong, Seo-gu, Incheon
　　　　－ The monument to participation of Colombia

3부

UN 의료지원단
UN Medical Assistance Group

UN 의료지원단
(UN Medical Assistance Group)

6·25 한국 전쟁 때 국제연합의 결의로 의료지원단을 파견했다.

6개* 나라다. 적십자 정신에 의거 한국에 파견된 연합군과 한국군의 선상사를 치료했다. 이 숭고한 정신을 어찌해야 하오. 찬양과 감사를 어찌할꼬.

파견한 6개국에 결초보은의 은혜를 잊지 말고 갚아야 하리‥

*♥ 덴마크, ♥인도, ♥이탈리아, ♥노르웨이, ♥스웨덴 , ♥독일

2021. 6. 13., 부산 영도 동삼동 산 14. 태종대 입구를 답사하고 참배했다.

부산 UN 묘지로 달려간 신삿갓이오.

During the Korean War, a medical support group was dispatched by the United Nations resolution. There are six* countries.

In accordance with the spirit of the Red Cross, They treated the Combined forces dispatched to ROK and the ROK Army.

How should I thank with this sublime spirit. How should I thank with praise and gratitude.

We have to never forget the favor of six countries which dispatched medical assistance.

*♥Denmark, ♥India, ♥Italy, ♥Norway, ♥Sweden, ♥Germany

On 13th June, 2021, I visited and paid tribute at San 14, Dongsam-dong, Yeongdo, Busan. Entrance to Taejongdae.
I am a gleeman Shin who ran to the UN cemetery in Busan.

韓國戰爭時　結國際聯合
醫療支援團　六個國派遣

赤十字精神　戰傷者治療
國際聯合軍　韓國軍治療
崇高業積焉　讚揚感謝乎
派遣國六國　結草報恩也

덴마크는 의료지원국 중에서 병원선을 파견한 유일한 국가였다.

8,500톤 규모의 화물선을 병원선으로 개조한 유틀란디아호는 360개의 병상, 4개의 병실, 3개의 수술실, 엑스선 촬영실, 안과와 치과 그리고 실험실을 갖춘 현대적인 해상 종합병원이었다.

덴마크 병원선은 1951년 3월 초, 부산항에 도착한 뒤 부산항을 거점으로 의료지원을 하다가, 1952년 11월부터 인천항에 정박하여 헬리콥터 테크가 설치된 이후 민간인 부상자를 대상으로 의료지원을 실시하였다.

유틀란타호는 유엔군 사령부에 배속되어 24개국에서 온 4,981명의 환자를 치료하고 6,000명에 달하는 한국 민간인을 진료하였으며, 등록되지 않은 민간인까지 합하면 12,000여 명이 넘는 한국인을 진료하였다.

Denmark was only nation which dispatched hospital ship among the medical assistance nations. Modern Hostital ship "Jutlandia" that was renovated form 8,500t class cargo ship had 360 beds, 4 rooms, 3 operation rooms, a X-ray room, an optical department, a dentist, and laboratories. The ship commenced its service in Busan in March 1951 and sailed to Incheon in November 1952. After established helicopter deck, it treated civil injuries. "Jutlandia" was attached to the UN Command and treated 4,981 soldiers from the 24 nations, and about 6,000 ROK civilians. if added unregistered civilians, total number of treated ROK people would be over 12,000.

덴마크

Denmark

- 참전기간 (Date of Participation) : 1951. 3. – 1953. 8
- 참전규모 (Troops Provided) : 병원선,
  유틀란디아호(Red Cross Hospital, Jutlandia)
- 참전연인원 (Total Participants) : 630
- 부상자 (Wounded in Action) : 0
- 전사자 (Killed in Action) : 0

1951년부터 1954년까지 주둔했던 노르매시(노르웨이 이동외과병원)에는 총 623명의 노르웨이 남녀 의료진이 근무하였다.

미 제8군 소속으로 의정부에 세워진 노르메시 부대는 최전선인 동두천으로 이전 후, 군인과 민간인을 포함하여 약 9만여명 이상을 치료했으며 10만여번의 수술을 시행하였다.

623 Norwegian men and women served at the Norwegian field hospital NORMASH from 1951 to 1954. The hospital was part of the U.S. 8th Army. NORMASH was established at Uijonbu, and then moved to the front line at Dongducheon. NORMASH treated more than 90,000 patients including soldiers and civilians and conducted around 10,000 medical operations.

- 참전기간 (Date of Participation) : 1951. 7. 18 ~ 1954. 10. 18
- 참전규모 (Troops Provided) : 이동외과 병원
                              (Mobile Army Surgical Hospital)
- 참전연인원 (Total Participants) : 623
- 부상자 (Wounded in Action) : 0
- 전사자 (Killed in Action) : 3

노르웨이

Norway

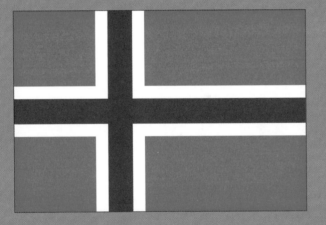

이탈리아는 유엔회원국이 아니었으나 한국에 의료지원 부대를 파병하였다.

이탈리아는 1950년 8월, 국제 적십자연맹이 6 · 25 전쟁의 전상자 치료 활동을 적극적으로 지원해 달라고 요청하자 의료지원 부대의 파견을 결정하였다.

이탈리아 적십자사는 군의관 6명, 행정관 2명, 약제사 1명, 군목 1명, 간호사 6명, 사병 50명으로 구성된 제68 적십자병원을 편성하고, 의약품과 의료 장비를 준비하여 1951년 11월 16일, 부산에 도착하였다. 150개의 병상 규모로 운영되었던 제68 적십자병원은 서울 영등포에 주둔하여 유엔군 장병과 민간인에 대한 진료 활동을 하였다.

Even though Italy was not a UN member, it dispatched medical units. In August 1950, the International Rrd Cross requested active support in treating the wounded during the war. Italy promptly decided to dispatch medical units. The Italian Red Cross organized the 68th Red Cross Hospital, which consisted of 6 army surgeons, 6 administration officers, 1 pharmacist, 1 military chaplain, 6 nurses and 50 soldiers. The unit left Italy with medical supplies and equipment by cargo ship and arrived in Busan on 16th November, 1951. The hospital with 150 beds had been based at Yeongdeungpo in Seoul and treated UN soldiers and civilians.

이탈리아

Italy

- 참전기간 (Date of Participation) :1951. 11. 16 – 1955. 1. 2
- 참전규모 (Troops Provided) : 제 68 적십자병원
    (68th Military Red Cross Hospital)
- 참전연인원 (Total Participants) : 189
- 부상자 (Wounded in Action) : 0
- 전사자 (Killed in Action) : 0ㅍ

인도는 유엔 안전보장이사회의 결의에 호응하여 1950년 11월 초 의료지원부대의 파병을 결정하고 의사 14명, 행정관 1명, 위생병 329명으로 구성된 제60 야전병원을 한국에 파견하였다.

제60 야전병원은 인도 공수사단 편제의 부대였던 관계로 공수 작전 능력을 갖추고 있었다.

미 제187공수연대 전투단이 공수 작전을 실시할 때에는 함께 편성되어 공수 작전을 지원하였다. 2개 제대로 나누어 본대는 영연방 제27여단에 배속되었다. 영국군을 직접 지원하였고, 분견대는 대구에 주둔하고 한국 육군병원을 지원 하였으며, 한국 민간인을 진료하기도 하였다. 제60 야전병원은 1951년 7월, 영연방 제1사단이 창설되자 사단 야전병원으로서 그 임무를 수행하였다.

India, responding to the resolutions by the UN Security Council, decided to dispatch medical units, the 60th field hospital, in early November 1950. The medical units consisted of 14 military surgeons doctors, 1 administration officer, and 329 medics. The 60th field hospital had capability to conduct airborne operations. Because it was organized unit of division. Thus it supported the US 187th Airborne Regiment Combat Group by organized with them. Hospital was divided into two units. The main unit was attached to the Commonwealth 27th Brigade and directly supported the UK troops. A detachment was based in Daegu and supported Korean Army hospital and treated Korean civilians as well. The 60th Field Hospital conducted missions aa division field hospital when the 1st Commonwealth Division was established on 28th July 28, 1951.

인 도

India

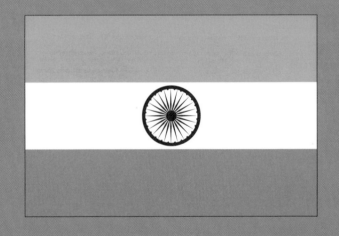

- ■ 참전기간 (Date of Participation) : 1950. 11. 20 - 1954. 2
- ■ 참전규모 (Troops Provided) : 제 60 야전의무대대
                                    (60th Field Medical Battalion)
- ■ 참전연인원 (Total Participants) : 627
- ■ 부상자 (Wounded in Action) : 23
- ■ 전사자 (Killed in Action) : 3

스웨덴은 한국에 최초로 의료지원부대를 파견하였다.

1950년 9월 23일 스웨덴 의사 10명, 간호사 30명 기타 행정요원 134명으로 구성된 스웨덴 적십자 지원단을 파견하였고, 스웨덴 적십자 야전병원은 미 8군사령부의 통제를 받으며 부산에서 의료서비스를 제공하였다.

200병상 규모의 병원으로 시작하였다가 그 후 점점 시설을 확대하여 450병상으로 늘어났다.

전쟁 기간 부상군인의 치료를 담당하였으나 전선이 소강상태에 이르렀을 때에는 민간인 환자의 진료와 한국의료진에게 의료기술을 지원하였다.

Sweden was the first nation to send a medical team to Korea. The Sweden government sent a Red Cross relief squad of 10 doctors, 30 nurses and another 134 staff members to Korea on 23 September, 1950. The Sweden Red Cross Field Hospital offered medical services in Busan under the control of the U.S. 8th Army. Initally, Sweden established a field hospital with 200 beds in Busan, which was eventually expended to 450 beds. The Swedish field hospital treated wounded soldiers during the waf. It treated civilians and transferred medical technology to the Korean medical staffs when the battles reached a stalemate

스웨덴

Sweden

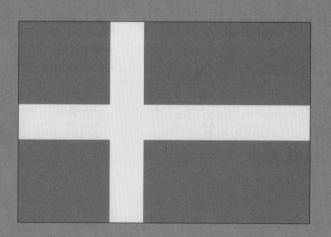

- ■ 참전기간 (Date of Partcipation) : 1950. 9. 23~1957. 4
- ■ 참전규모 (Troops Provided) : 적십자병원 (Swedish Red Cross Field Hospital)
- ■ 참전연인원 (Total Partcipants) : 1,124
- ■ 부상자 (Wounded in Action) : 0
- ■ 전사자 (Killed in Action) : 0

한국전쟁 시 UN의 결의와 적십자 정신에 의거해 독일은 부산에 '독일적십자 병원'을 열어 의료지원을 하였다.

한국전쟁 직후인 1954년 5월 인도주의적 차원에서 물자와 의사, 간호사를 지원하여 세워진 독일적십자병원은 수많은 한국전쟁 피난민의 목숨을 구하였다. 그 당시 부산은 전쟁으로 인하여 굶주린 피난민들로 북적이고, 의료시설이 제대로 없어 전염병 환자가 많았다. 가난한 피난민들을 치료해 준 곳이 바로 독일적십자병원이었다.

1954년 1월 독일 선발대가 도착, 부산에 있는 부산여고를 인수하여 서독적십자병원을 5월 17일 개원하였는데, 250개 병상에 내과, 외과, 치과, 방사선과, 산부인과, 약국을 운영하였다.

■ 참전기간 (Date of participation) : 1954년 5월~1959년 3월
■ 규모 : 독일 의료진 117명, 한국의료진 150명과 함께 진료
■ 외래환자 : 227,250명
■ 입원환자 : 21,562명과 대수술 9,306명, 간이수술 6,551명,
　　　　　　신생아 출산 6,025명 등을 진료하였다.

독일

Germany

　서독적십자병원은 한국에서의 1959년 3월 구호사업을 중지하고 부산의대 및 전남의대에 의료기재를 기증하고 폐원했으며 이후 간호학교를 졸업한 한국 간호사들이 1959년 처음으로 정식 간호인력으로 독일로 가서 1960년대 중반 정부가 주도하는 공식적인 파독 간호인력의 독일 취업을 위한 가교역할을 했다고 한다.

UN군 화장장 (연천)

위치 : 경기도 연천군 미산면 동이리

　1950년 6·25 한국 전쟁은 52년에 전선이 고착되어가고 고지 쟁탈전 양산으로 바뀌어 수많은 전사자 발생했다.

　혼령들은 얼마나 지쳤는지 아는 이 아무도 없다. 얼마나 힘들었는지, 얼마나 고된 전투 보냈는지도 얼마나 뼈를 깎는 노력을 했는지, 유리조각 쥐듯 얼마나 쓰라린 기억을 숨죽었는지 아는 이 없어 이제 육체 사멸되고 우리를 기억하는 사람은 아무도 없었다.

　2020년 10월 25일, 경기도 연천군 미산면 동이리에 있는 한국 전쟁 당시 유엔군 화장터를 답사했다.

　한국 땅이 어디 있는지도, 얼굴도 모르는데 달려와 별이 된 16개국에서 파병한 젊고 젊은 청년들 나라에 결초보은 은혜를 어찌해야 할꼬?

　오늘의 대한민국을 있게 한 혼백인데 정신 못 차리는 僞政者들 어찌 할꼬! 눈물만이 답하는 신삿갓 이라오.

　*마오쩌둥 몰래 38만 명 파병: 1950년 10월 19일

　25일 연합군 첫 공격; 이날을 抗美援朝(미국에 대항하고 북조선을 돕는다)기념일로 정했다. 6·25 사망자 중공군 36만여 명.

　★ 6·25 전사자

1. 국군 : 137,899명 (전투경찰 전사: 국군 22만 7천명/경찰 1만 3천
    명 전사)
(민간인 100만 명 피해, 과부, 고아 500만 명 발생, 이산가족 1000
 만 명 발생)

2. 미국: 36,574명 전사/카투사 7,174명 전사-추모벽에 4만 3748명
    새겼다.
(부상자에서 사망자 총합계 : 54,246 명 사망)
(부상; 103,284명, 실종; 7,578명, 포로; 7,245명 / 합; 154,698명)
3. 영국: 1,108명
4. 터키: 966명
5. 호주: 340명

 6. 캐나다: 516명
 7. 프랑스: 288명
 8. 그리스: 188명
 9. 콜롬비아: 213명
10. 태국: 129명

11. 에디오피아: 122명
12. 네덜란드: 124명
13. 필리핀: 112명
14. 벨기에: 99명
15. 뉴질랜드: 45명
16. 남아공: 37명
17. 룩셈부르크: 2명

☆의료지원국
1. 노르웨이 : 3명
2. 인도: 3명

UN Military Crematorium (Yeoncheon)

Location: Dongi-ri, Misan-myeon, Yeoncheon-gun, Gyeonggi-do

1952, the Korean War which broke out on 25th June, 1950 was going to be stuck.

The battles were changed to highlands battles. And they resulted in numerous KIA.

No one knows how exhausted the spirits were at the time.
How hard it was, how hard it was to fight

How hardly they fought like grinding their bone, like a piece of glass
I don't know how they held their bitter memories were, like grabbing a piece of glass.

Now their bodies were gone
And no one remembered them.

On 25th October, 2020, I visited the crematorium of UN forces which participated in the Korean War in Dongi-ri, Misan-myeon, Yeoncheon-gun, Gyeonggi-do.

They didn't even know where ROK was and how looked we were. In spite of they had ran to ROK and became stars.

What should we pay back to young people who had dispatched by 16 countries?

What should we do with the politicians who can't come to their senses about spirits which made a basis of modern ROK. I, gleeman Shin, just answer with tears.

* 380,000 soldiers were dispatched secretly by Mao Zedong: 19th October, 1950

The first attack against combined forces on 25th; China set this day as their anniversary which the day of helping nK against U.S.

More than 360,000 soldiers of Communist Chinese Army died in the Korean War.

★ Korean War KIA

1. ROK Armed Forces: 137,899 (227,000 Combat polices/ 13,000 Polices)
(One million civilians were damaged, 5 million widows, orphans, and 10 million separated families)

2. United States: 36,574 KIA / KATUSA 7,174 KIA – 43,748 were carved memorial walls.
(Total number of deaths from injuries: 54,246)
(Injured; 103,284, Missing; 7,578; POWs; 7,245 / Total; 154,698)
3. UK: 1,108 soldiers
4. Türkiye: 966 soldiers
5. Australia: 340 soldiers

6. Canada: 516 soldiers
7. France: 288 soldiers
8. Greece: 188 soldiers
9. Colombia: 213 soldiers
10. Thailand: 129 soldiers

11. Ethiopia: 122 soldiers
12. Netherlands: 124 soldiers
13. Philippines: 112 soldiers
14. Belgium: 99 soldiers
15. New Zealand: 45 soldiers
16. South Africa: 37 soldiers
17. Luxembourg: 2 soldiers

☆ Medical Support Nations
1. Norway: 3 soldiers
2. India: 3 soldiers

韓國戰爭　戰線固着
高地爭奪　多量戰死
生殘死鬪　極恨盡力
戰爭傷殘　骨刻努力
似琉破角　苦痛死命
魂靈切喨　誰知无焉
肉體死滅　記憶無也

♥ 대한민국은 16개국 국민들에게 말로는 할 수 없는 그들의
   은혜의 큰 빚을 지고 산다.

♡ 1964년 우리 1인당 GDP 100 달러.

♥ 지금은 세계 10위 경제 대국. 세계에서 유일하게
   원조받던 나라에서 주는 나라로 만든 주인공으로 만든 나라로
   발전의 밑거름은 바로 22개 지원국의 은혜를 받은 것이다.

♥ The people of ROK live with a big debt of 16 nations'
   people which is beyond words.

♡ ROK GDP was $100 in 1964.

♥ Now ROK has the world's 10th largest economy, ROK got
   22 countries' favor which made be modern ROK, the only
   nation that received aids from other nations into gives
   nation.

4부

특별작전 및
한국 단독 작전 기념비
Special Operations and ROK's Independent Operations

북한군의 기습공격으로 붕괴된 한국군은 북한군의 남진을 막기 위해 계속적으로 병력 재정비와 보충을 통해 군의 규모를 확대해 나갔다.

육군은 전쟁 초기 낙동강 전선으로 후퇴해야 하는 극한 상황에 이르기도 했지만 인적·물적인 손실을 보충하면서 병력과 장비의 증강을 도모하고 우방국의 지원을 받아 전세를 만회할 수 있었다.

개전 당시 8개 사단이었던 육군은 정전협정 체결 당시에 18개 사단으로 성장하였으며, 병력도 497,000. 여명으로 증가하였다.

The ROK military, which collapsed after a surprise attack by the KPA(Korea People's Army), continued to expand the size of its forces by restoration due to keep off the southward advance of the enemies. In early part of war, the army had been pushed to retreat till the Nakdong River defense line. But they recovered the war situation with the support of its allies. At the time of an armistice agreement between ROK and nK was signed, the ROK Army grew from 8 divisions to 18 divisions and soldiers increased to about 497,000.

대한민국

Republic of Korea

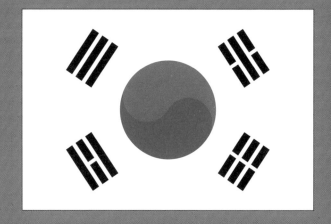

- 참전연인원 (Total Participants) : 621,479명
- 부상자 (Wounded in Action) : 450,742명
- 전사자 (Killed in Action) : 137,899명

대한해협 승전비 – 해군 백두산함

위치 : 부산시 영주동, 중앙공원

1950년 6월 26일 새벽 부산항으로 검은색 괴선박 1,000톤급 무장수송선이 남하했다.

울산 방어진 동방 3마일에서 수평선으로 검은 연기를 포착했다. 부산으로부터 30마일 (56km) 지점 백두산 PC-701함은 연기 있는 쪽으로 15노트(28km) 속도로 접근했다. 전투준비 완료 했다.

괴선박은 새까만 페인트만 친해져 있었다. 선체 표시도 국기도 없다. 국제신호 부호와 발광신호를 반복해서 보냈다. 응답이 없다.

함장(최용남)은 거리 3마일(5,500m)에서 위협사격 1발 발사했다. 적함은 기다렸다는 듯이 즉각 응사했다. 뒤에 달려온 YMS-518정도 37미리포로 적함을 향해 치열한 포격전이 20분간 계속되었다. 적함에 1,000야드(약 900m)에서 여러 발의 포탄이 적 함교를 폭파하고 마스트가 꺾여 나갔다.

적함이 검붉은 연기에 휩싸였다. 좌현으로 기울고 침몰하고 있었다. 01시 10분경 적함에 접근 300야드(270m) 3인치 포로 계속 흘수선을 때렸다.

적 600여명을 태우고 남하하는 적 무장함을 부산 오륙도 근해에서 격침했다. 기름 물결이 일렁이고 나무판자만이 떠다녔다.

조타수 김창학 수병과 전병익 수병이 적탄에 맞아 전사했다.

백두산함이 대한해협 해전에서 6·25전쟁 양상을 바꾼 한국해군의 첫 승리다.

2021년 9월 13일 부산 영주동, 중앙공원에 있는 한국해군의 대한해협 해전 첫 승리한 승전탑을 답사하고 참배하는 신삿갓이다.

♥ 상기의 기록은 '바다를 품은 백두산' 해군대령 최영섭(당시 소위, 갑판사관, 함장보좌임무)씨의 자서전을 읽고 쓰다.

The Monument to Victory of Koera Strait − Baekdusan, Naval Battle Ship

Location: Yeongju−dong, Busan, Jungang Park

Early in the morning of 16th June, 1950, a 1,000-ton armed transport ship, a black mysterious ship, advanced southward to Busan Port.

Friedly forces picked up black smoke from the mysterious ship on the horizon which 3 miles away from east of Ulsan defense camp.
30 miles (56 km) from Busan,

Paekdu PC-701 which was 30 miles(56Km) away from Busan approached the smokey side at a speed of 15 knots (28 kilometers). It was ready for battle.

The mysterious ship was only painted with black paint.
There was no national flag. Friendly forces repeatedly sent international signs and light signals.

There was no response.

The captain (Choi Yong-nam) fired one threatening shot from a distance of 3 miles (5,500 meters). The enemy ship responded immediately as if she had waited.

The fierce artillery battle continued for 20 minutes toward the enemy's ship with about 37mm gun, which ran after YMS-518.
Several shells which were fired 1,000 yards away from enemy ship blew up the enemy ship bridge and deflected the mast.

The enemy ship was enveloped in dark red smoke. It was leaning to left and sinking. At around 0110(I), she approached the enemy ship and continued to fire with a 3-inch gun away from 300-yard (270m).

The enemy ship which was moving southward with about 600 enemies sank nearby Oryuk Island in Busan.
There were a wave of oil, and only wooden boards floating.

Helmsman Kim Chang-hak and Seaman Jeon Byung-ik were Killed in action by enemy's bullets.
Baekdusan ship changed the aspect of the Korean War through Korean Strait battle. This is the first victory for the ROK Navy.

On 13th September, 2021, I, gleeman Shin, visited and paid tribute to monument to first victory of ROK navy in Korean Strait the Korean Strait in Jungang Park, Yeongju-dong, Busan

♥ The above record is based on autobiography of Navy Colonel Choi Young-seop whose nickname was 'Baekdusan which holds sea' (then a second lieutenant, deck officer, and captain's assistant mission)

釜山向進　武裝怪船
蔚山經由　黔燃捕着
釜山東北　五六指點
白頭山艦　戰鬪準備
武裝怪船　無表船體
發光信號　無應答也
五千移隔　危脅一發
卽各應射　赤艦發射
接近一千　赤船射擊
砲擊戰速　二十屬繼
適船艦上　爆破標臺
赤艦燃發　左舷沈沒

02

맥아더 사령관; 인천 자유공원

자유 평화를 수호하기 위함이었다.
포성 소리 잠시 그치고 지금은 휴전 중인데
괴뢰기 남침한 전쟁의 참혹함을 잊어가는 사람들을 보고 사령관*은
근심된 얼굴로 내려다보고 있었다.

*더글러스 맥아더 사령관
20년 7월 9일 목요일, 인천 자유공원 답사,
맥아더 사령관님께 맘속 일을 보고하니 "귀관이 계획한 것을 속히
시행하라" 라는 명령을 받았다.
맘속 깊이 존경을 표하는 신삿갓이오.

The Commander Gen. Douglas MacArthur; Incheon Freedom Park

It was only to keep the freedom and peace.

While the sound of guns stopped temporarily and now we are in the armistice.

As people of ROK forgetting the misery of the war of southward invasion by the nK puppet regime.

The commander, Gen. Douglas MacArthur is overseeing us

with a very anxious and troubled look.

On 9th July(Tur), 2020, I visited Incheon freedom park. The commander, Gen. Douglas MacArthur who had been reported my worries ordered me that "Do ASAP what you planed" I, gleeman Shin, respected the commander deeply.

自由平和　爲守護
砲聲止暫　休戰中
傀儡南侵　忘百姓
愁心顔色　司令官

맥아더장군 동상

03
故 백선엽 장군

꿈속 푸른 초원에서 백 장군을 뵈러 갔는데 꿈에서 깨어나니 새벽인시, 4시 반이었다.

민족 제2 영웅 서거 소식은 전쟁영웅 소천함에 국민이 낙담하고 우중조문 행렬 끝이 없어 6·25 전쟁영웅 애석한 마음 가득하다.

장군님 혼 혜성같이 일어나 천지를 밝게 해서 자유 대한민국 수호를 기원하옵나이다.

7월 11일 새벽꿈에 백 장군님을 못 만났는데, 오전 7시에 서진택 동지가 서거소식을 전해 왔었다. 12일 광화문 광장에 지팡이 짚고 우중에 경남 마산에서 올라온 박인애씨와 조문을 함께, 하늘도 울어버린 날에 신삿갓 입니다.

♡민족 제1영웅 ─ 이순신 장군이라 생각함.
백장군 추모 1주기
전·현직 연합 사령관 8명, 백선엽 장군 추모에 나섰다.

6·25 전쟁 영웅 고(故) 백선엽(1920-2020) 장군의 별세 1주기를 앞두고 전·현직 한미 연합 사령관 8명이 추모 영상 메시지를 보내왔다.

빈센트 브룩스 전 사령관은 "백 대장님의 용맹한 저항과 투지는 모든 미군에게 결의를 불어 넣었다"고 했다. - 조선일보 2021. 7. 9., A2면.

벨 사령관(2006-2008년)은 서한에서 "저는 백선엽 대장을 미국의 조지 워싱턴 장군에 비유해 왔다." 라고 했다. - 중앙일보 2021.7.9. 신문.

1950년 8월 낙동강 다부동 전투에서 30세였던 백선엽 1사단장은 후퇴하는 한국군을 가로막고 "나라가 망하기 직전이다. 미군은 싸우고 있는데 우리가 이럴 순 없다. 내가 앞장설 테니 나를 따르라. 내가 후퇴하면 나를 쏴도 좋다" 며 장병들을 독려했다.

결국 이 전투를 승리로 이끌어 패퇴 직전의 전세를 뒤집었다.

The Late General Baek Sun-yeop

I went to see General Baek on the green meadow in my dream
When I woke up, it was 0430(I) in the morning.

The news of the death of a second national hero were discouraged people of ROK.

There's no end to the funeral procession in the rain.
6 · 25 War Hero's mind was filled with sorrow.

I pray for the protection of the free ROK so that soul of General rose up like a comet and brighten up the whole world.

Yet I couldn't meet General Baek in my dream on 11th July at 0700(I), comrade Seo Jin-taek had reported General Baek's death. On the 12th, I paid my respects to him with Park In-ae, who came up from Masan, Gyeongsangnam-do, with a cane at Gwanghwamun Square. I was on the day which sky cried with me.

♡ National first hero - I think to be Admiral Lee Sun-shin.

the first anniversary of General Baek's memory

8 of former and present Combined Forces Commander stepped up to commemorate General Baek Sun-yeop. Before the first anniversary of the death of Baek Sun-yeop (1920-2020), the late hero of the Korean War. 8 of former and present Combined Forces Commander sent a video tribute message.

Former commander Vincent Brooks said, "Your brave resistance and determination inspired all U.S. forces." - Chosun Ilbo(daily report), 9th July, 2021, page A2.

The former commander Bell(2006-2008) said in a letter, "I have compared General Baek Sun-yeop to General George Washington of the United States." - JoongAng Ilbo(daily report) 2021.7.9. Newspaper.

In the Battle of Dabu-dong, Nakdong River in August 1950, Baek Sun-yeop, a 30-year-old commander of the 1st Division, blocked the retreating ROK soldiers and encouraged, "The country is on the verge of collapse. The U.S. military is fighting. How can we retreat. I'll take the lead, so follow me. If I retreat, you can shoot me." In the end, he led the battle to victory, reversing the situation on the verge of defeat.

夢中草苑　遇白將軍
醒夢起上　晨寅時覺
民族英雄　逝去所息
軍神消滅　國民落膽
雨中弔問　無極行列
戰爭英雄　哀惜滿也
似殞星起　光明天地
自由大韓　守護祈願

백장군 유성 묘지 비석

04

동락 전투(전쟁과 여교사)

위치 : 충주시 동락초등학교 내.

　사범대학 졸업 후 첫 부임지 충주 동락 초등학교 발령받은 여교사 김재옥 선생이 근무 중에 6·25 선생이 터졌다.

　승승장구 최선봉부대 북괴군 15사단 48연대가 학교에 들어와 정비할 때, 슬그머니 빠져나와 숨 가쁘게 달려서 4km 떨어진 국군에게 이 사실을 알렸다.

　패전에 패전을 거듭하며 후퇴하는 국군 7연대 2대대(임부택 중령)가 기습공격하여 적 2,700명 격멸하는 6·25 첫 승리를 달성했다.

　노획한 장비 중에 소련제를 확인함으로써 UN군 16개국의 지원받는 결정적 계기가 되었고, 이승만 대통령은 6사단 7연대 전체에 1계급 특진을 명령했다.

　1명의 여교사 김재옥 선생의 빛나는 애국심이 나라를 건져 올린 사건이 '동락 전투' 전사라고 한다네.

　20년 7월 27일 월, 여름 여행 2일차 충주 동락초등학교를 답사했다.

　김 교사는 그 부대 이득주 소위와 결혼해서 군인 가족이 되었다.

그 후 병기 장교인 이득주 소령과 고재봉 도끼만행 사건으로 비참한 최후를 맞는다. 다행히 아들 이 훈이 서울 외가에 가 있어 살아 남아있다.

동락 전투를 회상하며 6·25 비운에 한탄하는 신삿갓이오.

Battle of Dongrak(Schoolmistress)

Location: Dongrak Elementary School in Chungju.

The 6·25 Korean War broke out while Kim Jae-ok, a female teacher was in office at her first assigned place of Dongrak elementary school in Chungju after her graduation from a college of education.

When the spearhead nK army 48th Regiment of 15th Division which had been winning victory after victory entered her school and was tuning up, she ran off out of breath, sneaking out of the school, and delivered the news to the ROK Army that was 4 kilometers away.

And the 2nd Bn, 7th Regt, ROK Army, which was meeting defeat after defeat, made a surprise attack, destroying 2,700 enemy soldiers, the victory was the first victory in the Korean War.

Russia-made equipment collected among the tressure(booties) became a crucial momentum which created the support of the

UN forces from 16 countries.

The president Lee Seung Man of ROK ordered that a speci al promotion of one rank for all the soldi ers belonging to the 7th Regiment.

This case of the br illiant patriotism of one shoolmistress na med Kim, Jae-Ok, wh ich rescued our coun try, is called the historic story of the Battle of Dongrak.

동락초등학교
A photo Dongrak Elementary School

On 27th July(Mon), 2020, I visited the Dongrak Elementary Sh ool on the 2nd day during my summer journey.

The schoolmistress Kim got married to 2LT Lee Deuk-Ju of ROK Army and became a member of the military family. After that along with major Lee who served as an ordnance officer, she faced a miserable end by Go Jae-Bong's ax brutal event. Fortunately their son, Lee Hoon, was at the home of his mother's side. So he remains alive.

위치 : 경북 영천시 창구동 영천지구 전승비 공원

1950년 9월 6일, 영천이 9월 공세 북괴 15사단의 기습 공격을 받아서 피탈 당했다.

국군 8사단은 대구와 포항을 잇는 횡적 보급로가 동서 간으로 차단되며 최대 위기에 직면했다. 이로 인해 UN군은 한반도에서 전면 철수까지 고려했다.

최대의 위기다.

북괴 8사단이 국군 6사단이 방어하는 신령 지역에 주간공격을 감행했다. 맑은 날씨로 연합군 공군기가 폭격함으로써 6사단은 역공격을 가했다. 추가 지원을 받지 못한 북괴 15사단은 영천에 고립된 채 국군 8사단에 의해 각개격파 되었다.

국군 8사단은 7사 5연대, 1사 11연대, 6사 19연대의 3개 연대가 증원했다.

국운을 건 역습을 감행하여 9월 13일 영천을 탈환했다.

UN군이 고려했던 한반도로 부터 전면 철수계획이 백지화되었다.

1950년 12월 4일, 김일성은 압록강변 별오리 노동당 중앙위원회에서 "우리는 영천을 점령했을 때 승리할 수 있었고, 영천을 상실함으로써 패배하였다" 고 언급했다.

영천 전투에 얼마나 많은 기대를 걸고 있었는지 짐작된다. 6사단의 신령지역 방어에서 역공격 했다. 8사단의 영천 탈환이 국가존망의 위기에서 벗어날 수 있었던 것은 국군의 불굴의 투지와 불멸의 공로를 기념하는 장소가 되었다.

2021년 7월 27일 영천지구 전승비 공원을 답사하고 참배했다.

뙤약볕에 외기온도 36도가 넘는 날씨다. 용광로 속의 날씨와 한국전
쟁 때 국군의 불같은 투지가 넘치고 있었다.

시원하게 홀로 만세 부른 신삿갓이다.

The Monument to Victory of Yeongcheon District

Location: Jeonseungbi Park in Yeongcheon district, Changgu-
dong, Yeongcheon-si, Gyeongsangbuk-do

On 6th September, 1950, Yeongcheon was attacked by
surprise attack as a part of by nK puppet 15th Infantry Division
offensive operations in September. The ROK 8th Division faced
the biggest crisis due to the blocking of east and west due to
the horizontal supply route which was connected to Daegu and
Pohang.

As a result, the UN forces even considered entire withdrawal
from Korean Peninsula.

It was the biggest crisis.

The nK puppet 8th Division carried out day attacks on a
Sinryung area defended by the ROK 6th Division. The bombing
form Combined Forces bombers in clear weather so that the
ROK 6th Division launched a counterattack. The nK puppet
15th Division, which was not received additional support,
was isolated in Yeongcheon and was defeated by the ROK 8th
Division.

The ROK 8th Division was reinforced with three regiments: the 5th Regiment of 7th Division, the 11th Regiment of 1st Division, and the 19th Regiment of 6th Division. They conducted counterattack which could determine the fate of the nation and recaptured Yeongcheon on 13th September. To the Korean Peninsula, which the UN forces considered. From then on, the UN forces' plan for a full withdrawal was scrapped.

On 4th December, 1950, Kim Il-sung announced in the Central Committee of KWP(Korea Workers' Party) which took place at Byeolori along the Yalu River. "We were able to win if we occupied Yeongcheon, and we were defeated by losing Yeongcheon,"

I can guess how much expectations Kim Il-Sung the Battle of Yeongcheon.

The 6th Division conducted counterattack in defense of Sinryung. The 8th Division's recapture of Yeongcheon, ROK was able to escape the crisis of national survival. So this place became to commemorate the indomitable fighting spirit and immortal service.

On 27th July, 2021, I explored the Yeongcheon District's Victory Monument Park. It's over 36 degrees outside in the scorching sun.

The weather like a in the furnace and the fiery fighting spirit overflowing of the Korean War. I, gleeman Shin cried "Hurrah" alone

九月攻勢　永川彼奪
全面撤收　最大危機
美空支援　易攻擊也
永川孤立　各個擊破
國運一辦　易襲敢行
脫還成功　撤收白紙
永川傷失　敗北言及
不屈鬪志　不滅公勳

화령장 지구 전적비

위치 : 경북 상주시 화서면 문장로 288(화령장 전투기념관)

1950년 7월 북한군의 불법 기습 공격으로 국군은 후퇴를 거듭했다. 암울한 시기 6·25 전쟁의 흐름을 바꾼 전투가 화령장 전투다.

7월 17일~21일, 5일간의 기적이 화령장에서 일어났다. 상곡리와 동관리에서 국군 17연대(김희준 중령)가 상주, 대구방향으로 진출하려는 북한군 15사단 2개 연대를 매복전투로 섬멸했다.

승리할 수 있는 주요 원인은 주민(엄암회 씨)의 신고와 포로 1명의 진술로 이동로 제보, 휴식장소(송계분교)에 대한 정보입수다.

동리 주민은 국군에게 주먹밥을 해서 제공하고, 지형을 잘 아는 동네청년들이 도왔다.

기적적인 5일간의 전투로 적 600여명을 사살하고, 50여명을 생포하고 많은 전투 장비를 노획했다. 아군의 피해는 4명 전사, 30여 명이 부상을 입었다.

수적으로나 화력 면에서 적보다 불리한 국군은 지휘관의 사격통제와 주민신고, 식사제공, 지형안내로 승리할 수 있었다.

동관리 전투에서 연대장과 이 전투를 지켜보던 미 고문관 스카레이 소령은 "30년 군 생활 동안 이처럼 통쾌한 전투는 처음 보았다." 며 크게 감탄했다.

계속된 패배로 사기가 저하된 국군과 국민에게 희망을 안겨준 가장 통쾌한 소식이었다. 이에 이승만 대통령은 17연대 전 장병에게 1계급 특진의 영예를 부여했다.

2021년 9월 11일 토, 새벽에 출발하여 상주 화령장 지구 전적비를 답사하고 참배했다. 화령장 전투 전승기념관도 참관했다.

자유는 그냥 얻어지는 것이 아니다. 하늘은 스스로 돕는 자를 돕는다. 미국은 싸울 의지가 없는 나라를 위해 전쟁하지 않는다.

각 육해공 사관학교와 장교 임관자는 왜관 전적지와 화령장 지구에 다녀가기를 건의하는 신삿갓이다.

The Monument to Hwaryeongjang District

Location: 288, Munmun-ro, Hwaseo-myeon, Sangju-si, Gyeongsangbuk-do (Hwaryeongjang Battle Memorial Hall)

In July 1950, the ROK forces repeatedly retreated due to an illegal surprise attack by the nK KPA(Korean People's Army). In the dark period, the battle Hwaryeongjang changed the situations of the Korean War.

On 17th-21st July, a five-day miracle occurred at the Hwaryeongjang. In Sanggok-ri and Dongkwang-ri, the 17th Regiment of ROK forces(Lieutenant Colonel Kim Hee-joon) wiped out two regiments of the nK 15th Division by ambush which were trying to advance toward Sangju and Daegu.

The main reasons for winning were the reports of the residents (Eom Am-Hoe) and the statement of one prisoner which were the report of the moving route and the rest place(Songgye Branch School). The residents of Dong-ri provided rice balls to the ROK soldiers and helped by young people in the neighborhood who knew the terrain well.

In a miraculous five-day battle, more than 600 enemies were killed, 50 were captured alive, and many combat equipment was captured. In case of ROK forces, 4 soldiers were killed and about 30 others were injured.

The ROK forces which were more disadvantageous than the enemies in terms of numbers and firepower could win the battle due to the commander's control of firing, reports form residents, providing meals, and guiding terrain. Major Scaray, a U.S. adviser who was watching the battle with the regiment commander, said, "I've never seen such a satisfying battle in my 30 years military career."

It was the most pleasant news that gave hope to the ROK military and the people, whose morale was reduced due to continued defeat. In response, President Lee Seong-Man gave the 17th Regiment's former soldiers the honor of being promoted to upper rank each.

On 11th September, 2021, I departed at dawn on Saturday, and explored and paid tribute to the monument to the Hwaryeongjang district in Sangju. I also visited the Hwaryeongjang Battle Victory Memorial Hall. Freedom is not just earned. Heaven helps those who help themselves. The

United States does not fight for a country that has no will to fight. I suggest that every cadet of Army, Navy, and Air Force Academy and officers visit Waegwanjeokji and Hwaryeongjang district at least once.

北傀儡軍	不法奇襲
國軍後退	戰化寧場
上谷東觀	赤擊滅地
適進出慾	埋伏殲滅
勝利原因	住民申告
情報入收	埋伏壓勝
我軍數的	火力微弱
射擊統制	住民食給
國軍希望	通快消息
將兵全員	特進榮譽

화령장지구 전적비

제2차 세계대전 때 루스벨트 대통령의 큰 아들 제임스 루스벨트는 안경이 없으면 일상생활이 불가능한 고도 근시에 위궤양으로 위를 절반이나 잘랐으며, 심한 평발이라서 군화를 신을 수조차 없는 사람이었지만 해병대에 자원입대하여 운동화를 신고 다니면서까지 고된 훈련으로 정평이 나있던 해병대 제2기습대대에서 복무했다.

제2기습대대가 마킨 제도의 일본군 기지를 기습하는 매우 위험한 작전을 앞두고 대대장 칼슨 중령은 루스벨트 소령을 불러 '만약 현직 대통령의 아들인 귀관이 일본군의 포로가 되거나 전사하거나 하면 일본군은 이를 대대적으로 선전하며 전쟁에 이용할 것'이므로 작전에서 제외하겠다고 통보한다.

루스벨트 소령이 이에 강력하게 반발하자, 난처해진 칼슨 대대장은 태평양함대 사령관인 니미츠 제독에게 소령을 만류해 줄 것을 요청하고, 대대장과 생각이 같았던 니미츠 제독은 소령을 불러 훈련에는 참가할 수 있지만 작전에는 동행시킬 수 없는 이유를 간곡하게 설명했지만 이번에는 소령이 아버지의 '빽'을 동원했다.

대통령 루스벨트는 해군 참모총장 킹 제독에게 '내 아들은 제2기습대대의 장교다. 내 아들이 위험한 특공작전에 가지 않는다면 누가 그 작전에 가겠는가?' 라며 아들 루스벨트 소령을 반드시 마킨 제도 특공작전에 참가시킬 것을 지시한다.

그것이 루스벨트 소령이 제2차 세계대전 기간 중 대통령 아버지의 혜택을 본 유일한 경우였다.

소령은 소신대로 작전에 참가하여 혁혁한 전공을 세우고 돌아왔다.

루스벨트 대통령의 네 아들은 모두 이런 식으로 2차 대전에 참전했다.

미국의 입장에서 보면 자신들과는 크게 상관이 없었을 한국전쟁에서 그들 스스로도 잘못된 전쟁이라고 투덜대면서도 모두 139명의 미군 장성들의 자제들이 한국전쟁에 참전하여 그중 35명이 전사하거나 부상을 당했다.

그들 대부분이 평범한 집 자제들과 똑같이 최전선에서 싸웠으며 특별대우를 받는 경우는 없었다고 한다.

그들 중에는 52년 대통령에 당선된 아이젠하워 육군 원수의 아들인 아이젠하워 소령과 제3대 유엔군 총사령관이었던 마크 클라크 대장의 아들도 포함되어 있다.

특히 주목할 사람은 바로 한국군 전투력 육성에 지대한 공헌을 세운 제임스 밴 플리트 8군 사령관이다.

밴 플리트 대장의 외아들인 밴 플리트 2세는 야간 폭격기 조종사로 작전 수행 중 행방불명 되었고 공군은 장군의 아들을 찾기 위해서 필사의 노력을 다했지만 끝내 시신조차 확인하지 못한 채 실종 파일럿의 정규 수색 시간이 끝나가고 있었다.

이때 장군으로부터 전화가 걸려왔다.

외아들의 실종 소식을 듣고도 담담했던 장군은 이제 정규 수색 시간은 끝났으니 더 이상의 특별한 수색이나 구조 활동은 하지 말아 달라고 부탁한다.

모든 병사들이 최전선에서 죽음과 싸우고 있는 이 상황에서 내 아들이라고 해서 특별한 대우를 해줘야 할 필요는 없다는 것이 밴 플리트 대장의 전화 용건이었다.

외아들을 한국전선에서 잃었음에도 불구하고 장군의 한국 사랑은 지극했다.

전술 훈련과 체계적인 장교 훈련 프로그램이 미비했던 국군이었기 때문에 한국군이 전선에서 자주 패배를 당하는 이유를 간파하고 이후 장교들의 미군 참모학교 유학과 훈련 프로그램을 만들어 주었고 대한 한국 육군사관학교의 발전에도 많은 도움을 주었다. 그래서 육사 교정에 밴 플리트 장군의 흉상이 있는 것이다.

한국전쟁 중 대장으로 전역 후에도 장군은 전 미국을 돌면서 한국전쟁으로 피폐해진 대한민국의 전쟁고아들을 돕기 위한 모금 활동 연설에 나서는 등 한국을 돕기 위해 그 어느 한국전 참전 장군들보다 많은 일을 했다.

오늘날 한미 우호관계에 공헌이 큰 사람에게 주는 상의 이름이 밴 플리트 상인 이유는 외아들을 잃고도 한국 사랑을 멈추지 않았던 장군의 마음과 그의 노블레스 오블리주를 기리기 위해서이다.

미국인들은 한국의 고위층 관료들과 사고방식 면에서 상당한 차이가 있다는 생각이 든다. 특히 목숨이 위태로운 전쟁에서, 그것도 자기 나라가 아닌 타국에서의 전쟁인데도 불구하고 자식들이 용감히 싸워주기를 바라는 것은 진정으로 고위층 지도자들의 도덕적 의무인 노블레스 오블리주를 잘 실천하고 있다는 것을 보여주는 것이다.

이러한 점은 우리가 본받고 또 본받아야겠다.

Noblesse oblige in the United States

During World War II, Although President Roosevelt's the eldest son, James Roosevelt couldn't live a daily life without glasses because of high myopia and had cut the stomach in half with a gastric ulcer and had severe flat feet as much as he couldn't even wear military boots

He had volunteered to join the Marine Corps and served even wearing sneakers in the Marine Corps' 2nd surprise squadron, which had a reputation for hard training.

Ahead of conducting surprise attack which was very dangerous on the Japanese base in the Makin Islands, LTC Carlson, commander of the battalion, called major Roosevelt and said, "If you, the son of the incumbent president, are captured or killed by the Japanese Army,

The Japanese military will advertise it extensively and use it for war, so you will be excluded from the operation.'

When major Roosevelt strongly protested against it, the embarrassed Carlson battalion commander asked Admiral Nimitz, commander of the Pacific Fleet, help to dissuade the Major Roosevelt.

Admiral Nimitz, who had the same opinion as the battalion commander, called in the major to explain why he could participate in the training but could not accompany him in the operation. This time, the major pulled strings "his father".

President Roosevelt told Admiral King, Chief of Naval Staff "My son is an officer in the 2nd surprise battalion. Who would go to the operation if my son didn't go to the dangerous special operations?" and then the president ordered to take his son as a part of Markin Islands operation.
That was the only time major Roosevelt benefited from his

father during World War II.

The major took part in the operation as he believed and returned with a brilliant service in war.

President Roosevelt's four sons all participated in World War II in this way.

From the American's point of view, they complained that Korean War was wrong war, which would not have had much to do with them.

A total of 139 sons of U.S. generals participated in the Korean War, of which 35 were killed or wounded.

It is said that most of them fought on the front line just like ordinary soldiers and were never given special treatment.

They include major Eisenhower, the son of Field Marshal Eisenhower, who was elected president in 1952, and General Mark Clark, who was the third commander of the United Nations forces.

In particular, the person who we need to pay attention to is James Van Fleet, commander of the 8th Army, who made a great contribution to fostering the Korean military's combat power.

Van Fleet II, the only son of Van Fleet, commander of 8th Army was a night bomber pilot who went missing during the operation.

The Air Force tried desperately to find the general's son, but the regular search time for the missing pilot was ending without even identifying the body.

At the time, a call came from the general.

The general, who was calm after hearing the news of his only son's disappearance asked for stopping any more special search or rescue activities. Since the regular search time is over.

With all the soldiers fighting death on the front line,

There was no reasons his son had to be treated in a special way.

Despite the loss of his only son on the Korean front, the general's love for ROK was extreme.

He understood the reason that Korean troops are often defeated on the front lines

Due to the lack of tactical training and systematic officer

training programs.

Since then, he established overseas study and training programs for officers at the U.S. Army Staff School and helped the development of the Korean Military Academy.

That's why there's a bust of General Van Fleet on the campus of Korea Military Academy.

Even after being discharged from the military during the Korean War, the general traveled around the U.S. to deliver a speech on fundraising activities to help war orphans in the Korean War.

He did more to help Korea than any other Korean War general.

That's why the name of the award given to a person who contributes a lot is the Van Fleet Award in today to remember friendly relationship between Korea and the U.S.

Even after the loss of his only son
The general's heart that loving ROK and His Noblesse Oblige didn't stop.

I think there is a considerable difference in mindset from high-ranking officials in between American and ROK.

To want to fight their son bravely in the dangerous war which broke out in even not mother nation but other nation.

It truly shows good practice of the moral duty of high-ranking leaders, Noblesse Oblige.

We should learn from them.

龍門山, 전투 전적비

위치 : 경기도 양평군 용문면 신점리 산85.

마의태자 설움 안고 금강산 갈 때 심은 은행나무 천년 넘어 신목 되고 한국 전쟁 때 중공군 63 집단군을 국군 6사단이 치열한 전투 끝에 천추에 승리한 기점 용문산전투 방어에서 공세로 전환 진군 선봉되어 10만 호적 중공군을 파로호*에 수장하니 현대판 살수대첩* 시작되어 휴전 중인 조국이 평화통일 기점되는 龍의 門이 되기를 기원하네 ·

*파로호: 강원 양구와 화천 사이에 있는 호수이름.
*살수대첩: 고구려 을지문덕 장수가 수나라군대 113 만명을 살수에서 수장시킨 전쟁 그 후 수나라는 망했다.

2020년 9월 18일, 金 오후에 용문사의 1,100년 된
신목을 관조 후, 용문산 전투 전적비를 참배하는 신삿갓.
♥이승만 대통령은 대호를 중공군 깨뜨린 호수라며,
깨뜨릴 파, 오랑캐로, 호수호 : 파로호로 명 했다.

The Monument to Battle of Mt. Yongmun

Location: San 85, Sinjeom-ri, Yongmun-myeon, Yangpyeong-gun, Gyeonggi-do.

A ginkgo tree which planted when prince Maui went to Mt. Geumgang with sad feeling have become over thousand years old tree.

During the Korean War, After a fierce battle between the 63rd army of Communist Chinese Army and the ROK 6th Division Battle of Yongmun Mountain, It took a long time to win the battle.

Friendly forces turned defense to offensive. They were in the lead to bury 100,000 Communist Chinese Army in Paro Lake. The modern version of "Battle of Salsu" had begun

I wish the victory to be the gate of dragon for peace and reunification of the motherland in the armistice.

*Paro Lake: Name of lake between Yanggu and Hwacheon, Gangwon Province.

* Battle of Salsu: Gen. Eulji Mundeok of Goguryeo buried 1.13 million soldiers of Su dynasty in the water. After that, the Su dynasty went down the drain.

On Friday afternoon, 18th September, 2020, I, gleeman Shin visited 1,100-year-old holy tree at Yongmun Temple and paid tribute to the monument to the Battle of Mt. Yongmun.
♥ As president Lee Seung-Man said "it was a big lake which defeated the Communist Chinese Army" gave lake the name of Para Lake. The meaning is that The lake of which friendly forces defeated barbarians.

麻衣太子　錦鋼山之
植栽銀杏　千年神木
韓國戰時　中共軍滅
國六師團　熾烈戰鬪
千秋勝利　勝基執戰
防禦而也　攻勢進軍
十萬胡赤　破虜湖葬
現代判焉　殺水大捷
平和統一　龍門祈願

용문산전투 전적비

09

베티 고지* 영웅, 김만술 소위

위치 : 경기도 파주시 탄현면 성도리 670. (통일동산)

　6·25 한국전쟁 당시, 1953년 7월 15일 연천 서쪽 15km 지역 베티 고지에서 국군 1개 소대와 중공군 2개 대대 접전했다.

　중공군은 13시간 동안 인해전술로 공격해 오니 국군은 수류탄과 백병전으로 격퇴해 적 365명을 사살하고, 적 450명을 부상시키고, 3명의 포로 잡았다.

　김만술 소대장은 생사를 초월한 필승의 신념으로 최후까지 싸워 승리하니 금성 태극 무공훈장과 한국인 최초로 미국 '십자 훈장'을 받았다.

　1사단의 명예이며 국군의 영웅이 되었다.

*베티고지 : 연천군 서쪽 15키로 지역에 있는 고지명.

　2020년 12월 8일 화, 한국전쟁 전적비 답사 7개월 만에 문산역 동쪽에 위치한 문산 통일동산을 답사하면서, 개마고원 자유 의병탑, 육탄 10 용사탑, 1사단 충혼탑, 한국전 순직 종군기자탑을 답사하면서 베티 고지 영웅 김 소위님을 만난 신삿갓이오.

　♥ 김 소위 소속: 1사단 11연대 6중대 2소대장.
　　　　　 소대원 24명 전사, 12명 생환.
　　　　　 결과: 국군승리.

386

The Hero of Betty highland*, Second Lieutenant Kim Man-Sul

Location: 670, Seongdo-ri, Tanhyeon-myeon, Paju-si, Gyeonggi-do (Unification Hill)

During the Korean War, on 15th July, 1953, a platoon of ROK and 2 battalions of Communist Chinese Army were neck-and-neck at Betty Hill which was 15km away west of Yeoncheon.

Although Communist Chinese Army had been attacking for 13 hours with human wave tactics, ROK defeated them and killed 365 enemies, injured 450 enemies, captured 3 POWs with grenades and hand to hand fights.

The platoon leader Kim Man-sul finally led to victory with the belief of victory that transcends life and death.

He was awarded Golden Star Taeguk Medal of Merit and became the first Korean who received the U.S. "Distinguished Service Cross"
Received. Honor of the 1st Division and hero of the ROK forces.

* Betty highland: The name of highland in the 15-kilo away west of Yeoncheon-gun

On Tuesday, 8th December, 2020, seven months after

beginning to explore the monuments to Korean War. While exploring Munsan Unification Garden which located east of Munsan Station and Free Righteous Army Tower of Gaema Plateau, Tower of 10 heros who threw themselves to enemy's tanks, 1st Division Chunghon(spirits of royalty) Tower, and Tower of war correspondent who died in the Korean War I, gleeman Shin met Lieutenant Kim Man-sul, the hero of Betty highland.

♥ Organization of master sergeant Kim: 2nd platoon leader, 6th Company, 11th Regiment, 1st Division.
24 soldiers of platoon KIA, 12 survivors.
Result: ROK Forces won.

韓國戰爭　漣川高地
國軍小隊　對中共軍
人海戰術　長一三時
戰手榴彈　白兵戰夜
生死超越　必勝信念
勝利英雄　授與勳章

10

장사 상륙작전

위치 : 경북 영덕군 남정면 장사리, 장사상륙작전 기념공원.

　한국전쟁을 승리의 흐름으로 바꾼 전투는 인천상륙작전이다. 반면 이 작전을 성공할 수 있도록 추진한 전투는 바로 장사 상륙작전인데 성동격서 병법이다.

　1950년 9월 14일 밤에 학도병만으로 영덕 장사 해변에서 감행한 전투다.

　10대 학도병 720명이 열악한 환경 속에서 북괴군 2개 연대의 병력을 맞아 고군분투했다.

　2021년 금년이 한국전쟁 71주년이다.

　오늘은 7월 27일 68년 전 휴전한 날이다. 장사 해수욕장에서 소리 없는 총성이 들려온다. 이 전사를 잊으면 다시 또 재현된다는 역사의 교훈이다.

　2021년 7월 27일, 휴전된 날이다.

　이 전투의 결과는 학도병 139명 전사, 92명 부상, 수많은 학도병이 실종되었다.

　영덕 남정면 장사해변을 답사하면서 그날의 총성을 해변에서 듣고 있는 신삿갓이다.

　LST 문산호, 선장- 황재중, 부대장 이명흠 대위, 미 해군 쿠퍼 상사는 문산호와 명부대의 상황 보고를 했다. 명부대는 학도병들을 부대장 이름을 따서 명부대로 불렀다.

제안합니다. 대한민국의 남녀 고등학생이 3년간 수업 중에 이곳을 1
회 이상 답사하기를 제안합니다.

한국전쟁 때 같은 나이또래 학생들의 전투상황을 알게 하여 장래 나
라사랑을 실천할 수 있도록 교육이 이루어지기를 건의합니다.

Jangsa Landing Operation

Location: Jangsa-ri, Namjeong-myeon, Yeongdeok-gun,
Gyeongsangbuk-do, Jangsa Landing Operation Memorial Park.

The battle that turned the Korean War's situations into a
victory flow was Incheon Landing Operation.

On the other hand, the battle that drove Incheon landing
operation to succeed was Jangsa Landing Operation, which
applied military way of the SeongdongKeokseo which means
'After made a noise at west of enemies, attack east of enemies'.

The Jangsa battle was carried out only student soldiers on the
beach in Jangsa of Yeongdeok on the night of 14th September,
1950.

720 teenage soldiers fiercly fought against nK puppet two
regiments in the bad environment.

2021, This year marks the 71st anniversary of the Korean War.
Today is 27th July which was the day of the ceasefire 68 years
ago. I can hear gunfires without noise form Jangsa beach.

It is a lesson from history that if you forgot this history of war, it would be reproduced again.

On 27th July, 2021, today is the day of the ceasefire. The result of this battle was 139 student soldiers KIA, 92 WIA, and numerous student soldiers were missing. I, gleeman Shin was listening to the gunfires of that day on the beach while exploring Jangsa Beach in Namjeong-myeon, Yeongdeok.

● LST Moonsanho - Captain of LST Hwang Jae-joong, Deputy Captain Lee Myung-heum of the unit, and Sergeant Cooper of the U.S. Navy reported the situation of Moonsanho and the Myung unit. Myung unit was called according to commander's name of students unit.

● I would like to make a suggestion. I suggest that male and female high school students in ROK visit this place more than once during their three-year of school life. I recommend that education be conducted to learn about the combat situation of student soldiers of the same age during the Korean War so that they can practice their love for the country in the future.

韓國戰爭　勝利大流
仁川上陸　成功作戰
反面作戰　推進戰略
聲東擊西　長沙上陸
唯學徒兵　敢行戰鬪
十代學生　七百二十
戰北傀軍　二個聯隊
孤軍奮鬪　犧牲過多
六八年前　休戰調印
戰事忘失　再現歷史

장사 해수욕장

11

백마고지 전투 전승비

위치 : 강원도 철원군 산명리, 백마고지 전적지공원.

　30만 발 포탄 떨어진 격렬한 전투가 있던 곳.
　피·아 고지 주인이 24번 바뀐 백마고지.
　중공군, 인민군 2개 사단을 와해시킨 국군 9사단.
　자유, 평화를 죽음으로 지킨 군.
　배부르고, 등 따뜻하니 6·25 한국전쟁 잊어버린 백성들.
　UN과 지원한 16개국을 배은망덕 하는 무리 있지만 지각 있는 국민
다행히도 있어 한반도 자유 평화기도 행동으로 실천한다네.

　2021년 2월 17일. 철원 대마리 철의 삼각지 중심부를 답사하는 중
에 노동당사앞에서 한반도 평화 기도하는 불교인 부부를 보고 감동하
고 우국에 함께 기도하는 신삿갓이오. 6.25 한국전쟁의 많은 전투 중
1952년 10월 6일에 강원도 철원의 야산에서 가장 치열한 싸움이 시

작됐다. 철원 북방
395고지, 바로 '백
마고지 전투'이다.
　김일성은 철원의
광활한 평야에 목
숨을 걸다시피 했
으며 요충지였던
백마고지를 누가
차지하느냐에 따라

백마고지 전시관

전세가 바뀔 수 있었다.

　전투는 10일 동안 밤낮으로 물밀듯 밀려든 중공군 제38군단 6개 연대 병력과 국군 제9사단 30연대가 서로가 고지를 점령하기 위해 죽음을 무릅쓴 전투가 이루어졌다. 밤낮으로 이어진 전투로 포탄이 끊임없이 날아드니 야산은 허연 민둥산이 되어 깎이고 깎인 모습이 흡사 '백마'의 형상처럼 보인다 해서 '백마고지'라 붙여졌다.

　1952년 10월 6~15일에 걸쳐 벌어진 전쟁으로 한국군 사상자가 3,400여 명, 중공군이 14,000여 명을 기록했고, 24번이나 고지를 뺏고 뺏기는 치열한 전투가 이어졌다.

　'백마고지 3용사'인 강승우 중위, 안영권 하사, 오규봉 하사는 박격포탄과 수류탄 등을 몸에 지니고 적지에 육탄으로 돌진해 중공군의 기관총 진지를 폭파시키며 산화하면서 죽음을 불사르는 싸움으로 승리의 전쟁영웅이 되었다.

김일성은 철원평야를 잃은 후 3일을 철원평야가 바라다보이는 오성산에서 울었다고 한다.

당시 9사단을 이끌었던 전쟁영웅 김종오(金鍾五) 장군이 1952.10.5 백마고지 전투를 앞두고 장병들에게 내리는 훈시의 내용을 소개한다.

"전투에 임하는 장병들에게"

장병 여러분!
본관은 사단장 김종오 소장이다.
상승의 사단, 무적의 사단, 제9사단의 지휘를 맡고 있는데 대해 본관은 자랑과 긍지를 느낀다.
불굴의 감투정신, 타오르는 애국심을 누가 끄려한단 말인가!
이번 전투의 승패는 오로지 강철같은 의지력과 인내심의 결과 여하에 달려 있다.
이 일전은 또한 우리 한국군의 명예와 전투능력에 대한 평가가 달려 있다.
이제 우리는 승리의 순간만 기다리고 있을뿐 여기서 뭘 두려워 하랴!
수양제의 백만 대군을 살수에 장사지낸 을지문덕, 당 태종의 삼십만 대군을 섬멸하여 조국을 지킨 연개소문 장군이 구천에서 우리를 지켜보고 있다.

백마고지 전승비

누가 중공의 호적을 두려워하랴.

나를 비롯하여 사단의 모든 전우들이여,

여기에 우리의 뼈를 묻자!

그리하여 우리 9사단의 빛나는 명예를 지키자

이 전투가 백마고지 전투이다. 얼마나 치열했던지 국군 약 3500명과
중공군 약 1만명의 사상자가 발생했다.

The Monument to Victory of Baekma Highland Battle

Location: Sanmyeong-ri, Cheorwon-gun, Gangwon-do, Baekma
Highland Jeonji Park.

The site of a fierce battle that had fallen 300,000 shells.

The owner of the Baekma(white horse) highland changed 24
times during the battle.

The ROK 9th Division, which destroyed two divisions of the
Communist Chinese Army.

The ROK forces Kept freedom and peace of ROK with death
in honor.

There are people of ROK who forgot about the Korean War
because they were full and warm and bunch of ungrateful
people about United Nations and the 16 countries which
supported us.

Fortunately, there are people who has awareness. So they are
praying for freedom and peace on Korean Peninsula through
action.

On 17th February, 2021, while exploring the center of the Triangle of Iron in Cheorwon Daemari, I, gleeman Shin, was moved to see a Buddhist couple praying together for peace on the Korean Peninsula in front of the Labor Party and I prayed for my country together. (In the evening of 6th October, 1952, the Communist Chinese Army attacked with 44,000 soldiers the 395 Hill (Baekma Hill) in Cheorwon, Gangwon-do, which was guarded by about 20,000 soldiers form ROK and U.S.. Since then, They had made 12 wave attacks for 9 days until 15th October, but failed to succeed and was defeated. This is the Battle of the Baekma(White Horse) Hill. How fierce it was, about 3,500 ROK soldiers and about 10,000 Chinese soldiers were killed and wounded)

砲彈落下　激戰鬪
高地主人　變二四
滅中共軍　九師團
自由平和　軍死守

腹滿背溫　忘戰民
援十六國　背恩德
智覺國民　幸自覺
自由平和　實行祈

산화한 아군 3,428명의 넋을 기리고자 세운 백마고지 위령비

전적지 정상에 있는 백마고지 전적비는 전투에서 산화한 영령들을 두 손 모아 추모하는 형상으로 만들었다고 한다.

12

백마고지 참호전투

이강범(94세, 고지전투 생존자)

9사단 소속 이등 중사로 백마고지 전투에 투입되었다.

총은 지급받지 않았다. 소대장님은 카빈총을 휴대하고 있다. 소대원 전부가 소총이 없다.

첫 투입된 날 참호 주변은 11월인데 눈이 살짝 와 있다. 수류탄 안전 클립 재껴 수북이 쌓아놓고 대검만 차고 있다.

첫 야간전투 날이다.

잠잠하던 백마산 조경 능선 적막한데 난데없는 포성이 비 오듯 퍼붓고, 놈들의 연발포가 정신을 흔든다. 조금 지나니 살금살금 기어 올라오고 있는 것을 보고 쥐고 있던 수류탄을 던졌다. 정신없어 새까맣게 오르는 놈들보고 정신없이 던졌다. 사방천지 수류탄 소리 밖에 나질 않는다. 조용해 졌다.

상황이 어찌 되었는지 알 수가 없다. 조용해지니 공복이 왔다.

어제 오후 보국대(40대 노무부대)가 탄통에 담아온 소금 뿌린 황금보다 귀한 주먹밥 1개, 주변에 눈을 뭉쳐 목구멍에 밀어 넣은 것 밖에 없다.

여명이 밝아오고 아침 되니 우리 진지는 완전하고, 진지 밖 놈들의 시체가 즐비하다. 모습을 첨 봤는데 허술한 인민군 복장에 손에 방망이 수류탄을 가졌다. 나이는 15-17살 중학생이나 고등학생 정도. 놈들의 수류탄을 잡아보니 가운데가 잘록 한 것이 던지기에 용이했다.

백마산 전투는 주간에는 국군이 점령하고, 밤에는 인민군에 빼앗기기를 반복했다. 밤만 되면 놈들이 지랄하는 곳이다.

어언 전장에서 3개월 지나고 53년 2월이 되었다. 춥기도 하고 날은 빨리 어두워진다. 우리 진지 뒤편 기관총 좌에 폭음이 일어나고 동료가 공중에 떴다 내려왔다. 소련제 아시보 소총이 딱콩하더니 옆 참호 전우 철모를 관통했다. 즉사했다. 새까맣게 기어 오는 놈들 향해 얼마나 많이 던졌는지 알 수 없다.

그날 밤 '슈캉 소리' 와 함께 옆 전우와 적 수류탄에 당했다는 것을 직감했다.

동료는 좌측 몸 전체에 파편 맞았다.

난 우측 몸 전체에 파편을 맞았다. 겨울인데 우측 다리와 전투화가 축축하다. 나의 피가 흐르는 듯하다. 우수로 던질 수 없어 좌수로 던지다가 더 이상 버틸 수 없다. 쓰러졌다. 정신이 아물아물하다. 갑자기 이 자리가 포근하다. 꿈꾸는 듯 고향 거창 산천이 보이더니 어머니가 나타나 '아들아! 어서 일어나라' 소리 지른다. 정신차리니 야전병원이다.

한국전쟁 때 중공군과 가장 치열한 전투를 벌여 승리로 이끌었던 백마고지(해발 395m)

2021년 7월 25일 고향 방문차, 거창 보훈회관 방문하고, 이미 알고 있는 이강범 형님이 사시는 양평리 집에 인사를 갔다.

22세 입대, 현재 93세, 군번: 8831158 이등 중사, 9사단, 상의 제대, 유공자 5급, 아직 목과 머리에 파편있다.

경남 거창 보훈회관서 만난 이강범 형님 전사를 요약하는 신삿갓입니다.

The Trench Battle on Baekma(white horse) Highland

Lee Kang-beom
(93 years old, survivor of the Baekma highland battle)

He was a sergeant of the ROK 9th Division and was deployed to the Battle of Baekma(white horse) Highland. The gun was not issued. The platoon leader was carrying a carbine. The whole platoon had no rifles. On the first day of deployment, it snowed slightly around the trenches even it was November. The grenades which removed safety were piled up and the soldiers only wore a sword.

It's the first night battle day. The landscape ridge of Baekma Mountain was silent, but the sudden gunfire poured like rain, and their continuous gunfire shook the mind. After a while, he saw that enemies were creeping up and threw the grenade which he was holding. He threw it to the enemies who were going up fiercely. He could only hear grenades' bombing sound all over the place. It became quiet.

He didn't know what the situation is. When it became quiet, he felt hungry. The only thing that he ate was a salt scattered rice ball which precious than gold that Boguk unit(40s, Labor Unit) brought in a barrel of bullets yesterday afternoon and snow around trenches.

At dawn and morning, our positions were sound, and there were many bodies of enemy outside positions. He saw enemies for the first time, and they had a bat shape grenade in his hand in a sloppy People's Army costume. They looked about 15-17 years old students in middle school or high school. When he caught their grenade, it was easy to throw because the middle part was narrow.

The Battle of Baekma Mountain was repeatedly occupied by the ROK forces during the day and taken by KPA at night. It was a place where enemies acted rashly at night. After three months in battle place, it became February 1953. It was cold and got dark quickly.

There was a heavy sound on the machine gun's position behind his position, and a colleague floated in the air and came down. The Soviet Asibo rifles fired and penetrated the steel helmet of colleague in the next trench. He died instantly. He didn't remember how many grenades were thrown to the enemies crawling fiercely. I had a hunch with bombing sound that he was hit by an enemy grenade with my next comrade that night.

The comrade hit by fr
agments of grenade all
over his left body. Serge
ant Lee got shrapnels all
over his right body. Alth
ough It was winter, the
right leg and combat bo
ots are damp. He felt like
his blood was flowing.

이강범 형님과 필자

He couldn't throw with right hand so, he threw the grenades
with left hand but he couldn't endure any more. He was down.
He got distraught. Suddenly he felt that the place was cozy. As
if he was seeing his hometown, Geochang Sancheon, and his
mother appeared and shouted, "Son! 'Get up now,' When he
woke up, he was in the field hospital.

On 25th July, 2021, on a visit to my hometown, I visited the
Geochang Veterans Hall, and went to Yangpyeong-ri's house
where Lee Kang-beom, my old friend. He enlisted in 22 year
old, now he is 93 years old. Military number: 8831158 as a
sergeant, ROK 9th Division, discharged from service due to
hardships, meritorious grade 5, he still has shrapnels on the
neck and head. I, gleeman Shin, summarized Lee Kang-beom's
war fight stories at the Geochang Veterans Association in
Gyeongsangnam-do.

13

제2차 인천상륙작전

일시: 1951년 2월 10일, 17시
위치: 만석동 기계 제작소 해안, 기상대 고지, 시청, 월미도

중공군의 신정 공세로 1월 4일 수도 서울 함락되고, 37도 선상으로 방어선이 형성됐다.

7일 미 제 95호송부대 사령관 스미스 제독이 한국해군 단독으로 인천에 대한 소규모 상륙작전 가능 여부를 검토하게 했다. 701 백두산함은 영흥도, 자월도, 덕적도 해역을 경비하고 있었다.

미 순양함 헤레나함에서 해도를 펴놓고 작전방안 협의를 통해 한국해군과 해병대 단독 상륙작전을 세웠다.

701함 노명호 함장은 미리 적정을 파악했다.

감행할 지역 인천 적정을 정장들에게 설명하고 임무를 부여했다. 함과 정에서 차출 병력은 모두 73명이다.

10일 17시에 2척의 순양함과 1척의 구축함의 함포가 일제히 불을 뿜기 시작했다.

해군은 영종도 남쪽 해안을 돌아 18시에 만석동 인천 기계 제작소 해안으로 상륙했다. (현재 / 대한제분공장 위치) 적들이 월미도와 인천 역에서 사격을 가해 왔다. 해병부대는 기상대 고지(220m)로 향해 진격했다. 적은 따발총과 경기관총으로 대항해 왔다.

고지 정상 가까이는 각 분대장은 함성을 부르며 중대 앞으로, 대대 앞으로 하니 대부대가 공격해 오는 줄 알고 모두 도망쳤다. 21시경에 고지를 점령했다.

점령 후 확인된 적군 11명 사살, 아군피해 전무, 적 지휘소가 있는 인

천시청으로 진격 점령해 깃대에 있는 인공기를 내리고 태극기를 올렸다.

월미도 적들도 모두 도주했다. 포획물은 적 전차 1대, 야포 8문, 새벽에 만세 부르고 헤레나 함장에 보고했다.

제95호송 사령관 스미스 소장은 노 함장에게 한국해군이 감행한 인천상륙작전 성공으로 지상 작전에 큰 도움이 되었다며 공로를 치하고 노획한 적 전차에서 사진 촬영을 했다.

The Second Incheon Landing Operation

Date: February 10, 1951 at 17:00
Location : Manseok-dong Machinery Factory Coastal, Meteorological Observatory height, City Hall, Wolmi Island

On 4th January, The Communist Chinese Army's Lunar New Year's offensive led to the fall of the capital, Seoul, and made defense line on the 37th. On 7th January, Admiral Smith, commander of the U.S. 95th convoy unit, asked the ROK Navy alone to review the possibility of a small landing operation on Incheon. The 701 Baekdusan ship was guarding the waters of Yeongheung Island, Jawol Island, and Deokjeok Island.

ROK Navy and marine Corps discussed operational COA(Course of Action) with sea map to plan ROK only landing operation on the U.S. cruiser Herena.

Captain Roh Myung-ho of the 701 ship identified the appropriateness in advance. Captain Roh explained seaman the appropriateness of the local Incheon to be carried out and assigned the task. The total number of dispatched seamen from the ship were 73.

At 1700(I) on the 10th, the guns of two cruisers and one destroyer began to shoot fire at once. The Navy sailed around the southern coast of Yeongjong Island and landed on the coast of Manseok-dong Incheon Machinery at 1800(I). (Current location of Korea Mill factory) Enemies fired at Wolmi Island and Incheon Station. Marine units advanced toward the Meteorological Observatory height(220 meters). The enemies fought back with stun guns and light machine guns.

Near the summit of the highland, each squad leaders shouted "Company go ahead!", "Battalion go ahead!" The enemies thought were attacking them and ran away. Marine units occupied the highlands around 2100(I).

After the occupation, They found out 11 enemy soldiers were killed, no friendly forces' damages, and then they advanced to Incheon City Hall and lowered the nK flag and raise(Taegugi) ROK national flag.

Wolmi Island's enemies also fled. The capture were one enemy tank, eight field guns at the Wolmi Island. ROK soldiers hurrah at dawn and reported to Captain Herena.

RADM(U)(Rear Admiral Upper Half) Smith, the 95th convoy commander said "The success of the South Korean Navy's landing operation in Incheon greatly helped the ground operation." and took a picture with captured enemy's tank.

제2차 인천상륙작전

♥사진 설명 좌측부터 노 함장, 스미스 제독, 000, 000, 최영섭 가판장.
♥From the left, Captain Roh, Admiral Smith, 000, 000, boatswain Choi Young-seop.

14
장진호 전투

　1950년 11월 17일, 미 해병 제1사단과 미 보병 제7사단은 불과 얼음의 17일간 전쟁을 함흥북방 장진호에서 팽덕회의 중공군 12만 명과 맞닥뜨렸다.

　미군 격멸을 노려 영하 30~40도 혹한 속에서 총공세를 해, 미군 1만 8천여 명이 희생되고, 지상의 모든 것이 얼어붙어 운동화 신고 온 중공군도 5만 명이 얼음이 되어 죽었다.

　만약 중공군 5만 명이 죽지 아니하였다면, 남진하여 서울, 부산, 제주까지 쑥대밭이 되었을 것이다.

　혈맹을 상징하는 생존자 77명은 90세 넘고 대부분 세상을 떠났다. 남은 장진호 전투 용사들은 정례모임 갖고 행사 끝난 후에는 한국 민요인 아리랑을 부르고 강강술래를 하는데 역사를 잊으면 또 반복 한다네.

　혹한 속에 희생된 미군 1만 8,000명, 현재 생존인원 77명, 노병들은 대한민국 자유의 댓가는 미군이 지불했으니 우리 한국이 미국에 진 가장 큰 빚이다. 이자까지 갚아야 할 부채가 남아 있어 피 흘린 미군과 미 해병에게 고마움을 전하고픈 한국민은 많다.

　이 은혜를 갚을 기회가 얼마 남지 않았다네.

　20년 11월 17일, 한국전쟁 70주년, 장진호전투 70주년에 기록물과 책, 신문을 읽고 미국과 미군, 미 해병대에 감사를 올리는 초야에 묻혀 감사하는 신삿갓.

The Battle of Jangjin Lake

On 17th November, 1950, the U.S. 1st Marine Division and the U.S. 7th Infantry Division fought against 120,000 Communist Chinese Army of Pangdeokhoe for 17 days at Jangjin Lake in northern Hamheung.

The Communist Chinese Army conducted general attack to defeat U.S forces in the freezing cold of minus 30-40 degrees Celsius. So the 18,000 soldiers of U.S. forces were killed and everything on the ground was frozen. 50,000 soldiers of Communist Chinese Army who came wearing sneakers also died.

If 50,000 Communist Chinese Army had not died, they would have gone south and destroyed Seoul, Busan, and Jeju.

The 77 survivors, symbolizing blood alliance, are over 90 years old and most of them passed away. The remaining soldiers who fought in the battle of JangJin Lake have been having a regular meeting.

After the every meeting, they song Arirang, a Korean folk song, and did Ganggangsullae, a Korean folk dance.

The thing is if you forgot history, you would repeat it again.

18,000 U.S. soldiers were killed in the severe cold, 77 soldiers are now alive, The old American soldiers paid for the freedom of the Republic of Korea.

It is the biggest debt that ROK owes to the United States. There are many Koreans who want to thank the U.S. military and U.S. marines for their loss of blood as people of ROK still have debts to pay back including interest. There's not much time left to repay this favor.

On 17th November, 2020, the 70th anniversary of the Korean War and the 70th anniversary of the Battle of JangJin Lake,
I, gleeman Shin who are in the field read the records, books, newspapers, and thanked the United States, the U.S. Army, and the U.S. Marine Corps.

韓國戰爭　初期冬季
北長津湖　寒破戰爭
美軍擊滅　酷寒攻勢
美二萬犧　中共五萬
赤五萬命　戰鬪弗可
不可南侵　南全域棄
血盟象徵　生存勇士
定例會後　韓國民謠
美軍犧牲　得韓自和
結草報恩　機會短期

장진호 전투

15

세계 유일 UN군 묘역

위치 : 부산시 남구 대연동 776, UN 기념공원.

1950년 6월 25일, 한국전쟁으로 비극이 시작됐다.

51년 1월 유엔군 사령부는 전사자들을 부산 대연동에 묘지를 조성해 매장했다.

매년 11월 11일 오전 11시, 전 세계가 부산을 향해 1분간 고개 숙여 묵념한다. 한국전쟁시 유엔군 전사자가 안장된 부산을 향한다. 'Turn Toward Busan' 행사다.

이날은 1차 세계대전 종전일이자, 영연방국가 현충일이다.

유엔기념공원은 유엔군 용사 11개국* 2,311명이 잠들어 있다. 이곳은 세계에서 유일한 유엔군 묘지다. 70년이 지난 지금 전 세계에 자유와 평화의 소중함을 알리는 공간이다.

묘역은 축구장 18개를 합친 크기(13만 3701 m2) 한국 국민을 위해 목숨 바친 용사들 흔적이 A4 용지 1장 크기로 동판에 새겨져 있다.

미래 세대에게 자유 민주주와 평화 가치를 말없이 전하고 있다.

전쟁의 비극이 서려있는 이곳에 용감한 아들인 당신을 절대 잊지 못한다.

대한민국의 자유민주주의와 평화를 위해 희생된 참전용사를 기리고 젊은 세대에게 자유의 가치를 알리는 곳이다.

* 11개국: 미국, 영국, 터키, 남아공, 노르웨이, 뉴질랜드,
  네덜란드, 프랑스, 캐나다, 호주, 유엔파병 한국인.

2021년 7월 27일, 정전협정 조인 68주년이다.

한국은 전쟁을 하다가 잠시 쉬는 휴전 중이다. 내일이라도 전쟁이 일어날 수 있는 휴전국이다. 3번째 답사하면서 한국전쟁 때 산화하신 유엔군 참전용사에 묵념을 하는 신삿갓입니다.

The Only UN Military Graveyard in the World

Location: UN Memorial Park, 776, Daeyeon-dong, Nam-gu, Busan.

On 25th June, 1950, the tragedy began with the Korean War.

In January of 1951, the United Nations Command built a cemetery for KIA and buried them in Daeyeon-dong, Busan.

Every year, at 1100(I) on 11th November, the whole world heads to Busan and bow down for a minute and pay a silent tribute. It is called a 'Turn Toward Busan' event.

This is the day of the end of World War I and the Memorial Day of the Commonwealth.

The United Nations Memorial Park is home to 2,311 soldiers of U.N. forces from 11 countries.

It is the only United Nations cemetery in the world.

After 70 years later, now this place remains the world of the importance of freedom and peace.

The graveyard is the combined size of 18 soccer fields (133,701 square meters)

The traces of soldiers who sacrificed their lives for the ROK people are inscribed on a copper plate which the size of a sheet of A4 paper. It is telling future generations about the value of democracy and peace in silence.

I can't never forget you, the brave son at this place which has the tragedy of war.

This place remember the death in honor of veterans who sacrificed themselves for ROK's democracy and peace and teachs the value of freedom to younger generation

* 11 countries: United States, United Kingdom, Türkiye, South Africa, Norway, New Zealand, Netherlands, France, Canada, Australia, and Koreans who dispatched from United Nations.

On 27th July, 2021, it is the 68th anniversary of the signing of the armistice agreement. ROK is in the armistice.

It is a cease-fire country where war can break out even tomorrow.

I, gleeman Shin paid silent tribute to the U.N. military veterans who were killed during the Korean War for my 3rd visit.

韓國戰爭　悲劇始作
埋戰死子　釜山墓域
每年同一　向釜默念
戰死聯軍　釜山行事
紀念公園　世界唯一
自由平和　考知所重
爲國獻身　爲韓國民
銅版刻認　未來默傳
戰爭悲劇　各國勇士
自由價値　告永不忘

세계 유일UN군 묘역

자유는 그냥 얻어지지 않는다.

1975년 4월 30일 월남 사이공이 함락되고 월맹군에게 패망했다.

2021년 8월 15일 아프가니스탄이 수도 카불이 함락되고 탈레반에게 패망했다.

목숨을 걸어야 자유를 얻는다. 아무리 좋은 장비와 물자, 풍부한 예산이 있다 하여도 자유를 위해 목숨을 걸고 싸우지 않으면 자유를 얻지 못한다.

2021년 아프간 사태와 관련해 바이든 미국 대통령은 말했다.

"그들이 싸우려 하지 않는 전쟁에서 미군은 피를 흘리지 않겠다"는 선언이다. 너무나 당연한 말이지만 동맹국이 들을 땐 결코 예사롭지 않다.

탈레반의 공포에 휩싸여 생지옥을 겪고 있는 아프간 주민은 그동안 기본 선택을 잘못해온 것이다. 아프가니스탄이란 이름으로 우리는 타산지석으로 삼아야 한다.

자유는 남이 대신 지켜줄 수 없다. 베트남 전쟁에 이어 다시 한번 확인되는 잔인한 진리다.

우리는 북한의 기습 남침을 당한 후 순식간에 낙동강까지 밀렸지만 전선을 사수한 후 칠곡, 왜관 지역과 다부동 지역에서는 하루에 국군과 경찰, 학도병이 600명에서 700명이 희생되었다. 이 전투에서 시체가 산이 되고 피가 하천을 이루는 시산혈하로 사수한 후에 반격하여 국토를 되찾았다.

1950년 6월 25일 한국전쟁 당시에 북한군이 18만 8,297명이 남침했고, 특히 그해 10월에는 38만 명의 중국 인민해방군이 물밀듯이 쳐들어왔다. (한국군: 10만 3,827명) 전황이 바뀌면서 UN군이 급히 후퇴하는 긴박한 상황이 직면했다.

전투 중에 북한군과 중공군에 항복하거나 생포된 포로는 8만 2,000

명 정도로 추산한다. 휴전협정에 따라 8,300명 정도의 약 10명에 1명 정도 수준의 포로만 송환되었다. 수많은 포로들이 미송환되고 있다. 특히 상당수의 국군 포로들이 생존해 있으면서 인간 이하의 삶을 살아가고 있다.

탈북한 9사단 소속 육군 조창호 소위는 43년간 포로의 증언에 근거를 하고 있다. (1994. 10. 4. 중국으로 탈북)

국가는 송환에 필요한 모든 수단을 동원하여 반드시 해결해야 한다.

2021년 8월 15일 아프가니스탄이 탈레반에게 함락되었다.

한국정부의 아프간 재건 사업을 도왔다는 이유로 탈레반의 보복 위기에 처했던 현지인 391명, 영유아 100여명을 포함한 한국민이 대한민국 공군 수송기로 인천공항에 도착했다.

우리와 함께 일했던 동료들이 심각한 위기에 처한 상황에서 도의적 책임을 다한 것이다.

한국전쟁 때 포로로 잡힌 국군과 연합군은 지금은 90세가 넘었다. 어떤 협상을 해서라도 귀환시켜야 마땅하다.

2020년 5월부터 2021년 10월까지 UN 참전국 16개국과 의료지원국 6개 나라 22개국의 참전 기념비와 전투지역 전적비 약 80곳을 답사했다.

3곳의 전적지에서는 알 수 없는 눈물과 통곡이 터져 나왔다. (태국 참전 기념비, UN군 화장터, 왜관 작오산 45명 미군 학살 장소)

봄, 여름, 가을, 겨울 사계절을 답사하면서 나의 머릿속은 항상 6·25 전쟁 중의 상황을 생각했다. 특별히 영덕 장사 해수욕장인 상륙작전 지역에서는 학도병들의 모습을 봤다.

그곳에서는 우리나라 고등학생들이 3년에 1회는 이곳에 답사하게 해서 국가관을 키우고 싶었다. 그리고 경북 칠곡군 왜관읍에 있는 안보 교육장에는 우리나라 전체 초임 공무원에게 국가관을 심어주기 위해서 첫 임지에 부임하기 전에 꼭 한번 답사하는 것을 정례화하기를 건의합니다.

6·25 한국전쟁이 끝나고 71년이 지나는 동안 대한민국은 엄청나게 발전했다. 도움을 받는 나라에서 도움을 주는 나라로 변했다. 개발도상국들이 대한민국을 '롤모델'로 삼고 있는 것도 사실이다.

이제는 우리가 발전해 온 길을 돌아보고 우리가 어려웠을 때 우리를 도와준 사람은 누구이고, 그 도움을 준 나라와 그 국민에게 도울 일이 없는지를 돌아봐야 할 때라고 생각한다.

대한민국이 가장 어려웠을 때 희생하고 우리를 도와준 이들 또는 그 후손들이 도움을 필요로 할때 우리 대한민국은 마땅히 그에 부응해야 하고 보답해야 한다.

아! 어찌 우리 잊으랴!! 1950년 6월 25일 새벽 4시.

중공과 소련의 지원하에 북괴의 기습남침을!!

불굴의 정신으로 항전하고, 전 국민의 삶이 파괴되고 전 국토가 황폐화 되었다.

UN군 참전 6대주 22개국, 194만 여명이 달려와 항전한 대한민국 전사 4만명, 부상 10만명, 실종 4천명, 포로 6천명이 발생했다.

2018년에는 세계 12위의 경제 대국이 되었다.

UN 활동을 적극 지원하고 있다. 더 이상 늦기 전에 대한민국은 참전용사와 그 후손들의 손을 잡아 결초보은의 은혜를 갚아야 한다.

Freedom Is Not Free

Freedom is not just earned.

On 30th April, 1975, Saigon in Vietnam fell and was defeated by the North Vietnam Army.

On 15th August, 2021, Afghanistan was defeated and the capital Kabul was fallen by Taliban.

You have to risk your life to get your freedom. No matter how much money do you have, no matter what do you have, If you don't fight for your freedom, you won't get it. U.S. President biden said about the Afghan Crisis 2021 "It's a declaration that the U.S. military won't bleed in a war that they don't want to fight." It was so natural, but it's never unusual for an ally to hear. Afghans, who are suffering from Taliban panic, had made a wrong choice. We must learn from the case of Afghanistan.

Freedom cannot be protected by others instead. It is a cruel truth that was confirmed once again following the Vietnam War. After a surprise invasion from nK, we were pushed to the Nakdong River in an instant, but after defending the front line, 600 to 700 ROK people, polices and student soldiers were killed a day in Chilgok, Waegwan, and Dabu-dong. In this battle, the bodies became a mountain and the blood became a river, and then fought back and regained the country.

During the Korean War on 25th June, 1950, 188,297 nK soldiers invaded the ROK, and in October of that year, 380,000 Communist Chinese Army invaded like waves. (Korean military: 103,827) As the war situation was changed, UN forces were urgently withdrew. It is estimated about 82,000 prisoners surrendered or were captured by nK and ommunist Chinese Army during the battle. Only 8,300 prisoner, the number of one-tenth size of whole prisoners were repatriated under the armistice agreement. Countless prisoners were being remanded. In particular, a considerable number of ROK prisoners of war were alive and lived below humans. It based on the testimony from Second lieutenant Cho Chang-ho, a member of the ROK 9th Division who had lived as a prisoner for 43 years and defected from nK (He defected to China on 4th October, 1994) The state must solve it by all means necessary for repatriation.

On 15th August, 2021, Afghanistan was fallen by the Taliban. The ROK people who had been in the Afghanistan arrived at Incheon International Airport by ROK Air Force transport planes, The people including 391 locals and 100 infants who were on the verge of retaliation by the Taliban for helping the Korean government to rebuild Afghanistan. The nation fulfilled her moral responsibilities in serious crisis situations for our colleagues. The ROK military and allied forces captured during the Korean War are now over 90 years old. Any deal should be negotiated and brought them back.

From May 2020 to October 2021, I visited about 80 memorials and battle areas of 16 UN participating countries and 22 medical support countries. Tears and wailing burst out from the three battlefields(The monument to Thailand's participation to Korean War, UN military crematorium, the place of massacre of 45 U.S. soldiers in Jako Mountain, Waegwan). As I explored the four seasons of spring, summer, autumn, and winter, I always thought about the situation during the Korean War. In particular, I saw student soldiers in the landing operation area, which is Yeongdeok Jangsa Beach. I hope that Korean high school students visit this place once every three years mandatorily to develop a national view at there. In addition, I suggest that the head of the Security Education Center in Waegwan-eup, Chilgok-gun, Gyeongsangbuk-do, all first-time public officials in ROK should conduct regular viswit before they take their first post to instill a national view.

71 years after the end of the Korean War, the Republic of Korea have developed tremendously. It changed from a country of help to a country of help. It is also true that developing countries are using Korea as a "role model." I think it's time to

look back on the path we've developed and look back on who helped us in times of difficulty and whether there's anything to help the country and her people. When those who helped us or their descendants need help at the expense of the most difficult times in Korea, we should live up to it and repay it.

Ah! How can we forget that!! 0400(I), 25th June, 1950.

The surprise invasion of the nK puppet regime supported by the Communist Chinese and the Soviet Union!!

Although we fought with indomitable spirits, nK destroyed the lives of the entire people, and devastated whole country.

South Korea, where 1.94 million soldiers from 22 countries of the six continents participated in the Korean War under the name of UN forces. There were 40,000 soldiers were killed, 100,000 wounded, 4,000 missing, and 6,000 prisoners of war.

In 2018, ROK became to have the world's 12th largest economy. ROK is supporting UN activities actively.

Before it's too late, as the Republic of Korea has to join hands of veterans and their descendants, we should return the favor with the spirit of Returning the favor by weaving grass.

참전 16개국 전적지 답사기

The exploratory records to honor the favor in the War

|발행일| 2024년 6월 10일

|지은이| 신인범
|발행인| 안성윤
|발행처| 대한민국상이군경회 인천 계양구지회
　　　　인천 계양구 주부토로 426번길
　　　　(작전동 계양구 보훈회관)
　　　　전화_032-545-8275
　　　　이메일_shin514101@hanmail.net

|펴낸곳| 가온미디어
　　　　전주시 완산구 충경로 32(2층)
　　　　전화_(063)274-6226
　　　　이메일_ok.0056@hanmail.net

값 26,000원

ISBN 979-11-91226-22-5